My Own True Duchess

GRACE BURROWES

Published by Grace Burrowes Publishing, 21 Summit Avenue, Hagerstown, MD 21740.

Cover design by Wax Creative, Inc.

ISBN-13: 978-1-941419-62-5

CHAPTER ONE

"Anselm, why the hell didn't you warn me?" Jonathan Tresham spoke quietly, lest his ire be detected over the string quartet in the minstrel's gallery.

Anselm—as in the Duke of Anselm—lifted his glass of punch in discreet greeting to his duchess, who was wafting down the ballroom's main staircase. Dancers swirled and glided between duke and duchess, as if all of polite society were honoring the late-arriving lady.

"Warn you of what, Tresham? You are whiling away an evening in the most genteel of surrounds in the very best company—my own."

The duchess paused on the next-to-last step and flourished a lacy pink fan, which caused Anselm to set down his drink. This was the bow-and-curtsey opening to an intricate quadrille. Her Grace of Anselm would greet friends, kiss cheeks, and appear to wander about the vast game preserve where matchmakers stalked spouses for the unmarried and unwary.

Anselm would prowl in Her Grace's wake, making debutantes nervous, acknowledging acquaintances, indulging some dowager's need to hold forth about the weather. At the end of five minutes, Their Graces of Anselm would meet behind a potted palm, and Tresham's sworn ally would become utterly useless.

Again.

"You failed to warn me," Jonathan said, "that I'm a hunted man. Your duchess has probably been colluding with the coven at Almack's, reading tea leaves and forecasting my doom."

Anselm came as close to smiling as he ever did. "Your bachelorhood was doomed from the day you were born, Tresham. Ducal heirs marry as surely as mud puddles follow rain. An intelligent man would enjoy the benefits of such a fate, while you fume and pout."

Pout? *Pout?* "You liken my plight to a mud puddle? Marriage has destroyed the once formidable citadel of your reason, Anselm. Go pant at your duchess's heels like a good duke."

Anselm was a dark brute, every bit as tall as Jonathan and some years older. At public school, Anselm had been the bigger boy who'd occasionally intervened when Jonathan had been tempted to cross the line separating schoolyard justice from gratuitous—and gratifying—violence.

The duke arranged the lace at his cuffs and fluffed his cravat. "Tresham, you ridicule what you do not comprehend, and your ignorance alone excuses me from calling you out. My duchess has promised me her supper waltz."

Anselm bowed, eyes dancing, and prowled off to the land of unapologetic marital bliss.

For now. Sooner or later, that land would turn to a battleground or, worse, an expanse of boredom so endless and airless as to suffocate both reason and dignity.

On that gloomy thought, Jonathan sidled behind a gaggle of matrons watching the dancers and ducked into a servants' passage. He knew the Earl of Bellefonte's town house well enough to take cover when necessary, and with the supper break approaching, a respite from the ballroom was imperative.

His lordship had a decent library, and connected to that library was a lovely little study. Jonathan was halfway to safety when a footman with a tray of clean glasses winked at him as if a ducal heir lurking under the stairs was a common sight.

Jonathan emerged from the passage, looked both ways, then listened for approaching footfalls over the muted strains of Mozart. He looked both ways again and crossed the corridor to the library. A sense of guilty triumph filled him as he softly, softly closed the library door and surveyed a treasury of books and a crackling fire.

Half a dozen sconces sent shadows dancing across the cherub-bedecked clouds painted on the ceiling. The peace of the room settled over him, easing his temper, calming him physically. He could not ignore every invitation, but he could limit himself to accepting invitations from peers with quiet libraries, cozy studies, and deserted parlors.

He considered locking the door, but no. Any other bachelor seeking asylum would conclude the worst—a tryst in progress—which would start exactly the wrong sort of talk.

"How did Uncle endure all those years of being an unmarried duke?" Jonathan asked the angels dancing above him.

A head popped up from the sofa facing the hearth. "Mr. Tresham, I knew you'd come!" This exclamation came from a female, which Jonathan deduced despite the gloom by virtue of the mad profusion of ringlets, braids, and wildlife passing for the woman's coiffure.

Or the girl's. Jonathan would not have put her age above seventeen, while the ambition in her eyes was ancient.

"Excuse me, miss. I did not know the room was occupied. I'll leave you to enjoy his lordship's books." He bowed when he wanted to bolt for the door, though showing any hint of panic would hand the blighted female her victory.

"The other girls told me I was daft," the medusa said, advancing on Jonathan, "but I've paid attention. You take to the cardroom, pretend to smoke on the terrace, or find the library when the supper waltz comes around."

She manacled her fingers around Jonathan's arm. "I knew if I was patient, I could make this happen."

No. No, no, a thousand times *no*. History would not repeat itself, and Jonathan would not become a victim of twisted propriety.

"You mistake the matter," Jonathan said. "You mistake me, in fact. I don't know you and I have not behaved inappropriately with you, but I will leave you ruined if you so much as intimate that—"

The violins had gone silent to a soft smattering of applause. Voices sounded out in the corridor.

"Kiss me!" the young lady said, puckering her lips like a mackerel. "You must kiss me this instant."

Jonathan extricated himself from her grasp. "You are making a very great mistake."

A door opened, and fury gripped Jonathan. He would *not* be dragged to the altar, would *not* be forced to wed a stranger, would *not* be forced to conceive children with her, even if the presuming little baggage turned out to be Wellington's long-lost daughter.

"Mr. Tresham, has the supper waltz come around already?"

A brunette stood in the doorway to the study, a brandy glass in her hand. She looked to be about Jonathan's age—approaching thirty—and she exuded a subtle, worldly amusement.

"Madam," Jonathan said, bowing, though he'd never seen this woman before. "I was unavoidably detained by another lady's mistaken ambitions. The young miss and I *have not been introduced*."

The woman in the doorway took a sip of her drink. "Naughty, naughty, Dora Louise. Run along before I tell your mama what you're about. She would disapprove of such a desperate scheme, and you would end up back in Dorset for at least the next two years."

Dora Louise stamped her foot, making her ringlets writhe. "Mama would never chastise me for wedding a ducal heir! Nobody would!"

"I would," Jonathan said. "You'd be miserable married to me, and no amount of consequence or jewels is worth being unhappy for the rest of your life. You've had a timely rescue, I assure you."

As have I.

Dora Louise turned a quivering chin on him, and he had the damnedest, most abominable urge to pat her shoulder and pass her his handkerchief. Jonathan laid that absurd impulse at Lady Della Haddonfield's feet.

"Dora Louise," the lady with the brandy said, "you'd best not be missing when the introduction begins for the supper waltz. Be off with you. I understand your ambition, but Mr. Tresham is right. You deserve a spouse who finds you irresistible, not a fellow who objects to the whole undertaking."

Dora's gaze slewed from the lady to Jonathan, then she picked up her skirts and quit the library amid a righteous swish of embroidered hems.

"If that is not the definition of *to flounce*, I don't know what is," the woman said, leaving the doorway to pass Jonathan the brandy. "For your nerves, Mr. Tresham." She'd dropped the air of sophisticated amusement and become a disgruntled governess.

"My thanks," he replied, "for your intervention and for the medicinal brandy. Jonathan Tresham, at your service."

She inspected him, her gaze traveling from his dancing slippers, up his legs, then taking in his evening coat, pausing at his cravat—a simple mathematical anchored with a small gold and sapphire stickpin. Her expression said she was critical of whatever she saw, rather than pleased or impressed.

Smart woman.

"Did you mean what you said, sir?"

What had he said? "Might we repair somewhere less likely to attract the notice of an aspiring duchess?"

The woman returned to the study. She moved like a governess as well. No mincing or swishing, but rather, an economical stride intended to cover ground. She was attired fashionably in deep blue velvet rather than virginal white, and her dark hair was done up in a smooth twist. A single strand of pearls wound about her chignon, and that simple adornment held Jonathan's attention more effectively than all of Dora Louise's curls and nightingales put together.

Jonathan joined his rescuer in the smaller room and closed the door behind them. The study had its own entrance to a corridor, though few guests would know how to locate the side passage.

"You have closeted yourself alone with a female of marriageable age," the lady said. "Should I be insulted or flattered?"

In other words, was Jonathan immune to her charms or interested in them? "Neither. I accord you the good faith I'd attribute to any generous Samaritan. Would you like to finish your brandy?" He passed her the glass and poured a fresh portion for himself.

"It's too good to waste," the lady said. "I am Mrs. Theodosia Haviland."

The brandy was an appropriate tonic for the aftershocks of alarm running through Jonathan. He could even now be at the center of a domestic drama involving a weeping Dora Louise and her indignant papa, with Lord Bellefonte and his countess in the role of judge and jury.

"May I have a seat?" Jonathan asked as the quartet launched into a lively introduction.

"Of course." Mrs. Haviland took the chair behind Bellefonte's desk, which left Jonathan a wing chair near the fire.

"Are you often accosted by ambitious debutantes?" she asked.

"Dora Louise is the boldest of the lot thus far, but the Season is only half over. I've been kissed twice without my consent, my dance partners are prone to tripping straight into my manly embrace, and any number of fathers have approached me, singing the praises of their 'little fillies,' as if Tatts were having a mare's auction on Tuesday next. I'm told the ladies grow even more determined as the end of the Season approaches."

Why hadn't he seen this coming? Why hadn't he prepared himself to be the quarry in a hunt where the hounds wore muslin and the hunt staff stood smiling on the edge of the dance floor?

A soft tap sounded on the door to the corridor, and Jonathan nearly spilled his brandy. Rescued from one ambush only to be laid low by another?

"Mrs. Haviland," he said, "I hope you haven't presumed upon the trust—"

The look she sent him was complicated—humorous, disgusted, incredulous, and, most of all, exasperated. Jonathan fell silent.

She went to the door and opened it only wide enough to accept a tray. "Others must dodge unwanted attentions too, Mr. Tresham. Care to join me?"

Jonathan was hungry. He was tired. He was irritable, which was not only a function of fatigue and lack of sustenance, but also his general nature since returning to England. By day, his schedule was littered with business meetings, by night he dodged medusas and matchmakers.

"I'm sorry for my earlier comment," he said. "My trust in the fairer sex lately has been tarnished by unfortunate experience."

"Eat," Mrs. Haviland replied, resuming her seat. "Life isn't half so daunting when we're rested and well fed."

Who was she? Jonathan's commercial endeavors had kept him mostly away from England for the past ten years, as had a hearty disgust for so-called polite society. Lady Della had instructed him on the list of Diamonds of the First Dew, or whatever the term was, and other men's wives were absolutely incapable of capturing Jonathan's intimate interest for any reason.

He was at a loss with Mrs. Haviland. "Have we been introduced?"

She speared a bite of peach. "No, we have not. I'm the lady who makes up the numbers or chaperones the daughters of friends when the friend has more interesting things to do. I'm not of your ilk."

"I beg to differ," Jonathan said, helping himself to a cheese-laden pastry. "You don't put on airs, you don't hold with coerced marriages, and you know how to procure good food and privacy when a man's much in need of same. Mr. Haviland is a very lucky fellow."

"Mr. Haviland *was* a lucky fellow, from some perspectives," she replied, passing Jonathan the next forkful of peach. "His luck ran out five years ago, when he ignored a lung fever despite all warnings to the contrary. Try that fruit. It's exquisite. I don't even know what it is."

The gesture was friendly—take a bite of this, why don't you?—but nobody wore gloves to eat, and thus a brush of hands was involved. The brush of hands should have been awkward, as the entire exchange should have been awkward.

Though it wasn't.

"This is a peach," Jonathan said. "The Americans have taken to them, because the southern climes are suited to their cultivation. Peaches come from the Orient, and Bellefonte's older brother has found that they do well in walled gardens and sheltered arbors even here in England."

Not only were peaches generally good fruit, this peach in particular was luscious. Sweet, subtly spicy, juicy without being messy.

Jonathan passed the fork back empty. "Tell me about Dora Louise."

"Don't judge her," Mrs. Haviland said. "She's been raised to believe that she has no consequence, no value at all, beyond the status of the husband she can attach. These young women are fighting for their lives, Mr. Tresham. You spoke to her of happiness, but happiness is a luxury she cannot afford."

Mrs. Haviland tore one of the cheese pastries in half, letting the steam rise before she took a nibble.

"You speak from experience," Jonathan said. "You were Dora Louise once upon a time." She wasn't Dora Louise now. Now she was a woman of supreme self-possession, but then, she was a widow. The only female in all of English Society who lived with a modicum of independence was the financially secure widow.

"They are all Dora Louise," Mrs. Haviland said, glowering at her pastry. "They are taught that they are lucky—lucky—to be relegated to the status of broodmares and ornaments. A milkmaid has a skill, a trade, however humble, and she need not be pretty or risk having anybody's babies to be compensated for her trade. Let her marry, though, and her wages belong to her spouse, even if he beats her, drinks himself into a stupor, gambles, and otherwise disgraces—"

She set down the uneaten portion of her pastry. "I apologize. The Season takes a toll on us all."

Jonathan offered her the last of the peach. "I trust people whose anger is in plain view, Mrs. Haviland, and I removed myself from English society precisely because the hypocrisy of the peerage was beyond my tolerance. I gather Mr. Haviland was irresponsible with your settlements."

She accepted the slice of peach and bit off one corner. "Nobody is supposed to gather that. I work very, very hard to maintain the appearance of a widow of comfortable means. What you and I do not eat, for example, will come home with me."

The simple elegance of her dress and the single strand of pearls were apparently poverty disguised as good taste. How many other widows, matrons, and dowagers were engaged in the same fiction, and when would the reasons to detest polite society stop piling up?

Jonathan set down the last of the pastries without taking a bite. "You socialize to augment your larders?" A clever plan, if desperate.

"I socialize to keep my hand in. A widow who is perceived to have fallen upon hard times soon finds herself besieged with offers, many of which are dishonorable. I live a precarious life, Mr. Tresham, and the Countess of Bellefonte sets out a wonderful supper."

She finished the peach, nibble by bite, and set down the silver fork.

"You could charge me for your silence regarding Dora Louise," Jonathan said.

Mrs. Haviland's hand paused mid-reach for her brandy. "Blackmail is a crime."

Which apparently decided the matter for her. Alas, not so with the Parisian authorities.

"Letting girls fresh from the schoolroom have at bachelors such as myself should be a crime. Dora Louise is taking risks she can't fathom."

A shadow passed across Mrs. Haviland's eyes. She was blue-eyed and had doubtless chosen the color of her dress to emphasize that feature. More than the color, Jonathan noticed the intelligence of her gaze and a banked longing. She was eyeing the sweets on the plate, though cheese, ham, and spiced pears had yet to be consumed.

"I don't fancy chocolates," Jonathan said. "The French are wild for them, but I've never acquired the taste." Two small chocolates sat on the tray, satiny brown in the candlelight. "I'll leave you to finish this meal in private. I'm off to find Dora Louise."

Mrs. Haviland held one of the chocolates beneath her nose. "Why?"

"Because if I show her some favor, then the other fellows will take notice of her, and her desperation might drop from view long enough for some dashing swain to turn her head."

"A sound strategy." Mrs. Haviland set down the chocolate. "A pleasure meeting you, Mr. Tresham. Best of luck with the rest of the Season."

She offered him a smile, not a governess-smile or a widow-smile, but a friendly smile that suggested a timely rescue could be viewed as a lark rather than a brush with disaster.

Jonathan's thespian skills weren't equal to perpetuating such a miscarriage of truth. Dora Louise would have made him a terrible duchess, and he'd have made her a terrible husband.

He'd promised his uncle he'd find a wife this Season, though, so he bowed to Mrs. Haviland, listened for footsteps in the corridor, and withdrew.

* * *

Theo typically started her day with the comforting combination of tea served with buttered toast and jam, though those were scant fortification against Diana's curiosity.

"But did you waltz?" the child asked. "Did you twirl around the room and make your skirts fly out so all the gentlemen could admire the turn of your ankle?" She gestured extravagantly with her spoon, sending a glob of porridge flying onto Theo's plate.

"Di, you're *at table*," Seraphina wailed. "Please don't discuss ankles *at table*."

"And do try not to send your food sailing through the air," Theo added, though she'd offered her daughter that suggestion on other occasions. "I danced one waltz and sat out another." With a handsome gentleman, for once. Not with the wallflowers, widows, or trolling rakes.

"That was kind of you," Seraphina said, "to allow the other ladies a chance on the dance floor."

At sixteen, Seraphina believed fiercely in a world of propriety, civility, and graciousness, much as Diana, at seven, was devoted to dragons, unicorns, and magicians. They were equally fanciful worlds, but appropriate considering the ages involved.

Theo, by contrast, paid the trades, darned her stockings, and worried. "I learned something new last night," she said, adding a dab of jam to Diana's errant porridge and spooning it onto her toast.

"Something scandalous?" Diana asked. "Something appalling and *horrifying*?"

"Something delicious," Theo countered. "The Countess of Bellefonte served sliced peaches from the fruit-and-cheese portion of the buffet. I'd never had a peach before."

"What sort of name is peach?" Diana asked, swirling her spoon through her porridge. "Peach, reach, teach, screech, beach, each, leech… Peach doesn't sound like a fruity word."

Diana took after her late papa in more than his blond, blue-eyed good looks. She had a butterfly imagination that flitted about unpredictably. Alas, the quality Theo had first taken for charming whimsy in Archimedes Haviland had soon revealed itself to be lack of character. She was determined that Diana not take after her papa in that regard.

Seraphina aimed a look at her niece such as a mama cat turned on a kitten who certainly hadn't been among her litter when she'd gone mousing twenty minutes ago.

"*Leech*, Diana? You go from speaking of ankles to screeches and leeches?"

"Diana has a wonderful ear for a rhyme," Theo said, "and peaches are wonderful too. Sweet, juicy, spicy, and a lovely pink-orange color."

Mr. Tresham's attire had been severe by contrast, as all gentlemen's must be. Offering Theo the bite of peach on the silver fork, he'd been the image of temptation. Serious blue eyes, a nearly grim mouth, not a hint of flirtation. He was attractive in precisely the forbidding, direct manner designed to earn Theo's notice.

Her respect, even—possibly. Perhaps peaches were an intoxicant.

"Did you bring us a peach?" Diana asked. "Orange is my favorite color."

"Yesterday," Seraphina replied, "your favorite color was black."

"Yesterday, I was a Knight of the Round Table. Today, I want a peach."

Just like her father. "Peaches are very dear," Theo said, "and somewhat messy. I did, though, happen to bring home two chocolates that I simply did not have room for."

Diana sat up straight and put down her spoon. "Chocolates?"

Seraphina maintained a dignified silence, though her gaze was painfully hopeful.

Theo extracted the chocolates from her pocket and unwrapped the table napkin she'd tucked them into.

"One for each of you. You may eat them at the time of your choosing."

"I choose now!" Diana plucked the nearest sweet from the linen. "My favorite color just became chocolate brown."

Seraphina set the remaining chocolate on the edge of her plate. "Perhaps after luncheon or last thing tonight."

Theo had had the same sighing sense of self-denial where Mr. Tresham was concerned. She could have flirted with him. He was a man much in need of flirtation, and once upon a time, she'd been good at it. She might have bid him to stay rather than seek out Dora Louise, and he might have put aside his scheme to repair Dora's fortunes for at least another half hour.

Diana popped the entire chocolate into her mouth, her cheek bulging. "This is so good."

"Don't talk with your mouth full," Seraphina snapped before Theo could offer the same admonition in a gentler form.

"Don't let your chocolate get stale before you enjoy it," Diana retorted.

"Somewhere between heedless gluttony and endless denial lies a sensible course," Theo said. "I hope you both find it, though being scolded and judged and carped at never did improve my outlook. I'll be in the study this morning if either of you need help with your lessons."

"I'll help Di," Seraphina said, the martyred lament of an adolescent.

"Mama said *she* would help me," Diana replied, now sporting a dab of chocolate at the corner of her lips. "She knows more than you do."

Stop. Stop, stop, stop. Was this how Mr. Tresham had felt in Lord Bellefonte's ballroom? A beleaguered hare pursued by a pack running riot?

"Your mama has ledgers to deal with," Seraphina said, not meanly. "I know enough to sort out the occasional word, Di, and I like a break from my French."

"What is the French word for peach?" Diana asked.

Mr. Tresham would know—if the French had such a word. Dora Louise had caught him unawares through cunning and determination, but he'd not be caught the same way again.

"Will you finish that toast?" Diana asked.

Theo passed over the last, best quarter slice of toast. Diana was not stout—yet—but she was certainly sturdy.

"We'll go for a walk in the park this afternoon if the weather's fair," Theo said, which provoked rare matching smiles from both girls. "I'm hungry for sunshine and birdsong."

Which were free, unlike dancing slippers, bread, and jam. In the park, Seraphina would mince along at a ladylike gait, while peering about in hopes of being noticed by a handsome young gentleman. Diana would lark around like a kite in a breeze.

While Theo tried not to worry.

"Excuse me, ma'am." Williams, the maid-of-all-work, hovered in the doorway. "You've had a delivery."

Not another dunning notice. "What sort of delivery?"

"Flowers, ma'am, and a basket." Williams ducked back down the corridor and returned carrying a bouquet in a silver bowl.

That bowl will fetch a few coins warred with an inarticulate pleasure. The flowers were a combination of hydrangeas and sweet pea with sprigs of heather and ferns for greenery. The bouquet was neither exotic nor extravagant, but such an unexpected occasion of beauty that Theo was torn between burying her face amid the blooms and telling Williams to take them away.

"The ferns mean fascination," Seraphina said, studying not the flowers, but Theo.

"In this case, they mean shelter," Theo replied. "I shared a quiet respite from the dance floor with a gentleman." For who else could have sent Theo flowers? *Please let them be from him.* "Was there a note?"

"The footman who delivered them wore the Duke of Quimbey's livery, ma'am. No note."

Mr. Tresham was His Grace's heir.

"Heather is for admiration," Seraphina said, "or solitude. I'm not sure about the hydrangeas."

Diana had finished the toast and was watching this exchange with the alertness of a child who knew when something out of the ordinary had occurred.

"Hydrangeas are for thanks for understanding," Theo said. Not a romantic sentiment, but a gentlemanly one.

"What's in the basket?" Diana asked.

Williams retreated into the corridor.

"Sweet pea means thank you for a lovely time." Seraphina sipped her tea, her expression much too adult. "Sister, have you been indiscreet?"

"Of course not." *Though I was tempted. I was so, so tempted.* "The gentleman who sat out with me had been pestered by presuming young women, and they left him in peace while I was at his side."

Seraphina set down her tea cup. "Those hopeless ninnyhammers think you're fast. Merely because you're a pretty widow, they think bad things about you."

"Mama is good," Diana said. "Are those peaches?"

Williams had brought in a sizable wicker basket, a quantity of peaches stacked within.

"And chocolates?" Seraphina echoed. "He sent you a box of French chocolates for sitting out with him?"

"He sent three different kinds of cheese too," Williams said, as if cheese were gold, frankincense, and myrrh. "I do believe that's a box of gunpowder from Twinings."

"Flowers and chocolates from a ducal household," Seraphina said, tracing a finger over the curve of a fuzzy peach. "And ripe fruit, good tea... For *sitting out* with him."

"I barely know the man." Theo had known *of* Mr. Jonathan Tresham, because with Seraphina approaching a presentable age, keeping an eye on eligible bachelors had become prudent. "I'm off to do battle with the ledgers."

Leaving the room and getting away from Mr. Tresham's considerate gesture had become imperative, lest the flowers make Theo's eyes itch.

"May I have another chocolate?" Diana asked. "They're quite small."

"Not now," Theo said. "One treat with breakfast is more than enough. Williams, please take the basket to the kitchen. Cook can prepare us all a compote of the peaches for dessert tonight. We'd best use the fruit before it becomes overripe."

Williams, usually a staunch advocate of decorum, flashed a smile. "Cook will be at her recipes all afternoon, finding us the very best treat. I had a peach once. They're wondrous lovely."

The flowers were lovely too, and Theo was tempted to take them with her to the study. Mr. Tresham was grateful to her, and well he should be, for

Dora Louise Compton was a trial to the nerves, and she'd nearly succeeded in awarding herself a tiara.

"Foolish girl," Theo muttered, unlocking the study door. Her funds were kept in this room, as were the mementos of Archie she'd set aside for Diana. The rest of Archie's possessions—books, boots, shaving kit, his cherished collection of pistols—had been sold. Theo had made it through the winter without pawning his watch, but that was next on the list of lines she'd promised herself she'd never cross.

"Mr. Tresham mentioned blackmail," Theo announced to the empty room. "Said the word aloud. I nearly clapped my hands over my ears."

A widow who watched polite society closely learned many secrets—Dora's older sister had gone to Italy not with a lung fever, but with a child on the way. Lord Davington was rolled up, as he'd confessed to his paramour last week in another library where Theo had been lurking.

"But I cannot become the thing I loathe," Theo said, taking the seat behind the desk. She unlocked the right drawer and hefted the ledger book onto the blotter, then allowed herself a moment to acknowledge the hurt.

Pain ignored didn't go away. Pain embraced head on didn't either, but it sometimes subsided from heartbreak to mere heartache. Mr. Tresham would soon be married, a stolen moment with him meant nothing, a basket of peaches—and tea, and cheese, and chocolates—simply meant he was a gentleman.

The flowers were the problem. Every bloom had more than one meaning, and while hydrangeas might mean gratitude for understanding, they also meant good-bye.

Theo opened the ledger, picked up a pencil, and set the abacus at her elbow. Winter was over, but the social Season brought with it a host of expenses, and she really did not want to sell Archie's engraved gold watch.

CHAPTER TWO

"If I had my way, you'd be sold to the nearest coaching inn for use as an offside wheeler," Jonathan said. "But you'd gobble up their profits, slobber all over the common, and frighten the maids."

Debutantes, being three parts iron determination and one part guile, weren't put off by Comus. They and their chaperones fussed and cooed over the dog as if he were a spaniel puppy rather than fourteen stone of rambunctious mastiff.

Big dogs required room to roam, frequently, else big messes resulted and footmen grumbled endlessly. Thus Jonathan was in the park with his uncle's pet, rather than at the ducal residence wrestling with long-neglected ledgers.

Comus trotted along, head up, stride brisk, like a nanny ignoring a querulous toddler. The park was showing to advantage on a glorious spring afternoon, and no self-respecting canine could fail to enjoy a walk beneath the maples.

Jonathan, unlike the dratted dog, was preoccupied with thoughts of the previous evening. He'd sent the basket and flowers to Mrs. Haviland on impulse—unlike him, though motivated by genuine gratitude. Far better to be ambling through the park today than procuring a special license at Doctors' Commons.

"You want off the leash," Jonathan said, taking a side path. "I want off the leash too." His afternoon would be taken up with a board of governors' meeting for a boys' school, and the topic—the budget—was likely to be contentious.

How much nicer, if he'd been free to spend the afternoon reading in a back garden or pretending to read while stealing a nap.

When he and Comus had traveled enough distance to reach a secluded patch of grass far from the busier walkways and bridle paths, Jonathan unfastened the dog's leash.

"Go," he said, waving the leash. "Sniff and piss and roll, comport yourself like a dog, but don't leave this clearing."

Comus was already nose down in the grass and heading for the hedgerow ringing the clearing. Jonathan took the lone bench and considered a pretty widow whose quick thinking had averted disaster.

What sort of name was Theodosia?

Had she loved her late husband? She'd struck Jonathan as pragmatic, but not unfeeling. He liked to think of himself in the same regard, though his business associates would scoff at so soft a description.

Comus rooted around in the undergrowth beneath the maples, pushing through leaves and bracken on the scent of something interesting. Mid-snuffle, he stopped and raised his head, gazing up the path.

"Come," Jonathan said, rising. "Comus, come."

The dog padded over, and Jonathan was refastening the leash when a young girl pelted into the clearing.

"Hello," she said, careening to a stop and swiping blond hair from her eyes. "You are very handsome. What's your name?"

Forward little thing. And yet, for a child to consider Jonathan handsome was an honest assessment, rather than calculated flattery.

"Jonathan Tresham."

"Not you, silly. This gorgeous fellow at your side." She skipped up to Comus and stroked his head. "How lucky you are to have such a pet. I want a dog, but Mama says they are dear—everything is dear—and they need a lot of minding. I'm Diana."

The huntress? "This is Comus. He's not mine, but I'm tasked with exercising him."

"Lucky, lucky you. Does he do tricks?"

This conversation was inane, but then, Jonathan's whole purpose for being in London was inane. If he was successful in finding a spouse, children would doubtless result, and more such conversations would likely follow.

Pointless, inane, tedious… but then, Jonathan knew what it was to be a child for whom nobody had any time.

"He can shake hands. You stand in front of him and look him in the eye."

The girl complied. One of her braids was coming unraveled. The ribbon on the other had slipped precariously low.

"Like this?"

"Yes, and don't smile. He thinks showing your teeth means you're trying to start an argument. Hold out your left hand and tell him to shake."

She stuck out her hand. "Pleased to meet you, Comus. Shake."

The dog looked at Jonathan. *Translate that, please.*

"He's young," Jonathan said. "Doesn't have much confidence. You must be self-assured if you're to convince him of your authority."

The girl was giving Jonathan the same look the mastiff had. "What does that mean?"

Jonathan hunkered before the dog. "Shake, Comus."

A large, muddy paw was raised. Jonathan shook gingerly—the dog would be confused otherwise—and rose.

"Like that."

"Oh, you clever, clever boy. Good boy, Comus. Shake."

Diana, leave. Jonathan had wanted a quiet ramble to sort out his thoughts, and instead, he was beset with a prodigal child whose governess would chide her for getting her hands dirty, and likely chide him as well, while cooing at the dog.

"You can't confuse him with a lot of chatter," Jonathan said. "You say his name, give him the command with your voice, and show him the desired action with your hand. Name, command, cue. Try it."

The infernal girl spun on her heel. "I shall be a famous trainer of dogs! I'll teach them to do magic, and they will be the best dogs in all the world. Comus, shake."

Comus was peering up the path again.

"You must focus on him, so he will focus on you," Jonathan said, hunkering before the dog again. "Watch me."

Thus did Mrs. Theodosia Haviland come upon Jonathan shaking hands with a drooling hound, while a nattering little female extolled the virtues of dressing up a mastiff as a unicorn.

"There you are," Mrs. Haviland said, marching forward. "What have I told you about this behavior?"

About…? Jonathan was saved from making a fool of himself by Comus's tail whacking against his boots.

"Sorry, Mama," Diana said. "I had high spirits, and look, I made a new friend."

"Sir," Mrs. Haviland said, gaze swiveling to Jonathan. "I must humbly apologize for my daughter's—*Mr. Tresham?*"

"Mrs. Haviland." Jonathan bowed. Comus woofed softly. "A pleasure to see you again. I gather Diana is your daughter."

Diana was a little minx, peeping up bashfully from under the brim of her bonnet, her hand softly stroking Comus's head.

"My daughter and my despair. Diana, you know better."

"But I had high spirits, Mama, and the park is so lovely, and Comus is ever so grand." She graduated to scratching his ears, for which Comus obligingly lowered his head.

As a child, Jonathan would have had his ears boxed for such a retort. Comus, not having had the upbringing of a ducal heir, was shameless when it came to having his ears scratched. Any minute, he'd—

In the next instant, the dog was on his back, begging for a belly scratch. His tongue lolled, his tail brushed the grass, and in as much as nearly two hundred pounds of dog could wiggle, he wiggled.

"Comus, up," Jonathan said, lifting his leash hand. "*Up, now.*"

"Oh, but he can't scratch his own tummy." Diana dropped to her knees beside the dog. "What an aggravation that must be when such a nice, big, healthy fellow has an itch he's unable to scratch."

Jonathan did not dare glance at Mrs. Haviland.

"Diana Melisande, you will assist Williams with the dusting for the rest of this week," she said, "and you will not return to the park for the next seven days."

"I don't care." Diana scratched away as Comus's back leg twitched madly. "I've made a new friend, and Comus likes having his belly rubbed. When I grow up, I'll be a dog trainer, and I'll name all my best dogs Comus."

The dog was learning a bad habit, the child was being rebellious, and Jonathan did not want to be in London at all, but if he had to be in London, he'd take a clearing in Hyde Park shared with Mrs. Haviland over any other option, save solitude with his ledgers.

"Don't laugh," Mrs. Haviland muttered. "If you laugh, any hope of re-establishing order is lost."

Jonathan wanted to laugh—the dog was being ridiculous, the child was a scheming little baggage, and Mrs. Haviland was not the composed, self-possessed lady Jonathan had met the previous evening. He liked that aspect of the situation *quite* well.

He touched her arm and winked, then raised his leash hand again. "Comus, get up this instant, or you'll be pulling the knacker's wagon before sundown." Jonathan used the same voice he applied to unruly patrons at his clubs, the same voice that had faced down drunken lordlings, Paris criminals, and bumptious boards of directors.

The dog was on his feet so fast Diana leaped back and took her mother's hand.

"Good boy," Jonathan said, "though you forgot yourself for a moment. See that it doesn't happen again."

Diana was looking at Jonathan as if he'd doubled in height, while her mother was clearly pleased.

"The poor dog was tempted from proper decorum by an unruly child," Mrs. Haviland said. "One cannot blame a mute beast for undignified behavior when an otherwise intelligent girl sets such a bad example for him."

Diana's lower lip jutted at an angle Jonathan had recently seen from Miss Dora Louise.

"Diana, Comus is large enough to challenge a bear," he said. "He's fierce enough to kill a grown man, and if he shows the least bad manners, he'll lose his place as a trusted pet. He won't find another home willing to dote on him as my aunt and uncle do. If he forgets the habit of obedience, his life will be short and miserable. Don't risk his happiness for the sake of your momentary pleasure."

That jutting lip quivered gratifyingly. "I only wanted to pet him."

"Then you should have asked," her mother said. "Reward the dog for disobedience, and you condemn him to a terrible fate."

Comus sat panting and clueless at Jonathan's side, probably doing more to acquaint the girl with a guilty conscience than all the lectures in the world could.

"I'm sorry, Comus," Diana said.

"And?" Jonathan prompted, for he knew childish rebellion in all its guises.

"I'm sorry, Mama. I should not have run up the path by myself, and I should not have scratched Comus's belly without permission."

Despite the subdued tone and teary eyes, the girl was doubtless swallowing back a thousand arguments for why her behavior—tempting an enormous dog to ignore his master in public—really wasn't that awful. Jonathan took a leaf from the dog trainer's book and caught the pupil being obedient.

"Perhaps you'd like to walk Comus around the perimeter of the clearing?" Jonathan said. "Your mother and I can supervise from the bench. If Comus must heed the call of nature, you wait for him. Otherwise, he's to stay by your side while he investigates the undergrowth."

"I can walk him? Truly?" The teary-eyed gaze was gone like dandelion seeds in a brisk breeze. "You'll let me walk Comus by myself?"

"Anybody who has lost her park visitation privileges for the next week, who will be dusting the house from top to bottom, should take advantage of what liberty she has." Jonathan passed over the leash. "Yes, you may walk the dog."

"Diana, wait." Mrs. Haviland withdrew a black ribbon from her pocket and rebraided the loose plait, then retied the other ribbon more snugly. She accomplished this in less than five seconds, and then Diana and Comus were off across the grass.

"He seems like a good dog," Mrs. Haviland said.

"She seems like a high-spirited child." Had her mother ever been that independent and contrary?

"Let's sit. Keeping up with Diana can leave one winded."

"Have you other children?" Jonathan asked, escorting the lady to the bench.

"No, and that one is enough for any six mothers."

Diana held Comus's leash while the dog rooted in the hedgerow. She was talking to him, her words snatched away by the racket he created and the spring breeze.

"You worry about her." And clearly, Mrs. Haviland loved that contrary girl.

"To be a parent is to worry."

Jonathan's parents had worried—about their latest amour, their latest marital battle, the latest scandal, or the latest gossip. They had not worried about their son, when they even recalled they had a son.

"She's lucky to have you," Jonathan said, "as I was lucky to make your acquaintance last night."

In the afternoon sunshine, Mrs. Haviland's maturity was more apparent, or perhaps what showed in her eyes was fatigue. She was a pretty woman, and she'd likely been a beautiful young lady. Today, she was a tired mother, a bit overwhelmed, and in need—as Jonathan had been in need—of a respite.

"She knows," Mrs. Haviland said. "I don't know how Diana pieced it together so early in life—servants' gossip or native wit—but she knows if she'd been born a boy, our circumstances would be different. I lost track of her while searching for the missing hair ribbon. Waste not, want not."

If Jonathan made enough discreet inquiries, he might have unearthed the details of Mrs. Haviland's circumstances—and drawn attention to his interest in the lady. Perhaps that explained why Mrs. Haviland had volunteered what nearly amounted to a confidence.

"I take it an inheritance was involved?"

The dog was on his back legs, front paws braced against a tree trunk. In that posture, he stood taller than most men. Diana waited with uncharacteristic patience while Comus satisfied his curiosity about the path of a long-gone squirrel.

"A title was involved," Mrs. Haviland said. "My husband was in line for the Penweather viscountcy, though like you he was the previous titleholder's nephew rather than his son. Another nephew holds the title now, a fellow over in Hampshire. Any number of people will doubtless acquaint you with my history if Dora Louise mentions she saw us in the library together."

Comus watered a shrub, and again, Diana waited patiently.

"Dora Louise will keep her pretty mouth shut," Jonathan said. "I made it plain that young women who gossip about others raise questions regarding their own whereabouts at the time of any curious incidents."

"Thank you."

For that bit of prudence, Jonathan did not want thanks. "This troubled you?"

"I'm a widow, Mr. Tresham. Our reputations matter. I can be behind a closed door with you and not be ruined the first time it occurs, but a habit of being closeted with single gentlemen would see an end to my invitations."

"Because Society is nothing if not hypocritical. Diana is very good with the dog."

"You were good with her."

That observation had a whiff of *we must be going* about it. "Did my basket arrive?"

"And your flowers. You needn't have, but thank you. If Diana learns the chocolates were from you, she'll make you the hero of all of her fairy tales."

Jonathan had wanted to make Mrs. Haviland smile, not make her mouth pinch up in that resolute line. "I learned something while I danced a quadrille with Dora Louise."

Mrs. Haviland left off watching her daughter long enough to spare Jonathan a curious glance. "From Dora Louise Compton?"

"About Dora Louise. She titters." Jonathan affected a high-pitched giggle, which earned a puzzled look from the dog. "Incessantly, loudly, gratingly. The entire ballroom was forced to notice that I'd partnered her by virtue of that battle trumpet sounding at frequent intervals. I must marry—my uncle and his duchess are elderly, there is no spare—but thanks to you, I don't have to marry a tittering ninnyhammer."

Ah, a smile. "You make her sound like a variety of North American bird: the junco, the chickadee, the tittering ninnyhammer."

Jonathan took Mrs. Haviland's hand in his and raised her knuckles to his mouth, though, of course, he did not touch his lips to her glove in public.

"I am eternally in your debt. If you ever need anything, if you are in want of an escort, if that child needs a stern lecture, or if you develop a yearning for fresh peaches, you will apply to me, Mrs. Haviland."

He'd flustered her, which meant he'd at least made an impression. The girl and dog were edging closer, so Jonathan stood.

"Might I escort you home?"

"Thank you, no," Mrs. Haviland said, rising. "We follow a prescribed path, one intended to work off Diana's high spirits. The more routine I can impose on her, the less mischief she gets into."

"You are a very good mother," Jonathan said, letting go of the lady's hand. "You might err on the side of too much or too little discipline, you might bungle as a parent from time to time, but you see her and you love her. That matters to a child tremendously."

He'd said too much, and not on a topic remotely akin to flirtation. Jonathan tipped his hat, collected Comus, and took the dog snuffling and sniffing up the path. They were past the park gates and halfway home before Jonathan realized how extraordinary the encounter had been.

He'd conversed with an unmarried woman about topics other than the weather or fashion.

He'd enjoyed the exchange, despite the presence of a manipulative child and a drooling mastiff.

And he'd wanted to make an impression on the lady—a lasting, positive impression.

* * *

"Jonathan danced with Dora Louise Compton," Lady Della Haddonfield said. "He even spoke to her. I saw him all but whispering in her ear, and Dora Louise will *not* do, Nicholas."

Della was small and dark, unlike her tall, blond Haddonfield siblings, and while not mighty, she was a whirlwind. When Nicholas, Earl of Bellefonte, was near his youngest sister, he felt like a mastiff beset by a kitten. The little creature was pretty, sweet, and perpetually in motion, but what was one supposed to *do* with it?

"Tresham danced with any number of young women," Nick replied, etching tiny lines in the tail of the nightingale he was carving. "My countess does not suffer bachelors to sit out, and Tresham isn't rude."

"Not on purpose," Della replied, holding up the unpainted pigeon Nick had finished carving last week, "though Jonathan has a forbidding quality."

Tresham had an instinct for self-preservation. "Della, he's a ducal heir. He's a wealthy, single, *young* ducal heir, and the present titleholder is getting on in years." Quimbey was seventy if he was a day and had only recently married. His duchess was well past child-bearing years, and yet, the couple billed and cooed like the newlyweds they were.

Quite cheering, to see marital bliss among the elders.

"You're saying what everybody else is saying," Della replied, putting down the pigeon and making another circuit of Nick's woodworking shop. "Jonathan is Mr. Eligible. I hate that term, as if he's the last true bachelor in Mayfair."

Why didn't I take my countess driving when I had the chance? Why didn't I install a lock on the door to my woodworking shop?

"Della, you must not meddle. The worst affliction a bachelor can suffer is a meddling relation." Nick had warned his wife the previous evening along the same lines. Leah had kissed him, patted his cravat, and gone back to surveying her ballroom with the gimlet eye of a matchmaking general.

Della whirled, and by the very swish of her skirts, by the thump of her slippers against the plank floor, Nick knew he'd said something wrong.

"*Relation*," Della said, her voice low and bitter. "That's as close as you can come to admitting the truth. Jonathan Tresham is my brother, Nicholas. I have blood in common with him."

This anger in Della was new and bewildering. She'd always been a cheerful girl, a baby sister a brother could dote on... even if Nick's step-mama had conceived Della in an irregular liaison with Tresham's father.

"He's your half-brother, but what matters blood, Della, when we love you, we have always loved you, and the late earl loved you most of all?" Nick's papa had accepted his wife's by-blow in the spirit of a man who'd been no saint himself and who had, in his imperfect fashion, loved his countess and every child under their roof.

"Papa is gone," Della said, hefting an awl and holding it like a dagger, "and Jonathan is the only link I have to my real father. You'd toss Jonathan into the arms of any scheming henwit with the audacity to waylay him."

Somebody had waylaid Tresham. One of Nick's sleeve buttons had come loose at last night's ball, and he'd ducked up to his dressing closet for another pair. The shortest route had taken him past his study, from which Tresham's voice in conversation with a woman had drifted. A footman had come by with a tray bearing generous portions of food, and Nick had silently wished the lady good hunting.

Though a quiet tryst in a secluded study was an unlikely beginning to a courtship.

"Tresham has wit enough for ten bachelors, Della. You're the one trying to marry him off."

"I met him less than a year ago, Nicholas. If he must marry, I want him to marry the right woman."

Nick set aside his knife, for tail feathers wanted concentration, which was impossible with Della fretting and pacing.

"You are worried that Tresham will ignore his connection to you once he takes a duchess. That he'll marry a high-stickling prig whose self-importance ignores the realities of human nature and the existence of Tresham's only sibling."

Della came to a halt before the birdcage Nick had crafted for his nightingale. The wire was painted gold. A wooden facsimile of a lilac bush would provide the fake bird a fake perch. Leah could hang it in her parlor without a living creature having suffered for the sake of human pleasure.

Della opened and closed the cage door, which squeaked a bit. "Jonathan will be a duke. He can't marry just anybody."

Nick risked draping an arm across her shoulders. "His uncle held out against the matchmakers for decades, and Tresham is no fool. If he cuts you, if he ignores you, if he in any way hurts your feelings, Leah will do him an injury that jeopardizes the succession of his title."

And then Nick would kill him.

Della leaned against Nick's side and set the awl on the workbench. "I want to be his friend, Nicholas, but all I am to him is an inconveniently persistent nuisance."

Nick took Della by the hand and led her to the workshop's window seat, a perch where Leah read by the hour. This docility from Della would be gone in five minutes, so he'd make what use of it he could.

"Tresham isn't one of us, Della. He has no idea how to go on with a family. He was shipped off to public school at age seven, went straight to Cambridge, then undertook travel before he turned twenty. He was a brawler in the schoolyard, but became senior wrangler in mathematics at university. He's unfamiliar with polite society, unfamiliar with family, and not just any duchess will suit him."

"He was top wrangler? He earned the highest score in his whole class in the maths examination?"

"He earned spectacular marks in all of his academic endeavors, which is unusual in a ducal heir."

"And then he disappeared," Della said, leaving the window seat. "I didn't know he was a scholar. How could I not know that about my brother?"

"He's nigh ten years your senior. Do you know what Adolphus got up to while at Cambridge?"

Della sent Nick a peevish look. "Nobody knows what Dolph does in his laboratory. He scribbles a lot and occasionally causes explosions."

"So if you don't know what one brother is about, why would you castigate yourself for being unfamiliar with another brother?"

"Dolph is Dolph. I don't look like him."

Della did, unfortunately, bear a resemblance to Tresham. They were both dark-haired, had the same mouth, the same slightly aquiline nose, though Tresham was tall and Della petite. If they were seen together with any frequency, somebody would doubtless remark the similarity.

Somebody unkind and talkative. "Perhaps Tresham seeks to spare you talk. You've made your come out, but you haven't secured a match."

Della wrinkled her nose, which made her look about eight years old. "Secured a match, like a hunter filling his game bag. Nobody has secured *me*, Nicholas, and while you and Leah are doubtless happily wed, few Society unions can say the same."

Why did every subject with Della—every one—traverse boggy ground? She'd seemed smitten with Mr. Ash Dorning, brother to one of the Haddonfield in-laws, and a decent sort. As an earl's younger brother, Dorning suffered a predictable lack of means, though means could be found for a determined suitor.

Dorning was back in Dorset on some family business that likely had to do with unruly siblings, while Della was stomping around Mayfair, preoccupied with a half-brother who dared not openly acknowledge his connection with her.

"Promise me you won't meddle where Tresham is concerned," Nick said. "I was once an heir beset by the matchmakers, Della. A man in that position cannot be rude, but he cannot be friendly either. He trusts no one, though he's expected to be gracious to everyone. His every trip to the men's retiring room is a fraught excursion, and if he likes a woman, he doesn't dare dance with her twice in the same week. Tresham has his hands full."

Della rearranged Nick's collection of drill bits, so they were in size order rather than order of most frequent use.

"Socializing takes up a few evenings a week, Nicholas. Jonathan isn't seen at the fashionable hour in the carriage parade, he doesn't attend the theater, and he's not a member of Parliament. What is he *doing* with the rest of his time?"

What an odd, insightful question. "Learning the business of the duchy?"

"Quimbey's holdings are modest, as ducal estates go. Her Grace of Quimbey has said as much, because she's pleased the duke needn't spend half the year traveling from one property to another. What was Jonathan about when he wasn't in England, Nick? I don't see him as the sort to goggle at art and architecture, and nothing in the letters between my parents suggests Jonathan inherited great wealth."

She lined up the whetstones with Nick's whittling knives, just as she was trying to tidy up her understanding of her half-brother.

"He likely has investments," Nick said. "The present duke had only the one nephew and would have seen him provided for." Maybe. Every family dealt with heirs and younger sons differently.

"Jonathan isn't the type to live on family charity," Della said, "and even if he is a ducal heir, what if he's unable to support a bride, Nick? Respectable families encounter difficult circumstances all the time."

God, spare me from anxious sisters. Though Della's curiosity was justified. Everybody proclaimed that Tresham was the catch of the Season, a ducal heir, young, good-looking, and *wealthy*.

But nobody mentioned the source of his wealth, not in whispers, not in asides at the clubs. The rise of business speculation as a means of increasing wealth had also—as any form of gambling must—made losing a fortune that much easier as well.

"I'll make a few inquiries," Nick said, "though I expect Tresham has put money into the funds, the same as the rest of us. You will please not interfere in his affairs, Della. I'm asking you that as your brother, whether you think you're my sister or not."

She should have wrapped him in one of her signature hugs and told him not to be silly. Della instead remained across the workshop, arms crossed, brows knit, her gaze on the unfinished nightingale.

"Thank you, Nicholas. Please be discreet. Jonathan will not appreciate any more speculation aimed in his direction than he's already enduring."

CHAPTER THREE

"Merry widows and matchmakers," Beatitude, Lady Canmore, muttered beneath the chatter of Lady Brentnock's other guests.

"Bachelors and buffets," Theo murmured in response.

Bea was a friend from finishing school. Like Theo, she'd married up, been widowed early, and found herself in precarious circumstances despite a connection to a titled family. Not that she and Theo ever discussed finances, but the signs were there.

Dresses made over from Season to Season, refreshed with such lacework and embroidery as a lady could do herself.

A pretty brooch frequently worn last spring no longer in evidence.

A tendency to partake heartily of the buffets.

And a cloud of men watching from an interested, not always respectful, distance. Bea—poor dear—was beautiful in the blond, blue-eyed manner Society most preferred. She paused in the buffet line at the selection of meats and chose ham—cured ham lasted well—heaping several slices atop of her mashed potatoes.

Theo held out her plate. "I'm thinking of retiring to Hampshire. Two slices will do for me. Three, rather."

They moved on to the beef. "I would miss you," Bea said. "Do we have something to discuss over a cup of tea, Theo?"

Theo took two slices of beef still showing a hint of pink at the center, exactly as she liked it. "Diana would benefit from rural life. She finds too much mischief here in Town. Country mischief isn't as dangerous." Theo had found some mischief in the person of Jonathan Tresham. He haunted her dreams as Archie never had.

"Does the current Viscount Penweather know you're considering a repairing lease?"

"Not yet. I'm drafting a letter to him. Why are the plates always so small?"

Across the buffet, Lord Davington dipped a ladle into a gravy boat. "We savor those pleasures most that we enjoy in the greatest moderation, so m' pater claims." His smile was commiserating and a little flirtatious.

"True," Bea replied, "unless that pleasure is good company. The more of that we can have, the better."

She moved along to the curries, while Davington's gaze became speculative. Theo wanted to throw her plate at him, but remained silent until she and Bea had found a quiet bench outside Lady Brentnock's conservatory.

"Is there any quality more tedious in a man than a naughty mind?" Theo asked, arranging a side table before her. "That and a propensity for believing his own lies."

Even Bea did not know the exact circumstances of Archie's death, though Lord Canmore had been a merry wastrel.

"The two are related," the countess said, settling on the bench as gracefully as a swan navigates a still pond. "They are naughty because they believe themselves irresistible. Davington is at least handsome."

"The handsome ones can be the worst." Though Jonathan Tresham was handsome and hardly seemed to know it. "Would you like some of my bread? I was a bit too enthusiastic with the butter."

"I missed the bread," Bea said. "I wanted to get to the ham before the cardroom descended on the offerings."

The cardroom, meaning the hopeless gamblers, and the gentlemen who'd already served their penance with the wallflowers on the dance floor.

"If I remove to Hampshire," Theo said, "could I talk you into coming with me?"

Bea accepted a slice of buttered bread. "Afraid you'll lose your courage?"

Afraid I'll lose the roof over my head. Afraid I'll lose my reputation. Afraid I'll lose my wits.

"Seraphina will make her bow in two years. At that point, I must be in Town. The viscount is more likely to assist in her launch if he has at least a passing acquaintance with her. He has a town house he rarely uses, for example."

Bea set her plate aside. "I'm tempted. I'd be more tempted if Lord Penweather had extended any sort of invitation to you, Theo. Very bad of him to neglect a widowed relation." She rose and passed Theo her table napkin. "I forgot to stop at the retiring room. Guard my plate."

"Of course."

Bea glided off with the sort of deportment no governess could instill in a young lady. She knew all about negligent relations. All about negligent husbands too.

To eat in solitude was a pleasure, though when Theo had done justice to the beef and peas, she began to worry. Bea, in addition to being lovely, was also kind. Any dowager could accost her with a recounting of aches and ailments and be sure of a sympathetic hearing.

"While Bea gets cold ham." Theo moved the small table behind a pair of enormous ferns, lest hungry servants take the food back to the kitchen. The ladies' retiring room was one floor higher and toward the back of the house, though the shortest path was through the conservatory and up the back steps.

Theo emerged on the far side of the conservatory into a corridor far less well-lit than the public areas of the house.

"Please let go of me." Bea, trying for dignity, though Theo heard the thread of fear in her voice.

"You're a widow. You have needs." Lord Davington, exuding anything but charm. "I'm happy to oblige them."

The couple was in an alcove across from the back stairs, though Theo could not see Davington's face.

"I *need* a decent reputation," Bea retorted, "and you *need* to find another mistress. I am not interested in a liaison, my lord."

"I'm discreet. Ask anybody."

A tired rage urged Theo to "happen by" the scene and rescue Bea as she'd rescued Jonathan Tresham, though Mr. Tresham could probably have weathered the gossip. Davington risked Bea's ruin. If Bea could fend him off without assistance, then Davington's pride and Bea's reputation would both emerge unscathed.

"You are pockets to let," Bea countered, ire lacing her tone. "You can no longer afford a mistress, so you seek to take for free what you cannot purchase. I am not interested in what you're offering."

Bad idea, angering a man intent on a selfish goal.

"So the lovely kitty has claws," Davington drawled. "I like spirit in a pet."

"Let. Me. Go."

A thump sounded, possibly an elbow hitting a wall. Fabric tore.

"You little hellion," Davington said at the sound of a slap.

Theo marched into the alcove, grabbed Davington by the hair, and twisted as hard as she could. "Have you lost what few wits you were born with?"

Davington kept a hard grip of Bea's wrist and wrenched out of Theo's grasp. "Go away, Mrs. Haviland. The lady and I were having a private moment."

"I am not going away, and if you don't turn loose of her ladyship, I shall scream down this house." That was a bluff. If half of polite society came running from the conservatory to find Bea's gown ripped, Bea and Theo would both be leaving Town, and not for a cozy cottage in Hampshire.

"Perhaps you're jealous," Davington said, gaze traveling insolently over Theo's breasts. "Alas, I don't care for brunettes. They tend to show their age so much sooner."

Theo didn't hear Jonathan Tresham step up to her side so much as she felt him. A large, male presence, scented like a garden of exotic flowers upwind on a summer night.

"Kick him," Tresham drawled. "Kick him where he stores his pride, my lady. Keep your gaze locked on his, lest he divine your intention, and silently draw back your foot. Don't glance at the target—just let fly and demolish it. I'll be happy to do the same over pistols three mornings hence."

Davington turned loose of Bea and scurried back, stumbling into a potted fern. "Tresham. You're misconstruing the situation. We became a bit passionate, and the lady had a mishap with her décolletage."

"Or swords," Mr. Tresham said, drawing off his evening gloves, finger by finger. "The choice will go to the rodent whose behavior necessitated the object lesson."

Bea jerked her dress together and took Theo's other side. With Mr. Tresham, they blocked Davington's exit from the alcove.

"Your choice," Tresham said, as if discussing the offerings on the dessert table. "Name your seconds now, and I'll even leave you a week or so to brush up on your fencing and marksmanship. You'll want to put your affairs in order as well. *Pay off your debts of honor*, make a will. That sort of thing."

Davington had gone paler than moonlight, while Theo, who'd been married to a hopeless wagerer, got the sense that Mr. Tresham was bluffing and doing an outstanding job of it. Enjoying himself, even.

"Tresham, for God's sake," Davington said. "She's a widow."

Mr. Tresham backhanded his gloves across Davington's cheek—his right cheek. Theo hadn't sensed the blow coming and neither, apparently, had Davington.

"So sorry," Mr. Tresham said, pulling on his gloves. "I thought I heard you use the fact that a woman has been bereaved of her spouse as an excuse to prey upon her, ruin her good name, and violate her person. Surely what you meant to offer was an abject apology?"

Theo had read the *Code Duello* of sad necessity. After a blow had been struck, no apology should have been availing, and yet, Davington must apologize if scandal was to be averted.

"You will find it difficult to sully the reputation of two widows at once," Theo said. "I know what I heard and what I saw. I know that your finances are in disarray and that you conveyed that information to a certain baroness in Lord Petersham's library last week."

Davington sank back against the wall. He no longer looked like a dashing rake. He looked like a stupid, frightened boy.

"I would like to see both the ladies kick you," Tresham said. "Repeatedly. Make up your mind, Davington. Paris is far less expensive than London, and you are in the wrong."

Of the three arguments—the violent, the financial, and the honorable—the latter was clearly of the least moment to his lordship. That Mr. Tresham would include honor on the list meant a lot to Theo.

On Theo's left, Bea was ominously silent, likely battling rage and tears both. On her right, Mr. Tresham looked bored.

Davington stood tall and jerked down his waistcoat. "Apologies. Meant nothing by it. Bit of flirtation. No harm intended."

Mr. Tresham made a tsk-tsk-tsk sound. "Look the party you have wronged in the eye and admit fault. Offer to make reparation." He might have been instructing Diana.

Bea glowered at Davington.

"I am sorry, my lady," Davington said, running a hand through his hair. "I imposed and I took liberties. It won't happen again."

"I'll send you the bill from my modiste," Bea said. "If and when you do slink back from Paris, I will warn every woman I know to avoid you, especially the pretty widows."

That was clearly not the polite acceptance his lordship had anticipated. He stood, hands at his sides, looking helpless.

"Have my coach brought to the mews, Davington," Mr. Tresham said, "then repair your appearance and dance with every wallflower in the ballroom. The shy ones, the stout ones, the ones with meager settlements. Charm them and flatter them, but if you so much as steal a disrespectful glance, my seconds will be calling on you."

Mr. Tresham took a step back, and Davington bolted from the alcove like a tame rabbit fleeing the nursery.

"Thank you, Mr. Tresham." Theo wrapped Bea in a hug. The poor woman was shaking and her arms were cold. "I'll see that her ladyship gets home."

"Don't, Theo," Bea murmured. "You can make my excuses—the ham didn't agree with me or something. Nobody will notice if I slip out. It's after midnight, and…" Her voice trailed off as a shudder passed through her.

"We'll remove to Hampshire," Theo said, wishing somebody had delivered even a single kick to his lordship's *pride.* "Or to the Hebrides."

"While I hesitate to intrude on your plans," Mr. Tresham said, "if I fetch her ladyship's cloak, that will engender more talk than if another woman performs that courtesy. You, Mrs. Haviland, are the logical party to accomplish the task."

"He's right, Theo." Bea drew back and rubbed her arms. "And you haven't had supper yet."

"Bother supper."

And yet, Mr. Tresham's plan made sense, which was why, fifteen minutes later, Bea had been bundled into the ducal coach, the Earl of Casriel at her side. Mr. Tresham's friend had been happy to serve as escort, having, in his own words, *an aversion to the minuet after midnight.*

"Shall we pick over the remains of the buffet?" Mr. Tresham asked.

"I already have a plate," Theo replied. "I seem to have misplaced my appetite."

"That buffleheaded swine upset you. I really ought to have called him out." Mr. Tresham sounded unhappy with himself for that decision.

"Her ladyship's reputation would have suffered, regardless of the outcome. I cannot let good food go to waste," Theo said, making her way back through the conservatory. "You are welcome to join me, even if I am hardly fit company."

She was angry, with him, which made no sense, and with Davington, and of course, with Archie. Always with poor, departed Archie.

"Are you truly considering a move to Hampshire?"

"Yes."

They'd returned to the bench where Theo had left her supper. She rearranged the furniture and resumed her place, Mr. Tresham taking the seat beside her.

The food had little appeal. Removing to Hampshire had no appeal at all. Theo tore off a bite of beef and stuffed it in her mouth.

"Before you finalize those plans," Mr. Tresham said, "I have a proposition to put before you, if you're willing to listen?"

"If you are thinking to make me your mistress, I'll take a pistol to you myself, Mr. Tresham. I'm not yet that desperate, no matter how handsome and wealthy you might be."

"You are not that desperate *yet*," Mr. Tresham said, "which suggests soon you might be."

* * *

"You need not see me home," Lady Canmore said. "The coachman can set you down at your club."

She was a beautiful woman, also an upset woman. The first quality was a matter of indifference to Grey Birch Dorning, Earl of Casriel. The second meant he must pay attention to the lady, lest he aggravate her mood. Casriel had only two sisters, but those sisters had seven brothers, and thus the earl had a thorough acquaintance with exasperated women.

"I was spared the details," he said, "though I understand Tresham will ensure Lord Davington is on a packet for Calais by week's end."

Her ladyship gazed out the window, thus the occasional streetlamp illuminated a perfect feminine profile… also a tear trickling down her cheek.

"It doesn't matter," her ladyship said. "Davington can go to the Antipodes, and next week, another will take his place. I ought to dress in rags and carry a ferret, as Mrs. Haviland has suggested."

Tresham hadn't said anything about the countess being mentally unbalanced. "A ferret?"

"They have a disagreeable odor, my lord. Perhaps I can find a perfumer to bottle it for me so I can sell it as rake repellant."

Dealing with a furious woman required courage. Casriel switched seats, taking the place beside her ladyship when his every instinct prompted him to leap from the moving coach.

"Davington behaved very badly, didn't he?"

"Horridly, and the worst part is, Mrs. Haviland saw most of it, and Mr. Tresham had to intervene, and there was nearly a duel, and now I'm being escorted home like some truant scholar overdue for a birching. I'm also hungry." She swiped at her cheek.

"Open that compartment to your left."

She left off staring into the night long enough to flip down a panel built into the side of the coach.

"Sustenance," Casriel said. "We're in a ducal conveyance, after all."

Bread, cheese, two oranges, a pair of boiled eggs, and a few bites of shortbread, all prettily wrapped in a wicker basket and ready to be laid out on the tray latched to the inner side of the panel.

"Wine is not a good idea right now," the countess said. "But I will fight you for a fresh orange."

"I've had supper. Help yourself to the lot of it." This was a lie, but a man with eight younger siblings knew the restorative power of food when tempers were high and spirits low.

Her ladyship managed to create a cheese sandwich in a moving conveyance without making a mess.

"Shall I tell you a secret?" Casriel asked when her ladyship had peeled the orange and eaten half of it.

"I am not fond of secrets and confidences," she said. "I am very fond of this orange."

"This is a cheering sort of secret. Mr. Tresham can ruin Davington so thoroughly that his lordship dare not return from Paris without Tresham's permission. Tresham has connections all over the Continent, and Davington will be watched."

"Thankless job," her ladyship muttered, wiping her hands on the monogrammed linen provided for that purpose. "But as I said, the issue is not Davington himself. He's merely one of a horde of men who parade about in gentleman's clothing while behaving awfully. If one is too skilled at eluding them, then one is coldhearted, superior, and arrogant. If one is not sufficiently skilled…" She tore the skin from the remaining half of the orange. "I shall cultivate Mr. Tresham's acquaintance so that I might borrow this coach."

"If ever you need a coach, please consider my own at your disposal." The words were out, little more than a platitude, and yet, Casriel meant them. Lady Canmore had substance he'd missed when observing her from across a ballroom.

"Thank you, but your coach is crested. That too would start talk. Tell me more of Mr. Tresham. He's taken an interest in Theodosia—Mrs. Haviland—

something nobody else has dared."

No wonder Lady Canmore contemplated ownership of a smelly ferret. Even the way she licked her fingers was delicate and graceful.

"Tresham is exactly as he seems to be: a ducal heir prepared to marry for the sake of duty, one who has not been idling about since he came down from Cambridge."

"Not idling about London, you mean. Cambridge is an unusual choice for a ducal heir."

Rolling through Town with Lady Canmore was not the dull ride Casriel had contemplated. She had a lively mind, a righteous temper, and she paid attention.

Did Casriel want her attention for himself? The question was pointless. He must marry for money, and if Lady Canmore had substantial means, Davington would never have bothered her.

"Tresham and his papa had a predictable falling out," Casriel said. "Tresham refused to go to Oxford, and thus he was educated at Cambridge. Tell me of Mrs. Haviland. She seems a loyal friend."

A pretty, loyal friend. Her looks were understated, and she did not dress to call attention to herself. Casriel liked that in a woman. A man spoke his vows with a flesh and blood woman, not with a dressmaker's manikin or a milliner's artwork.

"Theodosia is very loyal, and she has contended with significant challenges. Any man would be lucky to win her notice." She tucked the second orange and a cheese sandwich into her beaded bag as coolly as if secreting foodstuffs was the stated purpose of reticules.

"I'm sure Mrs. Haviland is a lovely woman," Casriel said, "though she strikes me as formidable. Tresham does well with long odds and risky ventures, thrives on them, in fact. She could do much worse."

Her ladyship wrapped the shortbread in ducal linen and stashed that in her handbag as well. "Mr. Tresham has no chance at all with Theodosia, then, which is a shame. She disdains the company of idiots who thrive on needless risk or delight in stupid wagers. If Mr. Tresham enjoys that sort of diversion, she'll have no time for him whatsoever."

"Take the wine," Casriel said. "The vintage will be excellent, and you've had a trying evening."

She looked torn, so Casriel reached across her, extricated the bottle, and handed it to her.

"Tresham is not reckless," he said. "He's enormously wealthy because he understands risk better than any man I know. He seems to grasp the inner workings of chance as a veterinarian knows the insides of a horse. Everybody else climbs aboard and sends the beast cantering off toward a destination. The veterinarian reads horse dung like tea leaves and diagnoses a poorly fitting saddle from the minutest unevenness of the footfalls."

The lady was giving him *that* look. The one that said he'd lapsed into a country squire's musings when he was supposed to be an earl.

"My land is in Dorset," Casriel said, hoping to God his blush was not evident in the dark interior. "Our fortunes rise and fall with our flocks."

The carriage, mercifully, came to a halt.

Lady Canmore was smiling. Not a great, beaming grin, but a little quirk of amusement. That too, emphasized her beauty, though she could likely wear the rags she'd alluded to and carry the ferret and make even that ensemble alluring.

All without trying.

He stepped down first and turned to assist the lady.

"Mr. Tresham must divorce himself from any interest in risky ventures if he's to win Theo's notice," Lady Canmore said, joining Casriel on the cobbles. "Theo's late husband was not a prudent man."

Tresham was very prudent, but also… a financial adventurer. The various organizations on whose boards he sat always seemed to come right fiscally, while Tresham's personal finances were based on chance and speculation. Casriel hadn't met his like previously, though he'd come across plenty of resentful heirs.

Saw one in the mirror from time to time, in fact.

"I will leave Mr. Tresham to sort out his own fate with Mrs. Haviland," Casriel said, offering his arm. The lantern on the porch was unlit, an economy or an indication of domestic sloth. Either way, he didn't like it. The coach was in a porte cochere, meaning the entrance was private, but darkness and lone women were not a prudent combination.

"Theo will sort Mr. Tresham out," Lady Canmore said. "Thank you for seeing me home, my lord."

She was in better spirits than when she'd left the ball, and she had slipped the wine bottle into her reticule as well. Casriel wanted to ask if he could call on her, but… no. He must marry wealth.

Had to.

"Are you…?" Casriel stared over the top of her head. She was a petite woman, and yet, she had presence. "Are you well, my lady?" Clearer than that he could not be.

She faced him before her door, and such was the gloom that he could not make out her expression.

"People talk about your eyes," she said. "The Dorset Dornings have such beautiful eyes. Perhaps your eyes are a remarkable color, but I like that you see with your heart."

She leaned into him, only that. Her arms didn't come around him, but her weight rested against his chest. Casriel embraced her, and she sighed, becoming a smaller, softer bundle of female. A hug seemed to be all she wanted, a momentary respite from relying exclusively on her own strength.

"Tell Tresham to go gently with Theodosia," she said. "Mrs. Haviland needs flirtation and tenderness, lighthearted diversion and simple pleasures. Tresham might seek a duchess, but Theo needs a doting swain."

"What do you need?" The question was inane, imbecilic, beyond ridiculous, because Casriel had nothing of value to give her.

"I needed, for one moment, to be held. Thank you, my lord."

She slipped inside the house, leaving a hint of gardenia on the night air. Her departure—graceful, of course—was all that saved Casriel from asking if he might take her driving tomorrow at the fashionable hour.

* * *

Mrs. Haviland had pronounced Jonathan handsome and wealthy. She made both attributes sound like afflictions, and thus his confidence in his plan grew.

"I have avoided intimate entanglements of the nature you allude to," he said, keeping his voice down lest anybody strolling in the conservatory overhear. "I don't intend to give any woman the means to wreak havoc in my life. Mistresses all too often regard such drama as their right."

Mrs. Haviland stared at her plate as if Jonathan hadn't spoken. "I can't let this food go to waste, and I can't eat it. I want to do Davington a permanent injury."

So did Jonathan. "Davington is not the first man to disappoint you." And yet, even disappointed, Mrs. Haviland did not fly into hysterics, threaten public retribution, or cause a scene. Jonathan's parents would have done all three over a mere flirtation.

She tore off the crust from a slice of buttered bread. "My husband was a gentleman in name, and he wasn't a bad man, but he was untrue. That was a disappointment."

"You don't mean he was merely unfaithful. Half of polite society's marriages would collapse if infidelity were of any moment." Which baffled Jonathan. What did the vows signify, if not both loyalty and fidelity to one's spouse?

"Archimedes never had a mistress. A mistress expects to be housed, clothed, and fed, for which reasonable demand, I do not blame her in the least."

This conversation was not going where Jonathan intended it to, and the dancing would soon resume. He needed to police Davington's penance, but he also needed to secure Mrs. Haviland's agreement.

"While I'm sure you esteemed your husband greatly, I sense that the marriage was not entirely happy. I'm facing matrimony myself and hope the union is at least cordial."

She left off tearing up her bread. "You seek a love match?"

Laughter felt good. "Good God, no. I don't believe in fairy tales any more than you do, Mrs. Haviland. I seek a cordial partner with whom I am temperamentally compatible. I'll be a generous, faithful husband; she'll be a good mother to my children and a social ally. She will manage my households,

I will tend to our finances. It's a sensible system with room for considerable fondness. Nobody ends up disappointed, and much good can be accomplished without unnecessary histrionics."

Mrs. Haviland set her plate aside. "You make marriage sound like a business merger. Are you temperamentally compatible with your commercial partners?"

Again, she was disapproving. "I haven't any commercial partners."

"Then what makes you think you'll succeed at having a marital partner?"

Late at night, when the club had closed its doors to patrons and opened its windows to let in fresh air, when Jonathan's only company was the staff cleaning up after another night of aristocrats at play, that question haunted him.

"If nothing else," Jonathan said, "I've seen a fine example of how not to be married. One can learn from a poor example."

Mrs. Haviland sat back, leaving behind the posture of the proper widow. "That is a profound truth. What did you want to discuss?"

Archimedes had apparently been a rotter. Perhaps not in the same league with Jonathan's father, but the late Mr. Haviland had dimmed the joy in his wife's eyes and replaced it with grumpy honesty.

"I must find a bride," Jonathan said, trying to keep all emotion—all resentment, all anger—from the words. "I undertake this search not because the ducal succession requires an heir, but because I owe my uncle."

"Marrying for the sake of another is not well advised, Mr. Tresham." She fiddled with the cuff of her sleeve, tugging it down. She'd taken off her gloves to eat, meaning her arms were exposed. She had a fading bruise near her right elbow and wore not a single bracelet or ring.

"You speak from experience?"

"I married in part because my younger sister required a home. My father was significantly older than my mother, and Mama needed her widow's mite for herself when Papa died."

She rubbed her arms, and it occurred to Jonathan that she was cold. "Walk with me," he said, rising and extending his hand.

"I cannot allow this food to go to waste."

"It won't go to waste. The kitchen staff will see that it's used at the second table if it's not consumed before dawn."

Still, she remained seated.

"Madam, I'll send you a cured ham, a joint of beef, fifty pounds of potatoes, and a damned pineapple, but I'd like to conclude this discussion in the next quarter hour."

She picked up her gloves and drew the left one on slowly. "You needn't mock me."

"I am in complete earnest."

The right glove went on. "Not a pineapple. You want something from me."

"Nothing untoward."

She rose without taking Jonathan's hand. "Oranges and lemons, then. More peaches, next week. A loaf of sugar, cooking spices, a pound of gunpowder, and a pound of China black."

With that recitation, she'd given him all the leverage he'd need to get what he wanted from her, and her list was pathetically easy to provide.

"Done," he said. "Let's find a parlor where you will not be chilled and I will not be overheard."

She wrapped her hand around Jonathan's arm, adopted a pleasant expression, and permitted him—he had no doubt about whose decision this had been—to escort her from the bench.

CHAPTER FOUR

Once upon a time, Theo had loved the lyricism and passion of the violin. Trumpets blared across battlefields, drums reverberated throughout a city, but violins signaled polite society enjoying itself. Violins were creatures of refinement and leisure, made for beautiful ballrooms and genteel gatherings.

"You are frowning," Mr. Tresham said. "I can send the pineapple if you've changed your mind."

"A pineapple would draw significant notice, Mr. Tresham. You'll procure the peaches from your personal connections, and the rest are common luxuries."

"This is why I wanted to speak to you." He tapped softly on a closed door, waited a moment, then held it open.

The interior was warm, which mattered to Theo. Somebody had given orders that the fire was to be tended, though only one branch of candles had been lit. Portraits on the shadowed walls gave the little room the sense of having a gallery of ancestors eavesdropping on any conversations. The ancestors were a happy lot, ruddy-cheeked and smiling in their plumed and embroidered attire.

"I'll be brief," Mr. Tresham said. "I need two things. First, to not be compromised out of choosing my own bride. Second, to choose the correct wife, the one who will be a perfect duchess one day, and a good spouse for a man in my circumstances."

Theo crossed to the fire, the better to bask in its blessed heat. "Please elaborate. I am not a procuress, and virtually any debutante in all of Europe would be ecstatic to become your duchess."

Now, she was hungry. Now, she was preoccupied with memories of Cook's peach compote, which had been delicious, but lacked the dash of cinnamon that would have elevated it to perfection.

"I don't want a perishing debutante."

Mr. Tresham hadn't raised his voice, but he was exasperated, which pleased Theo. He'd handled the situation with Bea, handled Diana's obstinance in the park, and handled any number of presuming young ladies. Theo was cheered to think he'd found a situation he could not confidently manage on his own.

"What do you want? You are to become a duke, God willing. Dukes are married to duchesses and duchesses are chosen from the ranks of the debutantes."

"Might we sit? I'll spend the rest of the evening enduring bosoms pressed to my person while I prance around the ballroom with a simpering, sighing, young woman in my arms. My feet ache at the very prospect."

Theo began to enjoy herself. "Poor darling. You must have nightmares about all those bosoms."

He smiled, a rueful quirk of the lips that transformed his features from severe to… charming? *Surely not.*

Theo took a seat on the sofa and patted the cushion to her right. "Speak plainly, Mr. Tresham. The bosoms await."

He assumed the place beside her. "Plain speaking has ever been my preference. I left England after finishing at Cambridge and went abroad to make my fortune. In that endeavor, I was successful, but the whole time I ought to have been finding my way in polite society, forming the right associations, being a dutiful heir, I was instead making money."

Without any partners. "Why Cambridge? You would have met more young men from titled families at Oxford."

Theo really ought to scoot a good foot to the side. She'd taken a place in the middle of the sofa, and Mr. Tresham was thus wedged between her and the armrest. There was room, if they sat improperly close.

He was warm, however. Theo stayed right where she was.

"Cambridge offers a better education in the practical sciences and mathematics. I am something of an amateur mathematician, which skill is helpful when managing finances." He gazed at the fire, his expression once again the remote, handsome scion of a noble house.

Theo had the daft urge to tickle him, to make that warm, charming smile reappear. He'd doubtless offer her a stiff bow and never acknowledge her again, which was silly when they'd discussed marriage, money, and mistresses, despite their short acquaintance.

"You offered me plain speaking, Mr. Tresham, yet you dissemble. No ducal heir needs more than a passing grasp of mathematics."

He opened a snuffbox on the low table before them. Taking snuff was a dirty habit, one Theo had forbidden Archie to indulge in at home.

"Would you care for a mint?" Mr. Tresham held the snuffbox out to her.

Theo took two. "Tell me about Cambridge."

He popped a mint into his mouth and set down the snuffbox. "My father went to Oxford. He earned top marks in wenching, inebriation, stupid wagers, and scandal. I chose not to put myself in a situation where his reputation would precede me."

Most young men viewed those pursuits as the primary reasons to go up to university. "I gather he was something of a prodigy in the subjects listed?"

"Top wrangler. So I became a top wrangler at Cambridge."

Ah, well, then. "And you've taken no partners. Can't your aunt assist you in this bride hunt, Mr. Tresham?"

"Quimbey's wife doesn't know me, and she's too busy being a bride herself. She and Quimbey are…" He fiddled with the snuffbox again, opening and closing the lid. "Besotted, I suppose. At their ages."

Mr. Tresham clearly did not approve of besottedness at any age, and Theo had to agree with him. Nothing but trouble had come from entrusting her heart into the keeping of another.

"They are off on a wedding journey of indefinite duration," Mr. Tresham went on. "They are reminding me that soon Quimbey will not be on hand in any sense. He's an old man by most standards, and I have put off marriage long enough."

"They are also leaving you a clear field to make your own choices, which seems to be a priority with you."

He crossed his legs, a posture more common on the Continent. "Possibly. They also asked me to move into the ducal town house during their absence, supposedly to keep an eye on the staff and the damned dogs. Pardon my language."

"And you capitulated because of the dogs."

He crunched his mint into oblivion. "A pair of great, drooling, shedding, barking pests. Caesar and Comus. You've met Comus, who once belonged to my late father. Caesar is larger and more dignified."

"You want me to help you find a bride?"

"Precisely. I haven't womenfolk I can turn to for firsthand information, haven't friends from school who will warn me off the bad investments. In this search, I need a knowledgeable consultant, and I am willing to pay for the needed expertise."

A consultant, but not a partner, of course. "Why exert myself on behalf of a man I barely know? I could end up with another woman's eternal misery on my conscience."

Another smile, this one downright devilish. "Would you rather have *my* eternal misery on your conscience?"

Well, no. Mr. Tresham was little more than a stranger, but he'd been kind to Diana, he was dutiful toward his elderly relations, and he'd resolved Bea's situation with Davington.

Then too, Theo could not afford to turn up her nose at any legal moneymaking proposition, however unconventional.

"What are you asking of me, Mr. Tresham?"

"Your role has two aspects: matchmaker and chaperone. I will accept only those invitations where I know you have also been invited. You will simply do as you did with Dora Louise—guard my back. You will also keep me informed regarding the army of aspiring duchesses unleashed on my person every time I enter a ballroom."

Theo got up to pace rather than remain next to him. "And my compensation?" Five years ago, she would have aided Mr. Tresham out of simple decency. Archie's death meant she instead had to ask about money—vulgar, necessary money— and pretend the question was casual.

"We'll get to that," Mr. Tresham said. "You will be more effective as a bodyguard for being unexpected and for knowing my pursuers. I'm not buying merely your eyes and ears, though, Mrs. Haviland. Please be very clear that I am also buying your loyalty."

"My loyalty comes very dear." In some ways, loyalty was a more intimate gift than the erotic privileges a courtesan granted to her customers.

Mr. Tresham rose. Manners required that of him, because Theo was on her feet, but must he be so tall and self-possessed standing in the shadows?

"Name your price, Mrs. Haviland."

The fire warmed Theo's back, but the side of her facing away from the hearth was chilled. If she were home, the only flame burning would be the coals in the kitchen, which were never allowed to go out. Before she departed tonight's entertainment, she'd make another pass through the buffet and collect enough food to make her lunch tomorrow.

I hate this. She very nearly hated Archimedes Haviland too. Without question, she hated The Coventry Club.

"Five hundred pounds, Mr. Tresham."

Not by a quirked eyebrow did Mr. Tresham reveal a reaction to this demand. Theo needed ten times that amount to ensure her own old age was secure, though she could easily spend the entire sum launching Seraphina too.

Still… even a comfortable household would have trouble spending five hundred pounds in a year.

"Done," Mr. Tresham said.

Theo felt as if an auctioneer's hammer had fallen on the last remaining particle of her innocence. Mr. Tresham sought nothing illegal or immoral from her, but he'd required that she put a value on her loyalty. Perhaps this was how business was done and, for men, of no great moment.

"When will you provide payment?"

"You are wise to ask, because I will not have this agreement reduced to writing. I'll provide the whole sum immediately, and you will plan on a whole Season's worth of services."

He sounded relaxed, pleased even, while Theo was uneasy. "I've written to my late husband's cousin, the current viscount."

"How is this relevant?"

"Because he might well invite me to visit the family seat with Diana and Seraphina." Or his lordship might ignore Theo's hints and casual observations, as he had been for two years.

"Then put him off until summer or find me a bride posthaste."

Mr. Tresham's tone said either option was acceptable, for which Theo wanted to tell him to take his five hundred pounds and decamp for Peru. Beyond the parlor, the violins were tuning up, the undulating whine of open fifths scraping across her nerves. She dreaded to return to the ballroom, feeling as if she'd sold her soul in this dark little parlor.

"I'll send you a list of my planned engagements," she said, chafing her hands before the fire's warmth. "Do I assume we arrive and leave separately from these functions? Talk will ensue otherwise."

Mr. Tresham helped himself to two more mints. "Talk will always ensue, which is why you will not send me a list that prying eyes might come upon. I will call upon you tomorrow first thing in the morning. We have a bargain, Mrs. Haviland, and you have my thanks."

He possessed himself of her hand and brushed a kiss to her gloved knuckles—a Continental presumption—then withdrew, closing the door quietly behind him.

"I might even be home to you," Theo muttered, curtseying to the closed door, then dragging a chair near the fire.

Mr. Tresham had timed his appointment for an hour when polite society would still be abed. Prudent of him. But then, this whole undertaking was prudent on his part. Good decisions were made with all the details and possibilities in hand, a lesson Theo had learned only after she'd spoken her vows. She was not put off by Mr. Tresham's prudence.

She sank into the chair, untied her slippers, and stuck her feet toward the fire. The heat on her toes was lovely, but an ache persisted in Theo's heart. Mr. Tresham had noticed that she was in want of coin, though she worked hard to hide the state of her finances.

He had not noticed that she herself was among the women who would consider marriage to the right party under the right circumstances.

She nudged her slippers closer to the fire and tried not to feel angry.

* * *

Jonathan had neither a partner nor a mistress, but he had Moira Jones, and his regard for her eclipsed what either a partner or a mistress could have commanded. As he turned one of Her Grace of Quimbey's legion of god-daughters down the room for the good-night waltz, he considered whether to share tonight's developments with Moira.

"You are a very fine dancer, Mr. Tresham." The young lady stared at Jonathan's cravat pin while she offered that brilliant sally.

Jonathan dredged up the required riposte. "I am inspired by your example. Don't you think people are also somewhat more relaxed about the final dance of the evening? We know a soft bed and a soothing cup of chamomile tea aren't far off."

The young lady put him in mind of Della Haddonfield, though Della was dark and Miss Fifteenth God-daughter was blond. Della was more petite than this lady, and far more bold.

"You fancy chamomile tea, Mr. Tresham?" A spark of interest came through, suggesting even this mouse was hoarding details about Jonathan to share in the women's retiring room.

"At the end of the day, chamomile sometimes appeals. What is your favorite soothing tisane?" Even as he asked the question, he knew what her answer would be.

"Chamomile, of course. Nothing compares to it for restful slumber. I very much agree with your choice."

She would agree with everything he said, did, thought, and failed to do. Mrs. Haviland's words came to mind, about happiness being a luxury for polite society's unmarried women.

"What of lavender?" Jonathan asked as they twirled past a tired legion of mamas and chaperones. "Do you enjoy it as a flavoring, say a lavender ice or lavender custard?"

She stole a glance at his face, the merest flicker of reconnaissance. "Lavender is a very useful herb, and a lavender border can be attractive along a garden wall."

Somebody had schooled her well, because her answer neither committed to a position nor offended. In another life, she might make a skilled dealer for games of chance.

"Are there any young men whose company you particularly enjoy on the dance floor?" Jonathan asked as the world's longest waltz one-two-three'd into another reprise of the opening theme.

"The young men I've met in Town have all been very agreeable." She tried to bat her eyes, though the attempt came off much like a nervous affliction.

"Well, yes, we gentlemen try to be on good behavior in public," Jonathan said, "but I find your waltzing particularly graceful. Miss Threadlebaum has a lovely laugh. Mrs. Haviland's conversation is full of great good sense, and Lady Canmore exudes gracious poise. What of the young men?"

He should not have mentioned Mrs. Haviland, but she was on his mind. Thanks to her, his marital objective had become more attainable, success more likely.

"Mr. Sycamore Dorning is ever so dashing, but Mama says he isn't suitable.

The Dornings all have such lovely eyes, you know."

Eyes that shaded from periwinkle to gentian to lavender. Casriel, older brother to the unsuitable *parti*, claimed those eyes were a curse rather than a blessing.

"Mr. Sycamore Dorning is young," Jonathan said. "He'll grow up." Mr. Dorning would accumulate years, though whether he'd mature was another matter. "Who else?"

She regaled Jonathan with an increasingly enthusiastic list, until the waltz finally concluded and Jonathan could return his dancing partner to her chaperone. The next part was delicate. He must leave the gathering without being dragooned into accompanying any person or group to their next destination.

He did peer about for Mrs. Haviland, though, and saw no sign of her. That was a relief rather than a disappointment. Their bargain had pleased him enormously—she could have asked for ten times five hundred pounds and he would still have been pleased—but she'd seemed unhappy.

Then again, she'd had a trying evening. Jonathan's evening was about to go from satisfying to delightful. He went on foot the three streets to St. James's, the better to ensure his privacy and the better to give him time to ease away from the drudgery of wife hunting and into the invigorating business of owning a very lucrative enterprise.

He entered The Coventry Club by means of the establishment across the street from it, a once stately home broken up into bachelor apartments. Jonathan had a set of rooms here, though he also maintained rooms at The Albany.

He traversed the route through the kitchen to the pantries, to a small door that looked as if it opened onto yet another locked set of shelves or perhaps a wine cellar. In fact, it did open onto the wine cellar of The Coventry Club, a subterranean chamber that stretched for one hundred and fifty feet beneath both the street and buildings on either side.

Jonathan silently slid back the cover over the spy-hole, saw no movement on the other side, and used his key—one of only three to fit this lock—and entered the premises where his fondest dream had come true.

He made his way to the mezzanine offices, marveling, as always, at the quiet in some quarters of the club and the noise in others. The wine cellar was as peaceful as a chapel, while the kitchen was in riot. From the hazard room came raucous laughter, suggesting the cards were running against the house tonight, and the supper room bubbled with quiet conversations and late-night flirtation.

The vingt-et-un tables knit the whole together, partly social, partly earnest—for some, desperate—play.

He loved it all, loved how the club had moods, like a lively woman. One evening tense with excitement, the next full of chatter and casual play, another placid and friendly. He lingered on the screened stairway that shielded all of his comings and goings, and decided that tonight, The Coventry Club sounded happy.

Jonathan gained his office to find Moira sitting at his desk, looking as prim as a spinster, a pair of spectacles on her nose, a pencil in her hand.

"The waltz should be outlawed," Jonathan said. "Whoever imported it from the Continent failed to realize how thrilled the buttoned-up English would be to have an excuse to do more than bow and curtsey to the opposite sex."

Moira rose and poured him a brandy from the crystal decanter on the credenza. "And yet, there's never a shortage of English children, suggesting the English have sorted a few details out nonetheless."

She brought the scent of good tobacco with her. Moira would never smoke before the patrons, though she indulged in private. She was tall for a woman, with hands more competent than graceful. Those hands had made her rich, and Jonathan richer.

"I trust the evening has been uneventful," Jonathan said, accepting the drink.

She resumed the place behind his desk. Her movements were not consciously flirtatious, and yet, she was built to torment the male imagination. Jonathan hadn't noticed that at first. What mattered alluring curves, big green eyes, and glossy blond hair when a woman had taught herself how to count cards?

"I still do not understand why our food and drink must be free after midnight." She pulled off her glasses and rubbed the bridge of her nose. "We make a fortune at the tables, then spend it in the kitchen. Frannie is expecting."

The brandy was exquisite. Moira's mood was threatening to turn troublesome. "For God's sake, she still has one at the breast." Frances Mulholland was their bookkeeper, and for months at a time, she'd bring an infant with her to the club.

Moira idly flipped the beads on an abacus, arranging half on each side. "She's not due until September. We can hire a replacement this time, one who won't be gone for weeks to drop a brat, wipe its nose, or stay up half the night with it when the croup strikes. This is not a foundling home, to be overrun with infants during daylight hours."

Jonathan set his brandy before her. "Frannie has been with us since I bought this place. We do not replace her. I'll manage the books in her absence, the same as I've done for her last two confinements."

Though Frannie hardly knew what a confinement was. She rolled along through her pregnancies like a coal barge plowing through choppy seas. She might arrive to the club some days later than scheduled, but she delivered on her promises and did so with sturdy good cheer.

Mr. Mulholland was a lucky fellow.

"This wife hunting has addled your brains," Moira retorted, the beads moving with a steady *flick, flick, flick*. "By September, you might well be on a wedding journey. By September, you might have a duchess in an interesting condition. By September…"

Jonathan passed the brandy beneath her nose. "By September, nothing will have changed. Just because I've sold the Paris properties doesn't mean I'll sell The Coventry. This is where I proved to my disgrace of a father that I would not be him, that I would most assuredly never need his influence or emulate his folly."

She gently pushed the brandy aside. "Your father is dead. You've promised your uncle you'll take a wife. Things change, Jonathan."

To a boy raised amid chaos, change was the enemy, while predictability was evidence of a reliable order to the universe. Jonathan had made a mathematical study of predictability and applied it to card-playing. The Coventry was his temple to what he'd learned.

"My ownership of The Coventry won't change because I'm taking a wife. I won't allow it. Any duchess of mine will understand that certain spheres are hers to command, others are mine. This one is mine, and you really should have a sip of the brandy. It's exquisite."

She obliged him. One of Moira's many gifts was a sense of when to confront and when to compromise. Jonathan had occasionally considered marrying her and suspected she had considered marrying him. She was a gentleman's daughter—her papa was a vicar—but she'd run afoul of strict propriety in the wilds of Nottingham and become a lady's companion in Paris.

And that lady had enjoyed the occasional discreet game of hazard, and vingt-et-un, and roulette. Jonathan had first met Moira when she'd been hole-carding for her employer in Paris, spying on the dealer's hidden card in a game of vingt-et-un. When the dealer took a glance at his facedown card, Moira signaled her employer as to its value. The system had been subtle, involving casual gestures, facial expressions, glances, and slight movements of Moira's fan.

Jonathan had studied Moira and her employer for three consecutive nights before he'd drawn Moira aside and given her a choice: He would turn her over to the authorities, who were ready to arrest her as part of a periodic "raid" on Jonathan's premises, or he would become her employer.

Moira's smile at that offer had lit up the Paris night sky.

She wasn't smiling now. "Lord Lipscomb is playing too deeply," she said. "He hasn't left the table to so much as piss for four hours."

"Is he sober?"

"For him, yes."

"Then we do not intervene. He can stand the blunt. Davington will be leaving for Calais as soon as I can get him traveling papers."

"So he'll not make good on his markers."

"He'll sign over the contents of his stables to me before he takes ship. Tattersalls will do the rest. As long as he'll be in France, I'm doing him a favor by eliminating a large and needless expense from his ledgers."

Moira took another ladylike sip of her brandy and went back to twiddling the beads of the abacus. "Which do you enjoy more, the numbers, or playing

God with people's lives?"

The question was unlike her, both in its abstraction and in its resentfulness. "I do not play God. Davington accosted a woman at tonight's ball, a lady who wanted nothing to do with him, and he forced his attentions upon her. He brings his fate upon himself."

"You are turning into a duke," she said. "I feel as if I'm watching a season change, and no matter how many fires I light or how many potted plants I bring into the conservatory, the cold will overtake the land. You probably called him out, but he refused the challenge. Where would I be with you dead in some foggy clearing, Jonathan?"

Jonathan poured himself a half portion of the brandy, which was too good for a conversation this unsettling.

"Moira, *nothing will change*. I can keep the books from the Quimbey town house, in my apartment across the street, or at The Albany. I've done it before. I monitor the ledgers for several other enterprises and don't intend to drop those responsibilities either. What ails you?"

She was wealthy by any standard. If she chose, she could present herself as an heiress from the north, or she could resettle in Paris and call herself an English widow. She could marry a marquess's younger son and jaunt about with a courtesy title, and nobody would remark her resemblance to Mrs. Moira Jones, late of The Coventry.

If anybody even noticed.

"You aren't here as much as you should be," she said.

"I'm here more than ever. You managed this place on your own for weeks at a time when I still had properties in Paris. I come by almost every evening we're open, and you are in a pet about something."

The beads fell silent, and Moira lifted her glass to the branch of candles on the desk. "I turned twenty-eight today."

Not an occasion for celebration, apparently. "Go on."

"Frannie is four years younger than I am and soon to be a mother again. You are taking a wife. I sit here night after night, worrying about everything— the larders, the staff, the wine cellar, the dealers, the authorities, the coal, the everything. You assure me things will not change when you marry. I'm no longer certain that's a good thing, Jonathan."

She was beautiful by candlelight, and Jonathan was put in mind of Theo Haviland. The ladies shared a weary discontent with life, an air of determination.

"You have been away from Nottingham for ten years," Jonathan said, making a leap based on the cards he could see. "Go home for a visit, Moira. Arrive in style, take the ducal traveling coach, wear your finery, buy property in the area. Make the peasants see you for the success that you are."

He expected her to laugh, though he knew the value of proving oneself to those who'd offered judgment instead of support.

Moira shook her head. "If you think I'll turn my back on this place now, when you're larking about on a duchess hunt, when Frannie's back to casting up her accounts, and the authorities are itching to raid every establishment in the neighborhood, you have sadly miscalculated."

Her word choice was a dig—another dig. "Have I ever told you how much I appreciate your loyalty, Moira?" Jonathan had never had the luxury of *larking about*.

She rose and set the half-finished drink on the credenza. "You pay me a duchess's ransom in wages. I'm loyal to my salary. Was there anything else you wanted to discuss?"

Jonathan weighed whether to try to jolly Moira out of her birthday blue devils, to dive into the books, or to leave. If he dove into the books, he'd be here until dawn—a tempting prospect—but tonight his jollying skills were inadequate to Moira's mood.

"I'll bid you good evening," Jonathan said. "Send Lipscomb home at daybreak."

Play occasionally lasted around the clock, but Jonathan frowned on the practice for any but the most skilled members. Staff needed rest, and the authorities needed assurances that at least the veneer of a common club was maintained. The premises also required a regular airing and cleaning, which was difficult to do with a crowd gathered around a table.

Moira waved a graceful hand and put her glasses back on. "I'll escort Lipscomb from the premises myself, as Your Grace wishes."

"Don't call me that."

"Good night, *Mr. Tresham*." She lifted the abacus and shook all the beads to the left side.

He should stay, he should humor her, he should ask what she was working on, except that he knew better. Moira would recite every minor occurrence at the club, but she had never been able to simply report what troubled *her*. She either did not know herself, or she was constitutionally incapable of admitting that something bothered her.

She was entitled to her pride. That Moira was all but dismissing Jonathan from his own club was a petty display he would allow—this time. He'd need some rest if he was to be at his best when facing Mrs. Haviland in the morning.

Because his negotiation with the widow was not quite concluded.

CHAPTER FIVE

Theo took the bank draft from Mr. Tresham's hand without glancing at the amount. She had that much pride left, if only barely.

"Shall I have a tea tray sent up?" she asked.

Her formal parlor was seldom used, but Williams, bless her, was conscientious about the dusting and polishing. All the cleaning in the world couldn't hide a worn patch of carpet from the harsh morning light, or the fact that the candleholders on the mantel were empty.

"Tea won't be necessary," Mr. Tresham said. "Have you a discreet man of business to tend to that sum for you?"

She set the draft on the mantel facedown. "I'll deposit it myself."

He peered at a painting of doves Theo had done when she'd been about Seraphina's age. "Might I ask where you'll deposit that draft?"

Was he being concerned, nosy, or merely curious? "Why?"

"I wrote the draft out to 'bearer,' so that the recipient wouldn't be obvious until you endorse the draft. If we bank at the same institution, then the clerks will notice that money is being transferred from me to you. If you endorse the draft illegibly, then your privacy remains assured at my bank as long as we do not do business with the same institution."

What sort of ducal heir knew such stratagems? "I bank at Wentworth and Penrose."

"An unusual choice."

One her solicitor had disapproved of, though other widows patronized it. Wentworth's was a newer establishment and had not attracted many titles among its clientele.

"I am unlikely to see the same people at my bank that I see in Mayfair's ballrooms. Shall we sit, sir?"

Mr. Tresham bent closer to the bottom right corner of the painting. "Is that your signature?"

Theo had the same emotions now that she'd had upon accepting Archie's proposal of marriage: hope and dread, relief and self-doubt, all swirling inside her at once. Over a few weeks' worth of matchmaking?

And yet, her feelings were real and troubling, while Mr. Tresham was preoccupied with schoolgirl art. She took a place on the sofa, where the painting would not be in her line of sight.

"That is my signature. Have a seat, Mr. Tresham."

In his elegant morning attire, he made Theo's best parlor feel small and shabby. This was not his fault, of course, but she simply couldn't muster any gratitude for the funds he'd brought.

He'd purchased her loyalty, which had apparently cost him most of her liking.

"You have artistic talent, madam. The painting is wistful, poignant even. Is it a recent work?"

Small talk now? "I was sixteen when I did that. Doves sound so peaceful, and that year was difficult. My father was ill, and Mama was torn between terror at becoming a widow—my sister was only four years old—and terror that Papa should linger, such that our mourning would delay my come out. We need to coordinate our schedules, Mr. Tresham."

A tap sounded on the door. Theo mentally steeled herself to deal with a curious sister or daughter, but Williams appeared in a pristine apron, carrying a tea tray. The silver service, which Theo was on the point of selling.

"Thank you, Williams." Theo had not ordered this tray and had not explained to anybody the nature of Mr. Tresham's call.

Williams bobbed a curtsey and departed.

"Shall we close the door?" Mr. Tresham asked. "Talk of balls and breakfasts ought not to scandalize anybody, but I'm a guest under your roof. We must do as you see fit."

No, they must not, or she'd be escorting Mr. Tresham from the premises. "I'm having second thoughts."

"Ah." He took the armchair, his expression amused, as if this was a predictable phase in training a horse or tutoring a child. "If you will share those second thoughts, I will allay them."

Because of the angle of the sunshine slanting through the window, the worn patch of carpet was particularly obvious from the sofa. If Theo wanted to replace the carpet, she should lie to Mr. Tresham. If she wanted to buy the fabric she'd sew into a wardrobe for Seraphina's come out, she'd at least dissemble.

But, no. She owed him loyalty, and loyalty was a stranger to falsehood. "I have considered who among the unmarried women of polite society would suit you, and I perceive a problem."

"I'm not that choosy, Mrs. Haviland." He shot his cuffs, his signet ring winking in the sunshine. "I seek a cordial union with a woman who understands her responsibilities. I will be cordial as well, and loyal and faith—"

Theo had done nothing more than smooth a hand over her skirts, but it was enough to silence him. "A successful marriage requires friendship, Mr. Tresham. You've referred to your duchess as a social ally, but her loyalty will not be for sale."

Not if she was the right duchess for him.

"Her loyalty unquestionably belongs to her husband, madam."

"Why?"

He rose and resumed studying Theo's wistful doves. "You ask that question with annoying frequency."

"If you seek a cordial union, then you must bring to the marriage some genuine warmth, Mr. Tresham. You must pay heed to the lady. Empty flattery and false affection will not serve. If that's all you plan to offer your bride, then you must find yourself another matchmaker."

"And chaperone. I could sell this for you. The brushwork is ingenious, and I'm a competent flatterer, by the way."

And so modest. "Competence and facility are two different gifts, Mr. Tresham. When you tell a woman she's a graceful dancer, if her talent is only middling, she will know firstly that you lie and secondly that you've paid no heed at all to her on the dance floor."

"Perhaps you would be so good as to pour out." His tone suggested Theo had made her point, but he was wrong. She was barely getting started.

"Turn your back to me," she said, twirling a finger. "You hired me to find you a bride, and this is part of it."

He turned, and Theo regarded broad shoulders, a long back shown off by an exquisite mulberry morning coat that nipped in to drape over a muscular derriere then curved down to long, equally muscular legs. Archie had been handsome and used it to his shameless advantage. Mr. Tresham was breathtaking and made all the more impact for ignoring his own good looks.

"Tell me what I'm wearing," Theo said.

A male sigh huffed across the parlor. "A dress."

"Hilarious. I refuse to consign another woman to marriage with a man who cannot be bothered to *look at her* when she emerges from her dressing closet."

Mr. Tresham laced his hands behind his back. "You are wearing the same light blue dress you wore when we met in the park, suggesting you plan a walking excursion for later today. You wear no jewelry, not even a wedding ring, though I know you own a set of high-quality pearls.

"You wear them in your hair," he went on, "so perhaps the clasp is broken.

Your cuffs are white lace, not a stain on either one, and your fichu is lace as well, probably backed with silk, but without touching the material with my bare fingers, I can't be sure."

He'd recalled her dress, one of few she owned that she still felt pretty in. He should not to have mentioned her fichu, much less anybody's bare *fingers*.

"What scent am I wearing?"

"Jasmine. Faint, very pleasant. Good quality." He shot a brooding glance at her over his shoulder. "Have I passed?"

"Tell me something positive about myself that will surprise me, but is true."

He turned and studied her with a calm intensity that made the hair on Theo's nape prickle. What did he see besides an old dress and spotless lace?

"You dread the thought of a remove to Hampshire," he said. "Your friends are here, your independence is here. Mayfair is the battlefield you've conquered Season by Season, and scurrying off to the country to be a poor relation would be a bitter defeat."

Theo had reached for the teapot, but let her hand fall to her lap. "*That* is your notion of flattery?" He hadn't surprised her. He'd laid her out flat in her own parlor.

"Needs work," he said, resuming his seat. "I agree, but you also asked for honesty."

"Try again, then," Theo said, pouring out whether the tea was strong enough or not. "And I am not admitting that your observation is valid."

"You are courageous. Witness, you are doing business with me. I sit on the boards of several enterprises, and I'm told directors' meetings are much shorter and more convivial when I do not attend."

"Now you flatter yourself, sir, and proper society does not discuss commerce." Though he was trying, scrabbling about for something pleasant but personal to offer as a conversational gambit. "How do you take your tea?"

"Black, if I must take it at all. Years in France left me with a taste for good coffee and chocolate."

Theo passed him a cup of steaming China black, the very tea he'd sent in the basket, though this cup would apparently go to waste. The last two servings of peach compote graced the tray. If those were consumed, Diana and Seraphina would go into mourning.

"If you are to court a woman," Theo said, "the first step is to notice her. Not her settlements, not her bosom, not her dress, but *her*. What entertainments are you planning on attending next week?"

He recited a list and took a single sip of his tea before setting the cup and saucer aside. "I am not involved in politics, which means I am called upon to make up numbers almost any evening of the week."

"Send regrets at least one-third of the time," Theo said, mentally considering his schedule. "Make your attendance a coveted possibility, not a foregone conclusion."

She was invited to many of the same functions, though not all. A ducal heir moved in rarefied circles when it came to dinner parties. She named four entertainments she'd not been invited to, one of which caused her a small grief.

"I went to school with Lady Fulbright. She stopped inviting me to her home before I became a widow. I suspect my husband offended her husband." Archie had failed to pay debts of honor toward the end, and Theo could only hope that explained the old friends who barely acknowledged her.

"You could come as my guest," Mr. Tresham said.

"No, I cannot. If you are searching for a duchess, then you must not be seen to dally with a widow."

"Does polite society think of nothing else but flirtation and dalliance?"

Theo lifted her tea cup, the better to enjoy the fragrance of a strong brew for a change. "Scandal enlivens otherwise boring lives, Mr. Tresham. That is human nature. If dalliances aren't under consideration, then troubled finances make good grist for the gossip mill. I tread a delicate line avoiding both types of rumor."

"Then I will send my regrets to Lord Fulbright. I'll tell you something else that's true about you, Mrs. Haviland."

She wanted him to leave, so she could pace and curse and doubt herself in peace. She also needed to get that bank draft into her account before she changed her mind.

"Something positive?"

"Something true: Your late husband was a fool who didn't deserve you."

"You're right," Theo said. "Your flattery needs significant work. We will not discuss my late husband." She took a sip of tea and scalded her tongue.

* * *

Jonathan had spent enough time on the Continent to know good art from the kind that merely covered a stain on the wall. Mrs. Haviland's talent was significant, but she hadn't been encouraged to develop it. She had both the amateur's courage, where rules and conventions needed to be challenged, and the true artist's skill.

The painting had been thoroughly dusted, as had the rest of the parlor, and yet no fresh flowers brought color to the sideboard, no beeswax candles stood in the gleaming brass candleholders. The parlor was a mausoleum, preserving the memory of a happier, more secure household. Like most mausoleums, it showed signs of neglect.

While Mrs. Haviland became more interesting.

"Shall I go on?" Jonathan asked. "You were a bright child, but nobody thought to get you a proper governess, one who might have developed your interest in faraway lands or interesting philosophies. If you understand a chessboard, it's because your father taught you so that you might amuse him with the occasional game, but you soon learned to play at his level and to lose on purpose."

She studied her tea, hands wrapped around a dainty porcelain cup. Her expression suggested she was trying to place a far-off melody. Her grip on the tea cup spoke of strangled emotion.

Apparently, he'd overstepped. "Forgive me," Jonathan said. "Until my uncle intervened, I hadn't a tutor or governor worth the name. Before Quimbey took the situation in hand, I learned to command attention by being precociously bad, which worked for a time, though I became well acquainted with my tutor's birch rod. Once Quimbey involved himself, I had to be precociously intelligent, which wasn't quite as effective."

"And now you are precociously rude," Mrs. Haviland said, finishing a syllogism rather than passing a sentence. "But you *are* quite bright, so we will educate you. Wasting your hostess's tea is impolite."

He took another sip of tea, feeling like a bully. "I am not rude on purpose, usually. I suspect I am ignorant." The tea, now that he took the time to notice it, was a fine blend brewed to perfect strength. "I can talk about the weather if you like."

Though she'd likely have insights to offer about how even that topic was pursued. Abruptly, Jonathan was uncomfortable with their bargain.

"The debutantes all learn a trick," Mrs. Haviland said gently. "They learn to ask a gentleman questions and then listen to his answers. The trick is in the listening, in exerting enough effort in the conversation that a man feels important simply because he opens his mouth."

Jonathan was full of questions: What the hell had Mrs. Haviland seen in her husband that she'd entrusted her whole future to him? What had that idiot done to make her so wary and serious? Why hadn't she replaced the carpet by the door, where traffic had nearly worn the pattern away?

But then, he knew why.

"I'll start," Mrs. Haviland said. "Does the lovely weather tempt you to ride out on fine mornings, or are you more a man to read the newspaper page by page before embarking on your day? The question is personal without being intrusive, leaves you a choice of two perfectly gentlemanly pursuits, and allows you to ask about my mornings in return."

I love to spend my mornings with the ledgers from my club, because the damned park is full of the same buffoons who just spent their evening losing obscene sums in my establishment.

"Hyde Park is confining when a good gallop is needed," Jonathan said. "The paths are crowded on pretty days, even at dawn, and Roulette prefers to have room to stretch his legs. Compared to the freedom available at Quimbey Hall, hacking in the park feels like the briefest toddle. What of you? How does your day typically begin?"

Her gaze communicated humor, also approval and a certain friendliness. She wasn't smiling outright, but she was no longer biting back a rebuke.

"Roulette is an interesting name for a horse."

"He's a bay—red coat, black mane and tail. The name fits him." The gelding also alternated between angelic and diabolical moods, much like the roulette wheel.

"Tell me more about Quimbey Hall. I take it you have fond memories there?"

She was good at this. Jonathan was forming an answer—an honest answer—before he realized how good.

"My uncle cherishes that property, and when he saw what a naughty boy I was becoming, he sent me there. I thought I'd perish of fury, to be ripped away from my parents, but Uncle was right. I needed the peace and spacious surrounds, and even then, I suspect he knew I'd eventually be responsible for the place."

She offered him more tea. He accepted to be polite, though he longed for strong coffee or frothy chocolate.

"Were you angry to leave your parents?" she asked, "or angry that they'd let you go?"

Jonathan set his cup on his saucer carefully. "Both, I suppose." A silence sprang up, carrying a fraught sliver of vulnerability. Jonathan rallied before Mrs. Haviland could launch another soft-spoken rocket at his self-possession.

"What of you?" he asked. "Do you hold fond memories of a rural girlhood, and is that why you'd even consider a remove to Hampshire?"

The conversation wound on through the second cup of tea and several spoonfuls of the peach concoction, lest Mrs. Haviland scold Jonathan for wasting food. She knew when to press, when to retreat, when to offer up a small insight into her own situation—very small, which was doubtless another schoolgirl strategy about which nobody warned an unsuspecting bachelor.

At the end of an hour that had gone both quickly and slowly, Jonathan was on his feet, once again studying the trio of doves on Mrs. Haviland's wall.

"Will I do, Mrs. Haviland? Will I suffice as a husband as well as a duke?" He'd tried for a light tone and to his own ears sounded like a gambler asking for just a little more credit.

She considered him while he considered the pretty, docile birds so lifelike he could almost hear them coo.

"You have to *try*, Mr. Tresham. All those young women longing to be your duchess have been training for years to earn your notice. They care very much what sort of impression they make on you and the other bachelors. If you can't muster any regard for their opinion, then no, you will not do."

She was telling him no, telling him to take his bank draft and tear it into tiny pieces, despite the worn carpet and the empty candleholders. Unease Jonathan had been ignoring for the whole of this audition—for that was what it had been—coalesced into dread.

I must take a bride—the right bride—and I cannot find her on my own.

Mrs. Haviland's gaze held not anger, not even rejection, but sadness, and that made Jonathan even more uneasy. She could be hired, she could not be bought. She had an unerring social instinct and knew everybody. She was dignified but didn't put on airs, and integrity radiated from her every word and glance.

And she doubted his worthiness to speak vows with even the likes of Dora Louise. Genuinely doubted his ability to be a decent husband—and she might be right. Hadn't Jonathan said as much to Dora Louise himself?

The doves looked out at him from the painting, their little bird eyes at once calm and interested. He needed to be like the doves, settled, happy, sure of his life. He needed…

Mrs. Haviland was helping herself to his serving of the peach dessert, her expression as she slid the spoon from her mouth a mixture of bliss and guilt.

"You want me to be happy," Jonathan said, the truth of that insight lifting all manner of clouds. "You want me to find not merely an acceptable duchess, but the right duchess for me."

"Of course." Mrs. Haviland set his unfinished treat to one side on the tea tray. "Marriage is a partnership. If you aren't happy, your duchess will have a difficult time being content, and conversely. I understand that you seek a cordial union, but if you marry some fanciful girl and break her heart, if you marry a woman without scruples who appeals to your vanity, if you marry—"

"I understand," Jonathan said. "*I must try.* I must risk allowing the ladies to see the man they'll marry, not merely the tiara in his hands, and I must honestly assess their reactions to him. I comprehend." He must try, as he'd sworn in adolescence to never again try, to win somebody's notice and attention.

"Yes. This is not a pointless game of chance, Mr. Tresham. Finding your bride should come as close to a solemn quest as any undertaking you can imagine."

Next, she'd insist he trade in Roulette for a prancing white charger, and to secure her good offices, he might even do it.

"I do take the matter seriously, madam, else I'd not have retained your services, would I? Will I see you at the Gillingham musicale on Tuesday?" *Will you abandon me before our adventure even begins?*

"Call upon me Tuesday afternoon," she said, rising. "I will have a list of names to discuss with you."

"My Tuesday afternoon is already full of business meetings, none of which I can avoid. Might we reconvene Tuesday morning?"

Her brows rose, as if the notion that Jonathan had commercial interests surprised her. "If you prefer."

"Thank you." Jonathan meant those words. "Until Tuesday, and I will look forward to reviewing your list."

He bowed, and Mrs. Haviland escorted him personally to the front door, perhaps to assure herself of his departure.

"You won't meet with immediate success," she said. "We'll encounter false hopes and blind turns. Fortunately, the Season is only beginning and no betrothals have been announced, so my list will include a fair number of names. You must steel yourself for a forced march, Mr. Tresham, though I will be figuratively at your side for much of it."

So earnest, so sincere, and Jonathan had passed muster with her. He pulled his gloves on and tapped his hat onto his head.

"Your stalwart guidance alone will sustain me. If you'd like to ride in the park Tuesday morning, I can bring a lady's mount with me and call prior to breakfast."

"Thank you, no. My habit is years out of date, and the less we overtly associate in public, the better. I will not be the only lady coming up with a list of matrimonial prospects." She passed him his walking stick and moved to the door.

Well, damn. She could not be tempted from her mission, something else to like about her. Jonathan risked a kiss to her cheek and straightened.

"My sincere thanks for your time today, Mrs. Haviland. I'll look forward to our next encounter."

He jaunted down the steps, in charity with life for the first time in weeks and in charity with Theodosia Haviland. She should be on somebody's list of possibilities. She was pretty, sensible, kind in her rather stern way, thoughtful, intelligent, artistically talented, and she smelled good.

That last ought not to matter to Jonathan, but he did favor the scent of jasmine. He turned his steps toward The Coventry, mentally considering his many London acquaintances. Mrs. Haviland would make somebody a lovely wife, perhaps even a titled somebody. Casriel needed a countess...

But the idea of Casriel marrying Theodosia Haviland, having all that sense and dignity, all that subtle humor and latent warmth for his own, when the earl was mostly concerned with crops, tenant cottages, and wayward younger brothers... Casriel was a dear, but Mrs. Haviland would be wasted on him.

Not Casriel, then. Definitely not Casriel.

* * *

When Lady Canmore had suggested Theo keep her funds at Wentworth and Penrose Bank, her ladyship had offered a cryptic observation as well.

"Mr. Wentworth neither flirts nor flatters, and I'd trust him with my last farthing." Bea had likely done just that. Theo certainly had, though she hadn't understood Bea's remark until she'd laid eyes on the man.

Mr. Quinton Wentworth was the epitome of masculine pulchritude. He was decades younger than any banker of Theo's previous acquaintance, not a trace of gray in his sable hair. His eyes were a brilliant northern blue that should have been arresting, except that all of his features, individually and as a whole, were beyond perfection.

Lips slightly full, nose exactly proportioned to convey character without disturbing the symmetry of his face. He had height and brawn to ensure that understated sartorial elegance contributed to the impact he made at first sight.

And second, and third.

Theo had been lucky. The first time she'd had an appointment with Mr. Wentworth, she'd arrived a few minutes early. She'd noticed a man in a corner of the bank's fern-studded lobby, crouched before a small boy attired as a bank messenger. The man's back had been to Theo, but she'd seen the child's face.

The boy had been riveted by the adult who'd troubled to address a child at eye level. Man and boy were having a conversation that doubtless dealt with bank messenger business, though the gravity of the discussion suggested the safety of the realm was at stake. The child had not only listened, he'd replied, and nodded, and gestured in the direction of the stairs that led to the bank offices above the lobby.

Theo had been in few purely commercial environments, but she was sure that in all of London, no other well-dressed gentleman was having a serious discussion with a mere messenger boy on the premises of a bank.

The child fell silent. The man gently patted his shoulder, rose, and turned.

As the boy trotted away, Theo had pretended to search for something in her reticule. The man's gaze had been arctic, without sentiment of any kind. If she hadn't seen him touch the boy, hadn't seen the child hanging on his every word, she would not have believed her banker and that patient, considerate gentleman were the same person.

And yet, they were. In all the years Theo had dealt with Quinn Wentworth, she'd never seen him show any hint of affection again, never seen him smile, but she'd also never met his like for unfailing discretion or conscientious attention to detail.

"Mrs. Haviland." He welcomed her to his establishment now as he had then, with a bow to a correctly deferential level, no lower. "You are ever punctual."

And he had come down from his office to greet her, as he always did. She suspected Mr. Wentworth liked mingling with his customers, catching snippets of conversation while terrorizing his clerks.

Though the clerks were a cheerful lot at Wentworth and Penrose.

"Thank you for seeing me on short notice," Theo replied. "Let's be about our business, shall we?"

Another man might have been offended at her forwardness. Mr. Wentworth never gave any sign of offense. He was never rude, but he was reliably, wonderfully blunt.

"May I offer you tea, Mrs. Haviland?" he said when he'd closed the door of his office behind her.

"No, thank you. I've come on a matter of some delicacy."

He gestured not to the chairs before the enormous mahogany desk across the room, but to a tufted sofa positioned against the wall. A silver tray of biscuits sat on a low table, and a bouquet of daffodils spiced the air with sweetness.

"The biscuits are fresh," he said, flipping out his tails, taking an armchair, and lifting the tray in Theo's direction. "We order them from the bakery across the street. Help yourself."

"I'm too nervous."

He sat back and set the biscuits aside. "Then tell me what's on your mind. You have more privacy here than you'd have in a confessional, Mrs. Haviland."

She knew that. When Archie had died, she'd had to confide the situation—finances and all—to somebody knowledgeable and utterly trustworthy, and Bea had recommended Mr. Wentworth.

Theo withdrew the bank draft from her reticule and passed it to him. "I'm told that if I endorse that illegibly, nobody will know to whom Mr. Tresham remitted the funds. I am passing that document to you personally, so that the transaction remains confidential at this institution as well."

He studied the draft, turned it over, held it up to the window, and even sniffed it. "This is legal," he said. "Not that Tresham's word is suspect. But tell me, Mrs. Haviland, do I have cause to doubt his honor?"

The question was so quietly put, Theo at first didn't grasp… "Mr. Tresham and I have no arrangement of the sort you're implying, Mr. Wentworth."

Blue eyes regarded Theo with all the mercy of a winter storm bearing down on open country. "I ask, madam. I do not imply. You would not be the first widow whose situation left her vulnerable to the unscrupulous."

Mr. Wentworth's speech was that of a gentleman, but occasionally, she heard an echo of the West Riding in his vowels. In his reply, she heard more than an echo of a threat, albeit aimed at Jonathan Tresham.

"He knows little of the circumstances surrounding my late husband's death," Theo said. "Mr. Tresham is a ducal heir. He must marry soon and well. I am to ensure that he makes a well-informed choice."

Mr. Wentworth set the draft face-up beside the biscuits. To Theo, that was vaguely obscene, but Mr. Wentworth was a banker, and the draft was a mere commercial instrument to him.

"You know everybody in polite society," he said, "are seldom noticed among the chaperones and wallflowers, and won't send Tresham to a bad fate if you can help it. He should have paid you three times this sum."

"He should not have to pay me at all," Theo retorted. "I should assist a gentleman in distress out of simple human decency." Mr. Tresham would be horrified to hear himself described thus, though the term was apt. Theo had questioned him for more than an hour, and he'd never mentioned friends from school, neighbors at Quimbey Hall, old tutors recalled fondly, doting aunties…

not a single soul who cared for him.

Was there any greater distress in life than to be alone with all of one's joys and burdens?

Mr. Wentworth took the draft over to his desk. "Jonathan Tresham is something of an unknown quantity, but he's not in distress. He had substantial assets on the Continent, Paris in particular, and sold them all before removing to London. He does not bank with us, nor with the Dorset and Becker, which is where the ducal funds are kept. I can tell you little about his situation, except that you should be cautious."

Theo was always cautious, but that summary left her feeling encouraged as well. If Mr. Tresham were in difficulties or engaged in shaky investments, Mr. Wentworth would have known.

"More than usually cautious?" Theo asked.

He slipped the draft into a drawer. "Yes."

She waited while Mr. Wentworth resumed his seat.

"I was not born to all this," he said, making a gesture that included a silver biscuit tray, fragrant daffodils, and a desk that was worth more than all the furniture in Theo's house combined. "People know that, and they speculate: Where did Wentworth come by his fortune? I will tell you honestly, Mrs. Haviland, I worked very hard, I was very lucky. There's no more to the story than that."

There was likely much, much more.

"Is Mr. Tresham personally wealthy?"

"You decide: He has some of the best rooms at The Albany, though he doesn't appear to occupy them. His fancy coach is pulled by four matched grays, and he keeps teams waiting from here to the family seat at Quimbey Hall. He also has a private apartment in St. James's Street, three different country estates that I know of, a yacht he uses for Channel crossings when the mood strikes him.

"And yet," Mr. Wentworth went on, "Tresham is not an owner or investor in any business I or my partner have ever heard of. His name never appears on the betting book at White's. He doesn't keep a stable of hunters. His father, by contrast, was a legendary scandal. Public inebriation, liaisons that should have remained private, endless inane wagers and deep play he could not afford."

Theo helped herself to a biscuit. "If I expect polite society to overlook my late husband's faults, I can hardly hold Mr. Tresham accountable for the sins of his father. Mr. Tresham is a ducal heir. They aren't supposed to be paupers." And apparently, Mr. Tresham's differences with his father ran far deeper than boyish rebellion and aristocratic indifference.

Though Mr. Tresham had also mentioned business meetings. What had those been about if not investments or commercial enterprises?

"A ducal heir," Mr. Wentworth replied, "usually receives only a quarterly allowance, and the Quimbey dukedom is quite modest compared to most such titles." Mr. Wentworth looked as if he wanted to say more. "Be careful, Mrs. Haviland."

His sound advice had seen Theo through the worst months of her life. "So careful that I refuse his money?"

"If all he wants for that sum is matchmaking advice, then by all means, keep the blunt. I'll sign the draft and deposit it into one of the bank's operating accounts, then transfer the funds to your name. Such transactions are commonplace when discretion is necessary. I do have a suggestion."

The biscuit was heavenly, light, buttery, sweet, rich. It begged to be dipped in a hot cup of morning chocolate, not that Theo had had chocolate in the past two years.

"I have ever been one to heed your suggestions, Mr. Wentworth."

"Ask him about his charitable activities. If he hasn't any, then he might be just another conscienceless aristocrat, or he might have a reason for keeping his wealth quiet. When the charities know a man has coin to spare, they dun him without ceasing. If he has charitable causes, that will tell you much about his priorities."

Mr. Wentworth had charitable causes. How could Theo not have realized this? "You are certain he's wealthy?"

"As certain as I can be. I maintain a close watch over the funds, I have eyes and ears in unlikely places, and Mr. Tresham's name does not come up where it shouldn't."

Theo held out the tray to him. "These are exquisite. You must have one."

The moment turned awkward, with Mr. Wentworth considering the tray and then Theo, before shaking his head.

"I avoid sweets. One can grow accustomed to them."

"And a bit of sweetness in life is bad for us?"

He rose, and Theo did as well, rather than allow him to loom over her. "The lads…" He looked away, as if seeking guidance from the landscapes on the walls. "Any biscuits not eaten at the end of the day go to the messengers. They can eat them or sell them. One boy makes it a point to feed a few crumbs to the pigeons—his charitable project. I would not deny him that experience of generosity."

This admission embarrassed Mr. Wentworth. He'd once been a hungry, grubby boy without a crumb to give away. Theo was as certain of this as she was of his present wealth and integrity.

"You might consider marrying," she said. "My own brush with the institution left much to be desired, but I love my daughter beyond all telling. I'm not sorry I married."

"You're sorry you married Mr. Haviland. You'll choose carefully for Tresham and quietly. Shall I see you to the door?"

"I can see myself out, Mr. Wentworth. My thanks, as always." Theo paused in the doorway with him. "Have a biscuit every once in a while, Mr. Wentworth. Life can't be all about impecunious widows and crumbs fed to pigeons."

"Yes, ma'am." He was laughing at her, though his expression was more solemn than an undertaker's. "See what you can find out about Mr. Tresham's charities, and if I come across any relevant information, I'll pass it along."

"Thank you."

She left the bank feeling better than she had in months. So Mr. Tresham was discreet about his means. That spoke well of him. Theo was hundreds of pounds richer than she'd been a week ago, and all she had to do to earn that money was find some other woman for Jonathan Tresham to marry.

That notion made her so happy, she went across to the bakery and bought a half-dozen biscuits, though by the time she arrived home, only two remained in the box.

CHAPTER SIX

"Mrs. Haviland, I cannot be seen with the medusa on my arm at occasions of state." Jonathan spoke calmly when he wanted to shout.

"Dora Louise is not a medusa," Mrs. Haviland retorted. "She comes from good family, she is ambitious enough to make you a very creditable hostess, and she likely does not have any say over her coiffure. You were kind to her, you must have some regard for her."

They were in the dove parlor again, this time with the door closed. Jonathan was pacing a worn spot into the carpet before the hearth to match the one by the door.

"I am kind to any number of street urchins, impecunious scholars, and aged sailors, but I don't want to marry them," Jonathan said. "Miss Dora Louise schemes. Schemers are unpredictable and unscrupulous. A bad combination for a duchess."

Mrs. Haviland rose from the sofa. "Her *determination* indicates that she's highly motivated to gain and hold your notice. If she were a man, you'd call her enterprising. You'd say she shows ingenuity and initiative."

Of all the daft reasoning. "She is not a man, and she cannot be my duchess. What sort of woman exercises no influence over her own hairstyle?" What sort of woman ambushes a man who should have known better than to *be* ambushed?

Mrs. Haviland closed her eyes and rubbed the center of her forehead. She had an ink stain on her index finger, suggesting a late night with correspondence, or possibly with ledgers.

Lucky woman.

"Dora Louise is a young woman of good birth," she said, pressing her index finger to the spot between her eyebrows. "She is being paraded before polite society in hopes of making a match. How many times have I told you—?"

"Does your head hurt?"

She'd come to a halt before him, as if to stop his pacing. "A slight headache only. I spent too much time with the household accounts last night. I'm sure it will pass."

About twice a year, Moira was afflicted with paralyzing headaches. They were the only force Jonathan knew of that could honestly subdue her.

"A slight headache can turn into a megrim. Please have a seat."

Mrs. Haviland's expression said she wanted to argue, but now that Jonathan studied her, her gaze was less sharp than usual. Beneath her eyes, slight shadows showed against her cheeks.

"Please," Jonathan said again, patting the back of the armchair. "Perhaps we can make three lists. Impossible, possible, and encouragingly probable."

Mrs. Haviland sat, reminding Jonathan of a reluctant Comus. The mastiff did not obey him so much as he humored Jonathan's suggestions more or less begrudgingly. Jonathan's hostess would toss him from the premises if he aired that comparison, though the mastiff also had dignity and—when provoked—considerable ferocity.

She propped her elbow on the armrest and resumed rubbing her forehead. "What does probable mean to you?"

"The meaning of probable was the topic of a treatise I wrote at Cambridge. In many cases, probability can be predicted. In others, it can be narrowed to a discrete mathematical range, or so I theorized." He set his hands on her shoulders. "Relax your arms."

She sat up as straight as a new footman caught napping. "What are you doing?"

"Trying to prevent disaster." He set his thumbs against the base of her neck and pressed in small, firm circles. "If you've never had a megrim, count yourself fortunate. I've seen them fell formidable parties for days."

She was as taut as the shortest string on a harp. "I've endured my share. Your hands are warm."

"My apologies. Next time, I'll be sure to chill them prior to putting them on your person."

Her skin was warm and smooth as only a woman's flesh could be. Jonathan worked his way out across her shoulders and had a sudden image of Casriel touching the lady thus.

Which was absurd, of course. Mrs. Haviland was up to the weight of, say, the Duke of Anselm, a cantankerous, enormously wealthy, decent sort who, alas, already had a duchess. Casriel had younger brothers who weren't as fascinated with sheep as the earl was, but they were younger sons. Mrs. Haviland didn't need another genteelly impoverished dunderhead of a spouse.

"Do you ever think of remarrying?" Jonathan asked, beginning on the muscles that ran down either side of her hooks.

"All I can think about now is how irregular your behavior is."

"Shall I stop?" He'd done this for Moira any number of times and Frannie too on several occasions.

"If your duchess is prone to headaches, you'll need this skill. Dora Louise has been known to suffer headaches."

Dora Louise was a megrim in muslin. Jonathan's thumb found a knot of muscle beneath Mrs. Haviland's right shoulder blade. He explored gently, ignoring the fact that she was more gracefully curved than Moira, slighter, more petite.

Also prettier, as doves were prettier than peacocks.

"Dora Louise is the last name on my possible list. And now you will permit me to change the subject: What sort of man would you consider, if we were to look for your next match?" Jonathan slid his hands up to grasp her neck, his fingers tunneling into the warmth of her hair.

"I will not remarry."

"Bend your head forward. I'm not suggesting you remarry. I'm asking you about your own list in a hypothetical sense."

She obeyed, much to his surprise, though the result was to create a slight gap in her fichu that drew Jonathan's attention the way Comus's gaze would rivet on a bag of cheese rinds.

I am not a hound. Theodosia Haviland is not a treat. He braced a palm on her forehead and slowly, firmly squeezed her neck. A whiff of jasmine came to him—her version of the fragrance, which put him in mind of summer gardens under a quarter moon.

"I became interested in my husband because he had a fine sense of humor. He could laugh at himself, at Society, at ducks splashing in a puddle. After my father's illness, I longed for laughter."

"A sense of humor can be attractive." Jonathan lacked one, according to Moira. Anselm and Casriel laughed *at* him, though he was often at a loss to know why. "What else would you seek?"

"Archimedes's sense of humor turned out to be a frivolous nature. I did not want to see that. He was affectionate," she went on more softly. "He had a way of including little touches—a brush of his hand to my arm, an extra pat when draping my cloak over my shoulders. His nature was to touch who and what was around him. I hadn't come across that in a man before."

Mrs. Haviland's neck was turning pink—kissably pink, which was ridiculous—but Jonathan could not see her expression because her head was bent forward.

And then she sat up, her expression conveying that she'd endured as much helpful presumption from Jonathan as she was able to.

He withdrew his hands. "You miss your husband, for all his faults." Was it a relief to her, to be able to miss a man who'd disappointed her? A frustration? Jonathan shifted to take a seat on the sofa, and thus he and the lady were at eye level.

"The marriage grew troubled," she said. "Archimedes expected to inherit the title and all the wealth that went with it, though the previous viscount was vigorous in old age. My husband wanted more children, thinking that an heir would be expected of us, but if one cannot support a wife and daughter, how can one expect to support a son, or the next daughter and a son? Three daughters?"

"Don't dwell on the difficulties," Jonathan said, patting her wrist. "Every match has troubles, every family has troubles. I don't like to see you looking daunted."

Hated it, in fact.

"My head feels better."

She did not look as if she felt *better*. "You have some means now," Jonathan said. "Think about that, and if you'd like help choosing an investment, I can make a few suggestions."

"The cent-per-cents will do for me. Predictable growth on a modest scale is preferable to any wild venture, no matter how lucrative."

She sounded like His Grace of Quimbey, whose stewardship of the dukedom was conservative to the point of backwardness. Quimbey likely suspected Jonathan's involvement with The Coventry Club, but the old boy didn't pry.

"I'm sorry your marriage was difficult," Jonathan said, "but because your husband was a disappointment, you'll be cautious about choosing my duchess."

"You will choose her." Mrs. Haviland was very clear on that point. "I will merely suggest. Lady Antonia Mainwaring belongs on your probable list. She's kind, intelligent, pretty, and wealthy."

Theodosia Haviland was kind in a drill-sergeant sort of way, intelligent, and pretty. "As long as she doesn't fashion her hair into snakes or pop out of hidden stairways into the arms of unsuspecting bachelors, put her on the list."

Jonathan spent the next hour learning exactly how many well-born young women were in search of a wealthy, titled spouse. Mrs. Haviland considered everything—fortune, pedigree, location of the family seat, age, and the situations of any siblings or parents.

She knew all the secrets, which were relevant because they could become scandals. They were also bargaining points in the marriage settlements, as in the case of Dora Louise's older sister.

Mrs. Haviland had further troubled herself to learn the dispositions of the young ladies, sending two to the impossible list because they were—the eighth deadly sin again—frivolous.

"Are you perhaps being too cautious?" Jonathan asked when she'd consigned a marquess's daughters to impossibility for *silliness*. "A touch of lightheartedness in a duchess isn't the same as financial irresponsibility in a man."

The possible list was disconcertingly short. One widowed duchess, three ladies by birth, and two heiresses to old wealth.

Mrs. Haviland set her pencil aside. "The more a problem wanted solving, the more inane my husband's jokes became. I grew to dread his tread on the stair. He'd invest in idiot schemes and wager sums we could not afford on imbecilic bets at the clubs. If he was particularly cheerful, I knew he'd been especially stupid at cards and was hoping I'd never learn of his foolishness. A frivolous woman will be an endless liability, Mr. Tresham."

Jonathan had viewed admitting his dislikes, habits, and quirks as necessary, the same as a patient set aside dignity to discuss symptoms with a diagnosing physician. The greater awkwardness was these admissions by Mrs. Haviland.

The one man upon whom she should have been able to rely had betrayed her trust.

"Is there nothing about the married state that you miss?" Jonathan asked. "Nothing you'd like to have back, if you could have it without the disappointment?"

She glanced around at the parlor, as if she suspected the pantry mouser had sneaked into forbidden territory. "You will think me ridiculous."

"If I had to swear to one eternal verity, it's that you are not about to be ridiculous." Nonetheless, she needed some joy, even silliness. She needed flirtatious banter, mad gallops, and French chocolates.

"Sometimes, when we were courting, Archie would take me in his arms."

Jonathan waited, expecting a recitation of stolen kisses, and—heaven forefend—*silly* private endearments.

"He would hold me," she went on. "Just that. Stop the conversation, cease his flattery and grand pronouncements, lay aside his memorized verses, and take me in his arms. I thought it the most precious gift he could have given me." She twiddled the fringe on an embroidered pillow. "I believed his embraces when I ought to have paid attention to my own doubts. I gambled and I lost. I know better than to toss the dice again."

She had been content with so little—an embrace—and given her whole future for it. No wonder she undertook matchmaking with the solemnity of a questing knight.

"I'm sorry," Jonathan said. "I don't know what else to say." Didn't know what to think, say, or do. She'd given her heart to a bounder, which doubtless happened all over Mayfair annually, but the result had never before struck Jonathan as a tragedy.

"Say you will find the right duchess, Mr. Tresham, and that you will be the best duke to her you can be."

"I make you that promise." Though, of course, Jonathan was the one who would benefit most from such a vow. "Shall I see you at the Gillinghams' musicale tonight?"

"Yes, unless my headache returns. I will arrange for Lady Canmore to introduce you to Lady Antonia." She tidied the stack of papers on the low table and rose.

"Lady Antonia is the Earl of Waverly's heiress," Jonathan said, holding the door.

"Very good, Mr. Tresham."

Mrs. Haviland passed before him into the corridor, and Jonathan caught her by the wrist.

"A moment." He drew her back into the parlor and closed the door. "You will think I have taken leave of my senses." He wrapped his arms around her, carefully, gently.

An invitation. *Take this, have this from me.* Little enough to give when she was upending her schedule for weeks to see him comfortably settled.

She was unbending at first, but she didn't pull away either. Jonathan waited, feeling both surprise and indecision in her posture.

"No toss of the dice required," he said. "You don't even need to shuffle the deck."

Her arms stole around him. She laid her cheek against his chest, he gathered her closer. The embrace was sweet, not nearly as awkward as it should have been, and comforting.

"I miss my father," Jonathan said, though he hadn't intended to follow ridiculousness with true folly. "I miss having him to fight with. I hated him, detested everything he stood for, but I miss him." He hadn't connected the feeling with the words until that moment, and where discontent and annoyance had been, sadness settled.

A fair trade, and the realization shifted the tenor of the embrace, from Jonathan holding a woman to indulge an impulse, to two people sheltering in each other's arms. The experience was so unexpected that Jonathan forgot to bow on his way to the door.

But then, Mrs. Haviland forgot to curtsey too.

* * *

"I must be missing someone," Theo said, ignoring the lemon cake Bea had sliced for her guest. When Theo paid a call, the kitchen knew to cut the cake generously, for Theo would only ever permit herself a single slice, and she invariably chose the thinnest of the lot.

Today, she hadn't had even that one slice, though she'd been stewing and fretting over her little matchmaking project for more than half an hour.

"Mr. Tresham is a wealthy, attractive ducal heir," Bea said, toeing off her slippers and curling a foot onto the sofa cushions. "He can afford to be selective about his duchess."

"I'm the one striking possible duchesses from his list, Bea. This lady has an aunt who tipples. That one has a brother who gambles."

Bea chose the smallest slice of cake and bit off a corner. "My Aunt Dot can drain a flask as fast as any coachman ever did, and my brother Bert can't pass a card table without placing a bet. You'll have to raid a convent if your standards are that high."

Theo, the soul of serenity, got up to pace. "Mr. Tresham is not happy, Bea. He needs a lady who will bring him some joy. He all but admitted that to me, which had to have been difficult for him. A touch of lightheartedness, he said. His father ignored him terribly, and Mr. Tresham's response was to become top wrangler in his class at Cambridge."

To a widow, a life consigned to mathematics was a dire fate. "Only a passionate scholar achieves that honor." One with time to indulge his intellect and all the native talent to do so.

Theo straightened a hunt scene over the mantel that had been hanging perfectly plumb. "I need to find a woman who can hold the interest of a brilliant man while bringing him some joy."

That Theo *needed* anything where Mr. Tresham was concerned was puzzling. Bea took another nibble of her lemon cake. "If a healthy young man can't find joy in sharing his bed with a willing bride, then he's undeserving of happiness. This lemon cake is fresh, and I can't eat it all myself. It will go stale once sliced, so you'd best have some."

Theo's concern for poor, dear, unhappy Mr. Fabulously Wealthy Gorgeously Handsome Ducal Heir had apparently obliterated even her delight in lemon cake, her favorite treat.

She picked up a slice without even troubling over her choice. "We've both shared that bed with a willing man, Bea. That's not happiness."

"Then Archimedes was even more hopeless than I thought." Bea's foul mood was Casriel's fault. Why had he been such a dratted gentleman? Such an honest, likable gentleman?

"Marital affection was enough for a time." Theo tore off a bottom corner of her cake, for she always ate the icing last. "I wouldn't trade Diana for anything, but when Archimedes made an issue of having more children, even the sanctuary of conjugal intimacies was tainted by his impecunious habits."

Bea wanted to shake the late, perhaps-not-lamented Archimedes and the mama who'd allowed Theo to yoke herself to him. "He was worse than you let on, in other words. I'm sorry, Theo."

They ate cake in a silence more sad than companionable. Bea missed her husband terribly, but he'd been equal parts friend, lover, and rascal. Bea could be fond of the rascal now that he was gone and genuinely grieve for the friend and the lover.

Theo's mourning was for more than a departed husband.

"Who's on your list?" Bea asked, debating a second slice of cake.

Theo rattled off six names, all lovely women, all appropriate brides for a ducal heir, and not a single one of them lighthearted.

"What about you?" Bea asked. "You're eligible, pretty, you can bear children, and you seem to regard Mr. Tresham highly."

Theo rose, cake in hand. "I'll thank you not to jest, Bea. This is a serious matter. He's counting on me."

Very likely, Tresham had paid coin for Theo's expertise, which showed he wasn't all fine tailoring and dashing quadrilles.

"He trusts you, then, a fine foundation for a duke's marriage. You know everybody, you aren't a blushing doddypoll, you already have his respect."

Theo bit off a nibble of cake from the side with the sugar glaze. "I respect him too. You'd think a ducal heir would have had an upbringing to envy—shaggy ponies, jolly tutors, cricket matches, a bit of Latin. He's a mathematician to the bone, Bea. Life is an equation to him, and that attitude will not result in a happy marriage. I suspect he loves numbers as much as I hate them."

"Then he can do the bookkeeping. You like him for all his numerical inclinations."

Theo took the seat behind the desk, for they were in the study, not the formal parlor. This room had a low ceiling and only one window, which meant it was warmer than the airy parlor with French doors and bay windows.

Like all widows, Theo had doubtless learned what a desk was for: ledgers, bills, and that tribulation known as polite correspondence. She'd likely composed her carefully worded epistles to the viscount at a desk, and she'd battled her ledgers at a desk, wielding an abacus with the same skill she'd once practiced the language of the fan.

She looked more at home behind Roger's desk than she'd looked on the dance floor lately.

"I do like Mr. Tresham," Theo said. "I resent that I like him, I try to ignore it, I hope the liking will fade, but a deep vein of kindness runs through him. His father's bad example has made him tolerant rather than mean. He's honorable, Bea, and he..." Theo stuffed the last of the cake into her mouth, chewing absently.

"He has gained your notice. Why not have an affair with him?"

Theo choked on her cake. "I beg your—Beatitude, have you taken leave of your senses? I cannot... That is the most ridiculous... Beatitude Marie, have you been at the cordial?"

Cordial could be a dear friend to a woman who'd lost patience with polite society. "A fine idea," Bea said, crossing to the sideboard. "Strawberry, I think. It goes so well with the lemon cake."

"Not the strawberry. The Great Fire was doubtless started by your Aunt Dot's recipe for cordial, and that fable about a bakery is merely for children's history books."

"Definitely the strawberry," Bea said, pouring two glasses. "Such a pretty drink." She brought one to Theo and held up her glass for a toast. "To finding lightheartedness."

Theo touched her glass to Bea's. "To not making a fool of myself."

"I did," Bea said, resuming her seat on the sofa. "With Casriel."

Theo took a sip of her drink. "Do tell. He seems like a decent sort. Lovely eyes."

His eyes were only the start of his winning attributes, for they were kind as well as beautiful. "He was all that was gentlemanly when he saw me home, Theo. I was tempted."

"Ply him with a little cordial, and his clothes will miraculously start falling to your bedroom floor."

They shared a smile, not entirely humorous. "I don't want to become the merry widow, Theo, but I don't want to be the invisible widow either."

"We go quietly mad in our invisibility. Stitch more samplers than we have room for on our walls, do cutwork until we go blind."

"I could have invited Casriel in for a cup of tea," Bea said, running her fingers over the embroidery that rioted across the sofa pillows. More red, pink, and white roses than any bouquet could hold. She had an entire hothouse worth of such over-blooming pillows.

"But you didn't invite him in."

"He might have refused, and then I'd be pathetic. He might have asked to come in for a moment." Even a gentleman could say his good nights inside the front door, if they were brief good nights. "Share another slice of cake with me."

Theo left the desk and took the place beside Bea on the sofa. "You're saying the gentleman can't ask without risking offense, and we can't offer without risking pity."

Bea passed her half a slice of cake. "What an inane system." She dunked the other half into her cordial. "I hate it. You really ought to be on Mr. Tresham's list, Theo. He's a fool not to see that."

"I'm a poor widow whose husband died without honoring his debts."

Theo had said that exact sentence on more than one occasion, as if reciting a line from a play.

"You paid those debts."

"I'm paying the last of them off this week. Maybe now, I won't feel as if invisibility is my dearest friend."

"I thought I was your dearest friend."

Theo had taken only the requisite two sips of her cordial, but she was doing justice to the cake. "You are my best friend, Bea. Never doubt that. If you hadn't watched over me after Archie's death, I'd have been committed to Bedlam."

"Have an affair with Tresham if you won't put yourself on his list. It's time, Theo. Our husbands died, we did not."

Theo said nothing while she finished her half slice of cake, but Bea was encouraged. Never had Theo been tempted beyond the first serving of even her favorite treat. Jonathan Tresham was being a good influence, did he but know it.

Perhaps Casriel might have some ideas about how to aid the cause of romance—ideas best shared over a glass of cordial.

CHAPTER SEVEN

One night a month, Jonathan's rooms at The Albany became what he called The Lonely Husbands Club, though a few bachelors also joined the orphaned spouses, probably to gloat at the spectacle. Anselm's duchess held a Ladies Card Night—no husbands allowed—and the men congregated at The Albany rather than be seen haunting their clubs out of necessity instead of choice.

This month, Jonathan had invited his guests to join him at the Quimbey mansion, where the portrait gallery could serve as a makeshift bowling green.

"Makes one think," Anselm said from beneath the portrait of Quimbey and his duchess. "All the places we prohibit the ladies from going—our clubs, the floor of Parliament, Angelo's, Jackson's... where do they prohibit us to go?"

"To *paradise*?" Casriel suggested, hefting his ball.

"If your lady is declining to offer you her favors," Anselm replied, "then you aren't offering your own persuasively enough."

This provoked a snort from Hessian, Earl of Grampion, a connection of Casriel's. "Or perhaps you were too persuasive eight months ago, and the dear woman needs her rest."

He tossed his ball in the air and caught it amid good-natured laughter. Anselm and Grampion had children in their nurseries, as did several of the others. Of all the guests, the papas seemed the happiest. They were members of a fraternity of the not merely married, but the married and... something. Something that did not lend itself to words.

"Set the damned pins," Casriel yelled to Grampion's brother, Worth Kettering, who was ten yards away, near the portrait of the first Duke of Quimbey. "It's not like Tresham will hit any of them."

Jonathan never played cards with his acquaintances, unless the occasion was charitable, hence the evening was turned over to fencing, ninepins, chess, or—did the husbands admit this even to their spouses?—revisiting the repertoire of collegiate glee clubs.

And talking. Amid the bantering, drinking, and whining, interesting conversations ensued as the level of brandy in the decanters fell.

"I'll have the pins down before Casriel has refilled his drink," Jonathan called.

"Casriel never refills his drink," Sycamore Dorning retorted. Young Sycamore was away from university on a self-declared holiday, or keeping an eye on his titled brother. University apparently bored Cam Dorning, which dangerous sentiment Jonathan had shared until he'd stumbled into his first class in trigonometry.

"You steal my drink," Casriel said, firing his ball at Sycamore. "Hence it's in constant need of refreshment."

Sycamore caught the ball left-handed. "A thankless job, but I am nothing if not a dutiful younger brother. Let the play begin!"

Choosing teams was a ritual Jonathan didn't understand, though he sensed its importance, like deciding who on a crew team sat at which pair of oars. The discussion itself created a sense of team spirit, regardless of the actual arrangement agreed upon.

"Why aren't you off wooing some marquess's daughter?" Anselm asked Jonathan as Sycamore and Kettering got into an argument about how many teams should be formed.

"Because they're all silly."

"My duchess frequently accuses me of silliness."

Must Anselm sound so smug? "And to think I once admired your sense of decorum."

"My duchess admires my—"

Jonathan passed Anselm a drink. "Young Sycamore will provoke Kettering to blows."

"I tickle her," Anselm went on with the imperturbable air of an uncle determined to recite inappropriate stories at a formal dinner party. "She tickles me. Will you tickle your duchess, Tresham?"

I'll kiss her on that secret spot beneath her ear, where her flesh is tender and scented with jasmine. "I haven't a duchess. Mrs. Theodosia Haviland is advising me on how I might address this sorry lack." He should double her pay. Five hundred pounds to find a man's mate for life wasn't enough.

"Mrs. Haviland is an estimable lady," Anselm said. "When I stopped browsing the debutantes and heiresses, I realized that Mayfair is full of treasures blooming in deserted windows. I did wonder if her cousin-in-law the viscount would ever tend to her situation."

Kettering and Sycamore were standing nose to nose, pointing and shouting.

Anselm, who had four younger siblings, watched impassively. "Sycamore still hasn't learned to control his temper."

"Kettering hasn't learned to control his mouth. Let Casriel sort them out. They're his family. What do you mean about the viscount and Mrs. Haviland?"

Anselm clearly wanted to intervene in the gentlemen's spat, and he'd do it without offending anybody, or he'd offend both parties equally, which was the better choice in present company.

Jonathan, by contrast, wanted answers. "Let's visit the heirs, shall we?" He would not like to see Theo married to this negligent viscount cousin by marriage. She'd know she was a wife chosen out of expedience or duty, immured among the flocks of Hampshire far from her friends.

Far from Jonathan.

"I like this arrangement of paintings," Anselm said. "The parents beam across the room at their offspring, the offspring beam back."

"I set up the portraits so that no direct sunlight strikes any painting. Uncle paid a fortune to have the artwork restored, and I don't want my grandson having to do likewise with my own image. Tell me about the viscount."

Anselm sauntered over to one of the earls of Trenagle, a bewigged and powdered old gent with a spectacular hooked nose and a merry smile. He'd not become duke until he'd been in his fifties, and he'd spent the first half-century of his life setting a bad example for his younger siblings. His diary averaged two scandals per page, and Jonathan's father had spoken of him fondly.

"You are beginning to think like a duke if your grandson is on your mind," Anselm said. "I account myself amazed."

"Those of mean intelligence enjoy nigh constant amazement. Stop stalling, Anselm, for we're both about to be put on the same team as Kettering and Sycamore."

"I'll take Kettering. You can nanny Sycamore. He's frequenting The Coventry, isn't he?"

Anselm never referred openly to Jonathan's ownership of the club, so even a passing allusion was unusual.

"I might have seen him there. He does not wager excessively. He mostly watches." As Jonathan had sat in the shadows at too many clubs and watched his father fritter away his fortune and respectability, night after night.

"And he doubtless flirts, and he's as good-looking as any other Dorning. Did you ever wish you had the courtesy title?"

"Not once, for then my father would have been the duke, and the title dragged irreparably into penury and disgrace. I suspect Mrs. Haviland's cousin has acted disgracefully, but you are making me threaten violence to your person before you tell me the details."

Anselm took a leisurely sip of his drink. In the center of the room, Casriel was pacing off the distance from the pins.

"I'm ensuring we have privacy," Anselm muttered, "because one does not speak ill of the dead. Archimedes Haviland died in debt."

"He was an heir living on his expectations. They are notoriously prone to dying in debt." Jonathan's father certainly had.

"He was a worthless, philandering bounder too good-looking for sense, and he did not know how to quit on a losing hand."

The philandering part made Jonathan want to smash his drink against the earl's portrait. Quimbey had kindly put Papa's portrait in a small, unused parlor, for that image would have made a better target.

"You're saying he died deeply in debt."

"Scandalously in debt. The viscount paid the trades and the contractual debts by liquidating the trust that had supported Haviland in life."

"What fool wrote marriage settlements that liquidated a sum doubtless intended for Haviland's widow and offspring?"

Jonathan tugged his guest by the sleeve to the portrait of Jonathan himself. The solemn youth in the frame stood beside a bust of Euclid, as if anybody knew what that worthy had looked like. No faithful dog gazed up at the lad, no sagacious cat curled on his desk. Euclid's proof of the Pythagorean theorem had been sketched into the desk blotter. Behind the unsmiling youth, the room held a neat arrangement of oddities—a six-tiered abacus, a carpenter's square, a telescope, a beaker full of marbles.

Jonathan had loved sitting for that portrait, surrounded by his allies. The painting struck him as sad now, a boy in a mathematical laboratory rather than a playroom.

"I made some inquiries," Anselm said, "because I was one of Haviland's creditors, and the situation struck me as irregular. The wording of the will had been lax. After all of Haviland's *just debts* had been paid, the remainder of the fund set aside to maintain the family was to pass to the widow."

Jonathan recalled the empty candleholders, the worn carpet in Mrs. Haviland's best parlor. "There was no remainder."

"Not a farthing, and it gets worse."

Teams were lining up behind the pitch line, and Sycamore Dorning was going about topping up drinks as if he were the host, or at least the host's best friend.

While Jonathan stood six yards from his guests, plotting murder. "What is worse than a peer of the realm leaving a woman and child in penury when he's responsible for them?"

Jonathan's father had tried to leave him in penury and failed spectacularly.

"Viscount Penweather refused to pay Haviland's debts of honor. With those being unsecured by a contractual obligation, he reasoned that debts of honor die with the debtor."

"That is the law on the matter, to the extent a court has opined on it."

Gambling debts failed the criteria a court needed to find that a contractual relationship had been formed. Nothing of substance, no legal *consideration*, was surrendered in exchange for the money lost. More than a century ago, legislation had been enacted that left those collecting gambling debts without recourse to the courts.

Such debts were thus backed up by only the debtor's integrity and as a result were referred to as debts of honor.

"Haviland's creditors would not agree with Penweather's assessment," Jonathan said. "Debts of honor pass to the heir if the heir has any self-respect." Jonathan had paid off his father's vowels before the coffin had been covered with earth, the better to bury all of Papa's legacy at one go.

"The viscount is old-fashioned," Anselm said. "He reasoned that Haviland's cronies led him astray and failed to intervene as the debts mounted. Let those who gambled with him bear the cost of exploiting a weak man."

"Because," Jonathan said, staring at the boy alone in the gilt frame, "how will the weak man learn strength if friends and relations are constantly intervening to save the weakling from his own folly?"

Quimbey had used that argument to persuade Jonathan to leave his father's situation in life alone. Quimbey's position had been troubling then. It curdled the drink in Jonathan's belly now, though Jonathan espoused the same philosophy to allow men like Viscount Lipscomb to gamble away fortunes.

"That reasoning, that a weakling must learn strength, has a certain merit," Jonathan said, "but Mrs. Haviland was doubtless dunned by her husband's former friends regardless of the legalities, and she was blameless."

Dunned, propositioned, gossiped about. Jonathan abruptly needed to see her, to know that she was safe, to know that her aversion to marriage hadn't been compounded by ill treatment from supposed gentlemen after her husband's death.

"You look like you're contemplating cleaning your pistols."

"Tell me the rest of it, Anselm, and don't pretty it up." The bowling had begun, with Grampion setting the pins.

"Mrs. Haviland called upon me, for she'd found her husband's markers. She assured me I'd be repaid, no matter how long it took. She had a competence from an aunt, a small inheritance from her father, and intended to establish a payment plan with each of her husband's creditors."

"And be in debt for the rest of her life? Why? Why not allow a man's folly to be left in the laps of those stupid enough to trust him?"

Anselm finished his drink. "Who trusts a man more than the woman giving birth to his children? Haviland's death left a daughter and a sister-in-law without protection, and what chances do you think they would face in polite society if Haviland's irresponsibility became public?"

No chance at all, because polite society was vicious to those unprotected by wealth or standing.

"How much, Anselm? Tell me the extent of his debts, and I will—"

"You will do nothing, lest some gossip get wind that you are now paying the lady's bills and draw the wrong inference. The matter has been handled."

Casriel called to them. Jonathan ignored him. "Handled how?"

"When Mrs. Haviland came to me, I did form an arrangement with her. I saw to the sale of Archimedes's possessions. His coach and four, his phaeton, his pistol collection, even his clothes. I told Mrs. Haviland the proceeds were sufficient to settle most of the debts, but she knew they could not have also covered the amount Archimedes owed me."

Relief washed over Jonathan, leaving him in the same state a rare excess of spirits would. "You forgave the debt?"

"Mrs. Haviland would not allow it." Anselm slung an arm around Jonathan's shoulders and walked him toward the pitch line. "She insisted on paying back every penny, with modest interest, though it might take her the rest of her life. I'm setting the money aside for the girl, but I haven't told the widow that."

"How much?"

Anselm named an obscene figure. "That was the original amount, and Haviland's tastes were extravagant enough that his effects did take care of all the other debts. The balance remaining to me was paid off earlier this week by a bearer draft from Mrs. Haviland's banker. I assume the cousin's conscience bedeviled him into it at last."

"All neat and tidy, no trace of scandal." While Theodosia Haviland survived on buffets and determination. A snippet of conversation came back to Jonathan from his exchange with the girl, Diana. *Mama says everything is dear.*

The single strand of pearls with a clasp Theodosia couldn't afford to repair.

The fierce loyalty to Lady Canmore, another widow, and the unrelenting protectiveness of all the Dora Louises.

"Smile," Anselm said, his grasp of Jonathan's shoulder painfully firm. "The guests will think we've quarreled when all we've done is chat cordially about your marital prospects. Mrs. Haviland will find you a duchess, Tresham, if such a woman can be found in all of England. How many candidates are you considering?"

Anselm's duchess had doubtless taught him to change the topic like that.

"Six," Jonathan replied, casually taking the decanter from Sycamore Dorning's grasp. "No, that's not right. *Seven.* I'm considering seven." A lucky number since the days of the Romans, though Jonathan did not believe in luck.

"I started with a list of twelve. Most demented bit of arrogance I ever came up with, and my sisters abetted me. They likely wagered on the outcome, but my duchess foiled us all."

Foiled had never looked so fatuously content. Jonathan shoved Anselm's arm. "Go join what is sure to be the losing team. A man who needs a field of twelve potential duchesses to get him into the marital lists is a sorry creature."

"I have ever been one to thrive on challenges," Anselm said, passing Jonathan his empty glass. "The point is, I found the right duchess, or she found me, and she is all the treasure and happiness I will ever need. Enjoy courting seven women at once, Tresham, and get as much rest as you can. You'll need it."

Jonathan filled Anselm's drink from the decanter. "Who said anything about courting all seven? I'll consider six of them, but I intend to court only the one."

Anselm took his drink and lifted it a few inches in the air. "To your own true duchess, whoever she may be."

* * *

"The peaches are all gone," Diana said, dragging her spoon through her porridge. "Peaches and porridge would go ever so well together.".

The scent of cinnamon wafted up from her bowl, an indication of Theo's improved circumstances. She'd given Cook leave to replenish the spices, an unprecedented extravagance.

"All good things must end," Seraphina said, "and you oughtn't to play with your food."

Diana took a mouthful of her breakfast. "Peaches don't end. We could buy more."

"No," Theo said, "we cannot. They were a gift, and peaches are very dear."

"Dear," Diana huffed. "Rhymes with sneer, rear, fear, mere, jeer, drear… I do not like *dear*."

"Dear also rhymes with cheer," Seraphina retorted. "Clear, peer, and persevere. I like it very well."

Diana frowned at the spot two feet above the sugar bowl. "Chevalier. Leap year. Disappear."

"Your vocabulary is impressive," said a masculine voice from the doorway. "Dare I suggest the words atmosphere and belvedere?"

Jonathan Tresham wore riding attire and the beginnings of a smile. Theo's morning tea did a little dance in her belly, while Williams hovered behind Mr. Tresham, looking pleased with herself.

"Mr. Tresham, you must join us," Theo said. "Williams, another place setting, if you please."

Seraphina sat very tall, back not touching her chair. Diana watched Mr. Tresham as if he might steal her porridge.

"Thank you," he said. "I've enjoyed the morning air in Hyde Park, and some sustenance wouldn't go amiss."

"Do you mean you're hungry?" Diana asked.

Seraphina bowed her head.

"Mr. Tresham, you are joining us for a family meal," Theo said. "Otherwise, Diana would never forget her manners so far as to interrogate an adult guest."

"I am hungry," Mr. Tresham said, taking the seat at Theo's right hand, which put him next to Diana. "Also no great supporter of fancy words when plain speaking will do. I apologize for stopping by at such an hour, but my path took me past your door."

"Was the park *glorious* at dawn?" Seraphina was blushing. She had so little opportunity to converse with men that Theo applauded her courage.

"The park was quiet," Mr. Tresham said as Theo rose to fill a plate for him at the sideboard. "One forgets how precious natural quiet can be, how restorative."

"I find it so as well," Seraphina said, "though I've never been to the park at dawn."

Diana waved her spoon. "Why on earth would you leave a nice warm—?"

Theo set the plate before her guest. "We've more of everything." *Thanks to you.* The feelings that went along with having Mr. Tresham's money were complicated. Gratitude certainly, but also anxiety.

If Theo were to broach the outlandish possibility of an affair with him, would the discussion become sordid? Lucrative? Was she lost to all sense to even allow such musings into her mind?

"You should put salt on the eggs," Diana said. "They aren't as boring that way."

"Diana, if you're finished, you may take your plate to the sideboard," Theo said.

Seraphina's sigh of relief was audible.

"Thank you for the advice, Miss Diana. I'll give Comus your regards." He rose and came around the table to hold the girl's chair.

Diana, having never been shown such a courtesy, might have visited upon the moment some of the spectacular awkwardness she dispensed with heedless frequency. She instead left her chair with as much dignity as somebody in short dresses could, bounced a curtsey at Mr. Tresham, and skipped from the room.

"She *curtseyed*," Seraphina marveled.

"And," Theo added, "she smiled. Mr. Tresham, you must visit whenever you please."

"Yes, do." Seraphina passed him the salt cellar. "And if you send over more peaches, we might be able to bribe Diana into remaining silent the next time you call."

Mr. Tresham sent Theo a look over his plate of eggs and ham. His expression was solemn, his eyes were dancing.

"These eggs are good," he said. "My compliments to the cook."

"She will be delighted." Seraphina took a forkful of the eggs doubtless growing cold on her plate and went off into a desperate flight about the delights of mint tea first thing in the day.

Mr. Tresham murmured appropriate remarks at appropriate moments, until Seraphina's store of chatter was gone and his plate was empty.

"Seraphina, perhaps you and Diana might choose some irises for a bouquet,"

Theo said. "Mr. Tresham and I have a few matters to discuss." For he hadn't stopped by at such an hour to eat boring eggs and listen to Seraphina's equally uninspired conversation.

"We can choose the irises, Mrs. Haviland," Mr. Tresham said, standing to hold Theo's chair. "Let Miss Seraphina finish her breakfast in peace."

Oh, blast it all. Seraphina's gaze was nothing short of adoring.

"A fine suggestion," Theo said, rising. "Fina, please ring for Williams to clear when you're done."

For an instant, mutiny shone in Seraphina's eyes, making her look very much like Diana. The use of her nickname had done that, for which Theo mentally kicked herself.

"I will wish you good day." Mr. Tresham bowed over Seraphina's hand, as if he were her partner at a tea dance, and the mutiny was over before it had begun. "A pleasure to see you. The next basket of peaches will be in appreciation for your fine and gracious conversation."

That's laying it on a bit thick. "Come, Mr. Tresham. The irises are calling."

He accompanied Theo down the corridor that led past the kitchen steps, past the little back parlor that Theo used as her private sitting room. The floors in this part of the house did not shine with polish. The walls were bare plaster rather than covered in printed silk.

She was torn between embarrassment at the humble reality of her house and resentment that Mr. Tresham should even see the bare walls and cluttered office.

The garden, fortunately, was doing its best. The tulips had made a late start, while the irises, positioned against a sun-warmed stone wall, were being precocious. Still, Theo had never envisioned Jonathan Tresham amid her flowers, and with him at her side, her little patch of blooming ground felt... silly.

When a household lacked necessities, what mattered flowers?

"I was attempting polite conversation with your sister," Mr. Tresham said. "Did I pass muster?"

"Yes." A little too well. "I would never have known you were making an effort. You will please excuse Diana's lack of manners. Her only memories of having a man at the table go back to when Archie was alive, and he spoiled her shamelessly."

Though Archie had also on rare occasions offered Diana an effective, if gentle, reprimand.

"Shall we sit?" Mr. Tresham asked, gesturing toward the only bench in the garden. The fountain had been sold, leaving a circle of stones with a mere pot of herbs at the center. The bench sat on the shady side of the circle, opposite the irises.

"I deposited your bank draft," Theo said.

"I know."

"You sound serious, Mr. Tresham. Are you here to sack me? Perhaps you've found a bride on your own?" Which would be a relief. Also vexing in the extreme.

"I am here to confirm with you certain information that came to my attention earlier this week."

Theo settled on the bench, feeling like a prisoner in the dock. "Tell me the rest of it." Ever since paying off the last of Archie's debts, she had felt uneasy. She'd lived with the unrelenting anxiety of the debtor, and now…

Now, Mr. Tresham was calling upon her first thing in the day and enduring Cook's overdone eggs.

"The Duke of Anselm is among my acquaintances," he said, taking the place beside Theo. "He does not know the nature of my financial dealings with you. His Grace remarked in passing that the last of Mr. Haviland's debts had recently been paid. I encouraged the duke to maunder on—this was a private conversation between longstanding acquaintances—and it became clear to me that you have been the victim of significant misfortune."

Anselm had never promised Theo confidentiality, and Archie's debts had never been a secret among his friends.

Still, to be *discussed*… "Widowhood is considered a misfortune by some, not by all." The words surprised Theo, for their honesty and for their bitterness. "Forgive me, I'm not myself lately. I loved my husband and mourned his passing. Being able to resolve his debts will allow me to hold his memory in greater affection." The words were right. The unhappy tone was accurate too, though.

"Mrs. Haviland… Theodosia, shall I write to Lord Penweather? He has neglected you, Diana, and Seraphina shamefully."

Anselm deserved a hard kick in his ducal derriere. "Please do not. His lordship and I correspond, and he knows my situation. He did as Archie's will directed, and we cannot blame him for that. What did you come here to discuss?"

Mr. Tresham took Theo's hand. "How are you?"

She sensed the gesture was casual, like patting a mastiff. She could not discern Mr. Tresham's mood, though, as if he too had been disconcerted by the money that had changed hands.

"I am well, sir, and you?"

"I am furious at the way you've been treated, and I'm in no mood to be dangled before prospective duchesses. I spent half the night wondering if the most promising candidate for my bride isn't sitting right here beside me."

Theo very nearly looked to her right to see if another woman had joined them. "She's not. You are feeling protective, Mr. Tresham, and I esteem you for it, but we've come up with a list, and those are the ladies whom you ought to consider."

Motherhood had given Theo the gift of firm speech, though nothing would erase the sharp tug of despair Mr. Tresham's *wondering* provoked. An affair could be conducted nearly at arm's length. One needn't become entangled with a lover, but a man and wife could have few secrets.

Particularly if Mr. Tresham were the man and Theo the wife.

Still, he kept hold of her hand. "My flirtation needs work," he said. "My flowery speeches are a disaster, and my charm is nonexistent, but might I at least attempt to persuade you with a kiss?"

"You come calling at an unheard of hour to... to *kiss* me?" Theo wanted to laugh, to turn the moment to humorous incredulity, but Mr. Tresham's expression was serious.

She had spent nearly *all* of the night reliving their one embrace, a moment of such unexpected, undemanding comfort and closeness, she'd carried the memory into her dreams.

"I also stopped by to practice charming and flirting," he said, "but we know that's a lost cause where I'm concerned."

He'd charmed both Diana and Seraphina, and thus Theo as well. "I'm very much at sixes and sevens, Mr. Tresham. I was before you joined us for breakfast." That was thanks to him too, him and his bank draft, and the feeling of being able to surrender all burdens when held in his embrace.

"Tell me what has you upset, and call me Jonathan. If I've progressed to making a fool of myself in your garden, you should use my name when we are private."

"No, I should not." Theo should retrieve her hand, walk him to the back gate, and tell him not to come around again until he'd recovered his wits.

"What's bothering you, Theodosia? Tell me." He brushed his thumb over her knuckles, a tantalizing caress that a woman of mature years ought to be able to ignore. And to hear her name, spoken with such fierce assurance... Damn Archimedes for a selfish fool.

"You have me upset," she said. "You and your blasted money."

Mr. Tresham let go of her hand.

CHAPTER EIGHT

"What are they saying?" Diana asked, peering down into the garden.

"You needn't whisper," Seraphina replied. "They can't hear us." Theo and Mr. Tresham had likely also forgotten that every window on the back side of the house provided a view of the garden bench.

"But he was holding her hand. Mama never holds hands with gentlemen."

Diana was too smart, which resulted in all manner of problems. She took keen notice of everything and everyone around her and worried about all of it.

Losing a papa did that, as Seraphina well knew. "She holds hands with you, Di. We should come away from the window."

"I am not a gentleman, Fina. You go memorize some poem if you want to. I'm not letting Mama out of my sight."

"She and Mr. Tresham like each other. I think they are friends." Or were they something else? Cook had gone to market three days in a row and come back each time with an enormous haul. Last night, they'd had a joint of beef for supper, when a beef roast had become a rare treat even on Sundays.

At breakfast, before Mr. Tresham had arrived, Theo had mentioned buying fabric for new dresses. Diana's hems had been let down, let down again, and lengthened with sewn-on borders, though she didn't seem to care. Seraphina cared very much that, since they'd put off mourning, she'd had not a single new item of clothing other than a shawl she'd knitted herself.

"Mama does not look very friendly. She looks like she's had another letter from Cousin Viscount."

They referred to Diana's only male relation by indirection. Never Cousin Fabianus, never Lord Penweather. He frightened Theo, and because Seraphina had read her sister's private correspondence, he frightened Seraphina as well.

Nasty man. "Your mama and Mr. Tresham are merely having a discussion, Diana. Let's come away from the window."

Diana remained right where she was. "How will they cut irises without any scissors?"

"I'm sure Mr. Tresham carries a penknife."

"We should bring them the scissors."

Diana's suggestion was the result of knowing that Mr. Tresham brought with him the possibility of change. Seraphina hadn't decided whether it was a good change or a bad change, or simply a difference in routine. A stocked larder was good, a guest at breakfast was certainly interesting, but another letter had arrived from Cousin Viscount, and Seraphina hadn't found an opportunity to read it.

"The scissors," Seraphina said, "are in the locked parlor. If we retrieve them, then your mother will know we go where we ought not."

"Will Mr. Tresham go where he ought not?"

"You are too young to even ask that."

"Papa did. He went all manner of places he ought not, and he made Mama cry."

Diana ought not to have recalled that—she'd been a mere toddler when her papa had gone to his reward—and Seraphina wished she'd forget it. "She doesn't cry now, Diana."

Down in the garden, an earnest discussion was in progress, one Seraphina felt guilty for even watching. "We could bring your mother a basket to hold the flowers." Though first they'd have to find such a basket, which would take at least twenty minutes.

"A basket," Diana said, bolting for the door. "Mr. Tresham can hold the basket while Mama cuts the flowers, and that way, he can't hold her hand."

She was out the door, leaving Seraphina to take one last glance at the garden. The bench was empty, which was for the best. Seraphina had liked her late brother-in-law, until she'd realized that he wasn't a very nice man to be married to. Jolly and handsome, but fundamentally selfish and wed to a woman who had no capacity for selfishness at all.

If Mr. Tresham could teach Theo to be a little selfish, that would be a fine thing indeed.

* * *

Sometime while changing from evening attire into his riding clothes, Jonathan had taken to thinking of Mrs. Haviland as Theodosia. Morning light showed fatigue in her eyes, suggesting she had also passed a sleepless night.

Why?

"Show me your garden," he said, rising from the bench and holding out a hand. The little yard was a horticultural curiosity cabinet, with pots positioned on top of the walls, hanging from the branches of the lone maple, and lining the gravel walk.

The daffodils were fading along the east-facing wall, while the tulips were enjoying their finest moment and irises were only starting to bloom. Like Theodosia, the flowers weren't fancy, but they were lovely nonetheless.

"I'd rather show you to your horse," she said.

"I sent Roulette home with my groom." *Thank goodness.* "Are you anxious to be rid of me because I asked to kiss you, or because of my blasted money?"

She paused to twist off a potted hyacinth gone brown and droopy. "Let's start with the money. I've never had any of my own."

Few women did. "You mean funds, not merely pin money."

"I mean any sort of money. Archie was to disburse my pin money weekly, but I'd been married less than a month before I realized that system would be problematic. I had to go to my husband like a supplicant and remind him that another week had begun. He never forgot a luncheon at the clubs, never missed a Wednesday night card party, never failed to attend one of his friend's convivial evenings for men only."

She attacked another pot of fading hyacinths, casting the flowers onto a heap of dead leaves piled against the back wall. She had good aim.

"I thought Wednesday night was for dancing at Almack's." And those convivial evenings *for men only* did not sound like the Lonely Husbands gatherings.

"I thought Wednesday evening was for dancing as well. I learned otherwise. I eventually realized I needed to ask for a month's money and to make the request in front of others immediately after Archie's allowance arrived. Then he'd measure out the coin and make a great show of lecturing me about economies and prudent housewifery."

More dying flowers joined the heap of rotting leaves.

"Your husband was a fool."

She rounded on Jonathan, her hands fisted against her skirts. "Was he a fool, Mr. Tresham? Archie married me, and in return for dressing up and appearing at the church one Tuesday morning, he got an unpaid housekeeper, intimate favors, the use of my competence, and an increase in his allowance. For a fool, he did quite well for himself."

This emotional tempest had apparently been brewing for years, a particularly dangerous storm for being well hidden.

"Please tell me Haviland did not boast to you of his cleverness?"

She went after the next pot of hyacinths, pink this time. "When in his cups, Mr. Haviland could be devilishly honest. Then he'd forget, or pretend to forget, the hurtful words he'd spoken. I lived in dread of Diana waking up with a nightmare and getting a dose of her father's midnight demeanor. Bad enough that Seraphina saw more than her share. Then Archie would be his charming, handsome self come morning—or come noon."

Jonathan wrapped his hand round Theodosia's just as she yanked a perfectly lovely bloom from the pot.

"You are angry at yourself for failing to protect your sister, rather than proud of yourself for having protected your daughter, your domestics, your good name, and some of your memories of the man. His good name too, despite his every effort to the contrary."

She looked at the pink flower, which gave off a cloyingly sweet odor. "I must put this in water."

Jonathan took the hyacinth from her and propped it on the edge of the rain barrel in the corner of the garden next to the house. Theodosia watched him wending his way between her flowers, her expression suggesting he might make off with her blossom or crush it under his boots.

"I was wrong," Jonathan said, facing her squarely. "Your husband was not a fool, or not merely a fool. He was also a contemptible parasite. You might mourn his passing, I certainly cannot. He married you, knowing you had no family to speak for you or negotiate on your behalf. He betrayed your trust and failed to provide adequately. A man who lives off his expectations sometimes has little choice. A man who lives off his wife and child's security isn't a man."

The longer Jonathan considered Haviland's venery, the angrier he became, while Theodosia seemed soothed by his tirade.

"*Contemptible* sounds better when you say it," she murmured. "I lost respect for my husband. I tried not to lose compassion for him. Many men cannot moderate their consumption of spirits."

She wanted, desperately, to make excuses for a man whom she'd clearly also wanted to throttle. Jonathan still wanted to kiss her, though he understood better why Theodosia could not undertake such an intimacy lightly.

Nor should she.

"Many men drink to excess, Theodosia, but they do it without imperiling the security of their dependents. Even my father never jeopardized my mother's physical safety." What an odd relief to be able to say something positive about the man. "You told me the former viscount was vigorous in old age. What if the previous titleholder had lived another five years?"

She leaned against the tree, a venerable specimen that doubtless dropped leaves over the whole garden in autumn.

"At first, I thought Archie would settle down once he held the title, but since his death, I've admitted he was bent on ruin. He drank, he wagered, he gambled, he had affairs. God be thanked he had no bastards that I know of. If he'd inherited the Hampshire estates and income, he would have lost them on the turn of a card or through an inane bet with one of his friends."

Another Viscount Lipscomb, in other words. Mayfair was full of them, though solicitors and family usually limited the damage one ne'er-do-well could inflict on the inherited wealth.

"Instead, Haviland spent what you couldn't hide from him, and now that you have funds of your own, you vacillate between fear that the money will be snatched away and the compulsion to spend it all at once, so that nobody can steal it from you."

He'd apparently surprised her with that insight. He'd surprised himself too. Deductions, logical conclusions, algebraic variables, those he could manage handily, though insight seldom befell him.

"Exactly," Theodosia said. "I must be the least sensible widow ever to come into money. I am tempted to buy out all the shops one moment—so very, exceedingly tempted—and then I want to tell my banker never to let me withdraw more than a single pound at once."

Jonathan longed to hug her, to reassure her physically that her worries were normal. Instead, he offered her his arm.

"Let's enjoy the alley for a moment. You have a pretty little lane back there, and if I'm not mistaken, we are being chaperoned from the windows."

She pushed away from the tree and wrapped her fingers around Jonathan's elbow. "Oh, doubtless. Seraphina and Diana keep an eye on me, the way I used to watch Archie. If anything happens to me, life changes for them, probably not for the better. Have you ever been short of funds, Mr. Tresham? Ever wanted to fling money at every crossing sweeper until no more money remained to worry you?"

Jonathan led her through the gate, latching it behind them. "I was raised on a very strict allowance provided by my uncle. I counted every penny twice and deliberated over every expenditure. While at university, I came into some money as a result of my mother's passing, which I invested well. Some money became—by my standards at the time—a fortune. I grew obsessed not with money, but with figures, which was my salvation."

Theodosia took his arm again, this time without him having to pointedly offer. "So you are scandalously wealthy in your own right?"

In her present mood, he didn't dare name sums. "Afraid so. Does this bring us to the part about why you don't care for my kisses?"

They were ambling down the alley, a peaceful, sun-dappled strip of cobblestone shaded by tall maples and enveloped in the quiet of a placid neighborhood. Birds flitted overhead. The scent of horses came from the mews twenty yards on.

"Your kisses are much like the money," Theodosia said. "You are the first man to express a respectful interest in me since I put off mourning. I say this not to flatter you, Mr. Tresham. The prospect of your kisses strikes me rather like the prospect of buying out all the shops in Mayfair. Such a use of my resources would be unwise and unnecessary, and yet, I am sorely, sorely tempted."

Jonathan drew her into the shade of an oak. "If that's not flattery, then what is it?"

She looked up and down the alley, her expression stern. "That is a warning, Mr. Tresham."

Then she kissed him.

* * *

Theo dared not allow Jonathan Tresham to court her. Such a notion would be dangerous and absurd. But in what manual of bearable widowhood was it written that a woman could not enjoy a kiss with a willing swain?

Where was it written that she must deny herself even a moment's pleasure and comfort? The alley was deserted, and Mr. Tresham had haunted what few dreams she'd stolen from the night.

"Theo…"

She allowed him those two syllables, in case he sought to demur. Instead, he imbued her name with tenderness and humor.

Also with encouragement, so Theo looped her arms around his neck and dived into an exploration of the wonders of his kiss. Her first impression of Jonathan Tresham was his big, fit male body. Had her life depended on it, she could not have toppled him. Broad shoulders, muscular arms, long legs, and all of it pressed as close to her as clothing allowed.

Bodily sensations confirmed that she was, truly, intimately embracing a man she ought not to be touching: The hard bone and taut muscle of his shoulders, the more subtle feel of his watch chain trailing across his abdomen to a buttonhole. Below that, irrefutable evidence of masculine desire.

A bad moment ensued, when memories of Archie pushing himself against her without invitation tried to contaminate pleasure with anger. Mr. Tresh—Jonathan—must have sensed the intrusion, because he lifted his mouth from hers and cradled her cheek against his palm.

If Theo gave him the least indication, he'd doubtless step back, drop his hands from her person, and maintain a gentlemanly silence while she sorted her thoughts. That reliable consideration, that attentiveness, had her turning her face into his caress and kissing him again.

As a girl, she'd viewed kissing as a forbidden but safe pleasure. A stolen kiss seldom ruined a young lady, if it was a chaste stolen kiss.

Chastity had been nothing more than Society's window dressing on an ignorance that benefitted everybody but the young lady, and Theo was finished with honoring Society's convenience above her own.

She moved into Jonathan's embrace, pulled him closer, and seamed his mouth with her tongue. His lips curved, a smile, then a welcome, and holy celestial bodies, he knew what he was about. His hand on the back of Theo's head let her relax, giving him her weight and her balance. His arm about her waist was another assurance that all she need do is enjoy his kiss.

I have you. That message came through in the curve of his body, his confident stance, the deft touch of his tongue at the corners of her mouth. He was aroused, more so with each moment, but such was the patience and curiosity of his kiss that Theo need not monitor his responses. She could instead revel in her own.

To *desire* a man. To desire him, rather than endure marital pawing, dreading the possibility of conception. Oh, the years and years…

How could joy and sadness be so exquisitely present in the same instant?

Jonathan's hand moved over Theo's back in slow caresses as she eased away from the kiss. She needed his support to remain upright, so ambushed was she by sorrow.

Not for Archie. His situation had been tragic, but she'd given him the mourning he was due. The sorrow was for herself, for her innocence and trust in the world, for all that might have been and could not be.

"Do I take it," Jonathan said, "that you would allow me to pay you my addresses?"

His voice was rough, his breathing deep. How could any woman say no to such a question when she wanted to push the man who asked it against the nearest wall and resume kissing him?

And yet, she must refuse.

He brushed a lock of hair back from her brow and tucked it over her ear, the touch gentle and intimate, though not overtly seductive.

Except that for Theo, small considerations and caring gestures could seduce her common sense right to Bedlam. She must refuse him firmly and soon.

But not just yet.

* * *

"What on all of God's good green earth necessitated a social call at this unspeakable hour?" Anselm used his Duke of the Underworld tone, the one that often inspired his duchess into tickling him if they were private.

Sycamore Dorning was a bachelor, and for the most part, Anselm considered him a monument to youthful carelessness. Careless dress, careless speech, careless drinking, the same as many younger sons of titled families.

Today, he was dressed in immaculate morning attire, an enormous dog panting at his heels. Anselm's butler was ignoring the dog, which was nigh impossible for anybody but a duke's upper servants.

"This is when Samson takes his second walk of the day. I apologize for appearing with a canine in tow, but the pup takes his walks seriously."

And Sycamore, apparently, took the pup's welfare seriously—the pup who weighed a good twelve stone.

"Is it house-trained?" Anselm asked.

Sycamore lifted an eyebrow. The gesture should have been comical—a youthful attempt at masculine posturing—but Sycamore was maturing. He'd grown tall before going up to university, and he was developing muscle as well.

Perhaps he was even acquiring a scintilla of common sense.

"Very well," Anselm said, "come along and bring the beast. I warn you, if the children see him, they will demand to take him captive."

"He likes children, but then, he's a dog. He likes anybody who deserves liking. He doesn't judge people based on their youthful errors or common foibles."

Anselm attempted the same scowl that sometimes prevented him from laughing at his daughters' misconduct in the nursery. "While you call on dukes who ought to still be abed. Are we swilling tea?"

The click of dog toenails on the parquet floors was a comforting, domestic sound, and the beast seemed content to trot at Mr. Dorning's heels. Dorning's brother Willow was a highly respected dog trainer, though no power on earth had yet succeeded in devising a means of training unruly younger siblings.

"If tea will assist one of your ancient years to remain awake," Sycamore said, "then by all means, ring for tea. Perhaps a tisane might be in order as well, if you overtaxed yourself at ninepins."

Sycamore's team had won, in part because of his deadly accurate right arm. Anselm's team had… not won.

"Wait until next month," Anselm said, opening the door to the library. "We'll have an exhibition of swordsmanship and see who needs a tisane the next day."

He'd chosen the library because it looked out over the back terrace and gardens rather than the street. A front parlor was a public space, the drapes usually drawn back so any passerby might note the identities of guests.

The unusual hour of the call, the unusual nature of the caller, suggested privacy was in order.

"Somebody likes books," Sycamore said, twirling to take in the rows of shelves. "All manner of books. Have you many on mathematics?"

What an odd question. "A few. My younger brother is something of a scholar." Which was something of a surprise. "Why do you ask?"

Sycamore gestured with his hand, and the dog settled before the hearth. The mastiff made an attractive picture, panting gently, enormous paws outstretched.

"I have an interest in turning my few coins into many, the same as every other young man of imposing pedigree and unimpressive allowance. Casriel has his hands full with the earldom, and his resources are limited. I tell you this in confidence, of course, though the Dornings have long been known for having a wealth of good looks and poverty in every meaningful regard."

"Get to the point, man. I want you out of my house before my daughters learn I've allowed a dog on the premises."

Sycamore grinned, though his smile wasn't as boyish as it had been last Season. "The ladies love him too. If ever your duchess takes you into dislike, a nice, soft puppy with big eyes and a happy little tail—"

"I could toss you through a window and play fetch the twig with yonder mastodon. Your puppy would likely enjoy the game almost as much as I would."

"Insult me all you please, Anselm, but have the dignity not to insult a hapless creature. I have a problem."

The rebuke was deserved, the admission startling. "From all reports, you *are* a problem. You take stupid risks, drink to excess, refuse to attend university, and can't keep a civil tongue in your head." Though so far this Season, young Dorning had not been an object of talk.

"We could not *afford* to send me to university, so refusing to go seemed a kindness all around. Willow has set me up for this year—marriage improved his fortunes—but I found a way to rent my rooms in Oxford for a small profit, and thus I'm here trying to nudge Casriel in the direction of the altar."

"Bowling your elders into submission. What is the nature of your problem?" Part of Sycamore's problem was doubtless an abundance of siblings. Two sisters were happily married, but of his six brothers, only Willow had found a mate. The Earl of Casriel—Grey Birch Dorning, by name—Ash, Oak, Valerian, and Hawthorne were unwed and largely without independent means.

"I pay attention," Sycamore said, hands in pockets as he ambled along the French horticultural treatises.

"Younger siblings have a tendency to nosiness. I have four, and the trait bred true."

Anselm's guest took down a bound monograph on the propagation of tulips. The angle of the sunlight coming through the tall windows played a trick, making Sycamore Dorning look older than his years and scholarly. Contemplative, even.

The lingering effects of a surfeit of Tresham's good brandy were not to be underestimated.

"Does Jonathan Tresham own The Coventry Club?" Sycamore asked, leafing through the treatise.

He might just as well have asked if the French had invaded Yorkshire. "I beg your pardon?" Nobody knew of Tresham's association with the club, and it was certainly no business of an impecunious younger son.

"Tresham, our host last night," Sycamore said. "You and he are friends, or as good as. You don't have a private conversation that turns a man's countenance murderous unless you're either friends or enemies with him. Enemies are tedious. You have no patience for tedium. Therefore, you and he must be friends."

"You are blazingly confident in your syllogism."

"And you do not deny my conclusion. I mean the man no harm. In fact, I think he could use another friend. These illustrations are lovely."

"Tresham is a ducal heir. He must choose his friends carefully."

Sycamore reshelved the treatise where he'd found it. "Oh, right, of course, Your Grace. The rest of us can simply associate at will with all and sundry, no need for prudence or care. Swindlers and card sharps will do for us, while the likes of you lot must only associate with paragons and war heroes."

He wandered off in the direction of the biographies, the dog's gaze following him.

"Now that you've stuck out your figurative tongue at me," Anselm said, "why are you here?" Sycamore Dorning—*this* version of Sycamore Dorning—would not have willingly called on a duke.

"Tresham wears a particular fragrance, one that blends gardenia, tuberose, and jasmine. I came across it on him in Paris and assume it's either proprietary or quite expensive. I've smelled it at The Coventry on occasion as I sip my champagne in the little nook beneath the screened stairway. Took me an age to place the fragrance, but then I realized that the tread on the stair was familiar to me as well."

"How in the hell can you distinguish a man's footfalls?"

Dorning took a seat uninvited, appropriating the reading chair next to his dog. "You know your duchess's walk, Anselm."

"She is my duchess." Anselm knew her walks, her sighs, her smiles, her silences, and she knew his.

"When you begin life at the bottom of a large pile of siblings, you learn to pay attention to them. Who is home, who is out? Which brother is spoiling for a fight, which one needs a pounding? Which sister is prepared to deliver it to him? "One learns to pay attention," Dorning went on, "because nothing is explained, nothing is rendered sensible by adult interpretation. I can tell you which of my brothers is coming up the steps and whether he's sober, well-rested, exhausted, or furious based on his tread on the stairs—not that he'd admit any of that to me. This is why I like numbers. They behave rationally, except the ones that don't, and even those enjoy a fixed definition."

Dorning shot his cuffs, the gesture curiously sophisticated. "Tresham pops up three steps, then pauses to look about, then three more, like a well-trained cavalry patrol in unfamiliar territory. When he escorts his guests above stairs, the rhythm is unmistakable."

A problem indeed. "Assuming your recitation is true," Anselm said, "how is it relevant, and why present yourself and your hound on my doorstep before noon?"

The hound turned a patient gaze on Anselm, as if the duke, rather than Dorning, were the presuming upstart.

"I'm concerned somebody at The Coventry is cheating," Dorning said. "Tresham seems a decent fellow. If he's the owner, he needs to put a stop to it before harm results."

Another simple exercise in logic, with profound consequences. Anselm sank into the second reading chair, sorting and discarding possibilities.

"We will discuss hypotheticals," he said slowly, "and we will discuss them in confidence."

Dorning waved a hand. "Tresham is a decent sort, and he's awash in money. He has no need to run a crooked house. Somebody wants to ruin The Coventry or ruin Tresham. The play is honest. I've watched closely, and when the house takes a cut from every pot, crooked tables would be errant stupidity."

Dorning was a hotheaded stripling, but his assurance was so absolute, almost casual, that Anselm believed him.

"Explain yourself." *So that I might have time to think.*

"At The Coventry, the house keeps a percentage of every pot, which means a percentage of every bet placed, at every table, without exception. Revenue for the house is assured as long as the tables are busy. No need to create rules or break rules to keep the money coming in. The most imbecilic, irredeemable blunder the owner of the premises could make would be to allow rumors of crooked play to start."

Anselm knew this. He did not know what to do about such rumors. "You're certain the owner has committed such a blunder?"

Sycamore rose. The dog followed him with his gaze, but remained, chin on paws, before the hearth.

"What sort of question is that for a duke to ask about his friend, Anselm? You disappoint me, and we callow youths need our good examples. I'm sure that Tresham has not committed such blunder, but somebody has. A skilled player could do it, a team, an employee dealing at the tables working with a team. The place is busy. Many a sore loser would like to see it fail. I've watched for five straight nights and seen nothing beyond decks of cards reused more frequently than they should be, but then, I'm not a natural cheat."

"Keep watching, say nothing, and I'll tell… I'll let the owner know of your concerns. Why didn't you simply approach Tresham yourself?"

Dorning made a motion with his index finger, and the dog rose to sit beside him. "Tresham is reported to be hunting a bride. Having a brother in the same condition, I can tell you the hunt takes a toll on a man's disposition. Then too, I trust the word of my friends over that of other people's presuming younger brothers. Tresham needs to take the matter in hand immediately and silently. A rousing altercation with a noted young wastrel—regardless of the wastrel's obvious reform—in the middle of the day would be hard for even ducal servants to keep quiet."

He bowed and started for the corridor.

"Nobody considers you a wastrel," Anselm said, retracing their steps to the front door.

"Only because I haven't any means to waste."

"A helpful limitation for some, but your reputation is merely that of a young man in the process of learning self-restraint. Most of the House of Lords has yet to master the same challenge. Your brothers know this. They will do their utmost to assist you."

When they reached the front door, he passed Dorning a high-crowned beaver and a plain oaken walking stick.

"One doesn't want their assistance," Dorning said, setting his hat at a dapper angle. "One wants to *be* of assistance to them. I'm an uncle. Makes a man think. You'll not let Tresham know we've spoken, or he'll consider the source and ignore the message."

And that—knowing that a propensity for overimbibing and placing stupid wagers made one noncredible—also made a man think.

"I'll find a moment to tell him in the near future. My thanks for your concern."

Sycamore went on his way, the dog trotting at his side, while Anselm considered how to tell a very proud and private man that he had allowed a serpent to slither over his garden wall.

CHAPTER NINE

Being kissed by Theodosia Haviland brought a second dawn to Jonathan's day, one even more glorious than Hyde Park on a sunny spring morning. Her kisses shot straight past flirtation to a ringing declaration of desire, of intent to share intimacies long denied.

He stood in the alley, stroking his fingers along the resolute angle of her jaw, while the softness of her fragrance made him want to sniff every curve, hollow, and secret place on her body. A sense of having seized on a worthy ambition muted pure lust, for his dreams where Theo was concerned encompassed more than carnal appetites.

But what of *her* dreams? "You have had years to indulge in a discreet affair, Theodosia. At least some part of you must be attracted to me, else you'd never allow me liberties in a sunny alley."

If the patronesses from Almack's had burst through the nearest garden gate, she could not have leaped back more quickly.

"I am losing my mind," she muttered. "Perhaps senility has set in, despite being only halfway to my dotage. I've heard of such things." She paced away, skirts swishing.

"We kissed, Theo, and a marvelous kiss it was. Why castigate yourself for that?" Of all women, the widow alone was allowed to kiss whom she pleased with impunity, provided she was discreet.

She glowered at him over her shoulder. "Marvelous, indeed. Magical. This is your fault."

Marriage to her would be a marvelous, magical puzzle. "I should hope so, though as I recall, you initiated the magic."

"Very bad of me."

"Very wonderful of you." He held out a hand. "You are trying to talk yourself into a case of guilt, because you are supposed to be my matchmaker, not my duchess. We haven't executed a contract excluding you from consideration, and yet, I see you flagellating yourself with that nonsense."

She didn't take his hand, but she took his arm, wrapping her fingers around his sleeve. "I woke up this morning, expecting to spend my day in the agreeable pursuit of purchasing fabric for Seraphina's first ball gown."

Jonathan could buy the girl an entire shop full of ball gowns. If he said as much, he'd doubtless compound whatever muddle Theodosia was determined to visit upon herself.

"My kisses pale compared to an expedition to the mercer's?"

Ah, finally. A small smile. Self-conscious but genuine. "Your kisses outshine a Beltane bonfire. You cannot marry me."

"Why not?" Jonathan did not expect an honest answer. Theodosia was flustered, meaning she'd be all the more cautious with her truths. "List the excuses, madam, for that's all they'll be. You like me, you find me attractive, and you have every quality I need in a duchess."

She dropped his arm. "While you lack the humility needed in a duke. Good heavens, Mr. Tresham. Do you suppose I'd marry any man simply because I fancy his kisses? Look how that ended with Archimedes."

She twitched at her fichu, a gauzy bit of lavender lace that brought out the blue of her eyes—and reminded Jonathan of the pleasure of her breasts pressed to his chest.

Focus, man. Pay attention. Jonathan had taught himself to count cards, to keep as many as three decks straight in his head even in the midst of rapid play. He needed every bit of that concentration to deal with what troubled Theodosia.

"I see the problem," he said. "I must compete with Archimedes's unsainted memory for your trust. You are no longer that lonely, unsteady girl, Theodosia. If another Archimedes bows over your hand at tonight's entertainment, you will smile, curtsey, and dismiss him without a second thought. Please do not disrespect my honorable intentions by dismissing me similarly."

She patted his lapel. "I can dismiss whom I please, and there's nothing you can say to it."

She'd dealt him an ace, bless her. "Would that young woman, the one smitten with a handsome bounder, have delivered such a stunning and accurate set-down without a second thought, as you just did?"

Jonathan took her hand, put it on his arm, and led her in the direction of her garden gate. Her silence suggested a rearrangement of perspective, a crack in her mistrust through which the light of hope might shine.

This game they'd initiated was a greater challenge than winning at cards, also far more important.

"I am not that young woman," Theodosia said slowly, coming to a halt in the alley. "I am also not your duchess. I'm impoverished and of no great lineage. The only child I produced in five years of marriage was a girl. I'm not young. I have no political connections. I'm not... a *diamond* in any sense."

Oh, but she was, and she was also, as predicted, listing excuses.

"If I protest, you will bat aside my sincere compliments, so let us instead agree to disagree and to compromise."

Theodosia Haviland clearly did not like surprises, which was understandable when most of the surprises in her life had been nasty. A wolf in husband's clothing, a will that had done nothing to provide for her child. So Jonathan would give her time to adjust to the notion of becoming his duchess and give himself time to earn her consent.

A sound, logical plan.

"One does not compromise regarding permission to court, Mr. Tresham. One says yes or no, and I am clearly, firmly, unequivocally saying..."

She was clearly, firmly addressing the cobbles, not looking him in the eye, and that was not his Theo. He touched a finger to her lips.

"One can say, 'Not yet.' One can say, 'Let me think about it.' One can say, 'Sir, you have got above yourself, and a few weeks of torture on the rack of despair and hope—while I call the tune and you do the dancing—is the least a lady is owed.' You can say that, Theo. You needn't choose in this instant."

Now, she gazed at him, her expression at first unreadable, then breaking into a slow smile that gained certainty and joy as it rose to her eyes.

"You will dance with the six ladies on that list, Mr. Tresham. You will engage them in conversation, all six of them. You will be agreeable and interested in them, and if—*after* you've given them fair and open-minded consideration—you still want to renew your request to me, we will discuss it further at that time."

He'd won. He'd won as surely as if she'd shown him the location of every other card in the deck.

"I will dance with those ladies, exert myself to be polite with them, and even, if you insist, send them modest bouquets, but I won't kiss them, Theo." Wouldn't be tempted to kiss them, in fact.

"You must comport yourself as you see fit, Mr. Tresham."

She had regained her balance, as evidenced by her posture and by the flash of determination in her eyes.

He leaned near, almost within kissing range. Her scent teased at his self-restraint, and when he realized she was also breathing through her nose, he nearly yielded to the urge to steal another kiss.

But, no. The stakes were high. Concentration must not be broken.

"Call me Jonathan," he whispered, "when we are private." He remained close to her for one more instant, long enough to know he'd tempted her, before he stepped back and bowed.

She curtseyed. She did not smile, though as Jonathan strode up the alley, her laughter trailed after him.

* * *

The shopping expedition had to be put off until Cook and Williams returned from the market, because dragging an unwilling Diana from the glovemakers' to the milliners' would dim Theo's joy in the day.

She had stolen a kiss from Jonathan Tresham. He'd stolen her wits. The exchange, in the opinion of Theo's foolish, impractical heart, had been worth the risk.

She paced at the foot of the steps—paced!—waiting for Seraphina to come down. A knock on the front door nearly sent her preening to the mirror over the sideboard, like a young girl expecting her suitor to return on the pretext of having forgotten his walking stick.

The person on Theo's doorstep wasn't Jonathan, wasn't even male.

"Mrs. Compton. Good day."

Mrs. Compton was an acquaintance only, though her husband and Archimedes had been friendly. She waited on the front step, no maid or daughter with her, though a groom stood by a gig in the street.

"Mrs. Haviland."

"Won't you come in?"

She stepped over the threshold with the air of one admitted to a den of vice during daylight hours. Her curiosity was apparent, as was her unwillingness to be caught gawking.

"I won't take up much of your time," Mrs. Compton said. "This is a social call."

What else would it be? "The family parlor enjoys good afternoon sunlight," Theo said. "The formal parlor is better suited for earlier in the day."

Mrs. Compton was the sort who might be offended by a choice of parlor, but then, her oldest daughter was rusticating in Italy and Dora Louise might well end up waltzing in her sister's footsteps. An insistence on propriety was likely Mrs. Compton's only means of maintaining sanity.

"You are gracious to receive me," Mrs. Compton said when Theo offered her a seat in the family parlor. "We are not friends, but I have discussed the matter with my sister, Lady Hopewell, and she agrees with my decision."

Lady Hopewell had married a viscount. This fact found its way into almost all of Mrs. Compton's public conversations.

"I am always glad to welcome good company under my roof, Mrs. Compton. Shall I ring for tea?" Hammet, Theo's man-of-all-work, knew how to put together a tea tray.

"Tea won't be necessary." Mrs. Compton sat on the very edge of her seat cushion. "I've come to apologize."

Clearly, apologies involved gall and wormwood. "I am unaware of any reason you might have to do so."

Mrs. Compton had been pretty once, in the preferred manner of the blond English rose. She was fading now, into anxiety, middle age, and very likely, marital neglect. Her bonnet, reticule, and parasol were awash in lace, as if she'd bring a tide of consequence with her instead of the graciousness and warmth she might have claimed as a younger woman.

"When Clarice, my oldest, made her come out, Mr. Compton said you weren't good *ton*. I wasn't to encourage any connection between you and my daughter."

Jonathan had turned the morning into a delightful, if troubling, muddle. Mrs. Compton was threatening to ruin the day—if not Theo's life.

"Did you come here to insult me?"

Mrs. Compton rose on a rustle of silk and lace. "Certainly not. Mr. Compton is no judge of Society, but he is my husband. I heeded his wishes, because my daughters did not need the good offices of a common widow when Lady Hopewell sponsored them."

Ever since Archie's death, Theo had waited for scandal to find her. She'd waited for doors to close, whispers to start. How ironic that today, when she might have been courted by a ducal heir, Mrs. Compton should bring trouble to her door.

"Mrs. Compton, if the sad day ever befalls you when you too become a *common widow*, you will realize that nobody needs us unless we're willing to remarry and arrange our lives for another man's comfort and convenience. I'll see you out."

A hint of Dora Louise's determination shone in her mother's eyes as she resumed her seat. "Please hear me out. I came to thank you for preventing Dora from making an utter cake of herself at the Earl of Bellefonte's ball. She takes after her father in some regards—impulsive, convinced of her own genius. She's young, Mrs. Haviland, and terrified that her sister's circumstances will become known before Dora can secure a match."

As Theo was terrified for Seraphina and Diana.

Her ire faded, and curiosity took its place. "The threat of scandal should frighten any young lady, but Clarice is merely seeing the Continental sights in the company of a dear and generous family friend. Nobody will hear any differently from me."

This conversation called for a glass of cordial, though the parlor was stocked only with Madeira. Theo poured two glasses and brought one to her guest.

"Thank you."

Theo took the end of the sofa nearest Mrs. Compton's chair. "What did you really come here to say, ma'am?"

"You have held your tongue regarding Clarice's idiocy. You intervened when

Dora set herself up to be a laughingstock scorned by the best families or preyed upon by a cad as her sister was. You are a mother, you provide a home for your sister, and she will soon make her bow. I cannot openly defy my husband, Mrs. Haviland, but I can express my thanks for your kindness. You could ruin both of my daughters with an unkind word, and yet, you have not."

"Nor will I."

Mrs. Compton took a ladylike taste of her drink. "I don't think I could be as decent as you have been. Mr. Compton enjoys wagering, you see, though not excessively. I know what a mess Mr. Haviland left behind, because Mortimer passes gossip on to me."

Theo waited with a sense of inevitability. Would today be the day that Archie's death called in its remaining markers? Would today be the day that Theo wrote to Lord Penweather and insisted that he provide a home for Theo and her dependents?

"My husband will likely die in debt as well," Mrs. Compton said. "That is not my fault, just as Mr. Haviland's situation was not your doing. Gentlemen must maintain standards, though nobody is very clear on how that's to be accomplished."

So Mr. Compton's *not excessive* wagering was a problem after all. Theo sipped her drink, though she would have preferred some of Bea's cordial. Mrs. Compton did not know the whole of Archie's disgrace. God willing, she never would.

"Why are you telling me this?"

"So that you will know you aren't alone, Mrs. Haviland. Perhaps so that I know the same thing. Intemperance, infidelity, wagering... I could forgive him all of it, but then I see my girls. One ruined, the other desperate... They did not ask to have a bumbler for a papa. The worst part is, I love him. I love that he tries to do better. I love that he's never blamed me. I love so much about him, but he's wrong about you, probably worried that you'll spill some secret of his. After Mr. Haviland's death, Mortimer avoided The Coventry Club for an entire year."

Theo hated the very name. "There are too many clubs just like it, unfortunately. I do thank you for calling on me. Nobody else has."

They shared a silence, one that spoke of loneliness, self-doubt, and weariness.

"When I get Dora Louise situated, I'm going to Italy," Mrs. Compton said, peering into her half-empty glass. "I haven't told anybody that—not even Lady Hopewell—but Italy is much more affordable and very beautiful."

She had a grandchild in Italy, and with Mrs. Compton out of the country, her family could stop propping up an intemperate wastrel.

"Mr. Compton could end up in debtors' prison." Theo well knew how that prospect could haunt a wife.

"My brothers say the sponging houses have given many a man reason to stop squandering his coin and his life on drink."

"The people who say that have never been in the sponging houses, nor been addicted to drink. Have you anybody in mind for Dora Louise?"

By halting degrees, over another serving of wine, Mrs. Compton shared her hopes for Dora Louise and agreed when Theo suggested Lord Lipscomb should not be encouraged to stand up with the girl. Mrs. Compton passed along the name of a modiste in Bloomsbury whose prices were reasonable and who wasn't above adding some embroidery or a new underskirt to last year's creations.

The visit became almost pleasant and exceeded its polite allotment of minutes considerably. Theo saw her guest to the door, glad that Seraphina hadn't intruded.

"If you love Mr. Compton, you might suggest he accompany you to Italy."

"I have hinted," Mrs. Compton said, undoing the bow that secured her parasol. "I fear he loves his wagering and drink more than I love him. My brothers say I must put the choice to Mortimer, for surely he'll not disgrace his wife and daughters by drinking himself into penury."

Viscount Penweather had insisted on the same righteous reasoning, and Theo hoped Archie was haunting his lordship's nightmares.

"When the time comes, you'll know better how to proceed. Come back whenever you please, and I'll serve you a decent cup of tea."

"Tea grows tiresome," Mrs. Compton said. "Gunpowder is all Lady Hopewell serves." Resentment lurked at the edge of her smile, but so did a touch of self-deprecating humor.

On impulse, Theo hugged her guest, a firm embrace. Mrs. Compton looked slightly dazed by that presumption, but she didn't pull away. Theo felt as if she were hugging her former self, a woman doing the best she could with an impossible situation.

A woman whose husband had left the seeds of scandal scattered in his wake, seeds that still might germinate into ruin.

* * *

Jonathan enjoyed music. He did not enjoy musicales. Part of the problem was the quality of entertainment on offer. Young people with no other talent to their name save marriageability were put on display early in the evening, warbling through a repertoire that was meant for trained voices.

His usual strategy was to appear in time for the second half of the evening, but tonight he was prompt. Theo would be among the guests, and for her, he would endure *Caro Mio Ben* until his ears fell off.

"Are you avoiding me?" a soft female voice asked.

The first thought to spring to Jonathan's mind was, *Damnation*, followed by: The only force of nature more determined than a debutante pursuing a tiara was a long-lost half-sister pursuing her brother.

"Lady Della." Jonathan bowed over her hand as any gentleman ought to. He did not know Della Haddonfield well, but he knew she was intent on forming some sort of association with him.

"Answer the question. Are you avoiding me?" She smiled, though her eyes promised unending retribution if he answered honestly.

"Shall we peruse the buffet? I've yet to partake." He'd also yet to see Theo, who should have given up her buffet-prowling ways.

Della tucked her hand around Jonathan's arm lightly, as if contact with her might spook him into a dead gallop. Moira occasionally took his arm. The Duchess of Quimbey could hang on to a man more firmly than a barnacle affixed itself to a seagoing frigate.

With Lady Della, this common courtesy made him uneasy. "How have you been keeping?" he asked, because small talk was safe.

"Miserably. I have a brother who refuses to call on me, won't acknowledge me in public, and can't give me a reason why. You socialize with my siblings, but you won't socialize with *me*."

The buffet was lavish—Lady Westhaven was married to a ducal heir and entertained accordingly—and yet, no Theo appeared amid the throng circling the tables in his lordship's library. No Lady Canmore either, though Casriel was standing guard over a table of sweets and looking like a lonely mastiff.

"Are we not socializing at this very moment, my lady?"

"You can be a brother when the task requires sarcasm, but not when it requires acknowledging me."

"I've given you the letters." Jonathan kept his voice down, but he sensed Della was on the verge of making a scene. Perhaps she was always on the verge of making a scene. She put him in mind of Sycamore Dorning, prepared to engage in rash measures if necessary to achieve her ends.

Reckless, like Jonathan's father.

But then, his father was *her* father.

"Are you well?" Lady Della asked, for Jonathan had come to a halt in the middle of the library.

"Of course. What are you hungry for?"

"An honest argument, such as I have with my other siblings on any given day. We snap and snarl, sometimes we sulk and pout, then we make up. We even laugh together and cry friends. The concept isn't complicated, and you are rumored to be a well-educated man."

Rumored. She was listening to rumors about him. Annoyance laced with panic threatened to spoil Jonathan's evening. "I attended Cambridge and managed reasonably well."

Lady Della wore a paisley silk shawl that brought out the blue of her eyes. She was a small woman and not yet twenty, but she carried herself like a veteran of many Seasons. Her confidence was subtle. She might not even describe herself as confident, but she enjoyed an ease in polite surrounds that Jonathan did not.

"You were top wrangler," she said. "Why wouldn't you admit as much to me?"

"Because our sainted father ridiculed that accomplishment, ridiculed my choice of university, and most of all, ridiculed me for being intrigued by numbers when my birthright was to be intrigued by loose women and cheap drink."

"My mother was not a loose woman."

They are all Dora Louise. Theo's words came to Jonathan, and the retort he would have made died unspoken: *If you insist on being difficult, this will be our last conversation.* Papa had likely said as much to Mama, and she'd replied in kind, until half of Mayfair had been an audience to their farces.

"I apologize," Jonathan said. "I intended to state a fact about my late father and nobody else."

Della shoved a plate at him. "You need to work on your apologies. My other brothers have the knack, but then, they are married, all but Adolphus. You put me in mind of him."

"He also attended Cambridge?"

"After you graduated. He's a chemist. He likes to blow things up. I get on with him wonderfully."

I'm sure you do. Jonathan kept that observation to himself as well, because Della's recitation implied not only a protectiveness toward her lone bachelor brother—her *other* bachelor brother—but pride in his explosions.

She was not proud of Jonathan, as his father had not been proud of him.

Not that a half-sister's regard was a very great matter. "Of what dishes shall you partake?"

Della picked up a second plate. "I'd like a small serving of social interaction, perhaps a morning call with a short drive in the park. An accepted dinner invitation would make a nice side dish, and for dessert, you could sit with me at this evening's entertainment. Failing that, an occasional dance—I see you dancing nearly every set, Jonathan—or a pleasant exchange during the carriage parade."

Don't call me Jonathan. Any familiarity would be remarked by the gossips.

Lady Della was troubling over her food choices, picking up the spoon from a savory curry, then setting it back into the bowl without taking a portion. At the side of the room, the oldest of her enormous brothers—her Haddonfield brothers—made polite conversation with Lord Westhaven.

"Aren't you hungry?" Lady Della asked.

Jonathan put a pastry of some sort on his plate. "I am in search of a bride." He spoke very quietly, praying that this confession would meet with some sororal tact.

"More to the point, the brides are in search of you. I could help with that, you know." She chose a spoonful of some mushroom-laden sauce.

"Please don't help. Please, I beg you, don't help. They accost me in libraries.

They run me down in the park. They press their… persons upon me on the dance floor. If you laugh, I will cut you right here."

This threat pleased her. "Now you sound like a brother. Avoid the soufflé, unless you don't mind having a bad case of wind tomorrow."

He suspected that was a sisterly thing to say, and he put the serving spoon back into the pan. "I choose my entertainments carefully, so if our paths aren't crossing, it's because I'm avoiding the great majority of eligible young women."

She speared several slices of cold roast beef. "I am eligible. Do you know Mr. Ash Dorning?"

"I know a number of Dornings, though I consider only Lord Casriel a close associate."

Three slices of roast beef were added to Jonathan's plate. "Do you call anybody a friend, Jonathan? Anybody at all?"

Theodosia Haviland was his friend, though that wasn't all he'd like to call her. "What sort of question is that?"

"A concerned question. I have a list of theories regarding you. The simplest hypothesis that explains the facts is that you are a boor who tramples over my feelings out of overweening conceit."

She'd wandered to the dessert table and, to all appearances, was absorbed in a choice of sweet.

Jonathan added concocting theories to his list of her transgressions, though heeding rumors about him was bad enough.

"Is there a second theory?" He hoped so, because she made him sound very much like his father.

Their father.

"And a third and a fourth. The most likely alternative, which Nicholas espouses whenever I raise the topic of Jonathan Tresham, is that you have never had siblings, have never had a loving family. You are like a feral cat. You have a vague sense that sustenance can be had from some humans, but figuring out which ones and at what cost overtaxes your abilities. You look very pretty napping on a garden wall, and you might steal a few laps of milk from the bowl set out for you, but you are fundamentally ignorant of and unsuited to a domestic life."

Her words, delivered with the dispassion of a senior lecturer on the topic of feckless felines, carried an impact.

"So you will leave me in peace on my sunny garden wall?"

"Of course not," she said, cutting a fat slice of some orange-glazed torte. "I will set out as many bowls of milk as it takes, because you are my brother."

Don't say that. Don't say that.

The Earl of Bellefonte was watching this interaction, despite being in conversation with the gathering's host. Westhaven could blather about his parliamentary bills through the night, and thus he made a good decoy for an overprotective brother.

Lady Della was determined to forge a connection based on an accident of birth, for Jonathan's father had been that feral cat.

"I never read the letters." He'd given Della her mother's letters, and Della had offered to lend him his father's letters.

"You should. My parents were very much in love, very troubled. He let her go because he loved her."

Very likely, Papa had let the lady go because he'd moved on to another affair, and another and another, and the lady had seen what sort of bargain Papa offered any who cared for him.

"Perhaps family matters should be discussed at another time. Shall I escort you to Bellefonte's side, my lady?"

"Would you like to wear this delicious torte on your cravat?"

Bellefonte smiled and lifted his drink in Jonathan's direction, a great golden lion of an earl promising his prey a lively chase before the kill, because that was only sporting.

Jonathan smiled right back.

"Stop it," Lady Della murmured. "You only get to act like a brother if you intend to *be* a brother. Call on me."

Half of polite society had already seen Jonathan in conversation with the lady. The other half would note him calling upon her.

"If I'm to call on you, I want to call on *you*. I will not subject myself to the interminable inspection that will result if I show up at one of Lady Bellefonte's at homes."

"I'm an early riser. A hack in the park—"

Where all and sundry noted which lady rode with which gentleman. "I'll make a morning call in the next week or so."

Lady Della studied him. "A sweet plastered all over your evening attire would be such an improvement. I might call on you. Did you ever think of that? Would you be home to me?"

He wanted to say no, that the press of business seldom allowed him to idle under his own roof while waiting for callers, and that would even be the truth. He was scheduled to meet with a different directors' committee every day for the next week, and each meeting required preparation of meticulous financial reports.

And yet Lady Della... was his sister, and to treat her as extraneous, a nuisance, a presuming intruder in his life would be to walk too many steps along Papa's path.

"I will be home to you," he said, "should you and the earl grace me with a call."

Her smile was radiant, as if the dullest scholar had reasoned—not guessed, reasoned—his way to the correct answer when the headmaster had come to observe the class.

"I will be home to you as well, Jonathan." She sailed off to join her brother and Lord Westhaven, leaving Jonathan amid sweets he didn't care for. He'd made some concession in a game he didn't understand, played with a deck of cards whose markings he couldn't decipher.

Perhaps Theo might be of some help. She stood by the door of the library with Lady Bellefonte, a tall blond woman in conversation with them. Jonathan's intended made no indication that she'd taken notice of him, but to him, she appeared very much like an ace and a queen in the hand of a man who'd been losing at vingt-et-un since he'd taken his place at the table.

He set aside his plate and got all of two yards closer to Theo when Miss Pamela Threadlebaum stepped directly into his path, her smile promising him a full plate of inanities about the weather.

CHAPTER TEN

The evening should have been pleasant, not an interminable procession of smiles and arias, while Theo tried to both remain vigilant for Jonathan's sake and ignore him for her own. Bea's coach rolled five yards closer, among the last in the line on the street before Lord Westhaven's town house.

"I do fancy a talented violinist," Bea said, covering a yawn with a gloved hand. "But the ones on offer tonight were more enthusiastic than skilled."

"It's a difficult instrument," Theo replied.

The footman let down the steps and held the door open. Bea gathered her skirts and ascended, and Theo was preparing to do likewise when Jonathan Tresham appeared at her side.

"Perhaps you'd allow me to escort you home, Mrs. Haviland?"

"Do go on, Theo," Bea so-helpfully murmured from the depths of the coach. "Mr. Tresham will doubtless get you home faster than my sorry pair will."

Theo could argue, which would draw the attention of the guests chatting on the steps, or she could do as she'd been longing to do all evening and spend some time in Jonathan's exclusive company.

"I'll wish you good night, my lady," Theo said. "Expect a visit from me tomorrow." *And a lecture.*

Two minutes later, Theo was handed into a town coach that made Bea's little carriage look like a doll's hackney. The velvet upholstery was exquisitely soft, the cushions deep, the sheer size of the conveyance a testament to luxury.

How does he afford this? The question wandered through her mind as Jonathan came down beside her on the forward-facing seat.

"I will pay that violinist to tour the Continent in perpetuity," he said. "I've missed you."

Pleasure stole over Theo's determination to remain sensible, like night steals over day at sunset. Jonathan was being honest—the violinist had spent more energy tossing his dark hair about than coaxing melodies from his instrument—and Jonathan was also being swainly.

"You saw me yesterday morning." Had *kissed* her yesterday morning, or she had kissed him. Truly, madly, passionately kissed him and wanted to kiss him again.

Jonathan pulled the shades. "I sat with Lady Antonia Mainwaring, who insisted on discussing the music in the most effusive terms. I went through the buffet line with Miss Penelope Bainbridge, whose great fortune earned her a spot on your infernal list. I strolled at the interval with Miss Clytemnestra Islington, another sparkling gem who can discuss the weather more passionately than most MPs can debate the Irish question. Why didn't you warn me that being a gentleman is exhausting?"

"Would you rather they'd been pressing their bosoms to your person?"

He slanted a look at her. The carriage lamps were turned down, but streetlamps had been lit. His expression conveyed frustration and mischief.

"I'd rather *you* pressed your bosom to my person."

He sounded so disgruntled that Theo laughed. "You're lucky only three of your prospects were in attendance tonight."

His sour mood reassured her, which was very bad of Theo. She was glad he'd found the evening tedious, glad he was having to work to comport himself as a gentleman among his peers.

She was not glad she'd been on hand to see him succeed at that pursuit. Every one of the ladies present had regarded him with the sort of veiled yearning Diana reserved for French chocolates.

"You went through the buffet with Lady Della Haddonfield," Theo said. "You should consider her." Some demon prompted Theo down this path, the same demon that had warned her for years that she was doomed to penury and ruin.

"Don't, Theo. You chose your six names, I'm doing my penance, and you shall be my duchess when you're done watching me genuflect before the altar of polite ritual."

Genuine irritation marked those words, so Theo let irritation show in her reply. "I decide whose duchess I shall be, and I have not decided to be yours. Lady Della is young, but she's quite well connected, she's blazingly intelligent, and you're on good terms with her family."

"No, I am not. They tolerate me for Lady Della's sake."

The horses clip-clopped along. The coach swayed around a corner.

"You are upset," Theo said, though it wasn't a version of upset she recognized. Archie had stormed and threatened when in his cups. An unhappy Seraphina brooded in silence, while Diana scratched out rhymed couplets of juvenile indignation.

"I've told you how it was between my father and me," Jonathan said, taking Theo's hand. "You might think I judge him harshly, but Lady Della is my half-sister. She was told this, though I know not why, and she had letters… she has them still."

He stared straight ahead, into the shadows, and his voice was flat. Not angry, so much as resigned.

He'd surprised Theo, also relieved a worry. Lady Della had most assuredly not been flirting with him, and yet, she'd held his attention for the entirety of their conversation. Lady Bellefonte had pointedly ignored the whole business—*very* pointedly—while Theo's curiosity had been piqued.

"These situations arise frequently in polite society," she said. "A woman does her duty by the title, and then she's free to discreetly—"

"Don't make excuses for them, Theo."

"Don't judge them. Bellefonte has brothers and sisters in abundance. Lady Della is the youngest. You have no idea what the late Lady Bellefonte was enduring in her marriage when she indulged in an affair with your father. Bellefonte's father was no saint, and neither are you."

Jonathan turned his head to regard Theo in the gloom. A trick of the light reflected his gaze unnaturally, as if he were a lurking predator and not the same gentleman who'd shared such a lovely kiss with her.

"Explain yourself, Mrs. Haviland."

Not even Archie at his drunken worst had attempted that tone with Theo. "Comport yourself with an iota of manners, and I might."

A fraught silence, then a bark of laughter. Jonathan peeled off Theo's glove, his touch far from seductive.

"My nose was broken three times," he said, drawing her middle and index fingers down the slope of said nose.

The bone was uneven, though Theo would not have said his nose was crooked. "That sounds painful."

He linked his fingers with hers and curled her hand on his thigh. "Do you know what hurts worse than having your nose broken? Having it set. The Quimbey spare was not permitted to be disfigured by schoolyard brawling."

"This has to do with your father?"

"With my mother. Papa's philandering was far from discreet. Mama retaliated in a predictable manner. My classmates made sure I was aware of her every flirtation. I made sure they regretted passing along the gossip. I now sit on the board of governors for a boys' school, in part as a penance for having been such a disruptive youth."

"Were there duels?" *Please say no. Please say your self-restraint was adequate to the challenge of controlling your temper.* For if he said yes, Theo certainly could not marry him—not that she was considering such folly—and she couldn't in good conscience allow any decent woman to yoke herself to such a hothead.

"Of course not. I was twelve when Quimbey became aware of my temper. You know him as a dear old fellow with charm to spare. He stormed into the headmaster's office like the wrath of God and delivered me such a dressing down... I'd rather he'd gone at me with the birch rod. Until that day, I hadn't understood that I was the spare—the only spare. In some dim corner of my boyish mind, I recognized the theoretical possibility that I might be a duke someday, but not... *the* duke. Not His Grace of Quimbey."

In a sunny alley, Theo had kissed Jonathan the way a woman kisses when she knows what intimacy between the sexes is, in all its messy, glorious details. This conversation was intimate in a more complicated way, one that had nothing to do with pleasure.

"You stopped brawling?"

"I became a model student, for which I was regularly pummeled. I fought back, but no longer so hard that my opponent took two days to wake up or had to learn to write with his left hand."

"You were very angry." *Is he angry still?*

"I was very determined to gain my father's notice. In the end, I did, but whether he took note of my accomplishments no longer mattered."

The coach slowed as they turned onto Theo's street, which was mostly a relief. This conversation wanted pondering, as did Theo's entire situation.

"I did not like seeing you with those other women." She hadn't planned to admit that.

"Good. If I'm suffering, you should suffer too, though when I'm seen to choose you from among a throng of lovely ladies, your consequence as my duchess will be off on the right foot."

Oh, ye gods. "Jonathan, you must not assume I will agree to be your duchess. I am the—"

He thumped his head back against the squabs and stared at the coach's upholstered ceiling. "Penniless, aged spinster-widow, who bore only a girl child—though your daughter is a proper healthy terror—and who is so unattractive that mirrors crack when you pass before them. I know, Theo."

He did not know. God willing, she'd never have to tell him. "I'm glad you see the problem. I suggest you present yourself in the park at the fashionable hour tomorrow and exert yourself to be charming to the other three ladies on your list."

The coach slowed further, the coachman calling to the horses to halt.

"It's your perishing list, Theo."

"And my decision."

"Don't invite me in," Jonathan said. "I'm expected elsewhere."

At least he sounded unhappy about that. "I hadn't planned to invite you in."

The door remained closed, suggesting Jonathan's footmen were well trained—also accustomed to their employer tarrying in coaches late at night.

He folded Theo's hand between both of his. "I've told you my secrets, Theo. I have a sister I don't know what to do with. I had a terrible temper as a boy. My father was a disgrace, and I left England for years to remove myself from his ambit. At least assure me you aren't horrified."

How could he possibly think...? "I am beyond horrified *on your behalf.* I want to pummel your father and break his nose at least three times, then I'd like to deliver a sound scolding to your mother. Why Quimbey took twelve years to intercede I do not know, and you'd best hope I never ask him."

A great sigh escaped into the darkness. "I see."

No, he did not. Theo kissed his cheek, wishing she could take him in her arms and make him forget all those disappointments and betrayals.

"I'll bid you good night," she said, "and hope to see you at the Swanson's Venetian breakfast."

"You hurry away," he replied, trailing his fingers down her cheek. "I suspect I'm not the only person in this carriage with secrets, Theo. You might consider trusting me with yours."

Never. "Here's a secret. Seraphina waits up for me, so I must not linger conversing with you here, or she'll ask what I found to discuss with the handsome, charming Mr. Tresham."

He opened the door. "Handsome and charming. Now you dissemble when I've been nothing but honest. Sweet dreams, Theo."

She took the footman's hand and let him escort her to the door, then slipped inside the house lest any neighbors see an elegant town coach parked by her doorstep at such a late hour.

"You are handsome and charming," she said, closing and locking the door behind her, "and I cannot be your duchess."

* * *

"One generally rejoices to receive a duke on one's doorstep." Anselm handed Jonathan his hat and walking stick, as if Jonathan were the bloody butler. "You look like a man who doesn't know the meaning of the word."

Jonathan was a man not in the mood for His Grace's games. The night had been long, the encounter with Theo unsettling. Then Moira had started fretting again.

"Which word? Duke? I'm learning more about that sorry reality every day. For example, being a duke means employing a staff who claim venerable years. Said staff is prone to rheumatism, catarrhs, hay fevers, gout, and all manner of ailments about which one must be regaled at length. I conclude that whatever other faculties fade with an abundance of years, verbal stamina only increases."

Theo would scold him for whining, but the housekeeper, butler, and first footman were *all* laid low with one ailment or another.

"The word I referred to," Anselm said, "was rejoice. A handy verb. To feel joy or delight. From the Latin *gaudere*. One rejoices to behold my splendiferous self on one's doorstep."

"Rejoice," Jonathan said, leading his guest up to the estate office. "Rhymes with no choice and Miss Annabelle Boyce of the contralto voice. If I should become a duke—not that I wish for the day—will I also enjoy your handsome complement of humility?"

Anselm had the good sense to wait until he was behind a closed door. "Tresham, are you well?"

Had Jonathan indulged in even two hours more rest over the past few days, had Moira not been in such a mood last night, had the discussion with Theo not been so puzzling, had any of the various ledgers he was wrestling with balanced, he might have conjured up an appropriately witty reply.

"Why must women be so complicated, Anselm?"

"Because men are so thickheaded?" Anselm's answer sounded tentative, like a working theory developed after much thought, which made Jonathan feel marginally better.

"The hypothesis has merit. Are you in the mood for spirits, tea, or something else?"

The Quimbey estate office overlooked the gardens, an abundance of windows being conducive to accurate calculations. Compared to the tidy geometry of the garden, the office was a mess.

"I'm in the mood for friendly conversation." Anselm moved a stack of ledgers from the boys' foundling home to clear off a reading chair. "You've been busy."

The remains of Jonathan's breakfast tray sat on the blotter. The rest of the room was adorned with piles of correspondence, ledgers, wage books, and agricultural treatises.

"Quimbey is in love." Jonathan tossed himself into the seat behind the desk. As a boy, that chair had felt like an oversized throne. Now it felt too small for his weight and in need of new cushions. "And even the furniture in this household is ailing."

"Quimbey's affliction is relatively recent." Anselm helped himself to a slice of cold, buttered toast. "This office looks as if somebody has been battling the forces of chaos,"—he munched his toast—"and losing the fight."

"Quimbey has been relying on the same house steward for fifty years, Anselm. If I see Carruthers tap his forehead one more time and assure me, 'It's all up here,' I will not answer for the consequences. I like ledgers generally, I enjoy math, and make a contribution with my skills where I can, but this…"

"You don't enjoy math. You delight in it with a passion most men reserve for a new hunter or their first love. What's changed?" Anselm went after the cold tea next.

"Anselm, I can ring for a fresh tray, though it won't arrive before Michaelmas."

"No need for a fresh tray. This one's only half gone. I suspect the chaos in this room has something to do with a particular widow being complicated."

That hypothesis also had merit. "I generally find peace in numbers. These numbers reduce me to cursing. Quimbey must be the last peer in England to own unenclosed land, and I don't fancy the hue and cry when I rectify his oversight."

"My ducal seat remains unenclosed," Anselm said. "Enclosure is expensive. It puts a whole village off the land and invariably reduces the circumstances of any who remain. If the village retains an open common, then every family can have a decent garden, a cow or two, some sheep. England is no longer at war, so claims that every acre must be driven to maximum productivity ring false."

That was not an argument put forth by any other aristocrat of Jonathan's acquaintance. "But you lose money."

Anselm added a dollop of milk to his cold tea. "Those people have been loyal to my family for generations, Tresham. I have enough money. Do I really want a larger fortune at the cost of forty-five families' well-being? No, I do not. Be whatever sort of duke you please, but that is the sort of duke I am and intend to be. My duchess disapproves of greed, and I don't much respect it myself."

His Grace brushed imaginary crumbs from his cravat, though his words were either so backward as to be feudal or the stuff of reform.

"Theo disapproves of greed."

"*Theo*, is it? Well, then, I suppose you'll be offering for her." Anselm's supposition bore a certain inference, one redolent of pistols at dawn for a man who trifled with impoverished widows.

Which was surely one of the reasons Anselm was worthy of the name friend. "I've asked permission to court her. She's making me earn that privilege."

"Smart woman." The duke took a sip of cold tea, managing to look more elegant than Brummell in full evening regalia.

"She feels it necessary to remind me that I have many other options, but that she alone holds the power to accept a marriage proposal from me."

"Brilliant woman, rather. Has she discussed with you the circumstances of her husband's demise?"

"Very openly, I think."

Anselm's attention was absorbed with choosing a biscuit from the tray, though there were only three on offer. "Tread lightly. The late Mr. Haviland had faults, but he was her husband."

And now, Anselm, who never trod lightly, was stirring his cold tea.

"Go ahead and dunk your biscuit, Anselm. You know you want to. Dunk it in the milk, and I won't tell a soul."

"I am a duke," he said, dipping his sweet into the little pitcher of milk. "I am allowed my crotchets. What will you do with the club?"

How a man could look imposing while dipping a biscuit into the milk pitcher was a mystery known only to dukes.

"What has the club to do with anything?"

Anselm took a bite of his sweet. "Dukes are well advised to avoid illegal activities."

"You lent me money to help finance the purchase of the place."

"I was new to my station. I've since married a very demanding woman, and I know better than to give anybody grounds to create a scandal lest Her Grace be wroth with me. My children would be disappointed in me, and that is a penance with which no man should acquaint himself."

Slurp.

"A father who betrays his children's trust is a disgrace to the male gender," Jonathan said.

He got up to pace, because Anselm had put his blunt finger on an issue that Moira had tried to raise again last night. A gambling establishment was illegal, while a supper club where a man could have a game of friendly cards was entirely within the bounds of the law. The line was far from clear, but The Coventry operated on the wrong side of it.

"We won't be raided, Anselm. I take precautions."

"Well, then, what matters a little illegality in the hands of a peer's heir if you're taking illegal precautions to hide your illegal ventures? Hasn't it occurred to you that your competitors could easily join together and take other precautions and raise your bribe—or your bet? That business of offering free food and drink after midnight cannot sit well with them."

"Then they don't deserve to stay in business. The free food and drink more than pays for itself by attracting a greater crowd. When the house takes a percentage of every bet, the customers are assured I have no incentive to cheat. Moreover, certain rules—such as the dealer winning all ties—ensure that by a margin which runs true over time, the games favor the house. Add in the membership fees and the paid fare before midnight, and only a fool could lose money at such a venture."

Anselm finished his biscuit and dusted his hands. "You're a commoner now, Tresham. What sort of fool risks arrest, scandal, and the enmity of his clientele when he's trying to woo a prospective duchess?"

"One who has worked hard to earn his fortune and sees no reason to part with it. London is full of clubs doing exactly as The Coventry does, and that is no secret. Theo, by contrast, has not put all of her cards on the table."

"She owes you the unblemished truth while you court scandal in the shadows?"

A duke in a contrary mood was tribulation incarnate. "Nobody save yourself knows of my ownership—yourself and Moira, and the senior staff. A few of the junior staff have likely caught a glimpse of me, and the bookkeeper is an acquaintance of long standing, but I'm careful, Anselm. My coach doesn't await me in the alley. My comings and goings are discreet. My signature appears nowhere in public, and I own the property, so there's no leasehold to give my ownership away."

"Then there's a deed, Tresham, and anybody could deduce who the ratepayer for your address is. Mrs. Haviland's husband came to grief at establishments like The Coventry. She will likely take issue with your ownership."

"When she is my duchess, if my ownership of the club should ever become an issue, then we'll discuss it. I've sold all of my Paris holdings, but the day I bought The Coventry was the day I became truly free of my father, the succession, and anybody else's opinion of me. I tested my theories there before going to Paris. I learned how the cards work and how a club works. You didn't enclose the village at the ducal seat, and I'll not sell The Coventry."

Anselm dunked another biscuit. "Did you know that you can be recognized by your tread on a stair? You ascend three steps and pause to look behind you. Ascend three, another pause. A sort of waltz unique to you. Your pace is quick and steady, one might even say distinctive."

Munch. Munch. Munch. Perhaps this was a taste of what having a sibling was like. Intrusive, well-intended, irksome as hell. If so, no wonder Lady Della was extraordinarily tenacious. She had to be, with a herd of older, larger siblings to harry and be harried by.

"What's your point?"

"You are also, apparently, the only man in all of London to wear a scent that combines jasmine and tuberose, a Paris blend."

"My scent also contains gardenia, and as far as I know, it's blended solely for me. What of it?" Jonathan's question was dispassionate, but the accuracy of these details was unnerving. A lover might note such information, or an astute competitor.

Or a sibling?

"Your anonymity is subject to attack," Anselm said, rising. "So is your club. Nobody need cheat. The appearance of dishonesty will see you raided and ruined despite your precautions, and very likely jailed as well. The common man loves to see the aristocrat revealed for the parasite he can be."

Parasite? "My father was such a man, Anselm, while The Coventry is an honest club. I insist on that. I also insist on paying excellent wages and doing my bit for the less fortunate, but mostly, I simply run The Coventry according to sound business principles. A deck holds only so many cards that can be played in only so many combinations. Over time, the winning and losing hands balance out. Once I realized that, making a profit was simple."

"Profit is seldom simple, but far be it from a mere duke to instruct you on that point. I'm hearing rumors, Tresham. Rumors of crooked play, rumors regarding your ownership of the club. Have a care, or wooing Mrs. Haviland will be the least of your worries."

Jonathan sank into the chair behind the desk, a lump of cushion prodding him in the backside. "You are hearing rumors?" His tired brain tried to list possible sources of such rumors, enemies made in Paris, employees let go for cause.

Lady Della had also mentioned rumors.

"Rumors couched as musings intended to be overheard by somebody who's friendly with you. Warnings, I suppose you'd call them. I'll wish you good day and good luck. Mrs. Haviland will not succumb to your paltry charms without significant inspiration. A penchant for maths is fine for ruling in a gaming hell, but I doubt it will stand you in good stead if you aspire to serve in her personal heaven."

He swiped the last biscuit and sauntered toward the door. "I'll see myself out. You should get some rest. Wooing is hard work, and a man wants to put his best foot forward."

"Thank you for that stunning insight, Your Grace."

Anselm went on his way, closing the door softly in his wake.

Jonathan surveyed the estate office, which was not so much in chaos as in the midst of a reorganization. The Coventry's books were among the detritus, as were the ledgers from Quimbey Hall, the London house, and several other organizations with whom Jonathan had a business connection.

The lot of it—a great pile of numbers and patterns and calculations—should have called to him as seductively as a troupe of sirens sitting amid a heap of trigonometric formulae.

"I need a nap," Jonathan informed the Quimbey wage book. "Fatigue explains why I resented having to stop by the club last night." He took a sip of milk directly from the little pitcher on the tray.

Fatigue did not explain why he'd longed to follow Theo into her home last night, and bedamned to the club, Moira's dramas, and a few pesky rumors.

* * *

"I cannot marry Jonathan Tresham." Theo made this announcement in Bea's back garden, where no sister, daughter, maid, or footman could overhear.

"Are you trying to convince me or yourself?" Bea replied, snipping the end from an iris stem.

"I am stating a fact."

Bea's garden still sported a fountain, though at present, the fountain was quiet. Three broad ceramic dishes of water were stacked like a giant étagère beneath a statue of the Apollo Belvedere, whose proportions put Theo in mind of Jonathan Tresham.

But then, everything put Theo in mind of Mr. Tresham of late.

"You do not state a fact, Theo. You are trying to dissuade yourself from making a brilliant match. Pass me that pink tulip."

Theo passed over the flower. "I am nobody. I own nothing save one small house rapidly falling into disrepair. I can't be a duchess."

"My father was a vicar, and yet, I'm a countess. Somehow, my lofty status has given me no talent for flower arranging."

"You and your late husband were a love match. I want no part of love matches. You have to decide if your arrangement will be formal or informal, Bea."

The countess set the shears on the little wrought-iron table. "Flowers are flowers. They smell good, or they don't. They aren't formal or informal."

Theo removed the irises from the vase. "Because you're using a simple container, you can go either way. Strict symmetry, a limited number of colors and shapes, a bouquet that appeals equally from all sides. You could also attempt a less geometric approach, the balance achieved by assembling many varied elements with an originality that charms for its uniqueness."

Bea sipped her lemonade. "You lecture me only when you're vexed. Mr. Tresham's proposal vexes you, because you do long to marry him. If you did not, you'd thank him kindly, pass the you-do-me-great-honor sentence upon him, and go back to turning your dresses."

Theo started with a few stems of ferns, then three purple irises. "Who would not want to marry a ducal heir?"

"Precisely my point. You fancy him, or you'd send him packing. That already looks better than what I had." She walked around the table to stand beside Theo. "Tresham is handsome, wealthy, eventually to be titled, and not given to overt vices. The matchmakers are quivering to bring him down. I would never have thought to put the yellow irises in with the purple."

"Contrast enlivens most arrangements, and they are the same shape, which provides harmony and variety at the same time. Do you happen to know the basis of Mr. Tresham's wealth?"

"I do not. Why?"

"Because I left that inquiry to my parents' solicitors the last time I married, to my very great sorrow. I never hear Mr. Tresham discuss his investments, but when it comes to the ladies, I know this one is a coal heiress, that one will inherit thousands of acres in a specific county. We know what the ladies bring to the bargain. Why don't we know what the men offer?"

Bea passed her a pink tulip. "You're in love with him, aren't you?"

Theo jammed the tulip among the irises, where it looked ridiculous and out of place. "I cannot fall in love, Bea. Archie cured me of that malady."

"You're scared witless, because you want to be with Mr. Tresham, want to know everything about him. You fall asleep dreaming of his kisses when he hasn't so much as… Well, perhaps he has. We're widows. We may do as we please in certain regards."

Theo took the shears to the lone white tulip. "Find me a few sprigs of lavender."

"The lavender hasn't bloomed yet."

"I want the contrast in the greenery too. Mr. Tresham has not in any regard presumed on my person." Intimacies had been exchanged, though they'd been enthusiastically mutual.

Bea took the shears and knelt by the lavender border. "Mr. Tresham is an idiot if he hasn't made romantic overtures. You're smitten, and he's asking to court you. Where is the sense in pretending you're the last Puritan in Mayfair?"

Theo tried moving the tulip to the center of the arrangement. "Archie was no Puritan."

"Archie is dead, and I, for one, am glad. He was ruining your health and happiness. He left a mess when he died, but at least he spared you greater scandal. Is this enough?" She held a half-dozen long, silvery fronds of foliage.

"One more, so we have an odd number. I have been considering Mr. Tresham's request."

Snick. "And?"

"He does not know the whole of my situation, Bea. Viscount Penweather blames me for Archie's death. He said so to me directly. If I'd been a better wife, Archie would have moderated his vices."

Bea put the shears aside and hugged Theo, the scent of lavender wafting from their embrace. "I had no idea his lordship was so awful. You don't believe him, I hope? You cannot believe him."

Theo eased away. "The discussion grew ugly, but then, his lordship had lost a cousin and an uncle in the space of a month. We were both in rather a state. I informed him that had Archie not been made to live on a schoolboy's allowance, we might have been able to afford more children. We haven't spoken since. We correspond, or I correspond with his secretary."

The whole business sounded worse for being put into words. "Jonathan has no patience for family squabbles," Theo went on. "He detests his father's memory in part for all the gossip and scandal his parents caused."

Bea began jabbing lavender fronds in among the flowers and ferns. "One of the things I hate most about being a widow—and my list is endless—is that one's whole identity is tied up in a past event. I am the widow of a man who died years ago. His death defines me, not my life. I'm no longer my papa's daughter, my sister's sibling, or *myself.* I am only my late husband's widow. If Quimbey's duchess should predecease him, will we refer to the duke as Her Grace's widower? No, we will not."

Bea was in a passion about something, though she was also right.

"You put hock in the lemonade," Theo said, passing over another pink tulip. "No wonder it's delicious."

"Theo, if you are that hesitant about your estrangement from Archie's cousin, then put the matter to Mr. Tresham and let him decide. You are too wonderful a person to be held hostage to Archie's death for all the rest of your days."

Mr. Tresham thought Theo was wonderful. Wonderful enough to court. "I try not to think of myself, but if I were a duchess, Seraphina's and Diana's futures would be assured. Even if Mr. Tresham grew to hate me, he'd not treat them as cavalierly as the viscount has."

As cavalierly as Archie had, in the end.

"Stop trying to hide a perfectly lovely décolletage beneath a plain lace fichu. You want Jonathan Tresham, and he's worthy of your notice. Sample his charms, and if he can go on half adequately, then allow him to court you."

Bea tucked the pink tulip into the center of the arrangement, where it listed at an angle that matched the white tulip. The result was a cascade of color, a variety of shapes, and a very pleasing bouquet.

"I have argued and reasoned and exhorted myself without ceasing, Bea, but I come to the same conclusion you do: I will alert Mr. Tresham to the ill will between me and the viscount, and if that does not dissuade my suitor, I will allow him to court me."

Theo would do that much, and no more. The past was the past, and Archie's memory should be allowed to rest in peace.

Bea took another sip of her lemonade. "A man can be instructed on some matters. Others are beyond help. Sample Mr. Tresham's charms, Theo."

"I believe I shall." Theo raised her glass to her lips, though she was smiling so broadly, she felt like a whole bouquet of joy, and that had nothing to do with Bea's excellent lemonade.

CHAPTER ELEVEN

"Mrs. Haviland." Jonathan bowed before the woman who'd haunted his dreams and followed him—metaphorically—into the bath, the dressing closet, and any other place a man could be private with himself.

"Mr. Tresham."

"Might I have the honor of the next dance?" He'd ambushed her before the supper waltz, which she typically sat out with the dowagers or danced with some doddering colonel.

Not tonight. Tonight, Jonathan was determined to share some joy with her.

"The honor would be entirely mine."

Her smile was so lovely, so intriguing and feminine, and *personal*, that Jonathan forgot to let go of her hand. When she smiled like that, she was beauty incarnate, and Jonathan was the luckiest man in London.

"You'll waltz with me?" Jonathan pressed. "In front of all of Mayfair?"

The string quartet was still tuning up, so progress onto the dance floor could be leisurely. Jonathan wanted the whole gathering to see him dancing with Theo and to see her smiling at him.

"We will waltz with each other."

She wore the blue velvet again and the single string of pearls in her hair, and yet, she could not have been more radiant. Something had pleased her mightily.

Or *someone* had. "What have I done to earn this boon, Mrs. Haviland?"

"You have driven out, hacked in the park, danced with, and otherwise exerted yourself to be charming to every young woman on the list I handed you several weeks ago."

He bowed. She curtseyed, and Jonathan had the sense that something even lovelier than the waltz had begun.

"They have been the longest weeks of my life." Dancing attendance on women he had no intention of marrying had been tedious at first, but surprisingly agreeable when he'd taken the time to enjoy their company. Still, they weren't Theo.

"Lord Casriel said you are organizing the ducal finances. Surely you enjoy that undertaking?" She stepped into his arms, and for a moment, Jonathan lost the thread of the conversation.

Since kissing Theo in the alley, he had not presumed in the direction of any further liberties. He'd sent peaches and chocolates. He'd lurked in the park with the dogs in hopes of crossing paths with Theo and Diana. He'd lent Seraphina a book of French verse that used flowers for all manner of sentimental metaphors.

And he'd gone to bed restless and beset every night. The club was part of it. He'd changed out every deck of cards, for several had had random unevenness along the edges or odd smudges amid the pips. Not enough to call them marked, but a purposeful attempt to make them *look* marked.

He'd watched the kitchen staff from dim corners, dropped every casual question he could to Moira, and had found nothing. When worries for the club weren't troubling his slumber, longing for Theo bothered him without ceasing.

All the botheration stilled when he took her in his arms. The other dancers murmuring and shuffling into position faded, and the moment became a turning point, when hope blossomed and joy took hold.

The music started, they moved off, and for the first time, Jonathan *understood* the waltz. He understood the delight of dancing with a lady, not merely executing steps in tandem with her. He grasped why numbers and formulae could never be enough. He saw, in a wildly generous corner of his heart, why his parents had searched relentlessly for even an illicit echo of the joy that dancing with a true partner engendered.

Theo twirled, she dipped, she gave herself over to his leading and inspired him to a grace that was entirely her doing. When the music ended, she sank into a curtsey amid billowing blue velvet, and Jonathan nearly shouted at the musicians, *Again, damn you!*

"My thanks," Theo said, taking his arm. "You are a superb dancer."

He was also flirting with arousal that was simply there, his body rejoicing in her proximity. "I am motivated by your example. Might we find some cooler air while the buffet line forms?"

"The terrace will be crowded."

Oh, Theodosia. You didn't just invite me to… But she had. "Let's find some privacy." Jonathan knew Lord Tottenham's premises fairly well, because his lordship was one of Quimbey's familiars. The formal parlor was the cardroom for the evening, the gallery was hosting the buffet, and the library and music room were shoulder-to-shoulder with matchmakers and fortune hunters.

"And you did what you could," Jonathan said, "but you also had to protect your daughter and sister, maintain a household, and keep your fool of a husband from debtors' prison. Archie failed you, his daughter, and himself, Theo. The viscount was simply too ill-informed to see that."

"Ill-informed." She said the words as if tasting them and finding them disagreeable.

"People who have never been in the presence of rampant vice can't fathom it," Jonathan said. "If you've never seen a ragged child shivering on the steps of a great cathedral, then you can't believe such hypocrisy exists. If you've never watched a duke's son stumble from his coach and fall flat on his face amid the muck on the cobbles, then you don't believe it happens. You are not responsible for a grown man throwing away his health, his life, his means, and his family. You aren't."

Jonathan would make sure the viscount understood the magnitude of the wrong he'd done with his accusations, for somebody had to.

"Penweather isn't awful," Theo said. "He's principled in his way, just as Archie was unprincipled."

"Put both of them from your mind, Theo. They have troubled you too much and for too long. Penweather in particular does not deserve your concern. Tell me why you danced with me tonight."

As an attempt to change the subject, that gambit was clumsy, but Jonathan sensed Theo did not want to dwell on the past. Not now, not yet still more.

She slanted a considering look at him. "This takes us to the part about the kissing."

Thank God. "Do go on, Mrs. Haviland. Anything you have to say on the subject of kisses has my devoted attention."

"Enough talk," Theo said, rising.

For one moment, Jonathan thought she was leaving the room, concluding the discussion, a confidence shared, and a buffet not to be missed. He could content himself with that, if he had to. He could be her confidant, her waltzing partner, and assure himself that he was making progress in the desired direction.

Then she gathered her skirts and settled onto his lap, straddling his thighs, and every rational thought flew from Jonathan's mind.

* * *

"You are friends with Jonathan Tresham." Sycamore Dorning was being a gentleman, the most tedious and thankless undertaking ever to befall a feckless younger son. The buffet line would take until his next birthday to wind past the food, so Sycamore was hanging back, letting others go first, while he cornered his oldest brother.

"I am acquainted with him," Lord Casriel replied. "What *is* that knot you've put in your cravat?"

"I call it the Sycamore Cascade. It looks best on a tall man with broad shoulders."

"So why are you attempting it?"

Casriel stood perhaps an inch taller than Sycamore's six feet, one and a half inches. Casriel was well built, but Sycamore had taken up rowing because it was cheap and could be done as a crew of one. Then too, he was not done growing. Dornings were late bloomers, witness five of his idiot brothers still stumbling around without wives.

"I do not *attempt* this sartorial wonder, I define it, while you hide amid the potted palms hoping no matchmaker has planted an heiress among them."

"Or hoping I do find an heiress. The Season is both expensive and trying."

That Casriel would complain about expenses was simply what happened when he opened his mouth under most circumstances. But to complain here, amid his peers, and to his younger brother…

"I'm investing my allowance," Sycamore said. Though this was true only in a symbolic sense. "The Coventry has free food and drink after midnight, and you needn't play a hand to partake. You might consider sending Thorne and Oak round of a night. They eat like horses."

"You eat like a horse."

"I have better manners than my elders because every single one of my brothers took a solemn vow to correct me when I erred at table, usually by a prolonged and zealous application of his fists. Such fraternal love has created a paragon." Also a terror, in the words of Gentleman Jackson.

Casriel left off studying the buffet line—or the ladies in the buffet line— long enough to flick a glance over Sycamore. Something he saw must have caught his notice, for his inspection acquired a puzzled air.

"Is that my coat?"

"No. This is *my* coat. Yours are too narrow in the shoulders." A plain fact that made all those frigid mornings on the river a joyous memory. "Jonathan Tresham owns The Coventry Club, or owns a significant portion of it. You will please alert him to the fact that somebody is out to undermine his establishment."

Casriel ambled deeper amid the greenery under the minstrel's gallery, leaving Sycamore no choice but to follow. "One doesn't discuss such a topic in public, Cam. For shame."

"One has more privacy while the good folk of Mayfair are circling their feed trough than one has at our own breakfast table. I said something to Anselm more than a fortnight ago, and I can't see that he acted on my warnings."

"You expect not only a lowly earl but a duke to report his doings to you?"

The urge to smack Casriel on the arm, to shove him in the chest, was almost overwhelming. "To have this discussion here, where any gossip might lurk six feet away amid the ferns, is foolish. We had more privacy in plain sight."

He sauntered off, in the direction of the music room, batting aside fronds with a gloved hand. With the buffet set up, the music room would be empty, unless a canoodling couple was putting it to use.

Sycamore would certainly like to be canoodling with somebody, though doing his gentlemanly duty toward an acquaintance had to come first. An honest club was a thing of beauty, and all true gentlemen were bound to protect its good name.

Or some such twaddle.

The music room was empty, the quiet a pleasant shock to the ears. Casriel closed the door save for a few inches.

"Either leave it open," Sycamore said, "so we can hear and even see any who approach, or close it, so we have privacy of a sort." Something or somebody was distracting Casriel. As the eldest of a herd of rambunctious siblings, he ought to know about half-open doors, dense greenery, and eavesdroppers.

Casriel closed the door. "Say what you have to say, Cam."

"Tresham's club is using marked cards again. The decks were all changed out, but last night, I spotted another one. He has three new waiters, which is unusual for The Coventry, and one of them finds it necessary to pick up every used glass and plate left anywhere on the premises. I can't figure what he's about, but he makes that unreachable spot in the middle of my back itch."

Casriel ran a bare hand over the strings of the great harp. Once upon a time, he'd been an accomplished harpist. Cam hadn't heard him play for years.

"Isn't that what waiters do? Clean up the tables?"

"He marches around with an empty tray, doesn't seem to do much else besides that, unless he's setting the tray down and piling dirty dishes on it. He has a perfect opportunity to swap out a deck of cards or a pair of dice at the unused tables early or late in the evening. He's older, blond, skinny. Looks like a former footman down on his luck."

Casriel took the stool at the harp and bowed his head, as if recalling a tune. "Say something to Tresham. I'll pay your physician's bills, and you will have, as usual, created a great stir where none is warranted. People wear rings, Cam, they have sleeve buttons and other jewelry that can nick a card. You are imagining things, but be warned that Tresham is dangerously good with his fists."

A few delicate notes sang out from the harp, and Sycamore longed to sit as he used to and watch his brother play. The grace Casriel could summon with his hands—hands that spent too much time with the abacus and the ledger book—created an ache in Sycamore's chest and a sense of unnamed regrets.

He'd never be able to play like that, not if he studied for ten years.

"Use your imagination," Sycamore said over the ethereal beauty of some lament. "The cards don't have to *be* marked. They only have to *feel* marked. A slur on The Coventry's reputation will bring the authorities down in force. A raid will set the place back enormously. Of all the clubs, only The Coventry seems to reliably avoid entanglement with the law. And if you don't believe me about the cards, I suspect somebody is using a spotter."

"What's a spotter?"

How could Casriel play the harp and conduct a conversation? What sort of mind could do that?

"Somebody to assist a cheat by signaling the cards an opponent elsewhere on the table has in his or her hand." To speak when music like this was filling the air was blasphemy.

"Say something to Tresham. Try to use a bit of finesse. Drop questions, hints, suggestions, and stay out of punching range. I hope we taught you that much at least."

Sycamore's brothers had taught him to hit harder and faster than he'd been hit, though Casriel was leaving this challenge to Sycamore, which was a compliment.

Fancy that. "Shall I bring you a plate?"

"I'll drop by The Coventry later. This is a gorgeous instrument. It wants playing."

If the ladies of Mayfair could see the impoverished, staid earl romancing that harp, they'd beg him to strum and pluck any part of their persons he pleased to touch.

"And you do that instrument justice," Sycamore said, heading for the door. He left it open, the better to entice the ladies away from the buffet.

The Countess of Canmore was the only female in the corridor. "Who is playing?" she asked.

She was pretty, canny, and had a sly sense of humor. Sycamore liked her, but then, he liked most women.

"Lord Casriel. He sounds lonely to me, but that's just a baby brother's opinion. I do believe he's in want of an audience, poor lad. Playing all by himself seems a waste of his talent."

She wafted down the corridor and slipped into the music room, pausing only long enough to blow Sycamore a kiss. He caught it and tucked it into his breast pocket, then bowed and went in search of his hostess.

A goodnight was in order. The food was better at The Coventry than at Lady Tottenham's buffet. Then too, Jonathan Tresham had no younger brothers to look out for him, had no siblings at all, in fact, and even inheriting a dukedom could not redress that sad poverty.

CHAPTER TWELVE

A great weight had fallen from Theo's shoulders. She hadn't told Jonathan every last appalling detail of Archie's passing, but she'd told him enough, and he'd vindicated her trust.

She kissed him with all the relief and rejoicing in her, with all the hope and delight.

"Do I take it," he asked, framing her face in warm hands, "that I have permission to court you, Mrs. Haviland?"

"If you stop at simply courting me, I will be disappointed." She wrapped her arms around his neck, tucking his nose against her cleavage. "I have been disappointed before. I don't care for it."

He laughed, his breath warm against her skin. "We'll miss the buffet."

How she loved his laughter. "We'll share a menu of rare and special pleasures, while the other guests content themselves with mere truffles and champagne." Joy made her reckless, as she'd never been reckless with her husband. The few times Theo had attempted some creativity in the bedroom, Archie had scolded her for having a naughty imagination.

"You're sure, Theo? I cannot guarantee much finesse in my current state. You've haunted me day and night."

He was aroused and growing more so. How she reveled in the unmistakable intensity of his desire. How many times had Arche's arousal been unequal to anything but hurry and frustration?

"That I should haunt your dreams is only just," she said, nuzzling his ear. "I've stabbed myself with an embroidery needle more than once because some look you sent me across a ballroom intruded into my thoughts. I want you naked, do you hear me? Not a stitch on you, broad daylight, a bed to ourselves—"

He kissed her, and the rest of Theo's long list of plans for him flew from her head.

"We'll have all of that," he said, settling a hand over her breast. "For now, let us have a consummation of desire too long denied."

He spoke a greater truth than he knew, for celibacy had befallen Theo months before Archie's death. They'd stopped arguing. They'd stopped even speaking for the most part. Occasionally, he'd reach for her in the darkest hours, but his abilities often weren't commensurate with his aims. The sadness of that, for him and for herself, had driven Theo to keeping her hands to herself no matter how much she might miss marital intimacies.

"I can't guarantee you finesse," Theo said, arching into his hand. "I can promise you passion."

Jonathan wrapped his hand around the back of her head, the gesture both possessive and protective. For a moment, they remained thus, a tableau of desire that Theo could for once simply enjoy. Jonathan would not leave her unsatisfied, embarrassed, ashamed, and alone. They would share intimate, mutually gratifying pleasure, and as a couple, develop an even greater vocabulary of connubial joys.

Theo untucked her fichu from her bodice and let her sleeves fall far enough that she could wiggle her stays down. She was intent on untying the bow of her chemise when Jonathan's hands covered hers.

"May I have the honor?"

His question was curiously solemn. Theo responded by dropping her hands, though remaining passive was excruciating.

She meant to say: *The pleasure is entirely mine.* "Hurry, Jonathan."

"That, I cannot do." He untied the bow and brushed aside her chemise, leaving her breasts not only bared, but pushed forward by her stays. Theo was torn between arousal and self-consciousness, until Jonathan stroked a thumb over each nipple.

Self-consciousness fled, routed by shameless yearning. "Again, please."

He paid homage to her breasts, and Theo bore it. His caresses, his mouth, his breath on her wet flesh, varying pressures, and teasing kisses. His skills were many and diabolically expert.

"You," she managed. "Your falls. The buttons."

"Scoot back."

She did, though he kept a grasp of her left nipple, and the added pressure was exquisite. Then she was bereft of his touch, while he extracted a handkerchief from a pocket and laid it on the sofa cushions beside them. Next, he undid both sides of his falls, lifting his hips to rearrange his clothing.

Theo moved closer, a smooth, warm length of male flesh brushing against her sex. The wanting was a pleasure in itself, sensation to be savored rather than an anxiety to be assuaged.

How lovely to *enjoy* desire. To *delight* in longing, secure in the knowledge that satisfaction would come soon and thoroughly. Theo kissed her lover lingeringly, her frantic yearning coalescing into a pledge of mutual pleasure.

Jonathan must have understood her intent, for he sank lower against the cushions and guided himself to her sex.

The joining began without any other touching, Theo sinking down, Jonathan lifting up. His timing was perfect, her pleasure enormous. They teased each other, feinting and parrying, until Theo braced her hands on his shoulders and took him fully into her body.

"A moment," he whispered, holding her by her hips when he was hilted inside of her.

Without moving, without even kissing, pleasure welled for Theo. She could not have stopped the oncoming tide if she'd commanded the powers of heaven, nor did she want to. She purely surrendered to gratification, letting it lash through her like a scouring summer cloudburst.

"I am sorry," she said, dropping her forehead to Jonathan's shoulder. "I hadn't planned that."

"I planned that. Hold me, Theo."

She held *on to* him, while he moved, and she endured more of his *planning*. He knew exactly how to gauge tempo, depth, intensity, kisses, caresses, even stillness to render Theo panting, pleasure-glutted and utterly relaxed.

"I could do this until dawn," he said, moving lazily, "but you'd be sore, and our hostess would be scandalized."

Until dawn… Oh, marriage to Jonathan would be unbearably lovely. Theo wanted to weep, for all the lonely years, for the awkward moments she'd known as a wife, for sheer glee at having found Jonathan at last.

Jonathan, who was, in his indirect way, posing a question.

"If we must conclude this interlude," she said, "then use the next five minutes well. I can't be the only person to leave this encounter grinning like an imbecile."

She was giving him permission to spend. That he'd leave the decision to her was grounds to fall in love with him all over again. For she surely had— when he'd lectured Diana in the park, when he'd sent Seraphina the perfect book of French poetry, when he'd dutifully danced attendance on women whose consequence had been raised by his notice.

Theo offered him that love as he held her close and breathed with her, gave him that love as satisfaction bore down on her again. She hadn't thought pleasure could be more intense than what she'd already experienced, but with Jonathan intent on gratification, the joining became wild.

Not a wrestling match, for Jonathan's passions were measured and silent, but so intimate, so consuming, that Theo's past, her disappointing memories, her last regrets fell away in incandescent moments of oneness with the man to whom she'd given her future.

"Did I pleasure you all the way to sleep?" Jonathan asked, stroking her back in slow circles.

"Not to sleep, but to a place of perfect peace and joy." A holy place, one Theo had never visited with her husband. "The rest of the Season will be interminable."

She should sit up. She should sit up and tuck herself up and let Jonathan put himself to rights too. She bundled closer on a sigh.

"If you think I'll wait until July to speak my vows, Theodosia, you are much mistaken. A special license will suit. We can be married next week."

So fierce. She loved that about him too. "I have a household, a daughter, a sister, loyal servants. They all must be dealt with. You need to call on your solicitors. Besides, you haven't proposed. You must pay me your addresses first, and I must write to the viscount."

Theo wiggled to her feet, though Jonathan stole a last kiss before she rose. He remained on the sofa, tousled, casually exposed, and luscious.

"The viscount can go to Jericho, for all I care," he said, passing Theo the handkerchief. "Anselm will negotiate settlements for you, or his duchess will, and he'll carry out her orders."

Theo used the handkerchief and passed it back, which should have been awkward, but wasn't. "I barely know Their Graces."

Jonathan rose and began doing up his clothing. "That doesn't signify. Anselm's a duke. He'll meddle. If I didn't prevail upon him to advocate for your interests, then Bellefonte's countess would intercede on your behalf, or Her Grace of Quimbey would find some marquess or other to bedevil me, but it won't matter, Theo."

He gently moved her hands aside and gave her stays a firm upward tug, which was what they'd needed.

"I have my competence," Theo said, while Jonathan retied the bow of her chemise. "The settlements don't need to be much." She hadn't even thought that far ahead. Hadn't seen beyond confiding in Jonathan regarding the viscount's accusations.

"You are to be my duchess," Jonathan said, stepping close. "You will want for nothing, Theo. If you develop a craving for peaches, they'll be served to you daily. If you'd like Seraphina to attend a Swiss finishing school, you've only to choose which one. If Diana needs a pony, or Williams a pension, then that too can be—"

She laid a finger over his lips. His hair was a tempest, his cravat a mass of wrinkles. He had one shirttail out, and half his buttons were yet unfastened.

A wave of desire threatened to have her undoing the buttons he'd fastened. "Diana needs a step-father who can show her firm guidance and unwavering love. Seraphina needs an older brother who can help her navigate polite society upon her come out. I need a husband to love and esteem greatly. The rest will work itself out."

A stray thought intruded: She still did not know the source of Jonathan's wealth, though he'd reassured her he had ample means. For now, that was enough.

They argued as they adjusted each other's clothing, the bickering another form of intimacy. As Theo finger-combed Jonathan's hair into order, they agreed that she'd write to Viscount Penweather by express, and Jonathan would have the banns cried at St. George's.

Within a month, she would be a married woman again, but a happily married woman this time.

"Will I do, Mrs. Haviland?" he asked, fluffing his retied cravat.

"You will do splendidly, Mr. Tresham." They smiled at each other, a pair of cats who'd swilled the last drop from the cream pot. "Will you see me home?" Though truly, that was a rash idea. To be alone with him in that luxurious, roomy carriage… very rash.

"Alas, not tonight." He tucked her fichu more securely under her bodice. "The press of business calls. In fact, I'll make my farewells to my hostess and be on my way, though expect an early call from me tomorrow."

"I'd like you with me when I tell Diana."

"Shall I bring a dog?"

"Yes, please, but make no mention of ponies. Diana is nigh incorrigible, and a pony should be exhausted as a source of bribes before you consider purchasing one."

"No ponies, no puppies. Yet." He leaned in to kiss Theo's cheek. "Until tomorrow."

She clasped her hands behind her back rather than embrace him, because that too had become a rash act.

"Until tomorrow, Mr. Tresham."

She let him leave first, marveling that they hadn't thought to lock the door—though what would that have mattered? She was marrying him in a month or so, and engaged couples anticipated their vows from time to time.

She hadn't with Archie, not that it would have made any difference. Theo took a seat at the card table, for the first time noticing that she'd plighted her troth in a game room. A billiards table took up nearly one-half of the space. A chess set occupied the middle of one small table by the windows. A dartboard was anchored to a slab of pine at the far end of the room.

Archie had spent far too much time in surrounds like these.

Theo had intended to wait a full ten minutes before following Jonathan back to the ballroom, but she rose from the card table and headed straight for the door, not even pausing to listen for voices in the corridor before she quit the room altogether.

* * *

Jonathan took the usual route to the rooming house across the street from The Coventry with an odd emotion weighting his heart. He'd made this walk countless times. The streets themselves were as familiar as the jingle of the hackney harnesses, the *trit-trot* of the linkboys accompanying chattering groups of the well-dressed from one entertainment to another.

Usually, Jonathan was relieved to have the evening's social obligations behind him so that he could return to his pride and joy, the enterprise that never failed to please him.

Tonight, he *resented* having to spend the next hours at the club. Resented having to leave Theo amid the aging colonels and reckless debutantes. Resented not being able to dance the good-night waltz with her.

"I am permitted to prefer the company of my beloved to that of a bunch of idle gamblers." Theo *was* his beloved. He desired her, liked her, respected her. She blended common-sense kindness with unwavering propriety and a latent streak of passion.

Ye hopping devils, she had passion to burn.

Which only made the tasks ahead less appealing. Instead of verifying Frannie's bookkeeping entries, Jonathan might have been partnering Theo at a hand of whist. Instead of fencing with Moira's moods—would she be relieved or upset that Jonathan had chosen a bride?—he could have been sharing a dessert plate with his intended.

Floating amid these thoughts was the realization that Jonathan resented not being able to walk through the front door of his own… but then, why not? *Why not* walk through the door of his own establishment and see the place from the perspective of a patron?

His ownership was a closely guarded secret, and most of his acquaintances patronized the club. Anselm occasionally played a hand. Casriel's brothers came by for the food. Lady Canmore had taken a genteel turn at vingt-et-un in the company of some baron or viscount.

Jonathan entered through the front door, his first impressions being luxury and warmth. The candles were beeswax, the sconces burnished to a high shine. Battaglia, the club's majordomo and an employee who well knew that Jonathan paid his wages, greeted him with a professional smile that contained only a hint of surprise.

"Good evening, sir. Are we interested in a late supper tonight or a friendly hand of cards?" Battaglia was a dapper, dark-haired man whose Mediterranean appearance belied an upbringing in Chelsea. His French was flawless, and Jonathan had heard him conversing in excellent Italian and passable German as well.

"Both sustenance and entertainment appeal." Jonathan passed him his cloak, hat, and walking stick. The foyer was empty, and a hum of conversation came from the dining room and cardrooms. "I'm here as a casual guest. Nobody need be alerted that I'm on the premises."

Nobody meaning *Moira*. Jonathan would deal with her soon enough.

"Very good, sir. Would you like to start with the buffet?"

Theo might have some ideas for the buffet. "That would suit."

Battaglia gestured with a white-gloved hand in the direction of the main dining room. The guests were not to be harried by the staff or escorted from room to room like unruly toddlers. An evening at The Coventry should be like visiting a favorite wealthy uncle's card party, all gracious welcome and good cheer, save for the part about leaving substantially poorer—or richer—than one arrived.

Though this crowd could well afford to lose some blunt. Younger sons were much in evidence, as was the occasional title, the stray or straying widow. They could afford to play, and Jonathan saw to it that the proceeds of their frolics were put to good use.

Moira glided up to him and wrapped her hand around his arm. "Good evening. This is a lovely surprise. Spying on me?" She asked that question while bussing his cheek. Her smile was brilliant, though edged with uncertainty.

Good. She needed to recall who paid her salary and who owned the premises where she was employed.

"I'm enjoying one of the premier clubs in London," he said. "A ducal heir should be permitted that pleasure. Lipscomb must be winning."

The viscount was visible through a doorway that led to one of the private parlors. Should the authorities decide to drop by unannounced, the door locked from the inside, and the patrons could access the cellars by a servants' stair. From there, they could leave the building undetected.

Lipscomb was laughing, a stack of chips piled before him.

"He's winning for now," Moira said. "Shall I join you for a meal?"

"Isn't that the Marquess of Tyne and his new marchioness at the corner table? I don't believe I've seen him here before."

"Her ladyship is apparently being a corrupting influence, though his lordship's bets wouldn't feed a dormouse. I've sent them the requisite bottle of champagne all newlyweds are entitled to. Speaking of which, how is your bride hunt going?"

Moira asked him this at least weekly, though Jonathan did not want to air those developments amid his patrons.

"For thirty minutes, might I not simply enjoy the club's amenities, madam?" He was hungry, and Moira knew better than to cling to any guest.

A waiter glided by, an empty silver tray at his shoulder. Somebody at a hazard table must have had a lucky throw, for a cheer went up across the room. The house had an air of happy possibilities, a private world where chance was a friend and risk a diversion.

Jonathan did love this place. He did not love having Moira nanny him under his own roof.

"I can enjoy the club with you," she said. "Frannie will be leaving us."

No wonder Moira was unsettled. "We can discuss that when I join you upstairs, though Frannie has taken a leave of absence before. I truly do need to eat, Moira, and I am overdue for the pleasure of roaming the tables."

In Paris, he'd spent almost every evening visible to his guests and his staff. He missed that, though he did not miss being tethered to a commercial enterprise the way Frannie was tied to her infants.

"You needn't ambush me like this, Jonathan. I can have a tray sent up to you."

Moira was beautiful, and thus when she wound herself around a man's arm, other people took notice, particularly when that man was not a regular patron.

"I'm inclined to try the tables," Jonathan said, patting her hand. Though most of the guests would recognize one another at sight, she knew better than to use anybody's name, much less his. A gambling club was an illegal establishment, and protecting a guest's privacy was paramount.

"Just imagine," Moira said, beaming up at him. "If I owned this place, you could spend every night of the week here, enjoying the ambience, the tables, the comestibles. No more burying yourself in the ledgers—"

"I don't recognize that waiter."

"He's new. I have authority to hire and fire, have I not? I let that lazy Sutter boy go and found a willing replacement the very same day."

You don't hire or fire without consulting me. This was neither the time nor the place for an argument, but Jonathan insisted on a final interview with any person departing his employ, regardless of the cause. He presented himself as the owner's man of business, and nobody had questioned that status.

Every unhappy employee was one more breach in the security of the establishment, one more person who might reveal the club's secrets to the authorities. Severance pay and an agreement to protect the club's privacy let Jonathan sleep more soundly.

"We can discuss whether you have that authority at another time, madam. I have an empty belly now and The Coventry's offerings are said to be splendid. I'll see you in the office after I've had my supper."

He returned her smile for the benefit of any onlookers. From the table beneath the landing, Sycamore Dorning was watching this exchange. Younger sons were a troublesome lot, youngest sons more troublesome still.

"We have an audience," Jonathan murmured. "Exactly what I'd hoped to avoid."

Moira let go of his arm. "Enjoy the buffet, sir, and all the pleasures on offer here at The Coventry."

Another waiter whom Jonathan did not recognize hustled past, holding his silver platter high to avoid jostling a guest. Moira glided away and went back to spreading smiles and laughter among the guests. Jonathan filled a plate at the buffet and took the empty seat at Mr. Dorning's little table.

"Has luck abandoned you tonight, Dorning?"

Dorning was playing solitaire, or pretending to. He laid cards out on the table with the smooth, unhurried rhythm of a man who used card games as a form of meditation.

"Luck is a constant rather than a variable," Dorning replied, turning over card after card. "But when the house takes a portion of every bet, luck is a factor that need trouble only the patrons."

Jonathan speared a bite of ham. "You make a study of games of chance?" Dorning was studying something. Jonathan had seen him frequently at this table, which had a fine view of the whole cardroom.

"The games of chance are merely the attractions," Dorning said, "like the booths at a fair. An establishment like this essentially charges admission three times. Regular members pay the club fee, diners pay for the expensive fare before midnight, and gamblers play to place a bet. Whoever owns this place is making money faster than Fat George can spend it."

Not quite. "The expenses must be considerable for a business like this." The ham was excellent, slightly smoky, not too salty, almost sweet. The wine complemented it wonderfully—Battaglia's doing.

"The expenses are no more than a fancy restaurant would incur, while the profits are at least triple what's possible with a dining establishment. I do wonder why a place that has so much going for it would need to use marked cards."

Jonathan set down his wineglass carefully. "I beg your pardon?"

Dorning gathered the cards into a deck and passed them over. "I got this deck from the vingt-et-un dealer at the corner table. Gloss your fingertips over the short edges of the cards."

Jonathan had replaced every deck in the house more than a fortnight ago. The marks were more subtle this time, subtle as pinpricks and not on every card. Only somebody who knew where to look for the markings would feel them.

"This deck came from the corner table?" Where a *marquess* was playing?

"Not an hour past. Whoever owns The Coventry had better clean house thoroughly and soon." Dorning helped himself to a roll from Jonathan's plate, took Jonathan's knife, and applied butter to the bread.

"Have you said anything to Mrs. Jones?" Moira's nom de guerre, to all save Frannie and Jonathan.

"If I have an opportunity to address yonder female, I will not be talking to her about marked cards, Mr. Tresham."

"She'd snack on your conceit and laugh at your presumption."

Dorning dipped the roll in the ham gravy. "Know her well, do you?"

Damn. "I know her well enough. What will you do regarding your suspicions about the cards?"

"Nothing. I've spent the past hour examining that deck, card by card, and I can find no pattern, no system. Whoever marked the cards used six different sets of marks, but the seven of hearts has the same pattern as the nine of diamonds. The queen of spades has the same markings as the three of clubs. The marks won't allow anybody to cheat, not even at a game as simple as vingt-et-un."

"May I keep this deck?"

Dorning sent him a lazy smile over a half-eaten roll. "The deck belongs to the owner. Ask him or her if you may have it."

"Isn't Mrs. Jones the owner?"

Dorning tore a bite off his roll. "She wants to be. She looks at this place the way my sister looks at her infant. Part worry, part love, but without an air of ownership. This is excellent wine."

"That is my wine, Mr. Dorning."

"Whoever the owner is, his problems just grew more complicated."

Dorning made an elegant picture, the wineglass cradled in a long-finger hand. Was he marking Jonathan's cards? Playing some deep game? Watching the proceedings with a covetous eye?

"A randomly marked deck of cards is not a significant problem." It was a disaster, given that Jonathan had thought this problem solved.

"Perhaps not, but Lady Della Haddonfield and her brother Adolphus have joined the proceedings. If Bellefonte gets word that his baby brother has taken his baby sister to a gambling house, The Coventry's owner will need a good set of Mantons and excellent aim—whoever that owner might be."

CHAPTER THIRTEEN

"I'm in the mood for some adventure," Bea said as the orchestra took up a lively ecossaise.

"Such as having your toes mashed?" Theo replied. The entire room reverberated with the dancers' exertions, and the scent of warm bodies blended with the beeswax smoke from the chandeliers. The combination was familiar and unappealing, and Theo wished she'd had Jonathan take her home after all.

"The joy of mashed toes has befallen me more times than I count." Bea edged back among the ferns and beckoned Theo to follow. "Along with torn hems. On one memorable occasion, a flying slipper nearly struck me in the face, the scent of which was enough to chase me to the nearest window. The gentlemen don't worship at our literal feet for good reason."

They emerged into the cool and quiet of a corridor, the dancing creating a reverberation like distant thunder.

"What manner of adventure calls to you at this hour?" Theo asked.

Bea led her through a door that opened onto the buffet, abandoned now by all save the servants who were tidying up the remains of the meal and collecting half-empty plates.

Such a waste. Such a terrible, pointless waste.

"That is a very severe expression, Theodosia. I saw Mr. Tresham spiriting you away at the supper break. Did he transgress—or fail to transgress?"

"We discussed Mr. Tresham's social calendar." Upon which a wedding would soon figure. "I'm hungry." Perhaps that accounted for Theo's unhappy frame of mind, or perhaps Archie had left her incapable of trusting that any positive development could be the lovely news it seemed to be.

"I enjoyed a good meal," Bea replied. "Try the fish remoulade."

Cold fish sounded ghastly. "I'm in the mood for cheese." And in the mood to go home and consider the evening's developments. The pleasure of the time spent with Jonathan was trickling away, leaving doubts and questions in its wake.

"The dessert table is this way." Bea strode across the room like Wellington on the way to a parade inspection, while Theo was abruptly tired.

"When you referred to an adventure, were you intent on adventuring with anybody in particular?" Theo asked.

No clean plates graced the dessert table, though a stack of folded table napkins remained. Theo used one to assemble three cheeses—a bleu, a cheddar, and something pale laced with tarragon—and two slices of bread.

"That is hardly enough to sustain a bird, Theo. The Coventry has a very good chef. You should come with us."

Theo stepped closer, lest the nearest footman overhear her. "Beatitude, you are not suggesting that I visit a gaming hell, are you?"

"Yes, Theo. Yes, I am. Archie is gone. He wasted his money in hells, clubs, at private games, and God knows where else. That doesn't mean you have to live like a nun for the rest of your life."

The Earl of Casriel entered the room through a door at the far end of the buffet. When he spotted Bea and Theo, he pretended to become fascinated with the remains of the fish courses.

"Frequenting an illegal establishment," Theo said, "where I can do nothing but lose money doesn't strike me as an adventure, my lady."

Bea plucked a bon-bon from a silver tray on the dessert table. "You might win, Theo. Somebody wins every hand, after all. Sooner or later, you should face the devil that haunted your marriage. See that The Coventry is merely a place to pass a diverting evening, not some den of iniquity."

This conversation could not have been less appropriately timed, and Theo wanted to lecture Bea like an outraged chaperone.

"If these establishments are so harmless, why are they illegal?"

"Because Parliament hasn't found a way to tax them. That's what Lord Casriel says."

"And because they ruin lives," Theo countered. "An honest game is a contradiction in terms at most of these places, and if people can afford to lose money on a toss of the dice, they can afford to donate that money to worthy charities."

Bea selected another bon-bon. "I'm sorry, Theo. I hadn't realized that you were still so easily vexed on this topic. I won't raise it again, though many a generous patron of the charities has also enjoyed an evening at the tables."

A month ago, Theo had been considering selling Archie's watch, one of the few remaining bequests she could pass along to Diana. But for Jonathan

Tresham's good offices, that watch might already be at a pawnshop with a dozen other watches whose owners had likely gambled away the servants' wages.

"I am sensitive on this topic," Theo said. "I expect I always will be, Bea. The Coventry was the worst of the lot, with its free food, pretty dealers, and luxurious appointments. Archie spoke of that club as if it were the family seat, the site of fond memories and unspoken aspirations. I will never set foot on those premises, no matter how fancy their chef."

Casriel had worked his way to the beef dishes, and he was pretending he couldn't hear a conversation taking place twelve feet away. Theo did not care who overheard her on this point. She had agreed to become Jonathan Tresham's duchess, and the disgrace of her first marriage no longer controlled her choices.

"Theo, you have to let it go," Bea said gently. "You have to put Archie's betrayal behind you and look forward. Clubs are a part of life, men play cards, and women do too. They wager at the horse races, which is both legal and part of the fun of a race meet. I love you like my own sister—more than my sister, to be honest—but if you marry a man of an appropriate station, he's likely to engage in the same behaviors Archie did."

Not all of Archie's behaviors, please God. "My next husband had best claim far more moderation than Archimedes ever aspired to, and that includes avoiding all establishments like The Coventry."

Lord Casriel had found a clean plate and was taking three eons to choose a slice of beef. He was apparently to be Bea's escort for her adventure, which made no sense at all. Casriel was known to have limited means, and the sole purpose of The Coventry and venues of that ilk was to fleece its patrons.

"If you ever change your mind," Bea said, passing Theo a French chocolate drop, "I will happily join you at the tables. I will also understand if that day never comes, but I cannot approve of your choice, Theodosia."

She kissed Theo's cheek and wafted away, calling a greeting to the earl.

Lord Casriel left off dithering among the remains of the roasts and bowed to Bea. He also spared Theo a nod, his gentian eyes oddly serious for a man in contemplation of a diversion. But then, he could not afford to waste coin. Perhaps the outing for him was more about the company to be had than the diversion.

"Good hunting," Theo whispered as Bea took Casriel's arm and left the room.

Theo sat beneath a guttering sconce and made a sandwich of her bread and cheese.

Jonathan understood the damage Archie's intemperance had done, or understood as much as Theo had admitted, and Jonathan was a man of more than appropriate station.

"He won't expect me to throw money away at some notorious hell and pretend I'm enjoying myself." In every way, Jonathan Tresham was an estimable man.

Though Theo would ask him where his money came from. That was something a wife should know, and in a month's time, she would be his wife, his prospective duchess, and—God be thanked—his lover.

For exactly what sort of business called a man away from his intended in the middle of the night?

* * *

Jonathan was torn between admiration for Della Haddonfield's tenacity, pride that his sister should see and admire The Coventry, and lingering resentment from earlier in the evening.

Theo had given him permission to pay his addresses, the very last step before the formality of a marriage proposal. Why must the club have difficulties now? Why couldn't the place for once hum along without intruding into his other affairs? His obligations to other ventures and to the dukedom had only mounted, and his bride-hunting had run him short of sleep.

"Mr. Tresham." Della Haddonfield curtseyed. The blond giant beside her bowed, another one of her endless supply of legitimate brothers.

"My lady. Sir."

"Call me Dolph. My proper name is Maximus Adolphus, but my older brothers couldn't stand to call me that as I grew taller than all save the earl." His voice was a bass rumble, and the merriment of a younger sibling who'd had the last laugh shone in blue, blue eyes. A man this tall and striking would see no point in delicate fictions regarding the use of personal names.

"You're the fellow who likes to blow things up," Jonathan said. "Your sister has spoken highly of you."

Her ladyship was watching this exchange with an overly bright smile, while for Jonathan the encounter underscored an unwelcome truth.

Della looked nothing like her Haddonfield brother. He was a Viking, the youngest of a troupe of Vikings, while her ladyship was a Pict—short, dark-haired, petite. Her brows were slightly heavy—a legacy from her father—and her hair came to a widow's peak, another trait she shared with Jonathan.

"I'm a chemist," Mr. Haddonfield replied. "Explosions are one of the perquisites of the profession. I'm actually studying chemical reactions that bear directly on the means by which a leavened product—"

Lady Della wrapped an arm around her brother's elbow—her *other* brother. "If we allow you to start your discourse on the effects of heat on gases and the chemical results of fermentation, then I will never get to watch you play."

Watch him play. *Like a spotter?*

"I'm an evangelist for science," Mr. Haddonfield said, patting Lady Della's small hand. "But tonight, I am also a dutiful escort and instructor."

"I know how to handle the cards," Lady Della retorted. "You will teach me to gamble."

Foreboding roiled in Jonathan's belly, because Lady Della's blond brother might *be* the spotter. His height would give him an advantage in that regard, and he would support any effort on Della's part to bedevil a half-sibling she saw as negligent.

Sycamore Dorning was still at his post beneath the stairs, though he'd left off playing solitaire and was enjoying Jonathan's wine. Jonathan raised a hand in a gesture a patron might use to signal a waiter, and Mr. Dorning sauntered over, wineglass in hand.

"My lady, sir." Dorning bowed and came up sipping wine. "A pleasure to see you both."

"Good evening." Another curtsey from Lady Della. "I have come to learn about the pleasures of games of chance among the wealthy and wanton. You must never tell a soul you saw me here."

She was teasing, maybe. Too late, Jonathan recalled that Lady Della had seemed fond of Dorning's older brother Ash.

"One of the unspoken rules of this establishment," Jonathan said, "is that nobody sees anybody here. The authorities frown on gambling, and some hells go so far as to use dim lighting and to hand out masks at the door, so that nobody's identity can be reliably reported."

"But dim lighting," Dorning observed, "makes bad behavior easier to hide as well. The owner of The Coventry is happy to spend a fortune on candles, but then, he's neck-deep in blunt, so why not make sure we're all behaving as we misbehave?"

His smile was charming. Jonathan wanted to dash the wine in the bloody pest's face.

"Perhaps you'd be good enough to show her ladyship the rudiments of play at the vingt-et-un table," Jonathan said. "I'll accompany her brother to the dining room. I'm told the chef at The Coventry is among the finest in London."

Haddonfield seemed amused by the entire exchange, but then, a man who topped Jonathan's brawn by three stone and several inches could afford to be amused by much.

"Are you her spotter?" Jonathan asked as he and Haddonfield gained the quiet of the corridor. "Or is she yours?"

"Are your pistols clean?" Haddonfield replied in the same tone as he might have asked about Jonathan's elderly uncle. "Because I'm almost certain you've implied that our sister cheats. This is a degree of dunderheadedness worse than implying that I cheat, because a devoted brother is honor-bound to defend rather than malign his sister's good name. Perhaps that lesson was neglected at baby-duke school."

Jonathan kept going past the dining room, Haddonfield ambling at his side. The smaller of the private parlors was unoccupied, so he took a lamp from a sconce in the corridor, gestured for Haddonfield to follow, and closed the door.

"You certainly know your way around this place," Haddonfield said. "Della has a theory about that."

"A theory based on rumors, no doubt. Why on earth would a devoted brother escort his sister, who's all but a debutante, to a venue like this?"

Haddonfield took the lamp and squatted by the unlit hearth. "You don't know Della. She would have come without me. My brothers understand this, which is why they won't pummel me en masse for this escapade."

He peered up the dark chimney. "You could install a convection flue here," he went on. "Use it to turn a fan that would draw the smoke up from the table. A clerestory window would finish the job, and then the room wouldn't bear such a coal-smoke and tobacco stench. So is it to be pistols or swords?"

Anselm behaved with the same casual high-handedness. Jonathan had assumed the attitude was ducal, though now he suspected it was fraternal.

Theo had never mentioned siblings other than Seraphina, though he must ask about her extended family.

"I'm sure the owner of the premises would be very interested to hear your theories, Mr. Haddonfield. Some people associate that scent with late nights spent in pleasurable social pursuits. Why is Lady Della here?"

Haddonfield rose, the lamplight casting his features in diabolical shadows. He'd doubtless done that on purpose too.

"You are concerned for her," he said, setting the lamp in the middle of the table. "That means I can't call you out, because I am concerned for her too, but if you think she'd cheat merely to gain your notice, you're daft."

He slid into a chair, and even sitting, his height was apparent.

Jonathan took the seat across the table. "She wants my notice. I understand that, but I have embarked on the process of finding a bride, and my calendar has been busy. I sit on a half dozen boards of directors, and they all demand my time. I'm also trying to untangle decades of bookkeeping and the lack thereof for the Quimbey dukedom, another endeavor that is more time-consuming than it should be."

Haddonfield stared at the shadows dancing on the ceiling. "You are ashamed of her. She said you were smart, but I gather you're smart like an abacus. All manner of correct answers can be had from you, but in fact you're nothing more than wooden parts cleverly arranged by a chance hand."

Jonathan was tired, he was angry at Lady Della, and most of all, he would rather have spent the rest of this evening with Theo. Not even making love with her, simply talking. Simply holding her hand, holding *her*.

"Lady Della has an understandable interest in me, for we are related by blood," Jonathan said. "She has no concept of the gossip an association between us would stir. My parents made a Drury Lane farce look boring, with their unending and inane drama. If Lady Della is my sister, how many other dark-haired young ladies am I related to? She's the only one I know of, but until you've lived with such talk, Haddonfield, you don't know the damage it can do."

"Della has been dubbed the Haddonfield changeling. She knows about talk."

"No, she does not. When nobody offers for her, Season after Season, despite her settlements becoming more and more generous, then she'll have an inkling of the damage talk can do. When her daughters, should she escape the fate of an old maid, are treated to slights and whispers and her sons beaten bloody in the schoolyard, then she'll know. When an outing like this—innocent, if ill-advised—becomes common knowledge, and her reputation is sullied past all recall overnight, then she'll know."

Jonathan had not raised his voice, but inside, annoyance had escalated to indignation and then rage. Why couldn't Haddonfield see the peril he'd allowed their younger sister to blunder into?

"From the grave," Jonathan said, rising and leaning over the table, "our father has the power to ruin her. She does not grasp this. She who has brothers and sisters to spare merely wants to add to her collection."

Haddonfield sat across the table, his expression as impassive as a judge's. "You said you'd call on her."

Bloody hell. Jonathan sank back into his chair. "I will."

"Call on her tomorrow, if you value your sanity, and if you value that of her other siblings. You think she wants merely to flit about on the arm of a ducal heir to whom she has hidden connection. You do her a discredit. She wants to know who her family is, and she does not *grasp* how you can ignore her when she's the only sibling you have. She was raised as a Haddonfield. We do not turn our backs on family."

Jonathan was very glad he'd confided this situation to Theo. Her counsel would clearly be needed going forward, because Haddonfield was making some obscure point that Jonathan hadn't the patience to pursue.

"I will call upon Lady Della tomorrow afternoon," Jonathan said. "Somebody is trying to sabotage this club, and the less she's seen here, the better."

"Della would not betray family like that." Haddonfield fiddled with the wick on the lamp, turning the flame brighter, then to a tiny glow. "But how would you know that? You did not have a family, not worth the name. Such an existence bewilders Della, and she has made it a mission to console you for that terrible lack."

Which was, of course, what Della would tell a doting brother if she wanted his aid to gain access to the club.

"I have been given leave to pay my addresses to Mrs. Theodosia Haviland," Jonathan said. "I am hopeful that I will at least have a bride in the very near future and that family will follow in due time. This is a recent development, not common knowledge."

Haddonfield wrinkled an aquiline beak. "Does Mrs. Haviland know that Della is your half-sister?"

"Yes. I trust Mrs. Haviland's discretion utterly." Her loyalty, her discretion, her everything, and what a relief that was.

Haddonfield rose and collected the lamp. "If you're marrying the woman, then trusting her discretion should be a foregone conclusion. Mrs. Haviland is well connected in polite society, and my sister-in-law speaks well of her."

His sister-in-law would be... the Countess of Bellefonte. How Theo kept the whirling cast of polite society's characters straight was a marvel.

"You will please not disclose my marital aspirations, Mr. Haddonfield."

Haddonfield moved toward the door, the lamp in his hand. "You have much to learn, Tresham, but because I am not allowed to instruct you with my fists, I will attempt the less reliable route of instructing you with words: You will tell Della of your marital aspirations. You will bring Mrs. Haviland to call upon her. You will intimate that nobody, save perhaps old Quimbey, has been alerted to the news before you confide your joy in your only sibling. That's how it works with sisters, Tresham, unless you have some bosom bow from your boyhood whom you must inform first."

Anselm was hardly a bosom bow. Jonathan hadn't thought to write to Quimbey. "My thanks for your insights. If you'd see to it that Lady Della's visit is brief and uneventful, I'd appreciate it."

Haddonfield paused in the doorway, the light from the corridor making him appear as a looming shadow.

"She thinks you own this place. I think she's right. I wonder how Mrs. Haviland reacted when you confided that secret, assuming it's true."

"Good night, Mr. Haddonfield."

Haddonfield bowed, twirling his wrist to turn the gesture ironic. "My brother the earl claims there is no trouble so dire as woman trouble. He knows of what he speaks."

Jonathan rose as another snippet of memory prodded him. "Does Mr. Ash Dorning have woman trouble? Della seemed fond of him."

Broad shoulders slumped. "As best we can decipher, Mr. Ash Dorning has money trouble. He's a younger son without means. Bellefonte made it plain that Della will require a certain standard of living, though that lecture—which Dorning should have expected—doesn't explain why the man rusticates at such length. Perhaps Della is interrogating Mr. Sycamore Dorning on that very subject as we speak."

He withdrew, taking the lamp with him and leaving Jonathan in nigh complete darkness.

"I should tell Theo that I'm responsible for building this place up from its humble beginnings, for turning it into one of the premier venues of its kind anywhere in the world."

She's be surprised, but in Theo fashion, she'd take the news in stride. She might even have ideas for how to improve the club's appeal.

"But first, I must solve the mystery of who is trying to ruin my club."

That sequence made sense. Clean house—or stop Lady Della's mischief, if that was what the marked cards were about—then invite Theo for a tour. She'd be reassured to learn the true extent of Jonathan's personal wealth and to know how reliable The Coventry was as a source of income.

* * *

Diana and Seraphina were bickering, the weather had turned from sunny to a steady rain that might continue for days, and Theo was struggling to compose a letter to the viscount.

"Mr. Tresham has come to call," Williams said. "Shall I show him to the formal parlor, ma'am?"

Jonathan edged past Williams. "No need for that. Mrs. Haviland, good morning."

"Mr. Tresham." She rose, putting a self-conscious hand to her hair. "This is a pleasure—an unexpected pleasure. Williams, you are excused."

"Shall I bring a tray, ma'am?"

"Mr. Tresham?"

"Nothing for me, thank you."

He'd caught Theo in the breakfast parlor, which had the best morning light in the house. He'd also caught her with her hair in a single braid and in her oldest day dress.

Which was very old.

"How are you?" he asked.

"Please have a seat. I'm trying to compose a letter to Lord Penweather and my manners are failing me. The first draft informed him that if he was having a cow byre swept out to house his poor relations, he needn't bother. The second warned him that I might not recognize him should he deign to appear at the wedding."

Jonathan's hair was damp, his smile tired. "And the third?"

"Dear Viscount Foul Weather, you need no longer threaten me with sending Diana and Seraphina to some dreary school in the north. Our circumstances have improved, and you are an ass."

A gasp from the doorway revealed Seraphina in her best day dress. "You never said Cousin Viscount was threatening to send us away."

Jonathan rose. "Miss Seraphina, good day." He bowed, she curtseyed.

Theo wanted to toss the ink bottle at her dearest little sister. "Viscount Penweather has graciously intimated that should the need arise, he'd be willing to see to the education of the household's minor females. Was there something you needed, Seraphina?"

"I wanted to thank Mr. Tresham for the loan of the French poetry book. I've had to look up several phrases, and I love learning new vocabulary."

Seraphina was spying, in other words.

Diana sidled into the room. "Mr. Tresham, good morning, though it's a very wet morning. Did you bring Comus with you?"

"Good morning, Miss Diana. On a day such as this, Comus would track mud into the house and carry a certain fragrance which would endear him to no one."

"Oh. I can't find my slate, Mama." Diana had adopted her helpless and hopeful look, one of her most reliably endearing with strangers.

Theo sat back and crossed her arms. "While I seem to have misplaced my privacy."

Seraphina had the grace to look uncomfortable. Diana's expression became mulish. Theo hoped Jonathan was trying not to smile.

"Make your curtsey to Mr. Tresham, Diana," Theo said. "I'm sure Seraphina will help you look for your slate if you ask her politely."

"Rhymes with contritely," Jonathan said, bowing to both girls as they shuffled from the room. He closed the door behind them, flipped the lock, and resumed his seat. "They worry about you. Did Lord Pinfeather truly threaten to ship them off to school?"

"Yes." This admission made Theo angry all over again. "I hinted that we could use a respite in the country, not only to ensure Diana knew the head of the Haviland family, but also to allow me to conserve resources by closing up this house for a time, or even leasing it out. The viscount's response was to make a veiled offer to have the girls educated at his expense."

Jonathan put the cap on the ink bottle. "Is he a bachelor?"

"Yes, and something of a curmudgeon in training. To accept his charity would be a last resort."

"And you were considering it."

Less than twelve hours ago, Theo had been considering removing Jonathan's clothing. The notion still had significant appeal.

"Penweather considers me a bad influence, Jonathan. He holds me responsible for turning a fun-loving young man into a wastrel. His lordship hasn't demanded guardianship of Diana, in part because Archie made arrangements in his will naming me as her guardian." For which Theo was sincerely grateful.

"That is unusual."

"But not illegal. Had she been a boy, I'm sure Penweather would have intervened by now."

Jonathan covered her hand with his own. "You will never again be anxious regarding his lordship's neglect or his potential meddling, and I give you my word, neither Seraphina nor Diana will either. I shall settle sums on them both and name Anselm executor of their trusts in my absence."

He stood and drew Theo to her feet and wrapped his arms around her. The comfort of his embrace was profound, the comfort of his insight greater still.

"I hate having to ask anybody for money," Theo murmured. "Thank you."

He smelled of damp wool and whatever fancy floral soap was unique to him. Theo's mood eased, from dreary to peaceful, and yet, she was troubled.

"Shall I write to Penweather?" Jonathan asked.

"Please. I seem to have lost the knack of being a perpetually apologetic poor relation." How odd, and how wonderful, to remain in each other's arms. "May I ask you something?"

Jonathan eased away, stealing a quick kiss. "Of course."

"What business drew you from my side last night?"

He ran a hand through damp hair. "I don't have a mistress, if that's what you're wondering, and if I did, she'd be in possession of her parting gift by the end of the week. I saw the drama and misery that marital infidelity can wreak, and though it's old-fashioned of me, I will be faithful to you, Theo."

She hugged him tightly, apparently catching him by surprise. "Be old-fashioned, then. I will never complain of your loyalty." She had wondered, had tossed and turned, and doubted. What pressing business could have commanded his presence, other than informing a mistress of an upcoming wedding?

"Shall we sit?" Jonathan asked. "I came by to ask if you'd call on Lady Della Haddonfield with me. I've rearranged several business meetings to make myself available for a social call, but I'd like to bring an ally with me."

Pleasure bloomed, because in a sense, this would be calling on his family. "Of course, though I'll have to change."

He grasped Theo's braid and drew the tip along his cheek. "I like your hair down."

The door was locked, Jonathan had seen to that. Theo brushed a hand over his falls. "I was not expecting callers. Are you still willing to have the banns called?"

He dropped her braid. "Yes. Quimbey should be present for the ceremony. If I allow him several weeks' notice, he won't have an excuse for dodging off."

Now that Theo's immediate worries had been put to rout—Jonathan did not have a mistress, he would deal with Lord Penweather—she realized that he too was less than ebullient the morning after having become a suitor.

"Are you angry with His Grace?"

Jonathan took the place at the head of the table, where Theo had been composing her correspondence.

"His Grace married only recently, Theo. He's a duke, and he never married at a time in life when any other ducal heir would have done so."

"You came along. He didn't have to marry."

Jonathan lined up the quill pen and the penknife in the tray, and set the standish parallel to the tray. "He did not marry, because he could not afford to."

"I beg your pardon?"

"Quimbey has refused to modernize his agricultural holdings. I thought that decision was stubborn sentiment, him clinging to the old ways because he's not greedy or ambitious. I was wrong. He cannot afford to modernize. He keeps his aging staff because he cannot afford to both pension them and hire replacements. The pattern has been right before my eyes for years, but I've been too busy resenting my father to notice my uncle's difficulties."

Theo took the place at Jonathan's right side. "You are not your father, Jonathan."

He crumpled Theo's failed attempts at correspondence. "I have wondered why Quimbey was so late to notice my circumstances as his heir, why he took so little interest in his only nephew. He was overwhelmed with holding my legacy together, and I never suspected we were in difficulties."

Nobody referred to His Grace as anything other than *dear old Quimbey*. The duke presented uniformly sanguine countenance, and Jonathan would resent mightily the dishonesty in such good cheer.

"How bad is it?"

He tossed the wadded-up letter into the basket of kindling near the hearth. "The dukedom is not solvent. The revenue doesn't cover the expenses. Quimbey could not afford to enclose his commons. He hasn't the means to harvest his lumber. The previous two dukes were a pair of heedless libertines. Quimbey had nobody to show him how to go on, and then he was saddled with my expenses as well."

"You did not know this last night."

He shook his head, staring at the fire. "I've been working through the books a bit at a time, questioning the steward, trying to put the puzzle pieces together while I tended to other business obligations. This morning, a maid who looked to have been born in good King Hal's day shuffled in with my tray. I asked her why she hadn't retired. I nearly had to shout the question. She was horrified to think of making the dear duke both pay her pension and hire somebody who'd expect a full wage."

"And you figured out the rest. I'm sorry, Jonathan. I know what it's like to feel as if a tempest has destroyed one's finances. To feel as if the rosy picture you'd believed for so long about people you thought you knew is just that—a painting, not reality. Not true, a lie in fact."

He crumpled up the last of Theo's failed correspondence and tossed it straight at the fire. The paper caught, blue flames consuming Theo's rebuke to the viscount.

"Quimbey married a dowager who has her own means," Jonathan said. "I can't see that her finances in any way have been involved in putting his to rights. The dukedom is nearly bankrupt."

While part of Theo was horrified for Jonathan, another part of her rejoiced: He'd come to her with the news immediately. He wasn't concocting lies and evasions, pretending the world would come right with his next quarterly allowance.

"We'll have my competence," Theo said, getting up to draw the curtains. "I will sell this house. I will be the most frugal duchess ever to serve weak tea at my infrequent at-homes. I bring little to this union, Jonathan, but economies run in my blood. We needn't maintain your London quarters—lease them out. We can retire to the country with the duke and duchess. I've longed to return to the country and—"

She turned from the dreary day beyond the window and ran into a solid wall of male muscle.

"I love you, Theodosia Haviland," Jonathan said, taking her in his arms. "I love how fierce and protective you are, how practical and loyal, but we needn't subsist on sour gruel and stale oat cakes."

"I can," she said, burrowing into his warmth. "I can if we must. Many haven't even that much."

"I have properties, investments, and revenue independent of the dukedom, though even with my own fortune, bringing the Quimbey holdings around will take time. You mustn't worry."

"I do worry. I've learned it's better to anticipate trouble than be caught by it unaware."

Jonathan held her for a long, quiet moment, slowly stroking her back, and gradually, Theo's breathing eased, her body relaxed. She'd been ready to do battle with the forces of penury on Jonathan's behalf, too ready.

Of course he had means independent of the dukedom, or why would he be constantly tending to business, rescheduling meetings, or dashing off to attend them?

"I think I have found my balance," she said, "and then I realize that, no, I have not. My balance is precarious, my sense of peace hard-won. I nearly lost my temper with Lady Canmore last night because she made a casual suggestion that sat ill with me. Be patient with me, Jonathan. I am not frail, but neither am I as fierce as you might think. Your honesty and openness mean much to me."

"And your loyalty means everything to me." He kissed her cheek.

Theo caught him by the hair and kissed him back, at length. The discussion had been difficult, and she was still uneasy, but the kissing... oh, the kissing was a delight. Jonathan started undoing her braid—the wretch—and she trailed her hands down his chest, intent on unbuttoning his falls.

Somebody rapped on the door *hard*. "I found my slate, Mama. I drew you a picture. Do you want to see my picture? Mama?"

Jonathan swore in French while Theo hastily did up her braid. They waited until they'd stopped laughing to open the door.

CHAPTER FOURTEEN

Continents were shifting in Jonathan's heart, a bewildering sensation. He'd awoken to a revelation of the worst sort: Quimbey had not been honest with him. Quimbey, the one benevolent constant in his life, had pushed a bow wave of financial problems for decades and never once hinted to his heir that difficulties lay ahead.

Before bidding Moira a farewell last night, Jonathan had also learned that Frannie was not merely taking a leave of absence, she'd abandoned her post, and without a word to Jonathan. That development, in addition to Quimbey's difficulties and Sycamore Dorning's disquieting accusations, left too many questions and no answers.

Thank goodness Lady Della had been from home, and Jonathan's first social call with Theo had been thirty minutes of watching the Earl of Bellefonte attempt to charm Theo, while his countess smiled graciously and sent her husband affectionate glances.

"You are brooding," Theo said. "Come sit by me, please."

He'd given her the forward-facing seat in his town coach out of habit, for a gentleman did when all of Society was abroad to gawk at a passing carriage. Shifting to the place beside her felt right.

Theo took his hand, and that was welcome too. "You are worried about money?"

"Not money. I know how to make money—I'm good at it, in fact. Did Quimbey say nothing to me because he lacks the skills to perceive the problem? Is every dukedom teetering on the brink of ruin and I've simply not been aware of that?"

"You have other theories, I'm sure."

Well, yes. "Is Quimbey angry, such that his brother's son must be made to pay for all the drama and scandal of years ago?"

Theo should have scoffed at that notion, though she didn't.

Dear old Quimbey had shown Jonathan his temper once, in the headmaster's office. Since then, the duke had been a genial, not quite doting uncle. He hadn't been able to afford to dote.

"What evidence do you have of your uncle's vendetta?" she asked.

Good word. "None, save the debt."

"If he'd been intent on ruining you, might he not have done a more thorough job? Peers cannot be jailed for debt."

The anxiety roiling in Jonathan's gut eased. "Ruin is all too easy to accomplish. You're right. Quimbey is not intent on ruining me."

"I have faced ruin," Theo said, her head on Jonathan's shoulder. "It's terrifying. You worry most for your dependents. You worry that they'll be sent away to one of those horrid schools with high walls and short rations, where they learn misery and bitterness. To have disappointed Diana and Seraphina like that… The shame would have broken me, Jonathan. They rely on me, and I cannot fail them."

Jonathan tucked an arm around Theo's shoulders, for Lord Penweather—the man who should have protected her—had dangled this horror before her.

"You think Quimbey is ashamed?" Jonathan tried on that notion and found it credible.

"If the former duke was a wastrel like your father, then Quimbey was largely at the mercy of solicitors when he took on the title. The solicitors were useless to me when Archie died. Anselm stepped in, and that was helpful. My banker, a man who comes from nothing, was helpful. Lady Canmore sent the vultures packing when they began to gather even before the funeral. The lawyers, by contrast, fussed and sent bills."

"Not my lawyers," Jonathan said. "They damned well do as I tell them to do and they know that their invoices will be subjected to ferocious scrutiny. I sit on various boards of directors, and my greatest contribution to those organizations is my ability to inspect financial documents and detect errors and omissions others overlook."

Theo tucked closer. "Scrutiny is a cure for many ills. I look forward to the day when I can scrutinize you, Mr. Tresham, in a big, comfy bed with a cozy fire going nearby."

The rain drummed on the coach roof, the horses clip-clopped along on the wet cobbles, and Jonathan relaxed.

Theo had not failed him. She had not reacted to the bad news with drama, or worse, a suggestion that the wedding date be indefinitely postponed. That possibility had flitted through his mind like the stink of a dead mouse pollutes a spotless parlor.

Nasty, wrong, undeniable.

"I meant what I said," Jonathan murmured against her ear.

"I believe you. The dukedom will come right in time, and I will do all in my power to help."

She had faith in him. Perhaps Quimbey had faith in him too. Jonathan preferred Theo's version—honest and immediate.

"I meant it when I said I love you." He was glad she was snuggled against him, so he could hold her as a combination of terror and joy pushed aside thoughts of the ducal finances. "You did not fly into the boughs when I dropped looming tragedy in your lap. You did not castigate me for being the bearer of bad news. You are here, with me, plotting a solution."

To admit his troubles even to Theo was disquieting, but perhaps that had been the flaw in his parents' marriage: They had each remained alone, despite having spoken their vows. Their infidelities had likely begun outside the bedroom, rather than started there.

"If we are to be man and wife," Theo said, "and I dearly hope we are, then I will not tolerate being kept in the dark, Jonathan. I've seen that approach. It has nothing to recommend it when difficulties arise, and it further implies that all I contribute to the marriage are pleasures you can purchase elsewhere."

Theo had shared her difficulties with Jonathan, and her honesty had allowed him to see more clearly.

And to love her. "The greatest pleasures cannot be had for coin," he said. "I should get out here." He would rather have spent the rest of the afternoon with Theo, even in this coach, simply rolling from street to street in the rain.

"I don't want to part from you," she said. "You make a very comfortable pillow, and this conveyance has much to recommend it."

Jonathan could not arrive on Frannie's doorstep in a state. "Lady Canmore will know if we've been canoodling. She will tease you, and that will be my fault."

Lady Canmore had arrived at The Coventry last night with Casriel in tow as Jonathan had been leaving. She'd been too busy lecturing Casriel on some vital point to even glance Jonathan's way, not that he'd mention seeing her there.

"I thought canoodling was one of the pleasures of being engaged."

"I haven't properly proposed, Theo. You deserve the bended knee, showy ring, public announcement—the whole bit."

"I had the whole bit." She kissed his cheek. "I'd rather have a quiet wedding and you. No showy anything."

Truly, truly, he had found a rare and precious woman. "Is that a request for a special license?"

She sat up. "I leave that to you, Jonathan. I will not demand a lavish wedding breakfast for the sake of appearances. I know how to run a household, but this situation exceeds my expertise and I trust your judgment. If you'd rather marry by special license with Anselm and Casriel as witnesses, that will suffice. The size of the wedding matters not, compared to the quality of the marriage."

She was the perfect duchess for him. The perfect woman. "If I do not get out of this coach right now, I will have your skirts up, and this coach will be rocking so violently the horses will be scandalized." He rapped on the roof three times. "I'll procure that special license, and when we have more time to talk, we can decide if we'd like to use it."

"A fine plan, but do recall what I said about that big, cozy bed. Perhaps you'd be good enough to schedule a tour of the ducal residence for me on the next half day?"

"That would be Thursday. My regards to Lady Canmore." He allowed himself one last, swift kiss to her mouth, then leaped from the coach, though it hadn't even come to a complete stop.

* * *

"I have given Mr. Tresham permission to court me, and we—" Theo could not finish the sentence, because Bea had flown across the parlor and wrapped her in a hug.

"I *knew* you'd bring him up to scratch. I knew it. He's short on charm, but what does that matter when he's to become a duke and has sense enough to find a duchess hiding among the potted palms?" She gave Theo an extra squeeze. "This calls for lemon cake and cordial."

"No cordial, Bea, please. I'm awash in the Countess of Bellefonte's tea. Mr. Tresham and I paid a call upon Lady Della earlier today, though she was from home and we were left with the earl and countess for company."

Bea paused, hand on the bell-pull. "You must bring Mr. Tresham here, Theo. I insist. I want to know that he's properly respectful of the honor you do him. The man is hardly a debutante's dream come true, even if he is somewhat attractive."

She gave the bell-pull two tugs, then took the place beside Theo on the sofa. Though it was afternoon, Bea was still in a dressing gown, and her coiffure had a soft, barely pinned quality.

"Mr. Tresham might lack the lovely lavender eyes of a certain earl from Dorset," Theo said, "but he's kind and honorable and will make a fine step-father for Diana."

Bea scooted around on the cushions, arranging her skirts. "You are not marrying Mr. Tresham for Diana's and Seraphina's sake, I hope? Please promise me that you are not, Theo."

A footman came in bearing a large tray, which he set on the low table before bowing and withdrawing. The interruption gave Theo a moment to compose an answer, one that was honest but respectful of Jonathan's dignity.

She could not admit that he was Theo's dream come true, not so soon, not even to her best friend. The sense of being not only loved, but in love, was tender and private.

"I had my morning chocolate shortly before noon," Bea said. "Last night went quite late, and I'm famished. Help yourself, though I still say this is an occasion for cordial."

Theo accepted a cup of tea. "I am marrying Mr. Tresham in part because he can provide security for the girls and because he will remove any doubt from Viscount Penweather's mind that Diana is well cared for in my home. Diana is no longer an infant, and Penweather is the head of her family."

"Which exalted status," Bea said, pouring herself a cup of tea, "he recalls only when he wants to frighten you or lecture you. If Penweather ever comes to Town, you will alert me, Theo, so that I might cast aspersion on everything from his dancing to the knot he ties in his cravat."

The tea was hot but weak. Theo set her cup down after one sip. "You will receive Penweather graciously, Bea. Mr. Tresham has no tolerance for petty squabbles. Besides, I suspect we'll dwell mostly at the ducal seat, meaning Penweather's path will rarely cross my own."

Bea sat back and tucked her feet under her. She looked both seventeen years old and comfortably wanton.

"You do not win the hand of a ducal heir to drag him off to the shires, Theodosia. You deserve at least three Seasons to buy out the shops, enjoy his escort, and gloat at the cats who all but cut you after Archie's death."

Mrs. Compton's visit came to mind. "I suspect many of those women aren't cats, Bea. They were responding to their husbands' guidance and limiting their association with me. Archie was facing ruin, and for all I know, I was already in disgrace with half of Polite Society before he died."

Bea buttered a slice of apple tart. "Archie was certainly an object of talk. Tell me more about Mr. Tresham. Have you set a date, and where will you go on your wedding journey?"

"No date yet, though I expect our engagement will be brief. I haven't discussed a wedding journey with Jonathan. Oversight of the ducal estate has been lax in recent years, and I'm sure Jonathan will want to rectify that situation."

"Jon-a-than," Bea said around a mouthful of tart. "The look on your face when you say his name is the most encouraging aspect of this whole situation. I know you like him, Theo, but please tell me Mr. Tresham truly touches your heart, or I will have to dissuade you from becoming his duchess."

Bea was a good friend. A very, very good friend.

"He touches my heart. He's decent, Bea. He will never betray me as Archie did, appearing to be one thing by day while in fact he was quite another come nightfall. I can trust Mr. Tresham and rely on his honesty. That steadfast quality enthralls me, but he has other attributes that are also… very winning."

"He makes you blush," Bea said, hugging Theo with one arm. "If he makes you blush, then he's the right fellow. You will be a wonderful duchess, and you will make him a wonderful duke."

Jonathan would be a wonderful *husband*. "Is Casriel a wonderful earl?"

Bea made a face at her half-eaten tart. "We ran into his youngest brother last night. The moment was awkward. Sycamore has a talent for turning almost any moment awkward. He has limited funds, and yet, he was quite at home showing another young lady how to place her bets. He and Casriel were having one of those oblique arguments men have, all flaring nostrils and double meanings. Lord Casriel can be imposing. I would like to see more of that side of him, though not directed at me, of course."

And the night had gone *quite late*. "Are you toying with his lordship, Bea?" Her ladyship had been in search of adventure last night. Perhaps she'd found it.

The countess rose and went to the window, which looked out on a little patch of greenery gone dreary in the rain.

"Casriel either doesn't notice that I'm casting lures, or he's too much of a gentleman to reject me outright. He needs heirs."

That last was said softly as Bea finger-traced a raindrop trickling down the outside of the windowpane.

"Beatitude, at last count, there were seven Dorning brothers, all in good health. Casriel, of all the peers in England, does not need heirs. He probably needs friendship, affection, a woman to manage his households, and somebody to help him find matches for his brothers."

Bea turned, her smile determined. "You are right, of course, which means the problem is not a lack of heirs. It's that Casriel is not smitten. He was reluctant to escort me to The Coventry last night. If I'd known Mr. Tresham planned to go there, I would have imposed on him instead."

When Bea's words registered, Theo was taking another sip of her too hot, too weak tea. She nearly burned her tongue and almost dropped her tea cup.

"*Mr. Tresham was at The Coventry?*" Had asked permission to pay his addresses, made love with Theo, and then left for *The Coventry?*

"I'm almost sure I caught a glimpse of him, though he was leaving as we arrived. Whoever it was had his height and dark hair. Are you quite well, Theo?"

Theo set down her cup, for her hand had begun to shake. "Many men have dark hair and some height, Bea. Are you sure it was Mr. Tresham you glimpsed?"

Bea resumed tracing raindrops. "I am not sure. I was arguing with Casriel as we arrived, and the gentleman swept past me. He moved like Mr. Tresham, but I did not see his face clearly." She crossed back to her spot on the sofa. "You should have some of this apple tart, lest I eat it all."

"A small slice only. I must send Mr. Tresham's coach back to him before the afternoon advances."

Bea obliged and chattered on about somebody's lapdog's bad manners, while Theo murmured appropriate comments and choked down her apple tart.

Bea was a friend, a true, kind friend, but Theo could not tell if Bea had been concocting a lie, examining her recollection, or something of both when she'd said Jonathan *might not* have been at The Coventry.

* * *

Several years ago, when Jonathan had bought The Coventry, he'd occasionally stopped by Frannie's home. She'd had one infant then, a cheerful little creature who'd grabbed at Jonathan's nose and smiled on all and sundry. As the child had matured into a squalling, demanding whirlwind, and as another child had followed, Jonathan had ceased calling on Frannie at home.

"If this is a bad time," he said when she opened the door, "I can come back another day." The rain was intensifying, dripping from his hat brim straight down onto his nape in a cold, steady trickle.

Frannie remained in the doorway, an infant perched on her hip, another child clinging to her skirts and sucking its thumb. She had the beautiful eyes of the tired mother, and usually those eyes were lit with humor.

Her gaze promised Jonathan a slow, painful death. "What on earth makes you think I'd let you into my home?" She moved to shut the door, but the toddler let go of her apron and reached for Jonathan.

"Up!" The child hopped, arms outstretched. "Up! Want up!"

"Delphie, come away from him."

Jonathan hefted the child, a solid little person with Frannie's big blue eyes. "I won't stay long, and I think we need to talk."

Frannie gave him a look that would have cindered a man who wasn't sopping wet. "Five minutes, and then you leave and you do not come back. You can offer me all the money in the world, Jonathan, but after turning me off without a character, when you know my circumstances… I thought better of you."

The child in Jonathan's arms grabbed his hair. "Horsey."

"I am not a horsey."

"Horsey. Trot little horsey, don't fall down." The child bounced enthusiastically. "Trot little horsey, trot to town. Trot, trot, *trot*!"

"Delphie wants a piggyback ride. I want you out of my house. If you've come to apologize, then say your piece, assuage your conscience, and leave a bank draft if you must, but I'll tear it up, and James will light the pieces on fire for me."

James was her husband.

The child on Jonathan's hip smacked him on the shoulder and yelled, "Tally ho, Thunder!"

With the would-be jockey affixed to his back, Jonathan followed Frannie down an unlit corridor to a small sitting room. Every surface held books, papers, ledgers, or an embroidered pillow of some sort, meaning that to take a seat, he'd have to clear clutter away first.

"Delphie, that's enough," Frannie said. "Go find your bunny."

Delphie clambered from the saddle, pulling Jonathan's mane, then whacking his bum with a hearty, "Good pony, Thunder!" before cantering down the corridor, unruly curls bouncing.

"He's quite the horseman."

Frannie moved a few pillows and settled on the sofa, the baby in her lap. "Philadelphia is a girl. What do you want, Jonathan? You can't have fouled up the ledgers already. Even with Moira's help, that would take more than a week. Don't expect me to serve you tea. The children spill everything, and money will be tight now that you've found another bookkeeper *less likely to get with child.*"

"We seem to have a misunderstanding."

"I understand *your services are no longer needed* quite well. Don't drip on my carpets."

Her carpets were worn and needed a good beating. A wooden duck on wheels, a pony made of straw and sheep's wool, two storybooks, and a wooden beaker were scattered across the rug before her hearth.

Jonathan shrugged out of his greatcoat and set it on a chair near the fire so that the drips would fall on the hearthstones.

"I never told you that your services were no longer needed. Your services are very much needed. Now more than ever." Without the weight of his seven-caped coat, he was cold, and a chill that had nothing to do with the weather was spreading within him.

"If I'm still needed, then you should not have had Moira sack me, should you?"

"Moira and I discussed your situation weeks ago. I told her I'd handle the books while you took leave, the same as we've always done for your confinements. The club is quiet in late summer. It's the easiest time for you to be less in evidence. That is all I heard of the matter until Moira told me last night that you'd left us."

Not *taken leave*, apparently, but quit.

Frannie glowered up at him, the child snuggled to her shoulder. "Moira handed me five pounds and thanked me for all I'd done. She said a bookkeeper less prone to fits of motherhood would serve the club better."

"Moira overstepped." *Again.*

"You pay her to overstep, Jonathan. You can swan about, the owner, lord of all you survey from your screened stairway and shadowed balcony, while Moira has tantrums in the kitchen that make Armand look like the soul of decorum. She paints *the owner* as a demon to the junior staff, a mysterious, unreasonable despot who pinches pennies and expects perfection. One by one, you've lost the best staff, and she replaced them with…"

The baby fussed, clearly unhappy.

"Now I'm upsetting my offspring." Frannie held the child up in both hands and beamed at him. "No fussy, little man. No fussy for Mama. Mr. Jonathan will go bye-bye, and Mama can use all the bad language she wants to talk about him. That will be soooo muuuuuch fun, won't it?"

The baby continued to fuss.

"Frannie, I did not want you sacked, and I had no idea that Moira was annoying the staff."

"Annoying. What a genteel, lordly word. I suspect she insists on doling out the wages herself so that she can pocket some of the coin and make up reasons why the full amount isn't due."

The baby was starting to cry, a hiccup-y undertaking that scraped Jonathan's nerves raw. He plucked the child from Frannie's grasp and pressed his cold nose to the soft, little cheek.

"No displays of temper before the ladies, sir. Your mother has important information to pass along."

Big blue eyes stared at him, then a little pink mouth turned up in a merry smile.

"You like that," Jonathan said, brushing his nose over the baby's cheek again. "I like that you're quiet."

"For now," Frannie said. "Wait five minutes and prepare to be deafened. Moira claims you are turning the business over to her in all but name. You're preparing to step into the ducal shoes, and a gaming hell is beneath your notice."

Jonathan cradled the child against his chest. "Frannie, I love The Coventry and would never refer to it as a mere hell. My proudest day was when I acquired that enterprise. It's a model club, patronized by the best of polite society, and I make no apologies for that to anybody. Let those who can't enjoy a hand of cards take their custom elsewhere and leave me and my patrons to have our diversions in peace. Now you tell me that Moira has run daft, spreading lies, alienating my allies."

"That child doesn't like anybody, but he likes you. There is no accounting for taste."

"You are not sacked," Jonathan said. "You, especially, are not sacked. Why didn't you tell me what was afoot with the staff?"

"Because you are never on the premises during daylight hours anymore, and I was told that coming by in the evening, when James can watch the children, was no longer allowed. If I'd called upon you in your bachelor residences when my employment at The Coventry is known to the staff, I'd be jeopardizing your privacy. You need to have a long talk with Battaglia too. He's considering a position at White's."

The child was snuffling, so Jonathan began a circuit of the parlor. "Because?"

"Because Moira finds fault with him, no matter how flawlessly he does his job. She never compliments, she only criticizes, always in the name of the tyrannical owner. She's hiring younger dealers who haven't the temperament for a club of The Coventry's caliber, and she wants to dress the ladies like strumpets. Take an inventory of the wine cellar now or prepare to learn the joys of swilling gin."

Jonathan sat on the sofa next to Frannie, shoved two pillows out from under his bum, and passed her the baby.

"You are describing scenes from my worst nightmares. Turning The Coventry into a cheap hell, where decent patrons would never go when sober and the food isn't safe to eat."

"Boodle's is trying to woo Armand away, but he's stubborn and even Moira knows not to touch his wages. Then too, Armand, like Battaglia, knows who you are, and Moira is aware of that."

Armand was a genius, albeit a temperamental one.

"Frannie, can you manage the club?"

"No. I'm not..." She waved a hand about her person. "I'm a mother." She kissed the baby's fussy head. "Anybody can see that I'm a mother, and I have no interest in games of chance."

Despite the domestic surrounds—perhaps *because* of them—Jonathan battled outrage. Frannie had been with him from the first, and she had a family to support. Armand had five children. Battaglia was the sole support of at least three maiden aunts as well as his own children.

The dealers, the kitchen staff, even the charwoman depended on Jonathan to maintain The Coventry as the foremost establishment of its kind. Then too, Jonathan supported other enterprises with the revenue from The Coventry, and that resulted in more people and employees who were indirectly dependent on the club.

"Moira is sabotaging my majordomo, my chef, my dealers, my staff, my bookkeeper, and that's not the worst of it."

Frannie rubbed the baby's back. "What could be worse than all of that?"

"She's marking the cards, Frannie." And nobody save Sycamore Dorning had made Jonathan aware of that, but then... Frannie was right. Jonathan came and went like a ghost, peered down at the gaming floor from a hidden perch, and kept his identity secret. He'd built the scaffolding for his own execution out of prudence, privacy, and discretion.

Also misplaced trust. "Once a cheat, always a cheat."

Frannie rose, the baby in her arms. "Who said that?"

"Oddly enough, my father, and he was right."

"Will you close the club?"

"Of course not."

Delphie hopped into the room, a gray, floppy-eared rabbit clutched in her hand. She wiggled her nose at Jonathan, then hopped up onto the sofa. In his mind's eye, he pictured another little girl, one with Theo's blue eyes and Theo's brown hair.

"I have dependents," Jonathan said. "People have placed their trust in me, and I cannot fail them. The club's problems are mine to solve, and when I'm through, Moira Jones will be lucky to get a job scrubbing floors at a drovers' inn."

Frannie held the baby over her head, which inspired much waving of tiny fists and grinning.

"Be careful, Jonathan. Get a solid hold of the situation before you charge in and act the duke. Moira has allies on the staff now, and there's no telling what other trapdoors she's put in place. You really might be better off selling the whole thing to her."

Frannie meant well, and thus Jonathan ignored the river of anger her suggestion sent coursing through him. "I will never sell The Coventry, but it's time I managed the place like a responsible owner and not like Moira's dupe."

"You'll sack her?"

"Not immediately, but yes. She will be sacked, and I won't ever again allow another that much authority over my club."

"Best of luck," Frannie said, nudging the duck from the center of the carpet with her toe.

From the sofa, Delphie waved her rabbit. "Tally ho!"

Jonathan collected his damp coat and bowed. "Tally ho. I'm off to catch a fox."

CHAPTER TWO

Thursday took an eternity to arrive, and Diana apparently sensed that Theo's anxiety about inspecting the ducal residence was mounting. How grand a household would it be, and would the staff receive Theo graciously or with subtle disdain?

"I want to go with you," Diana said, bending over her slate. "Mr. Tresham is not from our family, so you should not be private with him."

"We won't be private. At least a half-dozen servants will be on hand." Theo paced past the schoolroom window, the best vantage point from which to spy a coach pulling up out front. "Besides, I am a widow, and I don't require a chaperone."

"That doesn't make any sense." Diana used a cloth to rub at her slate, while she kicked at the rung of her chair with one foot. "Married ladies have husbands, but young ladies and widows do not. If a young lady needs a chaperone, then a widow should as well."

"That's not how it works, Diana. What are you drawing?"

"A dog. Will Mr. Tresham bring Comus to call?"

"Likely not."

Diana looked up, her expression presaging a spate of grouchy rhymes. "I like Comus. I do not like Mr. Tresham."

Jonathan's matched grays trotted around the corner and drew to a jingling halt before the house.

"To dislike somebody who has given you no cause is unkind, Diana. You should be more concerned about whether Mr. Tresham has a good opinion of you."

Diana rubbed vigorously at her slate, making the school room smell of chalk. "Why should I worry about his good opinion of me?"

Theo wanted Jonathan with her when she informed Seraphina and Diana of the upcoming nuptials.

She also wanted to shake Diana. "Mr. Tresham's good opinion matters, because he is becoming a dear friend. I hope to see a great deal of him in the near future."

Down below, Jonathan emerged from his coach, looking splendid in morning attire.

"Will you marry him?"

Yes. "I might."

"Why?"

Diana takes after me. That realization came with equal parts relief and chagrin. The girl was stubborn, observant, and inquisitive, and those were not traits she'd inherited from her father.

Theo moved away from the window, lest she be caught gawking. "I might marry Mr. Tresham because I have been lonely since your papa died, and Mr. Tresham's company suits me." Two understatements so vast as to approach dissembling.

"Do you like him better than you liked my papa?"

What to say? "Your papa was my first love. He will always hold a special place in my heart." A sad, angry special place. "Besides, your papa gave me you, and I have no greater treasure on earth."

"I don't want Mr. Tresham to die."

Oh, dear God. The logic of childhood was simple and dire. "We all die, Diana, but Mr. Tresham is in great good health. I think he'll be with us for a long time, and he won't die simply because I marry him."

Diana put her slate on the ledge beneath the chalkboard. "Are you sure, Mama? Papa married you, and you had me, and then Papa died. He wasn't old. Seraphina said he wasn't old at all."

Theo knelt before her daughter. "Your papa was sick, Diana. He'd been unwell for a long time, and nothing anybody could have done would have kept him with us."

Diana looked so solemn, so unsure. Gone was the child with the attention of a butterfly, in her place was the beginning of a girl too serious for her own good.

"My father lived until I was of age," said a masculine voice from the doorway. "I still mourned his passing, still felt as if he was taken too soon."

Theo curtseyed. "Mr. Tresham."

He bowed, twice. "Ladies."

Diana curtseyed very credibly, which made Theo smile, though Jonathan looked tired and somber to her.

"Will you marry my mama?" Diana asked. "You have to promise you won't die if you marry her. She would cry and cry if you died, and Seraphina would go into a decline, and Cousin Viscount might send us to the north."

Jonathan sat upon Diana's desk. "The north is actually quite beautiful. Perhaps we can all travel to the Lakes some summer, and you'll see for yourself. Maybe you'd prefer a jaunt over to Paris, though the Channel crossing can be a challenge."

Still, Diana's regard was searching. "You've been to Paris?"

"I lived there for years. Nobody will ever replace your father, Diana. He was your papa, and you will always love him, but I hope you can love other people too."

"I could love Comus."

"That's a start. He's very sweet."

"Rhymes with bleat, treat, and neat," Theo said.

"Rhymes with meet, wheat, and complete." Diana twirled, her skirts billowing, her braids flying up.

"And balance sheet," Jonathan added. "Mrs. Haviland, are you ready for our outing?"

"And greet," Diana said, bending into a curtsey. "Also conceit."

"I am," Theo said, though in Diana's foolishness, she saw a hint of grace. "Diana, please have your sums finished before supper."

"You'll be gone until supper?"

If I'm lucky. "Perhaps. Mr. Tresham, shall we be on our way?"

He offered his arm, Theo took it, and they made a decorous progress down to the coach, Diana calling rhymes after them. The horses had not been given leave to walk on before Jonathan's mouth covered Theo's, and she'd wrapped her arms about him. His kiss tasted of humor and desire, but also a little bit of grief.

* * *

The past week had been among the most difficult of Jonathan's adult life. By night, he'd spent hours at the club, watching from his hidden locations, looking for a pattern, a formula, a detail out of place.

When that endeavor had proven fruitless, he'd taken to wandering the tables, though he hadn't gone so far as to play a hand in his own establishment. Sycamore Dorning was frequently in evidence, and Jonathan had ruled him out as a spotter or a cheat.

By day, Jonathan combed the club's ledgers and wage books for irregularities when he wasn't dealing with his other business ventures. Frannie's vigilance had doubtless prevented much harm, though Moira had clearly colluded with the trades to inflate invoices or generate bills for goods never delivered.

All the while, she'd smiled at the guests, flirted with those at the tables, and reminded Jonathan that a duke ought not to involve himself in illegal activities.

To which he'd replied, "I'm not a duke." *Yet.*

Nor was he yet Theo's husband, but the prospect filled him with such a sense

166 | GRACE BURROWES

of rightness that showing her around the ducal residence was a treat, a reward for the past days' labors.

"I've missed you," Theo said, as Jonathan's coach rolled past stately Mayfair homes.

"I've missed you too." An understatement, given the kiss they'd shared for the duration of the past two streets. "We should have the special license any day, but Quimbey and his duchess won't be back to Town until next week."

"We'll wait. Lord Penweather might want to attend."

Jonathan looped an arm around Theo's shoulders. "I wrote to him. No reply yet. If you don't want him at the ceremony, say the word, and he'll rusticate among the sheep until my duchess summons him."

Theo had the most delightful ability to snuggle in a moving coach. "I won't be that sort of duchess. Cousin Fabianus is old-fashioned and never sought the title. He's… difficult, but not dishonorable. Tell me about the staff."

"Speak to them loudly and slowly. They smile a lot. I'm not sure half of them can hear at all."

To Jonathan's confoundment, what staff was on hand demonstrated miraculously acute hearing in Theo's presence. She asked questions, she listened, she solicited suggestions, and she showed no sign of needing to drag Jonathan into a linen closet to have her way with him.

He, by contrast, was in a state simply from being near her. She aggravated his condition by taking his arm, leaning close, wearing that infernal jasmine scent, and coaxing a smile from Lear, the tall, white-haired African butler who'd served the household since the previous duke's time.

"I cannot recall seeing Lear smile in all the years I've known him," Jonathan said. "You have made a spectacular first impression."

They were taking tea—damned, wretched, useless tea—in the library, a room with enough windows to be considered public, though it faced the garden. With Theo on the premises, Jonathan noticed the haphazardly shelved books and the dingy fringe of the carpet near the hearth.

He'd not seen those before. Was this how Theo had felt when Jonathan had intruded into her formal parlor? Self-conscious and slightly dismayed?

"This is a beautiful house," Theo said, pouring out, "though it needs some love and care. The present duchess is doubtless attending to what tasks she can, or she will when she returns. You prefer your tea plain as I recall."

"Theo, right now, I don't care for tea at all. I don't want a perishing biscuit, and if you offer me an orange, I will pitch it through the nearest window."

She set down the steaming cup of China black. "You will?" No smile, no naughty innuendo.

She put Jonathan in mind of Diana, trying to sort out shifting loyalties and changing circumstances. Careful, watchful, unsure. Perhaps the grand residence had daunted her, or perhaps the condition of that residence had failed to impress her.

Jonathan rose and took Theo by the wrist. "I will throw *myself* through the nearest window if I can't have you in my arms, if I can't kiss you for more than a decorous four streets in a closed carriage."

He found the latch hidden on the underside of the biographical collection shelf and led Theo through a door disguised as just another bookshelf full of aging tomes. The little study was flooded with afternoon light, and the most private place in the entire town house.

"There's another door," he said, "at the top of the spiral steps. The latches are right beneath the sconces if you ever find yourself in here without me."

Theo stepped into his arms, and all the troubles at The Coventry, all the debts piling up on Quimbey's ledgers, fell away. Jonathan wanted to devour her, to fortify himself with the pleasure she could give him, but Theo was apparently of a mind to torment him.

She teased and hinted and implied, until gradually, Jonathan's passion eased from roiling to simmering.

"You're right," he said, shifting back half a step so Theo could undo his falls. "Better to savor, to take our time." Though they could do both—a heedless gallop followed by a leisurely trot.

Followed by another gallop.

"I have missed you," Theo said again. "Missed you mightily."

She stroked his rampant cock with a slow, cool hand, and Jonathan nearly spent like a randy stud colt.

"If you tell me that today is the day you demand to see me without all my clothing, I will survive the ordeal, but might I survive it fifteen minutes from now, Theo?"

Her smile was knowing and naughty. A lover's smile. "Perhaps twenty."

They were the most delightful, torturous twenty minutes of Jonathan's life. Frustration and pleasure clawed for the lead in a race to satisfaction that Jonathan was determined Theo would win.

She'd chosen the sofa for this interlude, chosen to have Jonathan on his back, leaving her free to plunder his charms and his wits with her hands, her mouth, her breasts—and, oh, ye cavorting Cupids—her sex.

This was what he'd needed, a bout of lusty, loving pleasure, an intimate interlude to chase the troubles away and bring the joys closer.

"You have utterly slain me," Jonathan said, stroking her hair. On the ceiling, somebody had painted a scene of fluffy clouds and golden doves, as if they'd known that this secluded chamber would earn top honors as a trysting place.

Theo sat up, her breasts rosy. She'd worn two chemises today rather than stays, and a dress that unbuttoned down the front of the bodice. A lock of hair cascaded over one shoulder to the lace frothing across the openings of her chemises.

Desire stirred, which should not have been possible.

"If you're slain, then I am as well," she said, stuffing a hairpin in her mouth. "A little slaying makes the day ever so much more enjoyable." She tucked up the errant lock with a dispatch that amused Jonathan, considering her breasts were on display and he was still inside her.

She shoved the hairpin into her coiffure and patted her chignon.

So brisk after such a thorough loving, so Theodosia. The thought wandered into Jonathan's mind that she might have already conceived his heir, and desire shifted to something vulnerable and precious.

"We will both be much slain following our nuptials," Jonathan said. "A wedding journey this summer to the Lakes isn't out of the question."

Theo lifted herself away from him, an indelicate moment. He hadn't thought to get out his handkerchief, but she withdrew one from her reticule, turned her back, and tended to herself.

Lying about like a happy satyr would not do. Satisfaction made Jonathan drowsy and content, but the line of Theo's back, the dispatch with which she'd risen, and the way she twitched down her skirts created a niggling unease.

She remained by the window, looking graceful and composed, arms crossed while Jonathan put himself to rights. Was she giving him privacy? Already back to thinking of linens and larders?

"Shall we finish our tea?" she asked, gaze upon the garden.

"Must we? I'd rather have you to myself for a few more minutes. The challenge of gentlemanly deportment in your company taxes me sorely."

Theo smiled and took the place beside him on the sofa. "I like taxing you sorely. I'm a bit taxed myself when you look so grave and handsome. You will make a very convincing duke, not that I wish your uncle a premature reward."

This nearly qualified as chatter. Jonathan reviewed the encounter, which had begun with greeting Theo and Diana in the schoolroom and noticing a resemblance about their features he hadn't seen before. They had the same eyes, the same way of smoothing their hands over their skirts.

"I hope I will not become duke for some time," he said. "I'd like to enjoy being your husband before less appealing duties befall me."

She smoothed her skirts again, which struck Jonathan as a tell. Gamblers gave away their motivations and plans with small, idiosyncratic gestures or turns of speech. Lipscomb read his cards, then arranged them, then cleared his throat if his hand was poor. If the hand was good, he'd sit up and smile.

Theo had something on her mind. Something other than Jonathan's winning smiles and lovemaking.

"Being a duke should have some appeal," she said. "Though I understand Quimbey will bequeath you problems as well as privileges. Are those problems the reason you've not been much in evidence socially?"

Such a casual question, though her gaze reminded him again of Diana, intent on unearthing sensible answers to thorny questions.

"I've been busy," Jonathan said, resisting the urge to wrap an arm about Theo's shoulders. "The dukedom is a tangled mess, and I suspect when Quimbey returns, he'll attempt to stop me from straightening it out. He'll be ashamed, he'll not want me meddling, and he'll fume and fuss and put wrong all I'm trying to put right."

This was true, and part of the reason Jonathan's days had become long and his fingers ink-stained. He was also reviewing finances for three other organizations, a task he took in his capacity as a director or governor.

"Do your responsibilities to the dukedom also prevent you from attending balls, suppers, and musicales?" Theo was off again, returning to the window. "I still have your list, Jonathan. You've given up any pretense of maintaining your social obligations. I ask myself, what could possibly detain you in the evening? What could keep you so busy, you haven't time to share a waltz with me, or take in a string quartet that does full justice to Herr Beethoven?"

Theo stopped short of asking the real question: *Why aren't you courting me?*

Guilt welled, because Jonathan himself had declared that Theo deserved to be courted. He'd seen how the attentions of a ducal heir raised a woman in Society's esteem, how a single dance merited notice.

"I'm sorry," he said, rising and taking Theo's hand. "I have been remiss. You shall have all the waltzes and promenades and formal dinners of me you please, but a problem at my club requires my immediate attention."

She withdrew her hand. "Your club? Your gentlemen's club?"

Her tone had acquired an edge, either worry or annoyance.

"A gentlemen's club, yes. In a manner of speaking." Though The Coventry was so much more, the situation was much larger than a mere problem, and the need for significant revenue beyond pressing.

"You are a suitor paying his addresses," Theo said, gaze on the garden. "Can't somebody else deal with this problem for the nonce?"

"Letting others handle the situation is how the problem arose, Theo. I apologize for the timing, but I assure you the difficulties are urgently in need of resolution."

Another look—skeptical, full of strategy and unspoken discontent. The look put Jonathan in mind of his own late mother working up to a tirade.

"Clubs have staff and managers," Theo said. "They have directors or some other managing body. What could possibly require your attention at a club, where gambling and wagering are of much greater significance than rare beefsteaks and overpriced libations?"

Too late, Jonathan realized that he'd misread Theo's mood. She'd been distracted and worried rather than intent on a slow joining. She'd been *upset*— with him. A hundred family meals from Jonathan's youth came back to him, with Mama muttering aspersions from one end of the table and Papa replying in veiled insults, while the servants pretended a marital brawl wasn't taking place in the formal dining parlor.

If Theo was intent on brawling, then she'd find herself without a suitor. "I expect your trust on matters relating to our finances, madam. If I tell you the problem is mine to solve, then it's mine to solve."

She faced him from her post at the window and damned if her eyes weren't sheened with tears.

Tears from his sensible, steady Theo? He hated tears, hated them especially from women with little to cry about. He hated even more that he'd provoked her to tears.

"I cannot attach myself to another wastrel, Jonathan. Archie's club and the wagers and cards available there were more of a threat to my marriage than any courtesan. You've secured my affections, and then I don't see you for days. Now you tell me you must sit night after night at some club that will doubtless claim half your affections after we're married. What am I to think?"

The question was chilling for its logic. He'd done exactly as she'd said: secured her affections, then neglected her utterly while wrestling with the problems at The Coventry. Hadn't sent a basket, hadn't sent flowers or a note. Hadn't dropped by for breakfast or brought Comus around to inspect the garden.

Hadn't *explained* his absence.

"You have no answer," Theo said, crossing the short distance to the spiral stairs. "I am determined that my first marriage will not haunt my second, but I truly do miss you, Jonathan. I want to know who your witnesses at the ceremony will be, and will you mind if I invite Lady Canmore. Should Seraphina and Diana attend? What if Penweather becomes difficult, and what are we to do about the settlements?"

An image came to Jonathan's mind, of his father stumbling as he climbed down from a coach, the footman staring straight ahead rather than presume to assist a lord far gone with drink.

Theo was not intent on drama. She was intent on answers. The relief of that insight was enormous.

"I've hurt you," Jonathan said, taking her in his arms. "I am so sorry, Theo. I am deeply, endlessly sorry. I've never been a suitor before, though I ought to know better. How can I make amends?"

She was quiet in his embrace, not cuddling. He could feel her thinking, feel her gathering her courage.

"Tell me the truth. Where do you go of an evening, and what has you so worried?"

Theo was to be his wife, his partner in all significant matters, the mother of his children. With her, he could and should be absolutely honest.

"I truly am tending to financial affairs," he said, stealing a quick kiss. "My primary source of income now is a club, and during my years in Paris, I've allowed it to fall into some disarray—serious disarray, of which I'm only now becoming aware. Somebody has set out to sabotage the venture. I'm almost sure I know who and why, but not how. I must find that answer before I can put the club back on solid footing, which will give the dukedom a healthy source of funds as well."

Theo's gaze was troubled. "You own a gentlemen's club?"

His idiot mouth was too eager to boast of his pride and joy, and his suitor's heart wanted only to be honest with her.

"It's a well-kept secret, but I am proprietor of the premier supper club and gambling establishment in all of London. The Coventry is mine, and I am pleased to include you in the small circle who know that. An employee of long standing has taken a notion to—Theo?"

She whirled away, as far away as the little chamber allowed. Her expression suggested Jonathan had confessed not to owning one of the best investments a ducal heir could aspire to, but rather, to ruling in hell.

* * *

"You have taken leave of what little sense you claim," Casriel said, fitting the tuning key to the little screw that adjusted the tension on the harp strings. "The Coventry is an honest house. You've made a pest of yourself there for the past several weeks and only discovered that, once again, an older sibling is right and you are barking mad."

Sycamore sidled past the harp, a great behemoth of an instrument with grapes and flowers fancifully carved all over the maple wood pillar.

"I have discovered that your friend Mr. Jonathan Tresham has more trouble afoot than he can handle on his own. What are you doing?"

Casriel gently plucked the string. "Having a polite difference of opinion with a venerable matron, a far more productive exchange than the one I'm having with you."

Sycamore folded into the chair behind Casriel's desk. "There's a pattern. I just can't see what it is."

Another pluck, infinitesimally higher on the scale. "Jonathan Tresham can spot patterns in the stars, in wind undulating across a field of ripe oats, in attendance at church on Sunday mornings. He can't help himself. If there were a pattern, he'd see it."

Another tiny increase in pitch.

"I can spot patterns too, and I know I'm seeing one. Lipscomb always sits in the same place, for example, across from the dealer at every table. Viscount Henries prefers any chair with its back to the wall. The most expensive food is always at the end of the buffet, so that patrons will have a full plate when they come to it."

Casriel bent closer to the harp and eased the tuning key a quarter turn. "And my youngest brother must stir up trouble." He plucked the string again, sending a gentle tone wafting through the office.

Of all the rooms at the Dorning town house, this one alone bore a stamp personal to the earl. Grey loved his acres, and thus the landscape on the wall was the view from the Dorning family seat in Dorset. A sheep-dotted checkerboard of green fields stretched away to the abbey ruins where Sycamore had played as a boy—or watched his brothers play while his sisters had scolded them.

On the opposite wall was a painting of Durdle Door, an arched rock formation on the beach near Lulworth that looked like a dragon drinking from the sea.

"If you miss home so much, why have all these reminders of it around you?" Sycamore asked.

Grey moved the tuning key up one string. "To remind me why I serve out my penance in the Lords. To encourage me when my daily bout of faintheartedness threatens. To show some hapless female just how rustic"—*pluck*—"her circumstances will be if she throws in her lot with me."

Sycamore stored away for later consideration the startling admission that the earl grew fainthearted nigh daily.

"The lady will be your countess, Grey. If you're marrying some cit's daughter, she won't care that rustication comes with it. She will care that you love your sheep more than you love her."

Casriel plucked the next string and turned the key gently, the tone rising as the tension increased. "You're an expert on courting heiresses now?"

"Lady Canmore is no heiress. Why did you bring her 'round The Coventry?"

Grey sounded the first string and the second in the *do-re* sequence that began the major scale.

"She brought me around."

"She's not an heiress, Grey."

Do-re-mi. "My brilliant sibling states the obvious. She also already has a title."

But does she have your heart? "Bad enough Ash has charged me with keeping an eye on Lady Della Haddonfield. Now you're mooning after an unsuitable lady too. Why is it, when surrounded by such nonsense, I'm the one who's accused of foolishness?"

Do-re-mi-fa. "Because if anybody is well suited to running an honest, profitable, well-respected gaming establishment, it's Jonathan Tresham. The very fact that you lurk under the stairs, looking askance at all and sundry while you yourself appear suspicious, is likely to start talk. You've said your piece to Tresham, now leave it to him to take action if action is needed."

Do-re-mi-fa-so.

"The G string is flat," Sycamore said. "You are so determined to view your brothers as a burden that you can't see what a problem it is for Tresham to have no brothers, nobody to guard his back. He hasn't any sisters either."

Sycamore let that observation vibrate in the air like a plucked note, because he was nearly certain he'd spoken in error. Della Haddonfield had the same cast to her features as Tresham, the same dark hair, the same widow's peak. She moved as he did, a cross between a saunter and a prowl, and she had taken to the tables with a natural aptitude for numbers.

"If Ash hasn't told you, then you didn't hear this from me," Grey said, "but Lady Della and Tresham share a bond of blood. Hush for a moment, please."

He fiddled with the G string, winding it too sharp, then easing it down a halftone.

"You'll break it, cranking it like that."

"Sycamore, is there no topic about which you admit ignorance? Are you an expert on every God's blessed subject?"

"Despite having six brothers who do know every God's blessed thing, I'm not quite up to their weight yet. For example, I'm only now learning how to cheat."

Grey sat back, the tuning key in his hand. "Must I beat you? A gentleman does not cheat."

"You left beating me to Thorne and Oak, for the most part. Valerian and Ash pulled them off of me, and Willow tattled to you when they got out of hand. I'm learning to cheat because gentlemen do cheat. They mark cards, they use spotters, stacked decks, hidden cards, sleight of hand, and more."

Grey tossed the tuning key onto the desk. "Never tell me you've observed that unscrupulous behavior at The Coventry?"

Sycamore rose and headed for the door. "Have I, or have I not, spent the last twenty minutes explaining to you that I smell a rat at The Coventry, but I haven't hunted the rodent down yet? Somebody has marked the cards twice now, to no apparent end. Tresham is haunting the place, so he must have taken my warning to heart, but the problem remains. Lipscomb loses even when he's sober, for example."

Do-re-me-fa-so-la. "Lipscomb is seldom sober."

"While I have eschewed inebriation of late. You should offer for Lady Canmore."

Grey strummed the lower registers of the harp, setting a wonderfully resonant minor arpeggio adrift in the office.

"I will not bequeath to my son the sort of mess Papa left for us, Cam. Willow is married. Ash is besotted. I'll marry well or not at all."

Do-re-mi-fa-so-la-ti. He twiddled the tuning peg this way and that.

"Papa was *happy*, Grey. He whiled away many a pleasant year in his greenhouses and gardens. He knew every tree in the home wood and every tenant's dog's name. When was the last time you were happy?"

"I'm happy right now. If you didn't learn to cheat at The Coventry, then where did you cross paths with all the scurrilous knaves wielding their dirty tricks?"

Do-re-mi-fa-so-la-ti-ti-*ti*...

"Where else? At that great bastion of learning and sophistication, to which all the best families send their young men for an education unmatched anywhere in the world."

"You're learning to cheat at university?"

"I'd rather learn to not be cheated. Be careful not to break the strings, Grey. That's a very pretty instrument, but like you, it has some age on it."

"Stay away from The Coventry, Cam. Whatever is going on there is not your problem."

Which statement all but confirmed that Grey too had felt the sour note in the club's air.

"Ask the countess if you can court her. Ladies aren't as concerned with money as they are with happiness. I like that about them."

"Be off with you, Sycamore Erasmus."

Do-re-mi-fa-so-la-ti-*spronnnng*.

Sycamore left amid the earl's soft curses. He did his older brother the courtesy of waiting until the door was closed before offering the empty corridor a quiet, long-suffering, "I told you so."

CHAPTER SIXTEEN

Theo wanted to clamp her hands over her ears or demand that Jonathan unsay the words he'd spoken.

"You own The Coventry?" Her voice was steady, while her heart hammered with dread.

"I have for more than three years. I gather this is a problem."

A problem he'd solve with patient good humor, apparently. "This is a disaster." Theo needed the bannister of the spiral staircase for support. "You will please sell that… that establishment."

Jonathan did not come to her, did not take her in his arms and offer soothing agreement. Instead, his posture shifted, becoming every inch ducal.

"The Coventry is the last hope the Quimbey estate has of avoiding bankruptcy. I'll not be selling it." He spoke gently, firmly, as one would to a fractious child. "In addition to the employees at the club and the Quimbey staff, others depend on The Coventry, and now of all times, I cannot step away from my responsibilities there."

Theo cast around for any gesture that might hint of compromise or reconciliation. "Would you sell it if you could?"

He leaned back against the windowsill, an aristocrat in Bond Street finery, lord of all he cared to survey.

"Why should I liquidate an asset that generates substantial income? What I learned in *that establishment* has made me a wealthy man, the envy of my peers. I can offer Quimbey hope of solvency because of The Coventry. I offer polite society honest play, good food, good company, while I make a well-earned profit and employ dozens who'd otherwise have no work. I am proud of that, Theo.

Why do you ask me to give it up?"

Because The Coventry killed my husband. How could Jonathan not see that?

Theo had grieved when Archimedes had been laid to rest. Nobody should die at such an age under such conditions. She'd also admitted to a guilty sliver of relief. With Archie for a father, Diana had been doomed to grow up cursed by scandal. His death had created the possibility of an upbringing amid genteel poverty rather than disgrace.

Not much of a silver lining, but Theo had seized it and dragged herself forward. Jonathan's loyalty to his club held no silver lining.

"You should sell The Coventry because gaming hells ruin lives," she said. "They aren't even legal."

Jonathan busied himself wrestling the window sash up a few inches. "The law is full of eccentricities, my dear. A Welshman who wanders into Chester after sundown commits an offense, while two hours of longbow practice for any lad over fourteen is still legally mandated. I can shoot a Scotsman in York with a bow and arrow on any day but Sunday, and a vast number of peers are engaged in selling illegal game to the better London restaurants. The law does not dictate moral absolutes, Theo."

He was *humoring* her. Attempting rhetorical arguments. Theo's despair edged toward rage.

"Gaming hells destroy lives, which fact—not moral conjecture, *fact*—I have had occasion to live firsthand, as have my daughter and sister."

Jonathan ran a hand through his hair and offered a patient smile. "Must we argue, Theodosia? I own The Coventry, but I do not patronize similar venues. We are to be married. Your pin money will be ample. Your daughter and sister will be well provided for."

Theo turned away, for she could not bear the sweet reason in his smile. "While my husband will be gone," she said, "night after night, plighting his commercial troth to an operation that is little better than a turnpike on the road to ruin. You serve your patrons free champagne so they lose their judgment as play deepens. You lure them in with free food after midnight. Your dealers are all so pretty and friendly, they nearly flirt the money from the pockets of their customers."

"Theo, it's not like that."

He was chiding her. *Chiding* her. "I haven't seen you for nearly a week, Jonathan, and that's your version of courtship when your club calls to you. You use beeswax candles because that is the scent of luxury rather than vice. You offer the gentlemen fine cigars for the same reason. Archie's clothes bore the stink for the last year of his life. You allow no hint of a common nuisance about your establishment, not because trollops cheapen the place, but because this lessens the probability that the abbesses in your neighborhood will resent your presence."

"Theo, please stop."

With her back to the room, she was addressing a portrait of a youth who bore a strong resemblance to Jonathan—very likely his father, hidden away in this secret room.

"You avoid the trollops because brothels are also illegal," she went on, "and the authorities delight in raiding them. I know so much more about running a successful gaming hell than any lady ever should."

Footsteps sounded behind her. Jonathan's hands landed softly on her shoulders.

"I do not own a gaming hell, Theo, and I will not quarrel with you about this. I grew up in the midst of pitched battle, and I refuse to allow my dealings with you to degenerate into endless conflict. We'll simply not speak of the club. I don't even gamble, and you must learn to distinguish between your first husband and me. I'll put the club to rights, and you will never hear me mention it by name."

He gently turned her to face him, and Theo saw in his eyes that he was offering the only truce he could. *We'll simply not speak of the club.*

Her despair was a palpable weight on her chest, a pressure in her skull. The longing to fold herself into Jonathan's embrace, to give in, wailed in her soul.

"I was married to a man to whom I could *not* speak, Jonathan. The silence grew, starting with his gambling and wagering, then to his erratic schedule, our miserable finances, his overimbibing, his failing health. Diana and Seraphina learned to *not speak* to him, as did the staff. He died amid a silence so loud, my heart broke to endure it. I love you, but I cannot base a marriage on ignored differences of this magnitude."

Jonathan's hands fell away. Another loud silence expanded as he stepped back. "A gentleman does not argue with a lady."

A gentleman does not own a house of ruin. Theo stopped short of that retort, because Jonathan *was* a gentleman. He was kind to Diana and Seraphina. He walked his uncle's dog when that was properly a footman's job. He'd sent peaches to a nobody of a widow and danced with women simply to raise their consequence.

"I am sorry, Jonathan, but I am not wrong."

Please, please capitulate. Give in, offer the smallest indication that we can weather this disagreement.

He took Theo's hand and kissed her knuckles. "Your independent nature was one of the first things I noticed about you. I'm sorry too, Theo, but I cannot fail my uncle, cannot fail those who depend on me, and most of all, I cannot leave an establishment I've built year by year to watch it sink under a weight of scandal and crooked behavior."

He kept hold of her hand, a comfort and a torment. Theo was tempted to drag him back to the sofa, to make love one more time, to rail at him until his parents' spats looked like the mere domestic altercations they'd been.

Anything to maintain a connection to him. Anything to maintain hope.

"I'll see you home," Jonathan said.

Theo allowed him that courtesy, because she wanted to linger with him as long as she could. He escorted her from the hidden chamber and past the laden tea tray. The aging footmen were cheerful, the journey back to her home silent.

Jonathan kept an arm around her shoulders the whole way, and she held his hand until the coach had pulled up in the alley. Only then did Theo permit herself to kiss him good-bye.

She made the gesture brief, but as she pulled away, Jonathan held her fast for one, endless agony of a moment.

"Good-bye, Jonathan. Be well." She left the coach the instant the footman let down the steps, and she did not look back.

* * *

"What else can you tell me about Archimedes Haviland?" Jonathan put the question to Anselm at another Lonely Husbands night.

For the first time, Jonathan was allowing an evening of cards under his own roof. He wanted to watch the play, to look for patterns, for he'd yet to put his finger on what, exactly, Moira was doing at The Coventry.

Perhaps she'd sheathed her claws now that Jonathan was on hand nearly every night, but at the vingt-et-un tables, the house was winning too many hands over too long a stretch of nights. The pots had grown larger, and that was attracting a different and less savory crowd.

Jonathan himself had passed out the staff's wages the previous week "on behalf of the owner" and had seen enough raised eyebrows to confirm that Moira was skimming from the payroll.

He was slowly working his way through the invoices from the trades and— no surprise there—had found the amounts charged padded, the difference doubtless shared with Moira.

Anselm touched Jonathan on the arm. "It's a fine night. Let's stretch our legs, shall we?"

Three tables of four players had been set up in the Quimbey mansion's game room, and the French doors were open to keep the room aired.

"The parlor across the corridor is unused," Jonathan said.

Anselm complied with that suggestion, thank the angels, and Jonathan was soon surrounded by a blessed quiet.

"We've already covered the topic of the late Mr. Haviland," Anselm said when Jonathan had closed the parlor door. "Why dredge it up again? His debts have been paid and you're smitten with his widow."

An eternal verity, however inconvenient. Jonathan had tried to immerse himself in work, but for once, numbers and ciphering were no consolation. He endured his endless meetings by daydreaming and fretting instead of preaching economy and accountability. Theo haunted him, waking and sleeping, as did the sense that he'd failed to solve a simple equation, failed to identify the only variable that mattered.

"Mrs. Haviland is no longer enamored of me."

Anselm took a wing chair by the fire. "My duchess was right, then. Araminthea said she hadn't seen you and the widow together for nearly a fortnight. Trouble in paradise and all that."

Trouble in purgatory. "Mrs. Haviland disapproves of my ownership of The Coventry. I disapprove of her late husband's intemperance, but she and I cannot find common ground or a way forward."

Did Theo want common ground? Had her love for Jonathan been scorched to cinders by disdain for his club?

Anselm crossed an ankle over his knee. "Don't suppose you've tried begging?"

This was proffered as a helpful suggestion, which implied Anselm had considered the same maneuver at some point.

"I all but did. I explained that I need the income from the club, that turning my back on The Coventry now would be a betrayal of everybody who has given me their loyalty over the years."

Jonathan was pacing, the habit of a man in want of self-possession. He made himself lean against the mantel, though the temptation to leave his guests and march over to the club—by way of Theo's street—was an itch in his boots.

"You mumbled a few vague words about needing funds," Anselm said. "Fine speeches elude us in the face of heartbreak."

"Did I not know you speak from experience, I'd take my fists to you for your presumption, Your Grace."

Anselm glanced about the parlor. "Lord Harlan used to indulge me in the occasional bout of fisticuffs. Even he has outgrown the need for horseplay."

A pouting duke ought to have been a gratifying sight, but Jonathan was too upset to enjoy Anselm's complaining.

Too heartbroken. "I refused to argue with her," Jonathan said. "I will not raise my voice to a woman, and I will not have her filling my house with strife."

Anselm rose. "Then do I take it that you seek to marry a well-trained spaniel?"

"Of course not. Theodosia is the furthest thing from—why would you say such a thing?"

"Couples argue, Tresham. Couples who love each other madly argue and disagree and even—I tell you this in confidence—raise their voices at each other. They also make up."

From across the corridor, a gust of laughter sounded.

"Your duchess *hollers* at you?"

Anselm's smile was stunningly sweet. "Her Grace counts it a victory when I am so far gone in a passion that I holler back. She says I'm too impressed with my own consequence most of the time and that I've learned too well to be the duke at the expense of being the man. You can see why I'm mad for the woman."

Mad for her and obnoxiously happy to admit it. "I cannot abide shouting."

"Then don't have children. Let the succession lapse or go to some fishmonger from East Anglia. Best thing, if you can't countenance a little volume in a discussion, is to avoid children altogether."

A little volume in a discussion? "Anselm, my parents shrieked at each other for days, then maintained weeks of cold silence, even at table."

Anselm snapped off a rose from a bouquet on the sideboard. "I'm not suggesting you hire the Hessian guard to tussle over who gets the Society pages at breakfast, Tresham." He tucked the rose into his lapel. "I'm merely pointing out that if you run from conflict when the first shot is fired, you'll never win the important battles. I thought every lordling learned this from his papa."

Anselm should have looked silly with the crooked little rose drooping from his lapel. He was a duke. His order in the royal succession had been established the day he'd ascended to the title.

He looked dear and wistful. Missing his duchess, no doubt, and she was probably missing him, drat the woman. Duke and duchess would cuddle up in the same bed in a few hours, tired and happy, and make tired, happy love while sharing gossip and inane pet names.

I miss my Theodosia. Jonathan missed her more than he missed the damned club, more than he'd missed anything ever.

"The problem, Anselm, is that even if I wanted to sell the club, I can't do that while Moira is poisoning the well." And Jonathan most assuredly did not want to sell the club, could not afford to sell the club, in fact.

"Then get rid of Moira Jones. Pack her off to Paris."

"If I do that, then the next manager can effect the same rig she's running. I hardly know most of the kitchen staff anymore, and some of the dealers were hired without my approval. Anybody who's in on her crooked game could start the whole business over again when she leaves."

Anselm brushed a finger over his rose. "Conflicting loyalties are always a problem. The peerage seems to understand that too well and always looks after their own. We'd do better to take the interests of John Bull to heart on more occasions."

Theo might say something like that. "No politics, Anselm, please. I have enough thorny conundrums on my plate."

Anselm admired himself in the mirror over the sideboard, then smiled, a ferocious expression featuring a quantity of teeth and self-satisfaction.

"Word of advice, not that you'll take it," the duke said.

"You'll give it, nonetheless."

"Solve the trouble with Mrs. Haviland first. Even with her husband's debts paid off, her circumstances cannot be comfortable. I sold everything the man owned, Tresham. Boots, pipes, nearly three dozen pistols, some of which were quite valuable, all save one in pristine condition. Rings, sleeve buttons, hats, even his night shirts. Perhaps the widow didn't want painful reminders, but I suspect her objective was simply to pay the trades before talk could ensue."

"I hate that Theodosia was put in such circumstances."

Anselm left off admiring himself. "She apparently hates more that you own a gaming hell. Peers own illegal ventures, but yours is shamefully successful. Perhaps the club failing is the best thing that could happen to you."

"I'm not a peer."

Anselm patted Jonathan's shoulder and sauntered toward the door. "Cling to that fig leaf while you can. I'm off to relieve a few earls of their arrogance. We peers benefit from regular set-downs, or so my duchess claims."

He went smiling on his way, while Jonathan stared into the parlor's gloomiest corner. Something Anselm had said... something about...

"They're all peers," Jonathan said softly. "The losers, the men whose luck never holds good for long, they're all peers. Lipscomb, Henries... Every time the stakes rise, it's never a banker, a mercer, or a half-pay officer with the most to lose. She's out to ruin the peers—and to ruin me."

* * *

"Theodosia, you are pacing. Ladies don't pace." Bea offered that great insight as Theo made another circuit of her ladyship's music room.

"Ladies don't cry off when they've secured the affections of a ducal heir." When they'd fallen in love with such a man and could not stop rethinking their last conversation with him, or the lovemaking that had preceded it.

Bea added a collection of airs to the stack of music accumulating on the piano bench. "Apparently, some ladies do. Who knew so much repertoire had been written for the harp?"

"I didn't know you played."

An imposing great harp stood near the windows, the instrument's pillar carved with leaves and flowers.

"I don't. That is Aunt Freddy's harp, or one of them. Casriel restrung it and tuned it for her. I'm keeping it until she returns from taking the waters at Bath. You could send Tresham a note telling him you've had second thoughts."

Theo took the free end of the piano bench. "No, I cannot. Did you know he owns The Coventry?"

Bea hoisted the stack of music and set it on the piano. "One isn't supposed to know such things. One can suspect. I'm not surprised."

Her ladyship was dressed to receive callers today, her hair coiled into a neat chignon, her gown a modest ensemble in a flattering shade of pale blue.

"Why doesn't one know such things?" Theo asked. "Had I known..."

"Would you have done anything different?"

"I would have decamped for Hampshire posthaste rather than involve myself with the owner of a gambling club." Theo was nearly certain she'd have been wise enough to do that, for Jonathan's lovemaking was as heady an intoxicant as any hand of cards had ever been for poor Archie.

Bea took the place beside Theo and pushed the cover off the keyboard. "Instead, you're breaking off an engagement and then turning tail for Hampshire. How can you abide the thought of relying on Penweather's charity?"

Theo pulled a handkerchief from her pocket and began dusting the highest octaves.

"Mr. Tresham wrote to the viscount to notify him of our situation."

"Of your impending engagement—that's now quits."

"Mr. Tresham never actually proposed. In any case, his letter must have gone into some detail about my circumstances, because Penweather wrote to me and extended an effusive apology for what he called a grievous misunderstanding."

Theo passed Bea the handkerchief to use on the lower octaves.

"Why do peers never simply admit they've wronged somebody?" Bea asked. "Why is the explanation always a misunderstanding or confusion, or—my favorite—a misconstruction on the part of somebody else?"

"Penweather was purposely misinformed. Archie told him I would want for nothing in widowhood. I had a competence and an inheritance, after all. The solicitors were forbidden to discuss my situation with Penweather, which was an insult to his lordship and also Archie's doing."

"Penweather told you this?"

"Not the insult part, but I read it between the lines. Cousin Fabianus sent me a bank draft, Bea, and asked that I consult him on the settlements with Jonathan—consult him, not defer to his wishes or allow him to handle the negotiations. I believe he was honestly mortified at his own behavior."

Bea rose. "You're saying we've misjudged Penweather?"

"I hope so. I'm removing to Hampshire for an indefinite visit within a fortnight. You are welcome to come with me, though I warn you that traveling with Seraphina and Diana will try your patience to the utmost."

Even being in the same house with the girls had become a tribulation. They bickered constantly, and Diana longed for peaches-rhymes-with-beseeches at least three times a day.

Theo had taken peaches into violent dislike, when she wasn't longing for them in a creamy compote.

"I'll send some cordial along to Hampshire with you," Bea said, "but I'll leave the rusticating to you and the viscount. If he's disagreeable, you will come back to Town straightaway, Theo."

Bea took the stool by the harp, making a pretty picture. Theo hadn't truly expected the countess to welcome a jaunt into the shires, not while a certain earl was still in Town.

"His lordship sent an astonishingly large bank draft, Bea." As much as Jonathan had paid for matchmaking services. Theo considered refunding

Jonathan's money, but he'd argue, and then she'd have to see him again, and then she might lose her resolve altogether.

"I can have Aunt Fred invest it for you," Bea said, resting the harp against her shoulder. "Whatever you do, you will accept that bank draft, Theo. It's not like you own a lucrative gaming hell."

Did Jonathan? He'd said The Coventry was in difficulties, though he'd also said it made him a fair bit of coin.

"I'd be too worried about being raided by the authorities, assuming I could overcome all of my other reservations."

Bea plucked a minor chord. "Tresham likely pays a king's ransom to ensure his club isn't raided. Either that, or having dukes and earls hanging from the rafters keeps the more ambitious reformers from bothering him." She turned the chord into a slow arpeggio, the notes halting and sad.

"But if The Coventry's reputation should suffer due to rumors of cheating and the like?" Theo asked. "Arrests would be more likely?"

"You aren't engaged to him, Theo," Bea said, tilting the harp upright. "Tresham can be arrested, and that's no concern of yours, but yes. If the rumors regarding crooked tables, reckless play, and other problems are true, then the authorities are more likely to interfere. Find me a cheerful tune, please. I'm at home to callers, and my only guest has informed me she's abandoning me for the company of some doddering sheep farmer."

"Penweather will never be doddering. He will be dignified until his dying day." Jonathan would be dignified as well, but not... not priggish. Not stuffy. He would not leave a widow to muddle on in penury when a wealthy relation should have seen to her finances. "I cannot abide the idea that Mr. Tresham's club is an object of talk."

"Then you'd best leave Town soon, for if the rumors are reaching my ears—a shy, retiring widow of limited means—they will soon be more than rumors."

Bea was about as shy and retiring as Wellington in pursuit of the French, though Theo's need to quit London was growing by the hour.

"Promise me something," Bea said, resuming her place beside Theo on the piano bench. "I am fanciful, I know, but I'm concerned for you, Theo. Promise me you aren't decamping to Hampshire to bear Tresham a child out of wedlock. You'd be that stoic, that principled. I know you can't marry a man who makes his living off of gambling, but I also know you aren't thinking clearly right now."

Theo slipped the cover back over the keyboard, for no cheerful tunes came to mind.

"No child, Bea. Thank all the merciful powers, there's not to be a child."

Theo was so relieved to report that recent revelation that she had to use the dusty handkerchief to blot her tears while Bea fetched two bottles of cordial.

CHAPTER SEVENTEEN

"The scheme victimizes men with titles," Jonathan said, keeping his voice down. "Not every time, but often enough that I consider it a pattern."

Sycamore Dorning turned over another card. "Lipscomb, Henries, Lord Welfaring, Lord Hamberton… I am loath to admit you might be correct, though I've sat here night after night and not seen the connections."

Across the room, three dealers were presiding over tables of vingt-et-un, a game that already favored the house by virtue of the dealer winning all ties. That Moira had further skewed the odds by cheating enraged Jonathan. His ire kept him at the club hour after hour, studying the play, moving from table to table, and spying on his own staff.

"If I know who the victims are, I'm more likely to spot the method," Jonathan said. "Though we're attracting fewer and fewer titles among our patrons."

"Who exactly is we, Tresham?" Dorning laid cards out in a long row, sometimes stacking cards atop each other, sometimes arranging them side by side.

We was Jonathan and perhaps a borrowed hound from the ducal residence. *We* did not include Moira, half the staff, Dorning, or the patrons themselves. *We* could not even include Frannie until the club had been put to rights.

Very little of which mattered, except that *we* certainly would not include Theodosia Haviland even when The Coventry was returned to sound footing.

"Now that I think on it," Dorning went on, turning more cards, "I haven't seen Lipscomb here this week, nor Henries. Hard to ruin men who have sense enough to keep their distance."

"Easy to ruin the ones who don't." Like Archimedes Haviland. Theo had not labeled Jonathan's ownership of the club a betrayal—she was fair, was Theo—but she'd clearly felt it as such.

Sycamore studied his cards while a waiter wafted by, a silver platter carried at shoulder height.

"Some men will find ruin if you hide it at the bottom of the deepest well," Dorning muttered when the waiter had collected a discarded wineglass. "You, for example."

"I am far from ruined, Dorning."

"You are one raid away from ruined, which is no different from any other club owner. I'm referring to your lack of marital prospects. Lady Della tells me you and Mrs. Haviland are no longer keeping company. She's concerned for you."

Hope leaped, a stupid reflex. "Mrs. Haviland is concerned for me?"

"Lady Della is concerned for you. She has threatened to look in on you here again."

God spare me from meddling sisters and resolute widows.

Moira appeared at the foot of the screened stairway. She was resplendent in a bronze silk gown that hugged her figure as closely as respectability allowed and showed off enough bosom to distract even a man holding a winning hand. A subtle reaction went through the room, the men standing a little taller, the women standing a little closer to their escorts.

While the dealers all smiled more broadly at the patrons.

"I do fancy a woman who knows how to carry herself," Dorning said. "But then, I fancy most women."

"Have you nowhere else to be, Dorning? Nothing else to do? Moira is even now scheming to bring ruin to this establishment, and yet, you long for her company."

And spare me from conniving employees too, please.

Dorning scooped up his cards and shuffled, though he was doing a false shuffle. The cards riffled audibly, but Dorning's maneuver hadn't disturbed the order of the deck.

"I do not long for the company of any who'd bite the hand that feeds them, Tresham. Like you, I'm trying to deduce her game. Your problem is you lack brothers. Never thought I'd say it, but a man without brothers is to be pitied. I could station Ash, Oak, and Valerian at the compass points, and we'd soon catch one of the dealers stumbling or fumbling."

Brothers might be useful, if they were less talkative than Dorning. "It's not brothers I miss."

"Hence my earlier comment about your ruin."

Jonathan was not ruined, but despair had taken up residence in his gut. He missed Theo waking and sleeping. He'd mentally posed all manner of arguments to her, though none would be availing.

The Coventry did not ruin lives. The Coventry provided honest employment and honest play to many. A lack of self-restraint ruined lives, and The Coventry—since Jonathan had become its owner—was more scrupulous than most venues at ensuring that patrons were protected from their own weak natures.

But The Coventry that Jonathan had built was dying, and he was tempted to let it expire. The tables gleamed with more silver and gilt than ever. The scent of beeswax hung over the lot, like some fancy undertaker's establishment. The stink had permeated his clothing, as Theo had said, and yet, he could not stay away.

"If a certain widow has seen reason and tossed you over," Dorning said, "you should resume your bride hunt. The hostesses are pining for your company, and the debutantes are said to be in a collective decline."

"Shuffle the damned deck properly, Dorning. The habits of a cheat have no place here."

Dorning effected another fake shuffle. "She's leaving Town, you know. Closing up the house to enjoy the bucolic splendor of Hampshire, though bucolic splendor has ever struck me as a contradiction in terms."

"Why don't you return to Dorset and study on the matter?" Dorning would actually do quite well in Paris. He had a backward charm, the ability to idle away hours at a time, and he did justice to his tailor's efforts.

"Casriel says it's a sorry man who can't enjoy a night of cards, and yet, you hardly ever sit for a hand. I suggested it's the drink and gossip you enjoy, but you drink about as much as a preacher's spinster sister. Anselm opines that lurking here night after night is no way to win back your future duchess."

The same waiter went past with the same silver tankard on his platter. The poor man never seemed to stop moving, but then, the patrons never stopped leaving their plates and glasses about.

"Anselm can take his opining straight to perdition," Jonathan said. "He quotes his duchess, and that makes him sound intelligent."

Dorning set the cards in a neat stack in the middle of the table. "You're not usually mean, Tresham. Perhaps you're short of sleep.'"

Jonathan cut the deck without being asked. He was short of sleep, but more significantly, he was short of dreams, the silver lining in a life of duty and decorum. He'd dreamed of owning the premier gaming club in London, but that dream was growing tattered before his eyes.

He'd dreamed of marriage to Theo, of raising children with her, of setting the Quimbey dukedom on solid footing, which would be an enjoyable, worthy challenge with Theo at his side.

Something to dream about, somebody to dream with. He wanted those back. Wanted the hope and the joy and all the silver linings that went with them.

"I won't find that here."

"Beg pardon?" Dorning asked, picking up the deck.

"This club has gold and silver aplenty, all shining with the false promise of wealth and ease…" Shining… shining.

Dorning turned over a card, the queen of hearts. "You are talking to yourself in philosophical asides, Tresham, and I know you are not the worse for drink. Get hold of yourself, man. You've a mystery to solve, and time to solve it is running out."

The busy waiter set his platter on the vingt-et-un table where Viscount Dentwhistle was amassing chips with ominous ease. Two or three hands on, those chips would move back across the table, and Dentwhistle would leave lighter in the pockets than he'd arrived.

Again.

Two cups and a wineglass were added to the silver tray, which the waiter then carefully raised to his shoulder like a porter wending through a crowd with luggage.

Candlelight caught on the underside of the platter, sending a golden gleam over the green felt tabletop. The dealer glanced up at the same moment as the waiter paused to redistribute the contents of his tray. Her gaze never so much as rested on the tray, but that look…

Jonathan remained seated when he wanted to bolt across the room and knock the waiter to the floor.

"It's the silver, Dorning. The platters, the tankards, the plates. The damned silver is how she's cheating."

* * *

"Does this bank draft require discreet handling, Mrs. Haviland?" Mr. Wentworth set the document aside and regarded Theo with the unblinking stare of a raptor who need not devour the particular mouse before him, though he might strike for the sheer pleasure of remaining in practice.

Theo had the odd thought that Quinton Wentworth would make a very convincing papa.

"You may cease impersonating a vexed headmaster, Mr. Wentworth. Lord Penweather was my late husband's cousin. These funds are a belated contribution to my widow's portion."

Mr. Wentworth offered Theo the plate of biscuits.

She was tempted, but his little speech about the bank's errand boys came to mind. "No, thank you."

"Are the mails in Hampshire so slow that you're only receiving these funds five years after the late Mr. Haviland's passing? I gather Lord Penweather could not afford to send his missive by express."

That slow, cutting remark was a version of humor, or possibly anger.

"Mr. Wentworth, please add the funds to my account. You may do so without any subterfuge. Anybody can page through Debrett's and see my connection to his lordship."

Mr. Wentworth rose to set the étagère full of sweets on the sideboard. He was such a well-proportioned man that his height came as small surprise whenever he stood. Jonathan possessed the same quality and a much more pleasing smile.

Though Jonathan also owned a gaming hell, from which he refused to part.

"Mr. Wentworth, might I ask you a question?"

"Of course."

"What do you know of The Coventry Club?"

He resumed his seat, a neat folding of masculine power into a well-upholstered chair, though Theo suspected Mr. Wentworth could give as good an account of himself in a noisome alley as he could in the elegant surrounds of his bank.

Jonathan would like Quinton Wentworth. More to the point, Theo trusted him.

"Why do you ask about such a place?"

"Because I want an answer."

A mere quirk of his lips met that retort. "I should clarify: What prompts your question now? I make it my business to remain abreast of financial gossip. When people cannot entice a bank to lend to them at the prescribed five percent interest, they often turn to riskier means of raising capital. The gambling hells can come into that picture, and I thus listen for mention of them."

Mr. Wentworth referred to *people* like Archimedes, who'd been as bad a risk as a borrower as he'd been as a spouse. Theo had never realized how the two qualities had become enmeshed, or how few options a well-born gentleman had when it came to making money.

"You've apparently heard something of note regarding The Coventry."

"For a time—for the past several years—The Coventry has been considered the best of the lot. Prior to that, it was just another mediocre venture. The management changed for the better, and now patrons are treated to free food and drink, and the house keeps a portion of all the winnings."

"That's unusual?"

"That *was* unusual. Other gaming hells are attempting to emulate The Coventry's approach, but they lack its clientele and its reputation for honesty. Then too, the authorities seem to leave The Coventry alone, but that's not unusual given the number of peers and courtesy lords who gather around its tables."

Mr. Wentworth spoke approvingly, admiringly, even.

"You're saying it's well run."

"Brilliantly run, Mrs. Haviland. What most people want in life is honest odds. We want to know the deck isn't stacked against us, that our hard work or upright behavior will merit us a decent living and a measure of respect. That doesn't change just because a man has money or a title. A game of chance can be a lively diversion, if the tables are honest. The Coventry offered that promise, and I didn't begrudge the place its success."

The Coventry killed my husband. The words stuck in Theo's throat, because they were one version of the truth, but not a complete version. Archie had gambled at many establishments, including the homes of his so-called friends and at his gentlemen's clubs.

He'd wagered on what color some woman's gown would be at her engagement ball, bet on horse races, and become a sot, all without specific prompting from any one club.

"You spoke in the past tense," Theo said. "You *didn't* begrudge The Coventry its success. Has that changed?"

"The Coventry has lost its cachet in recent weeks. The play is deeper, the wine cheaper, as the saying goes. Its titled clientele is drifting away, which means a different element is likely to find its way through the doors. The authorities will notice. I have wondered if the management hasn't changed hands again, because the rumors are so consistent. The previous owner would have known better than to let a goose laying golden eggs fly away."

He's been too busy courting me. The timing was likely not a coincidence. Jonathan had undertaken a bride hunt, and his club had become prey to a cheat.

"I'm glad to see your late husband's family developing a sense of responsibility where you're concerned," Mr. Wentworth said. "I'll see to your bank draft and send you a receipt."

Theo rose, wanting the transaction complete, lest she change her mind.

"Send the receipt to Hampshire, please. I'm removing to the country for an indefinite stay." *Where I will doubtless write many letters to Jonathan that will all end up in the dustbin.*

Mr. Wentworth was on his feet, but he made no move toward the door. "I have made inquiries, Mrs. Haviland."

Between listening to gossip and making inquiries, it was a wonder Mr. Wentworth accomplished any banking.

"Regarding?"

"Do you recall my mentioning that a man's charitable endeavors reveal much about his character?"

"Yes."

"I took it upon myself to research the charitable undertakings of a certain gentleman who had earned your notice."

Only Jonathan had earned Theo's notice. "And?"

"He's supporting two orphanages almost single-handedly, both of them sheltering the sons of enlisted men fallen on foreign soil. He contributes generously to a boy's school in the Midlands that takes in charity scholars, and he's on the board of a discreet establishment in Dorset for men seeking to overcome a propensity for intoxication. He apparently finds organizations in need of financial discipline and sets them to rights. The man clearly has a head for numbers."

Based on the banker's tone, no higher virtue could befall a mortal soul.

"He has other charities in France," Mr. Wentworth went on, "including a hospital that cares for poor women during their lyings-in and one in London that sends physicians to foundling homes. He's on the board of an organization that champions children injured in the mines, and he—Mrs. Haviland?"

Theo had sunk back into her chair. "He has a head for numbers."

"Are you well?"

Theo's thoughts were running riot, while an odd cool flush prickled over her arms and scalp. The same sensation plagued her when a summer storm was bearing down and had come upon her when she'd realized she was carrying Diana.

"Do go on, Mr. Wentworth. I am interested in your recitation." Interested in the man who used the proceeds of a gaming hell to look after women and children.

"You are also uncharacteristically pale."

Mr. Wentworth crossed to the sideboard and poured Theo a glass of something—lemonade, as it turned out. Not too sweet, not too strong.

"Thank you."

He set three biscuits on a plate. "You will consume these, please."

"You're saying Mr. Tresham is a philanthropist."

"A very active, shrewd philanthropist. I meet the obligations of my conscience, Mrs. Haviland, considering the degree to which fortune has smiled upon me. Tresham has taken on the betterment of the realm as a personal quest."

No, he has not. For Jonathan, doubtless, this was simply what one did in anticipation of a ducal title when polite society forbade one to undertake a trade.

"He robs from the rich to give to the poor," Theo said, biting into a biscuit.

"Is it robbery to offer wealthy people food, drink, and diversion in addition to an honest chance to walk away with great winnings? I, for one, am glad I am not called upon to refine on that distinction."

Theo finished her biscuits and lemonade in silence, and Mr. Wentworth seemed content merely to sit with her. He had a great stillness inside him, not restful exactly, but calm.

"How does one win at gambling, Mr. Wentworth?"

She'd surprised him, a small gratification.

Dark brows rose, then knit. "I cannot advise gaming as a means of increasing your wealth, madam. Slow, steady gain can be had from the cent-per-cents. You are a young woman, and over time—"

"Mr. Wentworth, I appreciate your concern for my welfare, but I cannot put that question to anybody else now, and I want—I need—to understand how gaming works."

He retrieved the biscuits from the sideboard—the whole lot—and resumed his seat.

"It's simple, really. The only way to honestly win is to play against yourself."

"I've been doing that for years. Explain how it works in the context of the card tables."

They ate half the biscuits and had demolished a tea tray before Theo left. In her head, she drew up a list of people upon whom she must call, starting with Jonathan Tresham's sister.

* * *

"You will take this one hundred pounds and leave England," Jonathan said, thrusting banknotes at Moira. "If I ever see you in an establishment I own, I'll call the authorities on you myself."

For one instant, a stunned woman gazed at the money. The next, Moira snatched the cash from Jonathan's hand.

"You're giving me the sack when I've made you wealthy?" she snapped.

"I'm giving you a chance to avoid prosecution, Moira. You've embezzled from the payroll of a respectable supper club, colluded with the trades to steal more funds, and threatened the staff with bodily harm if they refuse to participate in your schemes. You are finished here."

She lunged at him, and she was a substantial, fit woman.

"Moira, don't make a bad situation worse."

She fought like a trapped alley cat. Sycamore Dorning lounged outside the closed office door, making sure nobody intruded on this discussion, though having a witness to this altercation would doubtless only enrage the lady more.

Jonathan got a grip on her wrists, and because she would not give up her hold of the money, he eventually wrestled her to a standstill.

"You can't prove anything," Moira said. "You have no documents incriminating me."

"I have sworn affidavits from the kitchen staff that they were instructed to carry only highly polished silver trays and to position them in such a way that the dealers could see cards reflected on the trays. They did the same with tankards, goblets, and snuffboxes. A smart dealer need only be able to detect who is holding face cards to have a substantial advantage, and your scheme made that information plain."

She wrenched free and stalked across the office. "Your affidavits are useless, and you know it. You will never, ever close this place simply to spite me. I know you, Jonathan Tresham. The Coventry is your mistress. You will sell your soul before you give up on your precious hell."

She withdrew a lady's traveling bag from the bottom cabinet of the sideboard.

Packed and ready to go—of course. "I will warn the authorities in Paris of your impending arrival," he said.

"Then I won't go to Paris."

"I have connections in every major European city, Moira. Your career as a cheat is over. Every night, somebody who cannot afford to play is throwing the dice, risking ruin out of a compulsion he or she is helpless to resist. I owe them an honest throw."

She yanked a cloak from a peg near the door. "I cannot stand your righteous hypocrisy, Jonathan. You make up rules to comfort your conscience, but you're every bit as much a cheat as I am. You ply the patrons with drink, knowing it makes them reckless, then—when you decide it's time—you send them home in cabs you keep standing half the night from your own funds. Make up your mind whether you're a gentleman or a rogue. I can tell you which one I prefer."

She thrust a reticule into the traveling bag—a fat reticule no doubt also full of funds.

"The only part of your scheme I haven't figured out, Moira, is why. Did you think we'd marry?"

The look she gave him was so nakedly despairing, Jonathan wished he'd not asked the question.

"Would it have been so bad, being married to me? I'm not hideous, and I understand you aren't capable of loving a woman as she needs to be loved. But, no. Of course not. A future duke cannot ally himself openly with some lord's cast-off plaything, no matter how much sense that would make. Pardon me for getting above myself *again*."

"I am not a lordling, and I have never cast you off."

She opened the desk drawer and withdrew a fistful of sovereigns. "Don't try to stop me, Jonathan."

"I wouldn't dream of it. The more you take with you, the farther you are likely to travel from me and this club. You haven't told me what great wrong entitles you to act the woman scorned, Moira. You are not smitten with me. You are not worse off for having been in my employ."

"Always in your employ, never your partner."

Jonathan pushed the drawer closed before she could steal documents as well as coin. "You have won, Moira. The club's reputation is now such that I cannot sell it for what it's worth. My dukedom has been beggared by my uncle's unwillingness to inflict progress on his tenants and retainers or go more deeply in debt. My marital prospects…"

That was the worst hurt, though Jonathan couldn't lay Theo's decision at Moira's feet.

"Marry an heiress," Moira retorted. "That's what you lot do. Find a woman who can afford you and hand her a title to go with her stupidity. I wish you the joy of your union."

"While you do what?"

She stuffed the money into her pockets. "*You* have this club, I have coin, but I was respectable once, Jonathan. I didn't ruin myself. By an accident of birth that conferred both expectations and male gender on you, you will still be respectable when you're sitting in Newgate awaiting trial, while I'll be..."

She snatched a bonnet from the hook on the back of the door. "I would not have you now, Jonathan Tresham, if you begged me on bended knee."

That was pride speaking, and Jonathan let her grand pronouncement go uncontested. Moira was battling the past, building a life around an old wound, holding all and sundry responsible for pain that should have been laid to rest long ago.

He knew that road. Knew the ditches and hedges, the muddy ruts... and now, when he desperately longed to turn about... Theo was gone, had probably sold the vases and baskets he'd sent her, just as she'd sold every reminder of her feckless spouse.

Dozens of pistols, Anselm had said, and even the man's night clothes.

"This has to do with Lipscomb, doesn't it?" Jonathan asked. "You went after him relentlessly and have succeeded in driving him off. What did he do to you?"

The fight went out of her as if she'd lost the largest pot of the evening. She sank into the chair behind the desk, running her finger over the crest embroidered on Jonathan's handkerchief.

"Not him. His uncle. The previous viscount. The old hound wanted to play, then he pretended I'd encouraged him. Me, a decent girl who thought to be the helpmeet comforting him in his later years. The bastard."

"So you set out to ruin his heir?" That made a kind of rough logic.

"I considered marrying Lipscomb, but he made it plain I wasn't good enough for him. I'm not good enough for any of you."

This discussion—this drama—should have given Jonathan hives, but finally getting some answers was too great a relief. Moira, however, needed a solution, else she'd turn up in two years like a bad penny, bringing rotten luck and threats of blackmail with her.

"Lord Davington is in Paris. You have the means to resolve his debts, you will be able to wrest a proposal from him. Find a quiet corner of the world where you can be happy and make the effort to fit in there with or without him. You can be patient and reasonable, or go on with your tantrum like a spoiled toddler."

Like a child ignored by both parents.

She dabbed at her eyes with Jonathan's handkerchief and sniffed. "Davington's not bad looking."

"He'll beggar you in a year flat if you can't keep him away from the tables, Moira. Teach him to cheat and somebody will put a bullet through his handsome head. You'll also have to put the fear of philandering in him, or he'll meet the same end even sooner."

Jonathan could hear Moira's thoughts as if she were speaking them aloud: a titled, respectable widow... not an entirely objectionable outcome. A twinge

194 | GRACE BURROWES

of pity for Davington tried to nudge its way forward. Jonathan swatted it aside. Davington was a man grown and responsible for his actions.

Moira rose and tossed Jonathan's handkerchief to the desk blotter. She took a look around the office, an elegant, comfortable space that she'd appropriated for her own ends.

"You even have to be a bloody gentleman about this. Very well, I'll play the lady: The constables will be coming around early next week. They've been paid to ignore your bribes this time, to make an example of you, though I don't know when, exactly, they'll decide to pounce. Good luck with that."

Jonathan let her have the last word, remaining silent as he escorted her to the bottom of the screened steps and through the door that led to the wine cellars.

When he and Moira had passed into the kitchen of the rooming house across the street, Jonathan held out his hand.

"The keys, please." He'd change every lock, but that would take time, and Moira could not be trusted.

She passed over a key ring. "I only did what any other woman in my place would have done. Don't judge me."

"I don't judge you. Best of luck. My coach awaits on the street. Take it to Dover, for all I care. Don't come back."

He bowed over her hand. She hesitated a moment, then tossed him a curtsey and a saucy smile, before flouncing through the doorway.

The only emotion that accompanied her retreating footsteps was relief. Jonathan allowed himself the length of the wine cellar to puzzle over that—was such a parting sad? Overdue? Neither?

When faced with life's unfairness and low cards dealt by the hands of men, Theo had not taken to cheating or raging. She'd sold heirlooms, turned her dresses, and made economies without a word of complaint.

Theo, whom Jonathan missed terribly and hadn't seen even when he'd lurked in the park by the hour with a drooling hound at his feet.

He ascended the steps and took the passage into The Coventry's kitchen, which was the usual hot, busy pandemonium Armand preferred.

"Food's going to waste," Armand muttered as Jonathan paused to sniff a savory loaf of herbed bread. "This lot isn't interested in cuisine and good vintages. My talents are wasted, because all they can see are the dice and the cards."

"Then don't put as much out on the buffet," Jonathan said.

The authorities were planning a raid, the clientele was deteriorating, and the chef was preparing to defect to a competitor, but at least the tables were no longer crooked.

The Coventry might be doomed, but it would be doomed on Jonathan's terms. He was intent on searching the office for further evidence of Moira's mischief when Battaglia accosted him on the landing.

"Something's afoot, sir. You'd best be down at the tables."

"Now? I haven't time to humor a tipsy baroness when, for all I know, my safe is empty and my dice weighted."

Battaglia remained, blocking Jonathan's ascent. "Sir, I know we're in the middle of a rough patch, but I suspect it just got rougher. We're being invaded, and these are not The Coventry's typical patrons."

CHAPTER TWO

The Coventry's gambling floor looked to Theo like any titled lord's Mayfair gaming room, albeit this one had pretty young women dealing the cards.

Pretty, properly dressed women. No foul language peppered the air. No air of dissipation wafted over the patrons. The laughter was simply laughter—no hint of salacious trysts in secluded alcoves.

"You look disappointed," Bea said. "Expecting the debauchery of the Boxhaven masquerade ball, perhaps?"

"Lord Boxhaven's balls are genteel enough." Provided one left early and remained in the ballroom. "I am bewildered to admit The Coventry looks entirely proper."

But then, this was Jonathan's establishment. Of course it would be proper.

A liveried footman was collecting cloaks in order of precedence. The Duchess of Anselm first, then the Countess of Bellefonte, Lady Hopewell, Lady Della, and two of her sisters. Mrs. Compton was craning her neck like a curious goose, while His Grace of Anselm, Lord Casriel, and Mr. Adolphus Haddonfield stood by.

The gentlemen looked pleased with themselves to be escorting a platoon of respectable women to a gaming hell, but then, who could fathom the mind of the adult male?

"You all have your money?" Theo asked the ladies as the footman hurried away.

Mrs. Compton patted her reticule. "I might play a bit of my own, if the cards are kind."

"That is up to you," Theo said. "To the tables, ladies."

Brave words. Theo had no idea exactly how one joined the play or made a bid to enter a game.

Fortunately, her friends did.

"First, you watch for a few hands," Bea said, taking Theo by the arm. "Pretend you're carefully observing the dice, the other players, the cards. Look as if you're listening to a new string quartet and you haven't made up your mind about the cellist. Watch the other players as if you know their secrets. Pretend they aren't watching you."

"Rather like unmarried guests at a typical musicale."

Amid the beeswax, pomade, and perfume, Theo caught a scent, like a whole garden of flowers.

"Mrs. Haviland, this is a surprise."

Jonathan had sneaked up behind her. Theo thus had enough warning that she could compose her features and be again the wise, slightly weary widow he'd met weeks ago in a darkened library.

"Mr. Tresham, good evening."

Theo's curtsey was for the benefit of those watching, though her ladies were already assembled around tables, looking as avid as biddies awaiting their daily ration of corn, Mrs. Compton most eager among them.

Jonathan's bow was gentlemanly decorum personified. "I do believe one of your cohorts was expecting garish art and half-naked dealers. I admit to some surprise to find you here."

Tasteful nudes would not have been a surprise. "This is a rare diversion for me, I admit, while I knew exactly where you'd be. Lady Della regrets missing our call. The hostesses bemoan your absence, and Her Grace of Anselm says you've neglected your regular obligations as a host. Casriel says you haven't so much as taken a meal at your other clubs. You are here, always and only here, within sight of the tables."

His gaze fixed itself to the top of Theo's head. "I am not your late spouse, Madam."

A waiter went by, a wooden platter laden with wineglasses in his hands.

"I was suggesting," Theo said quietly, "behavior in common with your own father. I gather he was never home, but rather, he was single-mindedly devoted to his own pursuits regardless of other obligations. For him, the lure was diversion. For you, it's business—much of that business charitable. How do I join a table playing vingt-et-un?"

Jonathan leaned nearer. "Theodosia, what are you about?"

Oh, to hear him speak her name. Theo shrugged off that pleasure, because the stakes were too high for selfish indulgence.

"My friends and I left the Marquess of Tyne's ball letting all and sundry know our destination. Curiosity will do the rest when a lot of well-born ladies announce an intention to play away their pin money. Lord Tyne's guests should start arriving within the half hour."

The soft whir of a roulette wheel cut through the clink of glasses and chatter of the patrons.

"Theo, please assure me you haven't risked your own security for the sake of this club."

Jonathan's attire was immaculate, as always, but the folds of his cravat obscured the crested pin nestled among the lace. No elegant little rosebud graced his lapel. His gaze wasn't merely tired. He'd reached the stage of exhaustion that imbued the sufferer with saintly patience and wry humor.

"I'm enjoying an evening out with friends." Not as much of a fabrication as Jonathan might think, for Theo was enormously pleased to be *doing something*, to be taking an active role in another's welfare, rather than subsisting on the buffets polite society laid out for genteel widows.

Jonathan took her by the hand and led her to a quiet little table by the stairs. "Theo, I run an honest house. Please be honest with me now. You wanted nothing to do with this place. Now you're here with a personal platoon of Hessians in muslin, and I suspect you've staked them with your own funds."

She settled into one of the two seats at the table, the coins in her pocket an odd weight against her leg.

Jonathan's question was not as simple as it sounded: What was she doing? Why had nobody asked that when she'd accepted a proposal from a man she'd barely known? Why had nobody asked that when she'd weathered years of neglect from Penweather?

What was she *doing*, besides rolling the dice and hoping for the best possible outcome?

"I could not save my husband. Nobody could." That painful admission bore the seeds of self-forgiveness and maybe absolution for Archimedes too. "I don't flatter myself that I'm saving your blasted gaming hell, but you do not deserve to be alone in this, Jonathan. You would never fleece a patron, never break the unwritten rules by which such business is conducted. You use the proceeds for the best possible purposes. I'm here because I need to be."

He sank into the opposite chair. "You are *gambling* on my behalf?"

"My banker explained how to minimize the risks. I've divided my funds among my friends, and one or the other of us is bound to win occasionally if we mostly play against one another. This time next week, I will be on my way to Hampshire with the girls. Lord Tyne's ball was the last invitation I've accepted, so tonight is my only opportunity to see this place."

Say something. Stop me. Go down on your lordly bended knee.

Jonathan inched his hand across the table, just as a dapper fellow who looked to be a majordomo approached the table.

"Sir? The chef is demanding to speak with you."

A gaggle of couples came through the door, the ladies in their gowns and jewels, the gentlemen in evening finery.

"We will speak further, madam." Jonathan rose and bowed, then kissed Theo's cheek and strode away.

"You're welcome," Theo said to the seat he'd vacated.

The club was soon packed and noisy, preserving Theo from the need to join the play. Sycamore Dorning attached himself to her side, explaining each game to her, though many of them she'd learned prior to marrying Archie.

Mrs. Compton won a sizable pot. Bea's winnings were more modest. Her Grace of Anselm was a gracious loser, while Lady Bellefonte's luck changed constantly. Lady Della had disappeared into the kitchen more than once, the majordomo on her heels.

As Theo was preparing to leave, Lords Lipscomb and Henries arrived arm in arm, several friends on their coattails. The entire room gave a shout as Mrs. Compton won another substantial sum.

"Can you see me home?" Theo asked Mr. Dorning.

"You're leaving? The place hasn't been this lively in weeks, and you're leaving?"

Across the room, Jonathan was chatting with Anselm, the same as they might have at any ball or Venetian breakfast.

"I'm not sorry I came," Theo said, "but I still have packing to do." Jonathan would be here until dawn and be here again tomorrow night.

That hadn't changed.

Dorning offered his arm. "He can't leave the game just when his luck is changing, Mrs. Haviland. He gave his manager the sack, the chef is in a pet, and the club has been the butt of unkind rumors. You can't expect him to abandon his post now."

"This outing was a lark, Mr. Dorning, as all visits to a gaming hell should be. I've satisfied my curiosity. Mr. Tresham doesn't expect me to stay, and I'll not visit again. Let's be off, shall we?"

* * *

The Coventry had had its best night ever, the play continuing until dawn. Lipscomb had won a nice sum, as had many of Theo's friends. Jonathan's search of the office had revealed Moira's private set of books and a wad of banknotes sufficient to cover the club's expenses for months—or to convince the authorities that they need not trouble themselves to raid the club for the nonce.

He had no doubt more money had been secreted on the premises, but he'd fallen asleep before completing his investigations. He awoke to a jab in the ribs and a brisk female voice in his ear. Before the words made sense, his mind had sorted out the important message: This lady was not Theo.

"If this is your idea of how to organize a business, then it's no wonder you nearly lost everything."

Lady Della Haddonfield stood at the end of the office sofa. She wore a thunderous frown and a smart blue walking dress with a white lace underskirt.

"My lady, you should not be here."

"Neither should you. Their Graces of Quimbey arrived home from their journey late last night, and I understand they are expecting you to be engaged. You are very lucky your auntie was not among Mrs. Haviland's lady gamblers."

Jonathan's head hurt, his eyes were scratchy, he was famished, and he needed privacy. More important than all of that, he needed to see Theo.

"What time is it?"

"Time to get up. Well past noon."

He shot off the sofa and tripped over his own boots. "Bloody damnation."

"Language, Jonathan. You can't pay a call on Mrs. Haviland in your present condition."

He caught a glimpse of himself in the mirror over the sideboard. "Ye flying imps of hell." A ghoul stared back at him, cheeks unshaven, hair in wild disarray, shadows beneath sunken eyes.

Lady Della set about closing drawers, hanging up coats, and otherwise tidying the chaos Jonathan's search had created. She had the look of a woman preparing to exert dominion over a space, to arrange it to her liking.

"If you'd excuse me," Jonathan said, "I'll join you downstairs when I'm more presentable."

She passed him his favorite burgundy morning coat. "Don't tarry over your toilette on my account, though I suppose the charwoman shouldn't be needlessly frightened. Adolphus and Mr. Dorning have been touring the premises, prying into cupboards and trying to look knowledgeable. I suspect you will find them in the wine cellars."

She was leaving Jonathan a moment to collect his wits, which was more than he deserved where she was concerned.

"Thank you, Lady Della."

"For?"

"For joining the women last night, for being here today." *For not giving up on me.*

Her expression said she did not want his thanks.

Jonathan tried again. "You look like him, you know."

Her bravado faltered, revealing a very young and uncertain woman. "I haven't a likeness. I was hoping… never mind. I'll have the kitchen make you a tray."

She turned to leave on a soft rustle of skirts, and though Jonathan felt eight kinds of urgency to quit the premises, this moment mattered as well.

"A portrait of him—of Papa—hangs in a room off the library in Quimbey House," Jonathan said, sitting to pull on his boots. "He posed for it when he was a few years younger than you are now. The resemblance to you is uncanny. I will ask Quimbey to give you the painting."

She stared at the cluttered blotter, smiling at nothing Jonathan could divine.

"You walk like our papa," he went on, getting to his feet and searching his memory. "You have his flair for making an impression. Did you know his second middle name was Delacourt?"

Della wiped at her cheek. "I was named for my grandmother—for the Marchioness of Warne."

"I suspect if you look at the parish registry, you were baptized Delacourt Haddonfield, or you at least have that for a middle name. Lady Warne's nickname was doubtless a convenient afterthought. We can have a look sometime. Nobody need know of such an errand."

"I'd like that." She seized him in a tight hug, then whirled from the room when Jonathan would have offered more: Their father had been ferociously good at billiards, possessed of a fine baritone singing voice, and had been unusually patient with the elderly.

He'd been a poor father and a vexatious husband, but not a complete wastrel. Not even an entirely bad man, given the nature of the union he'd found himself in.

"Papa would have enjoyed last night," Jonathan informed the empty room. "He might even have been pleased for me." Jonathan had enjoyed last night, had enjoyed glancing up to see Theo amid her friends, Theo sipping champagne at the table by the stairs, Theo watching him.

Theo, who was departing for damned Hampshire.

Jonathan washed and shaved, found a clean shirt and cravat, and brushed his hair, all the while trying to recall what, exactly, Theo had said to him before she'd slipped away on the arm of Sycamore Dorning.

Perhaps Dorning had some insights to offer. Jonathan found his guest looking all too well rested and counting the bottles of claret.

"You've a fortune in wine alone," Dorning said, holding a bottle up to the lit sconce.

"What have you done with Lady Della?"

"She dragged Mr. Haddonfield off in the direction of the nearest milliner's. Said you would not be tarrying on the premises when you have a call to pay. This is an expensive vintage, and you must have two hundred bottles on hand."

"Two hundred forty-three."

Dorning tossed the bottle into the air and caught it. "Two hundred forty-two. What are the odds this call you're paying is on an attractive widow bound for Hampshire?"

"The odds coincide with absolute certainty. Come with me."

Dorning had moved to the next bin, which held a very fine cognac. "Why? You have a widow to woo, and I have a wine cellar to fall in love with."

"The widow might well have already left for the country, in which case I will have to renew my acquaintance with Hampshire. If she hasn't departed, then I have time to make you an offer you cannot refuse, but I don't intend to do it on an empty stomach."

Dorning collected a bottle of cognac and waved it in the direction of the steps. "Lead on, Mr. Tresham, though I warn you, I drive a hard bargain."

Jonathan took the steps two at a time. "I'm not inviting you to dicker, Dorning. Either you take the offer, or I'll make it to Lipscomb and Henries. I'd rather make it to you, provided you can inveigle your brother Ash to join you in the venture."

Dorning scampered up the steps, a bottle in each hand. "What's *he* got to do with anything?"

"*He* has caught Lady Della's fancy, and she can't very well bring him up to scratch if he's ruralizing in Dorset. I'm also told that siblings are a blessing of the highest order. Ash Dorning is proficient with numbers, and I like that in a fellow."

"I'm proficient with numbers."

One of the undercooks had set a place for Jonathan in the dining room. A plate of steaming eggs, a tray of bacon, a rack of buttered toast… hearty fare for a man with much to do.

"You are proficient at looking idle while spying. I persist in the hope that you have potential nonetheless. The Tresham family is tenacious, if nothing else. Find a seat and prepare to listen carefully."

"I'd rather find a wineglass."

Jonathan tucked a table napkin into his collar. "Save the boyish charm for the patrons, or for the magistrate. You might well be meeting with him later today in an attempt to persuade him to modify his plans for next week. I'll equip you with a substantial sum of money to use in any manner you see fit, though I suspect coin will figure in your discussion with the authorities—assuming you accept my offer."

Dorning took a seat and snatched a strip of bacon. "I accept. What are you offering?"

* * *

The garden was the only part of the London residence Theo would miss. She'd told her solicitor not to rent the property out just yet—a precaution, in case Cousin Fabianus proved to be impossible rather than merely dull.

Hampshire doubtless had flowers, but these were *her* flowers. She had separated the irises the year Archie had died, the *muguet des bois* the year after that. Those had grown from plants she'd taken from her mother's garden, and they'd thrived so well they needed separating again.

The garden was a small, important remove from the house itself, and Theo had needed that distance badly. Perhaps she should take a few cuttings to Hampshire as a gift for her host.

The gate creaked behind her, though Williams had departed with both girls for market not a quarter hour past. Perhaps Diana had forgotten her penny-rhymes-with-many again.

"Mrs. Haviland." Jonathan Tresham strolled around the potted herbs. He was resplendent in morning attire, though he still looked tired to Theo. "I knocked on the front door, and nobody responded. You gave me a very bad moment, madam."

Theo was having a bad moment—a good bad moment. "Mr. Tresham." She didn't bother rising to curtsey, lest she throw herself into his arms.

"May I join you on the bench?"

"Of course. How is The Coventry?"

He took off his hat and rested it on the rim of the herb pot, then sat a decorous foot from Theo's side. "We'll get to The Coventry. How are you?"

Miserable. Much of Theo's unhappiness was grief, a familiar and irksome burden. Not grief for a life wasted this time, but grief for a dream lost. She had set Jonathan aside, certain of her course. Now, she had time for regrets.

"I'm somewhat fatigued," she said. "Yesterday was busy, and last night went late, then I spent much of today finishing up my packing. I gather you were out later than I?"

Jonathan looked... different. Not as confident, not as self-possessed. Theo took a measure of satisfaction from the possibility that he was sorry to see her go, perhaps even troubled.

She was certainly troubled.

"I fell asleep as the sun rose," he said, "and had not Lady Della roused me with a hard poke to my ribs, I'd likely still be snoring amid The Coventry's bills and ledgers. We had our busiest night ever, thanks to you and your scheming ladies."

"My friends." That they'd rallied to her cause—a duchess, a countess, several other titles Theo barely knew—had been bewildering. She had been invited to Her Grace's card night for ladies, and she'd been assured that cards played little part in the gathering.

"Your friends," Jonathan said, snapping off a sprig of rosemary. "I hope you consider me a friend, Theodosia."

The piney scent of the herb cut through even the fragrance Jonathan wore. "I am not in the habit of wagering my savings on behalf of mere acquaintances, Mr. Tresham."

"Please assure me you won."

"I made fourteen pounds. I cannot believe... I did nothing to earn that money, but the ladies insisted I have it. That is two years' wages for some domestics and more money than many people ever see at once."

"Why did you do it, Theo? Why storm the gates of a place that cost you financial security and marital accord?"

"You asked me that last night. Archie had many haunts. The Coventry was only one of them. You didn't buy The Coventry until I was out of first mourning."

The garden was an oasis of peace, even if the fountain had been sold, even if the lilies of the valley were pushing up the bricks on the walkway. Theo did not want to say her good-byes to Jonathan here, not in this sanctuary.

She half rose, but Jonathan caught her by the wrist. "Something Anselm said has stuck in my mind, Theo. Something I need to clarify with you."

Theo sank back onto the bench. "Out with it, then. I'm leaving tomorrow morning, and I have no plans to return any time soon."

Stop me. Ask me to stay. Please...

"You told me Archimedes died amid a silence so loud it broke your heart."

Why would he recall those words, and why bring them up now? "I was the only one home, the only one with him." Very likely because Archie had planned it that way.

"Anselm assisted you by having your husband's personal effects sold, nearly all of them, from what the duke said. Rings, sleeve buttons, clothing, boots, his shaving kit and brushes, everything, including a collection of pistols, *all but one of them in pristine condition.*"

The moment condensed into dread, as many moments had since Archie's death. This one was worse than all the others, because Jonathan was here, speaking quietly and pronouncing himself Theo's friend.

"His Grace was most helpful," Theo said.

Jonathan moved closer. "Theo?"

A scalding droplet hit the back of her hand. "I think you should go." Another tear splashed onto her wrist, while a tearing pain welled from the bottomless pit in her belly.

"Archimedes took his own life," Jonathan said, so gently. "Rather than face ruin, he left you alone to cope with the aftermath. He did this, knowing you had both a daughter and sister depending on you, and he did this without alerting his own family to the straits you'd be left in."

Theo turned her head, unable to nod, speak, or reply in the face of a heartache so vast it nearly crushed her.

Another silence blossomed, this one patient and infinitely caring.

"Archimedes was not well, Jonathan. He was unwell in his mind, his body, his spirit. He was so sick, and I was so endlessly *upset*. I did not realize... I did not know..."

Jonathan enfolded her in an embrace, his arms tight around her as the tears grew into silent sobs. How long she cried, she did not know—an eternity of sorrow, a few minutes on a peaceful, sunny afternoon. Through it all, Jonathan held her and stroked her back, until the aftershocks of emotion quieted to an occasional shudder.

"I didn't want you to know. I never wanted anybody to know." Theo wiped at her cheeks with a handkerchief mangled past all hope. "He shot himself here." She tapped her chest. "The physician pronounced it an accident, but Archie had been so despondent… The doctor put forth a lie, admonishing me to protect the dignity of the deceased, and I was too… I did not contradict him, and my dissembling was not for the sake of the deceased."

"Guns do misfire, Theo."

How kind he was, how dear. "Archie left a note: *So sorry, my dear—for everything. Remember me fondly. Love, Archimedes.* I have never remembered him fondly, not since that day." She sat up, though Jonathan kept an arm around her shoulders. "You will think me awful."

"I think you courageous and honorable to your bones."

"I can't look at a gun. For months afterward, if somebody dropped a platter, if a stone bounced up and hit a carriage window, I jumped half out of my skin. The nightmares were terrible, and I could not be honest with anybody. Bad enough to die in debt, but to die by one's own hand… Diana and Seraphina would have had no future, and more than anything, I am still angry with Archie for that."

"And yet," Jonathan said, "you set aside your anger to rescue my gaming hell. Why, Theo?"

Because I am your friend too. "Because I know what it's like to need help and find all backs turned, all eyes averted. I know what a life without allies feels like, and I know about your list of charities, Jonathan. You aid so many, and you never mentioned that to me. You blathered on about Quimbey and tenants and employees, but your generosity goes beyond that. You are a good man, you were my good man, and I lost my courage."

He kissed her cheek and lingered close. "Why should you have to be brave all the time? Why should any of us?"

A fair question, and Theo would have the journey to Hampshire to ponder it. Jonathan would likely marry an heiress—six names came to Theo's mind, all wealthy women from excellent families. Jonathan—drat him—had made good impressions on every one of them.

"Will you write to me?" She was a widow. Widows could receive correspondence from friends.

Jonathan drew back and moved half a foot away on the bench. "Not bloody likely."

He enjoyed such a sense of clarity about his path. Always had, likely always would, while Theo felt as if she were setting out on a journey without a map, compass, or directions.

"You have courting to be about, I understand. The Coventry means much to you, and now you know—"

"No, Theodosia, you do not understand." Again, his resolve was evident in his tone. "I've arranged to sell The Coventry. Sycamore Dorning will take over its management with one or two of his brothers. Over time, if he's careful, he can buy me out. I'll remain landlord for now, but eventually, the Dorning brothers will become owners of the entire venture."

Theo had longed to hear those words, had not thought them possible, but now…

"Don't give up your dreams for me, Jonathan. If I cost you the one thing that gives you joy, the cornerstone of your financial stability, then resentment can only grow in its place. Others rely on you, and I did not take that into account."

Did not take many things into account, such as the need to fashion a life that was more than a defense against past hurts.

"I could not back out of the deal with Dorning now if I wanted to, Theo, and I don't want to. I'm told that gaming establishments are illegal, and I'm to be a duke someday. I no longer wish to cling to the diversions of my youth like some stubborn tot with a favorite stuffed rabbit.

"God willing," he went on more softly, "I'll become a father someday too. I refuse to allow my children to conclude that I stay out until all hours, bribe the authorities, and break the law because that is more important than reading them their bedtime stories."

Theo tried to make her mind work, but unburdening herself regarding the past had left her spent and muddled.

"You negotiated with Mr. Dorning before you came here?"

"I did not negotiate. I told Mr. Dorning how it would be, and he had the sense to seize the opportunity I presented."

Thank you, Sycamore Dorning. "You're certain, Jonathan? What of the dukedom?"

"I will do my best by the dukedom, Theo, and I hope that's enough for you, because I cannot contemplate marriage unless I'm married to you. I'll have some income from The Coventry for the next few years. I have investments. I'll make economies—I was hoping you could help me with that—and I'll raise my children to be prudent with their coin. I was hoping you could help with that too—the children part—unless you'd rather rusticate in Hampshire?"

He'd put The Coventry aside, and he wanted to have children with her. The great sadness Theo had carried for years broke into dust, and a breeze of joy blew it to the heavens. The sadness might come around again from time to time, but the joy would never leave her for long.

She leaned her forehead against Jonathan's shoulder. "Please do not consign me to Hampshire. I don't know anybody in Hampshire. I don't love anybody in Hampshire."

"Theo?"

She gazed up at the little dwelling where she'd struggled so, year after year. Just a house, worth some coin. Not a home.

"This place holds sad memories, Jonathan. That's what was driving me to Hampshire. The time has come to let go of what happened here, to move on, and to risk a bit of change. I cannot change the past. I cannot even fight it anymore."

Jonathan shifted, sinking to one knee before her and taking her hand. "Then I have a new dream that I'd like to discuss with you every morning, noon, and night for the rest of our lives. Theodosia, I'd like to discuss this dream with you in my bed, in the library, in the billiards room, and in about six different linen closets."

"And the music room," Theo said. "Do you still have the special license?"

He kissed her soundly. "Let's discuss the special license first."

* * *

"Tresham, why the hell didn't you warn me?" Anselm asked, over the lilt of the string quartet in the minstrel's gallery.

Jonathan smiled at Miss Threadlebaum, who was being led to the dance floor by no less worthy than an earl's heir. Dora Louise Compton's engagement to a young baron had been announced the previous week—Theodosia had had a hand in that—and Clytemnestra Islington had been walked home from services the previous Sunday by a widowed viscount.

Jonathan's pleasure in these developments was mostly on Theo's behalf, but also for the young ladies.

"You ignore me," Anselm muttered. "I put a direct question to you, and you are too busy watching that damned staircase—there they are."

"What could I possibly have to warn you about?" Jonathan asked, as Theodosia and the Duchess of Anselm paused at the top of the steps. The Duchess descended first, leaving Theo to shine before the whole ballroom in a gown of deep blue velvet. She wore a pearl choker that Jonathan had presented to her as an engagement gift, but other than the single strand of pearls in her hair, her only other ornament was a blazing smile.

For him. He lifted his glass, because the entire gathering, even the spectators gawking at the windows, should see the regard in which he held his wife.

"You might have warned me," Anselm muttered, "that some fool, some wretch with no sense at all, has made it fashionable for dukes and their heirs to dance with wallflowers, debutantes, widows…" His Grace trailed off as the duchess began a left-handed circuit of the ballroom.

"If you go that way, and I go the other," Anselm said, gesturing with his glass of punch, "we're bound to collect our ladies in the next ten minutes."

"Anselm, one does not collect ladies. Theo and I are meeting in the card room. You and your duchess are welcome to make up our foursome, or you can continue to fret and pout because your station obligates you to lend consequence to the unmarried women among us."

Anselm set down his drink. "You already sound like a duke—more like a duke than I do, and I do not pout."

Jonathan sauntered in the direction of the cardroom, Anselm stalking at his side.

"I pout, occasionally," Jonathan said. "When the wives are off having one of their gatherings from which we're excluded, and I'm consigned to pouring brandy for various lonely husbands, bachelor earls, and the endless procession of Dorning brothers. I pout like a toddler deprived of her favorite bunny."

"Ye heavenly intercessors," Anselm replied, nodding to Lady Antonia Mainwaring. "You should be having no dealings with stuffed rabbits. You've only been married a few weeks. The bunnies and horses and storybooks aren't supposed to figure into the equation for quite some time."

Jonathan fervently hoped Anselm was wrong. This time next year would do nicely for the bunnies to start showing up, but no amount of skill with numbers could predict such outcomes.

He reached Theo's side near the door to the cardroom. "Madam." He bowed over her hand, she curtseyed.

Anselm made a noise reminiscent of a crotchety bear.

"Your Grace," Theo said, offering her hand. "I believe your duchess mentioned a thirst for some lemonade. You might find her at the punch bowl."

Anselm spun on his heel and stalked off.

"You look delectable," Jonathan said. "All dignified and beautiful, with a hint of mischief in your eyes. Are you feeling lucky tonight, Mrs. Tresham?"

They'd shared a bit of luck as they'd prepared to go out for the evening. The bed had required making for the third time that day as a result, and Theo had sent Jonathan ahead to do his bit with the debutantes, while she put the finishing touches on her appearance.

"You look delectable too," Theo said, giving him a look that made him long for the privacy of their coach, or their bedroom, or his dressing closet, or the Quimbey conservatory, or…

"Shall we start your evening with a hand of cards, dearest wife? Lady Canmore is partnering the Earl of Casriel, and their conversation is always interesting."

"We should give them a nudge," Theo said, taking Jonathan's arm. "They need a nudge."

Whom Theo nudged usually ended up engaged, though in the case of Casriel and Lady Canmore, Jonathan suspected more than nudging was needed.

"We'll monitor the situation and compare our observations." They did that, regarding the ducal finances, Jonathan's charities, Diana's studies, what to purchase for Frannie's lying in gift. They conferred, exchanged honest opinions, and sometimes even grew heated in their debates, but—Jonathan would never admit this to Anselm—they also patched up their differences and apologized for words spoken too emphatically.

"Do you miss The Coventry?" Theo asked as Jonathan escorted her to the tables.

"Yes and no. I will always enjoy numbers, but I did not enjoy the moral conundrum that games of chance present, and I like the idea that Casriel's brothers are building on what I started."

He liked better—much, much better—that he and Theo were building a future together, one standing on far firmer ground than money, chance, appearances, and diversion.

"Prepare for defeat, Mr. Tresham," Theo said, taking a seat at Lady Canmore's table. "I'm feeling exceedingly lucky."

The earl and countess offered greetings, though clearly, they were barely aware that their table had become a foursome. After several hands, Casriel invited the lady to stroll on the terrace, and Jonathan once again had Theo to himself.

"They need a shove, not a nudge," Theo said, collecting the cards.

She'd revealed herself to be a ruthless and shrewd player, much to Jonathan's delight, though by agreement, any sums either of them won at cards or dice went toward their various charities.

Not that they gambled often or for high stakes.

"You have plundered all my reserves," Jonathan said, twenty minutes later. "Could I interest you in a stroll on the terrace?"

Theo set the deck aside. "Unfashionable of us, to socialize together, but if five pence is your limit for the evening, then to the terrace, sir."

Jonathan came around the table and bent low under the guise of holding her chair. "I will always prefer a moonlit garden with you to the feeble charms of the cards, Theo." He reassured her of that point frequently, and the lingering insecurities caused by her first marriage seemed to be fading, one moonlit stroll at a time.

"I can see why Archie became so enamored of games of chance," Theo said, slipping an arm around Jonathan's waist. "The cards promised him the possibility of financial independence, standing among his peers, and if nothing else, they alleviated the great sense of boredom and purposelessness an aristocratic son can be prone to. If we have children, we'll teach them to play well, but carefully."

She was offering Jonathan a reassurance of her own, one he needed to hear. He dropped in occasionally at The Coventry, and saw the Dorning brothers experimenting with this or that change to the establishment. That was hard, but then, Jonathan had his hands full with his own ventures.

And with Theo.

"I will sell The Coventry, Theo. The Dornings are off to a sound start, and they have ideas and insights I lacked. They'll make a go of it, and we'll get the dukedom set to rights that much faster for their efforts."

"I leave that choice to you," she said, pausing at a fork in the gravel path. "Are you in the mood for shadows and privacy or the well-lit path and its blooming roses?"

"You decide," Jonathan said, "and I will gladly accompany you either way."

Theo chose the private path—choice rhymes with rejoice—and Jonathan made a leisurely and loving tour of the garden's nocturnal splendors with her.

AUTHOR'S NOTE

Henry VIII tried to make it illegal for his army to gamble. Charles II appointed Sir Thomas Neale to shut down every illegal gambling den in London, and yet, by the late Georgian period, at least two aristocratic ladies were supplementing their incomes by running faro banks from their homes.

The history of British gambling is long and colorful, running between a nearly universal love of games of chance on the one hand, and an uneasy understanding of how a turn of a card could upset class expectations on the other.

As a young officer, the young Duke of Wellington came very close to gambling away his commission, and only the intervention of a friend prevented that disaster. Beau Brummel had to flee England due to unpaid gambling debts. Charles Fox and his brother in the space of just a few days lost the sum of 32,000 pounds (in Regency currency, which would be many times that amount now), and yet, every gentleman's club, Mayfair ball, and even Almack's assembly room offered card playing on the premises.

If aristocrats wanted to trade fortunes or parcels of land among themselves, that was one thing, but gambling also resulted in the ruin of many a titled family, and the overnight rise of men without blue blood. Hence the somewhat ambivalent regard for games of chance, which in the Victorian period, would blossom into crusades against "vice."

Those of you who read a lot of historical romances have doubtless come across that venerable gaming institution called Crockford's. William Crockford was born a fishmonger's son and began life in that trade himself. He had an aptitude for numbers though, and in particular for calculating odds and recalling anything he'd seen firsthand. He was also shrewd, patient, and in the right culture at the right time to end up as one of the wealthiest private individuals in Britain of the 1830s.

Crockford worked his way up, from casual games and working class establishments, to partnership in Watier's which eventually folded due to—it was whispered behind many a fan—employee graft. From there he opened his own club in 1828, and instituted many of the policies I appropriated for The Coventry: Free food and champagne after midnight, fabulous French cuisine, an elegant Mayfair-mansion ambience, and an invitation to membership extended to any prospective peer.

It's also the case that even as society's mood became less tolerant toward intemperate behavior, Crockford's was never raided by the authorities. Perhaps that's because "Crocky" paid enormous bribes, or knew enough to stay away from the game trade, or perhaps that's because he catered to such an exclusive clientele.

Crocky himself was the victim of swindling, when he bet heavily on The Derby horse race in 1832, and found himself involved in a notoriously crooked situation.

Too bad for him. He should have done as Jonathan and Theodosia did, and bet everything he had on true love!

To my Dear Readers,

I hope you enjoyed Jonathan and Cleo's story, because I had great fun writing it. I'm sure we'll hear more about the exploits of the Dorning brothers in future books, and particularly about the Earl of Casriel. What is up with that guy and his harps? I'd like to write a story for him in the next few months, but he's being coy about his happily ever after. So is Mr. Ash Dorning, about whom I would dearly like to know more. Stay *tuned* to the website (see what I did there?) for updates.

I do know, as in the probability converges with absolute certainty, that ***My One and Only Duke*** will be published in November. You doubtless noticed that Theo's banker was a little too cool for his cravat, and sure enough, Quinn Wentworth's tale is the first story in my new **Rogues to Riches** series. He is going to wish he'd sampled a few more biscuits before it's all over. Fortunately, Jane Winston comes along wielding all the sweetness one grouchy hero with a well hidden tender heart could ever need.

You'll find a vignette from ***My One and Only Duke*** below. I also got my paws on an exclusive excerpt from writin' buddy Kelly Bowen's upcoming September release, Last Night With the Earl, so you'll find a sneak peek at that tale too.

We just went through The Great Mailing List Botheration last month, wherein most of you confirmed that you'd like to continue to receive the occasional newsletter from me. If the dragnet missed you, you can sign up again at http://graceburrowes.com/contact/. Another way to stay in touch is to follow me on Bookbub at https://www.bookbub.com/profile/grace-burrowes. You'll get alerts about deals, pre-orders, and new releases without a lot of blah-blah or tub-thumping (as if I would ever...)

Happy reading!
Grace Burrowes

MY ONE AND ONLY DUKE

When Quinn Wentworth and Jane Winston spoke their wedding vows in Newgate prison, neither expected the result would be a lasting union. But here they are, a month later, no longer in Newgate, very much in love, and not at all sure what to do about it...

Having no alternative, Quinn went about removing his clothes, handing them to Jane who hung up his shirt and folded his cravat as if they'd spent the last twenty years chatting while the bath water cooled.

Quinn was down to his underlinen, hoping for a miracle, when Jane went to the door to get the dinner tray. He used her absence to shed the last of his clothing and slip into the steaming tub. She returned bearing the food, which she set on the counterpane.

"Shall I wash your hair, Quinn?"

"I'll scrub off first. Tell me how you occupied yourself while I was gone."

She held a sandwich out for him to take a bite. "This and that. The staff has a schedule, the carpets have all been taken up and beaten, Constance's cats are separated by two floors until Persephone is no longer feeling amorous."

Quinn was feeling amorous. He'd traveled to York and back, endured Mrs. Daugherty's gushing, and Ned's endless questions, and pondered possibilities and plots—who had put him Newgate and why?—but neither time nor distance had dampened his interest in his new wife one iota.

Jane's fingers massaging his scalp and neck didn't help his cause, and when she leaned down to scrub his chest, and her breasts pressed against Quinn's shoulders, his interest became an ache.

The water cooled, Jane fed him sandwiches, and Quinn accepted that the time had come to make love with his wife. He rose from the tub, water sluicing away, as Jane held out a bath sheet. Her gaze wandered over him in frank, marital assessment, then caught, held, and ignited a smile he hadn't seen from her before.

"Why Mr. Wentworth, you did miss me after all." She passed him the bath sheet, and locked the parlor door and the bedroom door, while Quinn stood before the fire and dried off.

"I missed you too," Jane said, taking the towel from him and tossing it over a chair. "Rather a lot."

Quinn made one last attempt to dodge the intimacy Jane was owed, one last try for honesty. "Jane, we have matters to discuss. Matters that relate to my travels." And to his past, for that past was putting a claim in his future, and Jane deserved to know the truth.

"We'll talk later all you like, Quinn. For now, please take me to bed."

She kissed him, and he was lost.

Order your copy of *My One and Only Duke*
at http://graceburrowes.com/grace-bookstore/

Read on for an exclusive sneak peek from Kelly Bowen's
Last Night With the Earl.

It wasn't the first time Eli had broken into this house.

The rain seemed to lessen slightly as he headed for the rear, toward the servants' entrance near the kitchens. The doors of the house would be bolted, but there was a window with a faulty latch, something he had taken advantage of a lifetime ago when he would stumble back from town in the dead of night after too much whiskey. Eli gazed up at the empty windows that lined the upper floors, relieved to find that the vast house was dark and silent. Avondale would be operating with only a skeleton staff—aside from maintaining the structure and grounds, there would be little to do.

Eli slipped his fingers under the edge of the low window and tapped on an outside corner while gently pushing upward. The window inched up slowly, though with a lot more resistance than he remembered. Above his head another roll of thunder echoed, and he cursed softly as the rain once again came down in sheets. Quickly he wrested the window the rest of the way up and swung himself over the sill, then lowered the window behind him. The abrupt cessation of the buffeting wind and the lash of rain was almost disorienting.

He stood for a long moment, trying to get his bearings and listening for the approach of anyone he might have disturbed. But the only sounds were the whine of the wind and the rattle of the rain against the glass. He breathed in deeply, registering the yeasty scent of rising dough and a faint whiff of pepper. It would seem nothing had changed in the years he'd been gone.

The kitchens were saved from complete blackness by the embers banked in the hearth on the far side. Eli set his pack on the floor and wrenched off his muck-covered boots, aware that he was creating puddles where he stood. A rivulet of water slithered from his hair down his back, and he shivered, suddenly anxious to rid himself of his sodden clothes. He left his boots on the stone floor but retrieved his pack and made his way carefully forward, his memory and the dim light ensuring he didn't walk into anything. Every once in a while, he would stop and listen, but whatever noise he might have made on his arrival had undoubtedly been covered by the storm.

He crept soundlessly through the kitchens and into the great hall. Here the air was perfumed with a potion of floral elements. Roses, perhaps, and something a little sharper. He skirted the expanse of the polished marble floor to the foot of the wide staircase that led to the upper floors. Lightning illuminated everything for a split second—enough for Eli to register the large arrangement of flowers on a small table in the center of the hall as well as the gilded frames of the portraits that he remembered lining the walls.

He shouldered his pack and slipped up the stairs, turning left into the north wing of the house. The rooms in the far north corner had always been his when he visited, and he was hoping that he would find them as he had left them. At the very least, he hoped there was a hearth, a bed, and something that resembled clean sheets, though he wasn't terribly picky at this point. His stocking feet made no sound as he advanced down the hallway, running his fingers lightly along the wood panels to keep himself oriented. Another blaze of lightning lit up the hallway through the long window at the far end, and he blinked against the sudden brightness.

There. The last door on the left. It had been left partially ajar, and he gently pushed it open, the hinges protesting quietly, though the sound was swallowed by a crash of thunder that came hard on the heels of another blinding flash. He winced and stepped inside, feeling the smooth, polished floor beneath his feet, his toes coming to rest on the tasseled edges of the massive rug he remembered. This room, like the rest of the house, was dark, though, unlike in the kitchen, there were no embers in the hearth he knew was off to his right somewhere. Against the far wall, the wind rattled the windowpanes, but it was somewhat muffled by the heavy curtains that must be drawn. Eli took a deep breath and froze. Something wasn't right.

The air around him was redolent with scents he couldn't immediately identify. Chalk, perhaps? And something pungent, almost acrid in its tone. He frowned into the darkness, slowly moving toward the fireplace. There had always been candles and a small tinderbox on the mantel, and he suddenly needed to see his surroundings. His knee unexpectedly banged into a hard object, and something glanced off his arm before it fell to the floor with a muffled thud. He stopped and bent down on a knee, his hands outstretched. What the hell had he hit? What the hell was in his rooms?

It hadn't shattered, whatever it had been. Perhaps it—

"Don't move."

Eli froze at the voice. He turned his head slightly, only to feel the tip of a knife prick the skin at his neck.

"I asked you not to move."

Eli clenched his teeth. It was a feminine voice, he thought. Or perhaps that of a very young boy, though the authority it carried suggested the former. A maid, then. Perhaps she had been up, or perhaps he had woken her. He supposed that this was what he deserved for sneaking into a house unannounced and unexpected. It was, in truth, his house now, but nevertheless, the last thing he needed was for her to start shrieking for help and summon the entire household. He wasn't ready to face that just yet.

"I'm not going to hurt you," he said clearly.

"Not on your knees with my knife at your neck, I agree." The knife tip twisted, though it didn't break the skin.

"There is a reasonable explanation." He fought back frustration. Dammit, but he just wanted to be left alone.

"I'm sure. But the silverware is downstairs," the voice almost sneered. "In case you missed it."

"I'm not a thief." He felt his brow crease slightly. Something about that voice was oddly familiar.

"Ah." The response was measured, though there was as slight waver to it. "I'll scream this bloody house down before I allow you to touch me or any of the girls."

"I'm not touching anyone," he snapped, with far more force than was necessary, before he abruptly stopped. Any of the girls? What the hell did that mean?

The knife tip pressed down a little harder, and Eli winced. He could hear rapid breathing, and a new scent reached him, one unmistakably feminine. Soap, he realized, the fragrance exotic and faintly floral. Something that one wouldn't expect from a maid.

"Who are you?" she demanded.

"I might ask the same."

"Criminals don't have that privilege."

Eli bit back another curse. This was ridiculous. His knees were getting sore, he was chilled to the bone and exhausted from travel, and he was in his own damn house. If he had to endure England, it would not be like this.

In a fluid motion, he dropped flat against the floor and rolled immediately to the side, sweeping his arm up to knock that of his attacker. He heard her utter a strangled gasp as the knife fell to the floor and she stumbled forward, caught off balance. Eli was on his knees instantly, his hands catching hers as they flailed at him. He pinned her wrists, twisting her body so it was she who was on the floor, on her back, with Eli hovering over her. She sucked in a breath, and he yanked a hand away to cover her mouth, stopping her scream before it ever escaped.

"Again," he said between clenched teeth, "I am not going to hurt you." Beneath his hand her head jerked from side to side. She had fine features, he realized. In fact, all of her felt tiny, from the bones in her wrists to the small frame that was struggling beneath him. It made him feel suddenly protective. As if he held something infinitely fragile that was his to care for.

Though a woman who brandished a knife in such a manner couldn't be that fragile. He tightened his hold. "If you recall, it was you who had me at a disadvantage with a knife at my neck. I will not make any apologies for removing myself from that position. Nor will I make any apologies for my presence at Avondale. I have every right to be here."

Her struggles stilled.

Eli tried to make out her features in the darkness, but it was impossible. "If I take my hand away, will you scream?"

He felt her shake her head.

"Promise?"

She made a furious noise in the back of her throat in response.

Very slowly Eli removed his hand. She blew out a breath but kept her word and didn't scream. He released her wrists and pushed himself back on his heels. He heard the rustle of fabric, and the air stirred as she pushed herself away. Her scent swirled around him before fading.

"You're not a maid," he said.

"What?" Her confusion was clear. "No."

"Then who are you?" he demanded. "And why are you in my rooms?"

"Your rooms?" Now there was disbelief. "I don't know who you think you are or where you think you are, but I can assure you that these are not your rooms."

Eli swallowed, a sudden thought making his stomach sink unpleasantly. Had Avondale been sold? Had he had broken into a house that, in truth, he no longer owned? It wasn't impossible. It might even be probable. He had been away a long time.

"Is it my brother you are looking for? Is someone hurt?"

The question caught him off guard. "I beg your pardon?"

"Do you need a doctor?"

Eli found himself scowling fiercely, completely at a loss. Nothing since he had pushed open that door had made any sort of sense. "Who owns Avondale?"

"What?" Now it was her turn to sound stymied.

"This house—was it sold? Do you own it?"

"No. We've leased Avondale from the Earl of Rivers for years. From his estate now, I suppose, until they decide what to do with it." Suspicion seeped from every syllable. "Did you know him before he died? The old earl?"

Eli opened his mouth before closing it. He finally settled on, "Yes."

"Then you're what? A friend of the family? Relative?"

"Something like that."

"Which one?"

Eli drew in a breath that wasn't wholly steady. He tried to work his tongue around the words that would forever commit him to this place. That would effectively sever any retreat.

He cleared his throat. "I am the Earl of Rivers."

Order your copy of *Last Night With the Earl*!